epic

CONOR KOSTICK was a designer for the world's first live fantasy role-playing game, based in Peckforton Castle, Cheshire. He now lives in Dublin where he teaches medieval history at Trinity College Dublin. He is the author of several historical works, numerous political and cultural essays and one strategic board game. He is the chairperson of the Irish Writers' Union. In between historical research, writing and political agitation he somehow finds the time to play a number of online games. *Epic* is his first fantastical futuristic novel. He co-wrote *The Easter Rising: A Guide to Dublin in 1916*, and co-edited *Irish Writers Against War*, an anthology of writings by Irish authors in response to the threat to invade Iraq.

EPIC

CONOR KOSTICK

THE O'BRIEN PRESS
DUBLIN

First published 2004 by The O'Brien Press Ltd,
20 Victoria Road, Dublin 6, Ireland.
Tel: +353 1 4923333; Fax: +353 1 4922777
E-mail: books@obrien.ie
Website: www.obrien.ie

ISBN: 0-86278-877-3

British Library Cataloguing-in-Publication Data
Kostick, Conor, 1964-
Epic
1.Computer games - Fiction
2.Science fiction
3.Young adult fiction
I.Title
823.9'2[J]

1 2 3 4 5 6 7 8
04 05 06 07

The O'Brien Press receives assistance from

Typesetting, editing, layout and design: The O'Brien Press Ltd
Printing: Cox & Wyman Ltd

Heartfelt thanks are owed to many people for helping
to shape this book. They include:
*Aoife, Ballanon, Barbara, Barthabus, Brajakis, Compte, Conor, Creno,
Glarinson, Hanna, Ishy, Jillumpy, Juno, Kalpurnia, Mindgolem, Roisina,
Rubblethumper, Sarant, Semefis, Spinespike, Sliperi and especially my editor, Susan.*

CONTENTS

Chapter 1

A Death in the Family

A sea mist had coated the window of the farm's kitchen with minuscule drops of rain. Erik was trying not to think of the terrible gamble taken by his mum. His nervous attention was focused on the droplets. Erik sat perfectly still, watching the flecks of water as some of them joined together to form larger drops, and these in turn amalgamated. Eventually, a raindrop grew to the point where it could no longer cling to the glass, and with an erratic plunge rushed downward, moving all the swifter as it gathered up the water in its path – a catastrophic event in the world of the million mist droplets.

Next to Erik, apparently paying equal attention to the faded patterns in the wood of their well-worn table, sat his dad. Neither of them had spoken in over an hour and their shoulders were hunched from tension. At long last, hollow footsteps rang out, changing in tone as they moved from wooden stair to tiled floor. The kitchen door latch was raised and his mother entered.

'Well?' asked Erik. But as soon as his mother had set foot in the kitchen, he could see from her gaunt, pale face that the news was bad.

'I'm dead,' Freya replied, a tremble in her quiet voice.

Harald stood up and pulled out a chair for her. She grasped the chair with shaking hand and slid into it, not meeting their anxious eyes.

'The poison did no good service, then?' enquired Harald gently.

'No.' She shook her head. 'I didn't penetrate his armour.'

Taking her hand in his, Harald tried to comfort her. 'You did your best. We knew it was nearly impossible.'

'At least she fought.' Erik stood up suddenly, energy flooding through him after so much stillness. His dad was a kind man, but Erik was unable to control the bitterness that came from nowhere to rage through him. Mum at least had entered the arena on their behalf; she was the truly brave one. Harald had hidden; he always hid.

'We will find a way.' Harald pointedly ignored Erik, and put an arm around Freya.

'Will we?' She let out a gulping half-cry, a sound that shook Erik with the realisation that she had run out of answers too. It was frightening to see someone who had been so steady all his life unable to control herself. 'Let's be honest with each other. At least we have that.' Her eyes were tearful. 'We are going to be reallocated.'

Reallocation. Work on the farm was hard. But not as hard as in the coalmines, or on the saltpans, or a great many of the other tasks that had to be done on the planet of New Earth. Reallocation would mean leaving Osterfjord and his friends, and probably it would mean being parted from his parents. Their lives were no longer their own.

'Why don't you issue a challenge, Dad?'

'Stop it,' Harald snarled angrily. 'Still you will not take my word.'

'No. I won't. Not any more. It doesn't make sense.' Erik could feel shrillness rising in his voice and paused to take breath. 'What can be worse than being reallocated?'

'There is worse,' replied Harald ominously.

'Leave it, Erik. We've had this out a thousand times.' Freya looked up for the first time since entering the room, and met his eye. 'Your father cannot fight for us. That's the end of the matter.'

'But why?' Erik pleaded.

'I cannot say.' Harald was grim-faced.

'Blood and vengeance. I'm fourteen now. I'm old enough. Tell me.'

'No.'

Even before he knew he was going to do it, Erik threw the clay mug he was holding against the wall. It cracked apart crisply, the clatter of shards resounding around the kitchen as they fell to the tiled floor, leaving a reddish mark on the whitewash. All three of them stared at the remains in silence. He knew what they were thinking: a massive catastrophe was about to overwhelm the family, yet they were regretting something as inconsequential as the loss of a mug. Almost at once, his anger subsided and Erik felt embarrassed and guilty; it was indeed a waste.

As they paused, each uncertain as to what needed saying, footsteps could be heard running through the yard. Hurriedly rising from her chair, Freya began to gather up the jagged pieces of pottery. Then came a rap on the door.

'Come in!' Either Harald did not care that the visitors would see the broken mug, or else he actually wanted them to.

A golden-haired girl flew in, bringing a breeze and her stocky brother in her wake.

'Injeborg, Bjorn, welcome,' Harald greeted their young neighbours. Freya placed the shards of clay behind a basket and stood up.

'Hello. We're very sorry about the duel,' Injeborg said earnestly. Behind her Bjorn added his condolences with a nod.

With a forced smile, Freya lifted a stray hair back behind her ear. 'Thank you. And thank your parents for the sword and the potion. They must have been worth months of effort. I'm sorry they went to waste.'

'Oh don't worry, they don't regret it. Yours was a good cause. We will miss you terribly if you have to go.' Injeborg's eager face suddenly clouded over as though she wished to take back her words.

'Erik, take your coat and go with your friends. Your mum and I have much to talk about.' Harald gestured to the door.

'Aye, and behind my back as always.'

Erik slammed the door as he left, the latch rattling and failing to catch. He noticed Bjorn and Injeborg exchange a glance of alarm, but no one spoke. The three walked in silence away from the farm, the hoods of their woollen jackets up over their heads, putting them each in their own world. Erik set a fast pace, even though it meant Injeborg was having to skip from time to time in order to keep up. Bjorn, however, plodded along behind with measured strides. Only when they had crested a hill and brought the sea into view did Erik relent from his moodiness. There was no point fuelling his anger and despair, especially in front of his friends; they only wanted to help.

Behind them were acres and acres of olive trees, set out in neat but tedious rows that radiated out towards infinity from a small community of six farms and a large round building that held the olive press. This was his home, the village of Osterfjord. Ahead, towards the sea, the hillside was sandy and bare. Nearby was a particularly large boulder that gave shelter from the sea breeze. It had served them often before, and they went to sit underneath it now.

'Don't be upset, Erik,' Injeborg said, tentatively moving to place her warm hand on his. 'It might not be so bad. Even if they reallocate you, it could be to the saltpans. That would mean you living in Hope – not so far away.'

'And in any case,' added Bjorn, 'Central Allocations won't make a decision before graduation. That gives you a chance.'

'Did you watch?' Erik changed the subject.

'Yes. We were all in the arena, everyone from Osterfjord at least and many from Hope.' Bjorn looked cautiously at Erik out of a broad, fleshy face in which watery green eyes were holding a question.

'I couldn't bear the waiting. And anyway I wanted to be at home for Mum.' Erik paused. 'Did she fight well?'

'Very well!' exclaimed Injeborg. 'She really knows how to wield a scimitar. But you know what she was up against. Ragnok must have had ten thousand bezants worth of armour alone.'

'More,' Bjorn knew a lot about the value of arms and armour.

'It's so unfair.' Normally Erik considered self-pity a sign of weakness, and never let it take form in his own mind, let alone allow his friends to see it. But these were not normal circumstances. Not only was he likely to be placed among complete strangers and set to some painfully arduous work, but his own parents considered him a child still, untrustworthy and unequal to a discussion on a future that would affect them all. In his own mind he was loyal, dependable and could hold his tongue if a secret needed to be guarded.

'Of course it is unfair. Totally unfair and unreasonable. It's not your family's fault the solar panel broke. That could happen to anyone. Why should you be punished?' When Injeborg was angry, her pale cheeks flushed red – only then could you see the resemblance between the slender girl and her stocky brother.

'Ya. And it's not as if a new family could fill the quota without that power. It doesn't really make sense to reallocate you.' Bjorn tied up the neck of his jacket as he spoke, trying to keep out the cold damp air.

'Do Central Allocations even think about what it means to split up friends and families? But what can we do? Even to challenge them on a small decision is to be killed in the arena like your mum. Let alone if someone suggested a really radical change.' Injeborg was worked up, talking as much to herself as to Erik.

'Did you ever daydream about duelling Central Allocations and winning?' he asked her, the thought soaring up from the bottom of his heart, from where he normally hid it, saved for those moments when he lay thinking of the future.

'Always.' Injeborg looked up at him, their eyes met and Erik saw total understanding. He was glad now he had blurted out his wish.

'Not I,' Bjorn said with a shrug to convey his pragmatism. 'It's too unrealistic.'

A chaffinch landed near them, looking for shelter, head flicking busily so that everything around it could be surveyed by its two tiny black eyes. The warm hand that covered Erik's tightened as Injeborg unconsciously stiffened, holding herself still so as not to frighten the bird. Erik tasted a happiness that was all the more precious for the bleakness that surrounded him. The affection and solidarity of his friends was a great comfort and the prospect of losing them more painful than the thought of having to labour in a coalmine.

The breeze, which was merely ruffling the tiny feathers of the chaffinch, making it seem like the bird was wearing a fur collar, suddenly gusted. The chaffinch was gone.

In those few moments, deep within Erik, a decision had been made. It was a decision he relished. Impossible as it sounded, he was going to fight Central Allocations and avenge the death of his mother.

Chapter 2
In praise of Beauty

Dead again.

Erik sighed aloud and rubbed his ear in exasperation, anticipating the despair in his mum's voice when she found out. Struggling to find a way to challenge Central Allocations, Erik was taking risks in Epic like never before. He was quite prepared to die in pursuit of the revenge and information he needed. But his mother would not understand. Her one hope was that Erik would escape reallocation by doing well in the annual graduation tournament. From that perspective each death was a disaster, wiping out any wealth and equipment Erik's character had obtained. If he was not careful, he would be entering the tournament practically naked, an easy victim to any ten-year-old who had got as far as obtaining a rusty dagger.

Just as Erik reached up to unclip from Epic, the thought struck him that he should at least prepare a new persona. And that was a way to postpone telling his parents the bad news.

gender: female

The selection had been made almost without thought and Erik surprised himself. It was the first time he had ever chosen a woman. Usually people stuck to their own gender; indeed they generally tried to match the character as much as possible to their own figure, possibly because many marriages eventually came about from meetings within the game. In any case, the impulse pleased him. Perhaps he would be luckier as a woman.

He flicked through the enormous database of women and picked a figure. He settled for one that was small, pale-skinned with red hair, green eyes and a few freckles. In build, his character conformed to him, although Erik, like his mother, had dark hair and brown eyes. Then, perversely, he allotted all his start-up points to beauty.

Serious gamers, and the whole world consisted of serious gamers, never wasted a point on beauty that could be spent on more practical attributes, or combat skills, craft skills, weapons, magic items and spells. As a result, Epic's population of players consisted entirely of dull, grey-looking humanoids.

His friends were in for a shock; it would be impossible to explain his choices to them, as there was no rational argument in favour of throwing away every practical advantage in favour of beauty. Perhaps he could just say the creation of an attractive female character was a whim, because he knew she was not long for the world. That would be partly true, but at the same time Erik felt that she was a genuine reflection of the mood that he was in, a mood of nonconformity, of wanting to defy the usual conventions of the game.

Looked at from every angle, she was an impressive creation. She was stunning. Lacking any armour, she stood in tunic and trousers, looking lithe and confident; you could feel the glow of energy from within her.

#smile

She grinned cheekily at Erik and his heart skipped; the vividness of the facial animation was lifelike. A smile command issued to any of his previous characters would have seen the grey polygons of their head shuffle in a gesture indistinguishable from a snarl. He chuckled aloud, the cloud of his recent death lifting. This was fun. She might not last a week – especially given his plan – but he already felt a fondness towards his new alter ego. She would stand out and be the cause of a lot of questioning. She looked more like an NPC – the computer-generated Non-Player Characters – than a player's character.

#wave farewell

She waved goodbye.

Unclipping his headset and gloves from the computer, Erik stood up and stretched. He rubbed his ear again where it was sore from supporting the device for four hours – four precious hours given to him so that he could start catching up with the other Epic characters of his age group.

Dusk had stolen over the land while he had been immersed in Epic. His parents and the neighbours would be in from the fields. They were probably cleaning their iron tools carefully against rust, or preparing their evening meals. A flickering light from the corridor showed that a fire had been lit downstairs. Time to face the music. Erik moved slowly and quietly down the bare wooden staircase.

'Damnation!' it was Erik's mum from the kitchen.

'What is it, Mum?' Erik walked into the room.

'Oh, Erik, I didn't know you were there,' she sighed. 'The stove is not working properly. There is no hot water at all.'

She looked tired, but then her face brightened hopefully. 'Did you make progress today?'

'Well, yes and no.' Hating to disappoint her, Erik moved to the table and took a seat, looking at the straw placemat.

'Yes and no?'

'I died. But I learned ...'

'Oh, no. Not again. Oh, Erik, why can't you get on in the world?

The graduation tournament will come soon and you won't have a chance.' She stopped herself abruptly. They both knew the speech. She sat at the table and looked at him until tears started to form in her eyes. Unable to look at her, Erik stared at his hands, deeply unhappy. He understood her perfectly, but stood by his new, dissenting approach to the game.

'Erik, listen to me for your own sake. Dad and I will be reallocated somewhere soon, but you still have a chance to win some choice over your future. I just don't understand why you are throwing it aside.'

Erik did not respond, not wishing to upset his mum further, but not yet ready to accept her perspective.

'Let's see what your dad has to say,' Freya got up and opened the door onto the yard. 'Harald, can you come in?' she called.

'Dinner already?' Erik's dad brought an armful of logs with him from the woodshed. He smiled at Erik but quickly caught the mood, 'What's the matter?'

'Erik died again.'

'Just a moment.'

They stayed silent while Harald took the logs through. Erik's stomach tightened with anxiety. His dad came back, brushing the chips from his jumper.

'What got you, son?' Harald's voice was non-committal.

'The Red Dragon again.' Erik was reluctant to admit this; it sounded like he was stupid. It was hard to explain.

'Again? That's how many. Three?' Harald sat down opposite him.

'Four.'

Harald nodded slowly. 'How many more before you give up on it?'

'Dunno,' Erik said curtly. 'Look. I'm not giving up on it until I'm convinced that it's impossible. But I have my reasons. It can be done.'

'But if that is true, why has no one else killed Inry'aat, the Red Dragon?' His mum was standing beside the table, arms folded.

'Because they've been too busy fighting to see what I saw.'

'Which was?' asked Harald.

Erik glanced up from the mat he was toying with. A note of genuine interest had replaced parental severity in his dad's voice.

'The attack pattern of the dragon,' Erik hurried on. 'See, it doesn't charge for the nearest opponent but the one who is doing the most damage.'

Harald nodded. 'Intelligent creatures usually do that.'

'Yes. But, it turns mid-charge, if it decides a new person is the greater threat.'

'Go on.'

'The timing would have to be precise, and the amount of damage would have to be consistent. But if a group of three or four were in the right places, you could get it to keep on re-targeting without actually reaching anyone.'

Harald shook his head. 'I understand what you are saying. But Epic is too well designed. They would never leave such a loophole on a dragon. Wishful thinking, son.'

'If I showed you, you might believe me.'

His mum banged a cup angrily on the table. 'That's not fair, Erik. You know your dad can't enter Epic.'

'You getting at me again, son?' Harald sighed, but he did not seem angry. He reached over and patted Erik's hand. 'Listen. You are a great player. You have been since you first put on a headset. Your reflexes are excellent and you understand the tricks and games that the world throws at you. But you are so far behind now. Look at Bjorn ...'

Erik interrupted his dad with a snort of derision.

Harald scowled. 'Bjorn is very solid. Every group needs someone like him. Hard working. Slow gains, but safe ones. And now a good strong character. The best in the school, perhaps.'

'In a tiny district agricultural school, perhaps. But he is nothing compared to the Mikelgard players. And that means we will never get anything from Central Allocations Bjorn's way. I mean, look, we are going to be reallocated. How can we avoid it? We have to aim high.'

'Well. Erik has a point. When was the last dragon killed?' Harald glanced at his son, then smiled unexpectedly; they both knew the answer.

'Thirty years ago, a group from Mikelgard University killed M'nan Sorth – the Black Dragon of Snowpeak Mountains.'

'And where are they now? Mostly employed by Central Allocations, I shouldn't wonder,' Harald answered his own question.

Clearly exasperated with the turn in the conversation, Erik's mum got up. Soon drawers of cutlery were slamming.

Harald looked at Erik with a steady, blue-eyed gaze that seemed to be taking his measure. He whispered, 'Listen well, Erik. Your mum is ill. She cannot sleep at night.' Then his dad spoke loud enough that Freya could hear too. 'Seriously though, Erik. If you clip up every night after work, you might still get somewhere in time for the graduation competition.'

'We could even give him more time during the day,' added Freya, turning to face the table. 'There's no point even trying to meet our targets now.'

'True,' agreed Harald. 'So how about it, son? No more deaths. No more dragon.'

'Very well.' Erik's heart sank at the thought of the hours and hours of boring accumulation ahead of him, so that he could acquire enough copper bits for his character to have even the minimum of basic equipment.

'Promise?' Freya's eyes narrowed, detecting the reluctance in Erik's voice.

'Promise,' he answered.

Chapter 3

A note, a map and some advice

It was raining outside, turning the soil too muddy for the transfer of the delicate olive shoots from their clay pots to the fields. So Erik had been sent inside by Freya to start his new character in Epic. He was resentful at having to promise to go nowhere near Inry'aat, the Red Dragon, but when he clipped up he remembered with pleasure that he had defied convention. His new persona was a woman with no significant attributes other than beauty.

Erik harmonised with the equipment and a small music box chimed, unwinding its colourful sides and raising a platform on which stood his red-haired selection.

#wave

She waved cheerfully, making Erik smile.

Before he could enter the world as this woman, he still had several decisions to make. Lacking all attributes but beauty, she would not perform well in any of the major disciplines. Therefore he looked through the less common options: footpad, swashbuckler, chevalier, gambler, tumbler, drifter – the list went on into the hundreds.

Patiently Erik read through the summaries of the disciplines that interested him, returning to the one that stood out by its unusual description.

swashbuckler

The swashbuckler is similar to the pirate, a warrior whose true home is on the high seas. However, the swashbuckler has the manners and style to make an impression in urban environments. They combine a lightly armoured fighting skill with much of the knowledge of a thief and the 'je ne sais quoi' of a court dandy. When it comes to swinging on a chandelier across a hall full of enemies, fending off sword-cuts from below, having stolen the jewels from a crown, swashbuckling is the only discipline to have.

Erik couldn't imagine that this discipline would be particularly good, as in all his hours of playing Epic he had never come across another swashbuckler. But then again that could be because no one ever experimented as the game's designers had intended. It was thought that centuries ago the game had been designed to amuse colonists travelling in a half-frozen state through the vast distances of space. It was not supposed to be about the slow accumulation of pennies, nor even for conflict resolution – although that made more sense to Erik. No, the designers had created the game for fun. And his newly discovered, light-hearted description of the swashbuckler discipline was further evidence that the designers had not created the world for the dour professionals of Central Allocations.

So, she was a swashbuckler, and Erik would find out shortly the wisdom of that decision. Now the final choice. Always a tricky one. What would his new name be? For once it could not be his own name, as was conventional. Perhaps Freya then, after his mum? No. Too many Freyas already. Something with 'je ne sais quoi', whatever that was. Cinderella. That was nearly right, but maybe he should not use an exact copy of the fairy-story name. Sinbad the sailor. There were a few of those around already and of course they were male. How about Cindella the sailor? Now that sounded right.

Erik confirmed his decisions. A moment of silence and darkness then a rushing sound that grew rapidly in volume to a shout, accompanied by an explosion of light.

★★★★

He was back in the world of Epic.

Where was he? This felt like the day he was introduced to Epic. As you looked around for the first time, you just could not help being amazed by how stunningly detailed and lifelike were the sights and sounds.

An attic, cobwebs, simple furniture, a window – with a little broken pane. Outside a seagull, tucked up on the ledge. A bed, with someone? Beyond the room the wind gusted and rattled the loose window frame. Inside a heavy breathing, like a snore.

One step toward the window, then another. Cindella moved well; Erik could feel a nimble response to his slightest command. It would take some practice not to oversteer with her. Erik reached out a hand towards the window. It was amusing that instead of a big muscled fist from a fighting character, he had a slender woman's finger. A breeze was blowing through the broken pane. He let it wash over his fingers and arms. Touching the glass, he left a slight mark in the grime. On the ledge outside the window, the seagull shifted. It turned a bright eye to look at him through wind-ruffled feathers.

With a shriek of discontent, the seagull leapt into the air and, suddenly veering, was thrown out of view by the wind.

How long would his mark last on the window? If he went away for years would it still be there? Just how sophisticated was Epic?

The view from where he was standing allowed Erik to make sense of his location. The street outside was narrow and dark, but there was enough of a gap between the grimy buildings to see the masts of a tall ship in the distance. He was high up in an attic in the seedy dockside area of Newhaven, one of the great Epic towns. For a moment he felt slightly disappointed. Newhaven was very familiar to Erik, while the unknown was always thrilling. But on the positive side it meant he could meet up with his friends easily. Like the vast majority of newer players, they were to the north of the city, hunting kobolds, goblins and wild animals.

Time to check his inventory.

weapons: throwing dagger, rapier.

magic:

food: loaf of bread, two apples.

drink: flask of water.

armour:

pouch:

purse: four silver ducats, eighteen pennies.

Fairly disappointing. The money was not bad, but with no armour at all, he would be extremely vulnerable in a fight. He would have to buy a shield and that would take up most of the money.

Next Erik called up the skills menu.

combat: fence, throw dagger, dodge, parry, riposte, mock.

Thieves: move silently, pick locks, appraise jewellery, climb.

Others: sail, swim, ride, sing, dance.

Now that was excellent. The swashbuckler description had not let him down. No wonder they hadn't listed all the skills. He'd never had this many for a new character; nearly all the start-up thief skills, and some great fighting skills. Plus there were two skills listed that Erik had never seen before: mock and dance. Dance was fairly self-evident, although who could say when it would ever be used? Mock, though, as a combat skill? Curious. He would have to ask Bjorn – or try it out and see what happened.

Looking again at the combat skills, it was clear that he should not buy a shield or even much armour. Dodge, parry and riposte were all abilities whose effectiveness was reduced by too much weight. Instead he was going to have to rely on swiftness of movement.

Well, time to move on. Perhaps some shopping first, before going to the fighting grounds – the incredibly boring fighting grounds. There was a massive and complex world to explore, but he had promised his mum he was going to survive this time. And that meant hacking away at the same creatures, again and again, taking pennies from their purses or selling their skins if they were wild animals.

Partly to put off having to go to familiar territory, and partly out of genuine curiosity, Erik looked again around the room. Ah, of course, the sleeping person. Approaching the bed, Erik could see a white-bearded, elderly man, wrapped in his blanket, facing the wall. He could tell at once from the extraordinary detail in the man's face that it was an NPC. One of the hundreds of thousands of people controlled by the computer which was at the heart of Epic. He reached out a slender hand and touched the man's shoulder.

'Huh? What?'Tthe harsh breathing stopped. His eyes opened.

#smile

'Oh, it's you, Cindella.' The bearded man suddenly smiled back. 'It is always a pleasure to look at you, my daughter. You are so beautiful.'

There was a pause.

'The pleasure is mine,' tried Erik.

No response. The old man remained paused, broad smile on his face.

'Daughter?' offered Erik. Usually the conversation of an NPC was extremely limited and tended to follow certain key words in the previous sentence.

'Ah, you have been like a daughter to me, ever since I found you and brought you up aboard the ship. You remember the *Black Falcon*?'

'I remember the *Black Falcon*.' Erik went along with the storyline.

The old man suddenly scowled. 'A curse on Duke Raymond. When he betrayed us and sank the *Black Falcon*, he condemned us to this life of poverty. I am too old to begin the pirate life again, but you, you will go far. And you will avenge us all, myself and the crew.'

'I will avenge us all,' Erik replied dutifully.

The old man smiled with satisfaction. 'I know you will. Sadly I have nothing I can give you apart from a note, a map and some advice.'

'What advice?'

No response.

'What note?'

'This is a letter of introduction. Just give it to the captain of any ship and there is no doubt that you will be taken on as a member of the crew. It tells of your sailing skills and has my seal: "Captain Sharky of the *Black Falcon*".'

A scroll with a red wax seal appeared in his hand, which he promptly reallocated to his pouch. This was fun, thought Erik. Much more interesting than his previous characters. None of them had a quest of their own from the beginning. Or perhaps they had, he suddenly realised, but he had never noticed because he hadn't taken the time to talk to the nearby NPCs.

'What map?'

'Aha, young Cindella. I have guarded this map for years in the hope of gaining a ship once more, but now it is getting too late for me. This map shows the location of the treasure we buried after capturing the *Queen's Messenger.*'

Another scroll appeared in Erik's hand. He opened it. It was a nautical map of a group of islands – the Skull Islands. Two long lines were drawn which crossed at a point marked '!'.

'Where are the Skull Islands?'

'The Skull Islands are a long way to the west. You will have to sail to Cassinopia and get detailed information from there.'

'What treasure?'

'There are hundreds of gold pieces hidden there and much more besides.'

'What else is hidden there?'

No response.

'What was the *Queen's Messenger*?'

The old man remained silent, staring up at Cindella.

Putting the map away in his pouch, Erik tried another question.

'What advice?'

This time, the old man grabbed Cindella's hand and held it earnestly.

'Trust no one. There is no captain I know who would share the treasure with you. If they knew you had the map, they would steal it from you, or worse. To get the treasure, you will have to get your own ship. And it will need to be a well-protected ship. Many dangerous creatures reside in the Skull Islands.' He fell back with a sigh.

'What creatures? What protection?'

With a mental shrug, Erik prepared to leave.

#bye

'Goodbye, my daughter. Fare well on your voyages. And come to visit me from time to time.'

'I will visit you from time to time.'

'Thank you, Cindella. I will miss your beauty. But it is time for you to make your own way in the world.'

#bye

Captain Sharky gave a tired wave from his bed and turned over.

Erik almost skipped from the room. This really was enjoyable. This was a proper adventure. If you had plenty of time, you could gradually earn the money to make a voyage to Cassinopia, hire a ship, and get the treasure. The only problem was, Erik did not have a lot of time. The Epic graduation championships were to take place in less than two months.

Outside, the wind was still gusting, swirling leaves through the street. If he could feel the cold through his character, no doubt he would be suffering. Cindella moved quickly through the alleyways, until Erik brought her to the merchants' stalls on the quays. Time for a bit of shopping.

Newhaven was a great cosmopolitan city, and here on the quays you could buy almost anything you wanted – except that you would hardly waste your money on anything inessential.

Elves from the great forests were here with their produce: baskets of strange fruits, fine wines and delicately woven clothing. In the tall, gold-bordered tents of the sombre Sidhe elves, it was possible to buy exquisite weaponry, including their famous rune-carved longbows and glittering silver chain mail. The cheapest item from the Sidhe elves, a throwing dagger, cost around fifty silver ducats. Out of curiosity, Erik had once asked them the price of their chain mail. Nine hundred bezants seemed very reasonable in terms of the economy of the game. But for an ordinary player that represented more wealth than they would be able to accumulate in a lifetime of standard play.

Friendly-looking dwarfs from the mountains had their stands a little nearer to the town walls. All the metal items that you could wish to buy were on display, from pots and pans to fish hooks and solid, practical pieces of armour. In contrast to the tents of the elves, the dwarven stalls were crowded with grey player characters asking prices and checking their savings of copper bits, to see if they could afford a new piece of armour.

Erik almost laughed aloud to see the players with their patchwork appearance: one armguard here, one greave there. Whatever Cindella did, she was not going to go down that road. Leather armour perhaps, but she was not going to look like that warrior ahead of her who was unarmed except for a solid helm. He looked like a child who had borrowed a pot for a helmet and was pretending to be a soldier. The warrior took off the helm, and Erik realised with a chuckle that it was Bjorn's persona, inevitably called Bjorn.

****

It was with a great sense of accomplishment Bjorn hit the #agree command and the trade with the dwarf took place. Gone were his old greaves, gauntlets and linen tunic, and in their place he had a shiny bronze helmet. Not only was this a significant boost to his overall armour score, but, vitally, it should allow him to tackle kobolds single-handed, and that would really accelerate his earnings just in time to acquire either an upgrade to his warhammer or some more armour before the tournament.

Bjorn was just thinking how pleased his father would be when he heard his name.

'Hey, Bjorn! It's me Erik! Are you in from the rain as well?' The voice came from somewhere near a red-haired, attractive NPC, a human woman with a stylish rapier and a sheathed dagger in her belt. Looking slowly back and forth, Bjorn was puzzled.

'Erik? Where are you?'

The NPC bowed. 'This is me, the female swashbuckler.'

'Female? Swashbuckler? I've never heard of that character type. What are you up to?' Bjorn was bewildered and worried. What was his friend doing? Had the stress of his family troubles caused him to have some kind of nervous breakdown?

'Is that a new helmet?' the swashbuckler asked.

At this question, Bjorn's concerns were replaced by the surge of pleasure his important breakthrough gave to him, 'Yes, I had to trade in the greaves, gauntlets and tunic, plus two bezants. But isn't it great? I believe I've boosted my armour score by about twenty percent.'

'It *is* great, Bjorn. Well done.' Erik's character smiled and that was an extraordinary sight. Bjorn was so used to the inexpressive grey polygons of players that it was still hard to believe he was not interacting with an NPC of the game. Erik must have started his new character with a maximum investment in beauty, which was absolutely a waste and another sign his friend was cracking up under the strain of imminent reallocation. The poor kid obviously no longer cared; he probably felt that it was too late to perform at all well in the tournament.

'I'm going back to fight the kobolds. I should be able to solo them now ...' Bjorn paused. 'Do you want to come?'

In that moment of hesitation, Bjorn had struggled with himself. The etiquette when killing monsters was that everyone in a group shared the small amounts of loot equally, regardless of who did the most work. In this case, there was no doubt that Bjorn had no real need for Erik's help and that his warrior would be crunching up kobolds with his warhammer far more quickly than would a female character whose starting points had all been spent on beauty. In effect, Bjorn was offering to tow Erik along. It would have been easy to convince himself that Erik was not serious about his new character and that any loot divided with it would be wasted. But friends were friends and, regardless of Erik's irresponsible choices, it was right to make the offer.

'Sure, Bjorn, that would be good. I won't be much help though.'

'Don't worry. Everyone has to start somewhere.' Bjorn hoisted his warhammer over his shoulder and the two of them walked north along the quays. As they did so, Bjorn revised down the amount of new copper bits that he had hoped to make this afternoon.

While they made their way through the flapping canvas and rope of the market stalls, Bjorn noticed something unusual. The NPCs were not stationary; their heads were turning towards the two players.

'Erik, look at the merchants.'

'Hmmm. That's odd.' Erik's character made the actions that arose from the #wave+smile command.

A nearby seller of herbs smiled and waved back.

'You try.'

Bjorn had his big warrior wave. Nothing.

'They like me!' The inflexions of a player's voice carried through into their character's speech, and it was clear that Erik was delighted.

'Come on. I want to see how effective this helmet is.'

As they walked on, Erik continually waved and smiled at the NPCs, many of whom waved back. Even a frightening-looking desert mystic, selling spells for magicians, gave a slight nod of his head towards Cindella. Admittedly it was extraordinary, but Bjorn was becoming a little impatient with Erik's frivolity. The sooner they made it to the kobold plains, the better.

At the end of the quays were streets with permanent shops. Standing outside a jeweller's was a guard in full plate-armour, resting his hands on his two-handed sword. Theoretically a thief, or a gang of players, could try robbing shops, but the various defences employed by the merchants would almost certainly kill them. The elderly shopowner waved back at Erik's gestures and surprised them both by calling out, 'Cindella. What a joy to see you!'

Erik turned to Bjorn, and even through the medium of the game, they exchanged a significant look. That a merchant should call out to a player was totally unexpected.

Turning to the merchant, Erik tried a number of phrases:

'It is a joy to see you, too.

'Thank you.

'Hail, merchant.'

'Erik, the sign!' Bjorn pointed up to a wooden marker that said 'Antilo the jeweller'.

So, after a slight pause, Erik tried simply, 'Hail, Antilo.'

'Come in, my dear. I've something I've been saving for you.'

'Come on, Bjorn. We have to check this out.'

'Let's not be long though, Erik.' Bjorn tried to keep the irritation out of his voice.

They followed Antilo into the shop, waiting a moment to adjust to the darkness.

'Here you are – a present. When it was sold to me, I immediately thought of you. It matches your hair perfectly.'

A pendant appeared in Cindella's hand. It was silver with a garnet that twinkled with red sparks. Erik equipped it to his neck.

'Here, look,' Antilo said, pointing to a mirror.

For some time, the merchant and Erik's character stood still, admiring the silver pendant on her pale neck.

'Are you done, Erik?' muttered Bjorn quietly.

'Thank you, Antilo.' Cindella turned away from the mirror.

'No need to thank me, Cindella. To have such a beauty as you in my shop is reward enough. But should anyone ask, tell them this pendant came from Antilo the jeweller.'

'I will tell them that this pendant came from Antilo the jeweller.'

There was no further response from the smiling shopowner, so it did not take any extra effort to get Erik to leave the shop.

'Good. Let's hurry.' Bjorn set off.

'Wait, Bjorn. Look at me. What do you think?'

'What?' He turned. 'That pendant? Surely it's a worthless trinket?'

'True, but even so. Have you ever heard of a merchant giving anything away?'

Bjorn had to agree the encounter was strange, unprecedented. Curious, he looked more closely at the jewel.

'Actually, that's really strange. It's pretty good, might be worth something. Ten silver maybe.'

'Let me try my appraise jewellery skill,' suggested Erik.

There was a long silence.

'Well?' asked Bjorn eventually.

'I don't believe it! IT'S WORTH OVER A BEZANT!'

Bjorn stood silent. At home he was simply stunned. If his warrior had greater facial detail, Erik would have seen its jaw drop. In a few minutes of existence, Erik's joke character had just obtained more wealth than Bjorn had gathered in a year of patient fighting. Bjorn's thoughts were a whirl. Part of him bitterly resented Erik's instant success. And a lot of uncomfortable questions arose. Was there another way to play the game that meant his years of accumulation were wasted? Did many other people know about this? Was he being stupid all this time that he had prided himself on his careful banking and tiny increases in copper coins? On the other hand, Bjorn felt a surge of excitement too. Perhaps Erik had made an important discovery about the game? Already with this new wealth he could buy some decent equipment, get off to a flying start. From nowhere Erik could now hope for some modest success in the graduation tournament, and if Bjorn could help him, then of course he would do so.

Chapter 4
The Law of violence

A row of distant figures stood shovelling salt into barrels, filling them and then working together to lift them up to rest beside each other on a narrow track. Later, a cart would be pulled along that path, and the heavy barrels of salt would be raised by teams of workers and stacked onto it. But for now they were doing the backbreaking work of hacking through the crust and lifting layer after layer of white salt into the barrels. After digging down to a depth of about three feet, the salt turned yellow and was still damp with the estuary mud. This they left. Erik was studying the process intently. The haze of salt dust that rose around the workers looked unpleasant. On a hot day, it would be choking. He could imagine the dryness of the atmosphere, all moisture absorbed by the salt; eyes half closed against the stinging dust; pores clogged with salt; skin worn to an ancient leathery texture. Everyone could recognise a lifelong salt worker by the roughness of their skin. But more dangerous still was the work of those who were out on the dykes. Up to their waists in tidal water, they were letting the sea gush into the great rectangular flood plains that had been marked out by the dykes. Then, when the tide was it its height and on the turn, they had to fill the breach, hurriedly piling stone and mud to seal the water in, so that the sun could evaporate the trapped sea, to leave yellowing piles of salt for the shovellers. Two or three dyke workers a year died in the struggle with mud and tide.

'Erik.' Her voice was tentative.

'Inny.' He didn't turn around, but was glad that she had found him.

'Can I join you?'

This time he glanced up, and smiled. 'Of course.'

'Bjorn says you have a female character, and that she has gained a bezant already.'

'Yes. It's amazing. I've never experienced anything like it. I really think that I have connected to the game in a way people usually miss out on. It's made me wonder what more is possible.'

'That's wonderful, Erik. You might have time to get somewhere before … you know.'

They sat close together. A few strands of Injeborg's long blond hair were lifted by the breeze to touch Erik gently on his cheek.

'The saltpans are bad news, Inny – look.'

'I know. But at least you would live close to us still.'

'Even that is still an unlikely allocation. I should put in a request I guess. But I still hope … I hope that I can find a way to make a challenge myself. Or maybe that my dad finally comes out of hiding and is successful.'

'Erik. Can I ask you something personal?' Injeborg looked serious. He was so used to seeing her in a playful, tomboyish humour that Erik was slightly shocked by a sudden insight into the adult woman she would become: thoughtful, intelligent, and, he had to admit, beautiful.

'Yes. Ask.'

'Why doesn't your dad play Epic?' She quickly added, 'You don't have to say if it's a secret.'

'Oh.' His gaze shifted uncomfortably from hers back to the workers in the estuary. 'I wish I knew. I wish they trusted me, but whatever the secret is, they keep it even from me.' He was embarrassed to admit it. Suddenly Erik felt tearful, 'You know I can be trusted, Inny, don't you?' Instinctively he rubbed his tongue across the rough bottom edge of one of his front teeth.

'Of course. Every time you smile, I know you can be trusted.'

Erik grinned then, and they cast their minds back seven years.

****

The September olive harvest was a rare opportunity for fun for the children of the village. The adults would lay down netting around the small trees, then stand back and let the children run wild. They would shake the branches, or hit them with sticks, or even climb into the thickets to rock the tree, until the ground was strewn with olives and debris. The olives were then gathered in the nets and poured through a bucket and moving platform device to sort out the twigs and leaves from the black and green olives.

Erik rode on the shoulders of Big Erik – or B.E. as they all called him – grabbing tree branches and shaking them until all the olives were down.

'That one done?' asked B.E.

'Aye. Finished.'

'Quick then, there's Injeborg!' B.E. was a bold scoundrel nearly twice Erik's age and Erik loved to be involved in his games.

'Yes, hurry, hurry!' Erik drummed his feet onto B.E.'s chest as they galloped to the next tree. Injeborg, holding hands with her chubby brother Bjorn, ran up just behind them.

'Ours!' Erik was gleeful.

'But there's not many left,' complained Bjorn.

'True, true, you can help us with this.' B.E. loosened one of his hands from its grip on Erik's legs to gesture at the tree.

For a few minutes they were silent, busy pulling tree branches back and forth. Then, with some difficulty because of Erik's weight on his shoulders, B.E. bent low and moved the two of them stealthily up behind the girl, who was crouching, back towards them, in order to reach the lower branches. Erik giggled, knowing it was bold, and vigorously thrashed the branches above her head. B.E. could barely keep his balance as olives rained down on Injeborg.

'Oh!' She ran out, hands over her head. 'Did you do that deliberately?' Injeborg challenged them, little hands on hips, her fair hair a tangle of twigs and leaves.

'Of course not,' replied B.E. innocently. 'You know the rules.'

Injeborg eyed them suspiciously. 'Ya. And I also know you two.'

Bjorn came over. 'Are we finished?'

'That was the last one,' answered B.E.

'Then let's go get a drink.'

'Wait. Carry me.' Injeborg always gave as good as she got, which is why it was good to tease her. She pulled her brother down so she could get on his shoulders. 'Now, you two troublemakers,' she hailed them imperiously. 'Let's play Epic.'

'Oh, Epic!' shouted Erik.

'How?' B.E. was puzzled.

'We are knights. And the first one to fall over loses,' explained Injeborg.

'Is that allowed?' asked Bjorn.

'Probably not,' replied B.E., hoisting Erik up more firmly and gripping him tightly.

'Well, I don't know,' Bjorn was uncertain.

Erik felt the excitement in his mount and knew from the tension of the frame beneath him that B.E. was ready to move.

'Charge! Charge!' Erik yelled at the top of his voice before being abruptly cut off as B.E. jumped towards Bjorn. He recovered his position, only to have Injeborg grab him by the shoulder and pull hard.

Erik was on the ground, B.E. beside him, laughing.

'What was that cracking sound?' Bjorn leant over Erik. 'Oh no. Poor little Erik.'

'What?' B.E. sat up immediately on hearing the deep dismay in Bjorn's voice.

'Look,' Bjorn pointed.

'Oh,' B.E. looked sadly into Erik's face. 'Does it hurt?'

'Whath?' replied Erik.

'Your tooth.'

'Let me see! Let me see!' Injeborg pushed the two big children away and leant over. She was serious for a moment and then tried to hide a smile. 'You look daft.'

'Are you all right, Little Erik?' asked B.E. again.

'Ya. I'm thine.'

'Let's look for it. Maybe it can be stuck on.' Injeborg dropped to her knees and began parting the grass.

'I don't think they can,' said Bjorn slowly. 'Remember Greta, she had to have the whole tooth removed when she broke hers.'

'Oh, don't worry.' Injeborg spoke as if she was an adult and not just seven. 'Little Erik is young. He'll grow a new one.'

Erik was happy that Injeborg was so cheerful. He would have been very distressed if he had only Bjorn and B.E. to look at. They were exchanging glum looks as they helped search for the piece of broken tooth.

The children were visibly disheartened by the time Harald and Rolfson approached them. Bjorn explained what had happened.

'Oh, son,' Rolfson said faintly, as though he had been struck. He shook his head and looked to his neighbour. 'What do you think? Was it a violation?'

Harald shrugged. 'First things first. Are you well, Erik?'

'I'm thine, Dad. It dothen't hurt a bit.'

Harald crouched in front of his tiny son and, pushing Erik's lip to one side with his thumb, stared for a while at the broken tooth, 'Hmm. It might function all right. But you are going to have a crooked smile for a long time.'

'There is no way of capping it?' asked Rolfson.

'Maybe in Mikelgard.'

There was a long pause.

'What about the violation. Can we say it was an accident that occurred while shaking for olives?' Rolfson was pale and stuttered.

'We could.' Harald gave a severe glance to the children. He scowled at Injeborg. 'You do understand that people never, ever fight or hurt each other.'

The little girl gave a violent nod.

'Our ancestors left their home planet centuries ago because of violence, and for all we know that planet was destroyed by war, as we have been on our own ever since. Those first settlers brought with them one rule, a rule that we have obeyed ever since. There is NEVER any reason for violence.'

The children had heard this lecture a hundred times, but suddenly it sounded far more important than ever before.

'We weren't fighting, sir,' interjected B.E. 'We were just playing Epic.'

'Epic? How?' asked Rolfson.

'We were being knights,' replied B.E.

Harald gave a wry grimace. 'The whole point of the game is to provide an alternative to fighting – not to cause it.' He squatted so that he was eye level with Injeborg. 'Now, children. Can you all keep a secret?'

They nodded earnestly as his gaze moved from one to the other, assessing them.

'What you did might be considered fighting. And if that's so, Bjorn is old enough to get into a lot of trouble. A judge could even exile him, taking into consideration that Erik was hurt.'

'I'm noth hurt, Dad.'

'Listen. If you are asked, you must say Erik broke his tooth getting olives. Understand?'

They all nodded again, impressed by the seriousness in Harald's voice.

'Let's hope for the best,' Harald sighed and glanced at Rolfson.

'Do you have to tell Freya?' Rolfson asked him, still sounding anxious.

'Yes. I tell her everything. But don't worry. Neither of us will say anything more on the matter.'

Rolfson nodded several times, trying to reassure himself.

****

Later, as a treat, Erik was riding Leban the donkey as it walked around and around, forcing the press down on the olives, their juice running thick and lumpy into clay pots. His dad led the donkey by the halter.

'Of everybody involved, you are the one who is most likely to forget our secret.' Harald looked solemn.

'Why, Dad?'

'Because everyone else will soon no longer need to talk about it, but you, you will have that broken tooth and people will always ask.'

'Don't worry. I won't tell.'

'Good boy. You understand why it is important?'

'Not really. We were only playing.'

'I know. I know. That's why I'm not cross with Bjorn or Big Erik. But it's the judges. They can be very, very strict about fighting. You know the only rule of our society.'

'Yeth. Never harm anyone.'

'They might think Bjorn harmed you deliberately.'

Erik laughed, 'It wathn't him. It was Injeborg!'

'I'm not blaming anyone. And don't you either, or when you are older you will feel bitter about your looks.'

'No. Anyway,' Erik said, giving his dad a broken smile, 'I broke it jumping for olives.'

Harald smiled back with the same proud expression he had worn when Erik had unclipped after his first Epic session.

Chapter 5
A Glitter of Metal Panels

'Olives again?' Erik groaned as he joined his mum at the table.

'With bread and cheese, it's a very good diet. You will live a long time if you eat like this every day,' his mum lectured him, cutting the bread as she did so.

'Hello, hello.' Freshly scrubbed, Harald came into the room.

For a while, there was silence as they all ate, Erik making a pattern from his olive stones.

'I think that we have to ask to be reallocated to coal mining,' Harald said without looking up. Freya stopped eating.

'You want to work in a mine?'

'It's the only guarantee we can stay together as a family.' Harald paused, still looking at his plate. 'Rolfson says it's not too bad.'

'But he only did it for a year.' Freya sounded resigned rather than seriously opposed to the idea.

Harald tore apart a great piece of bread in his hands. 'There is another option though.' Erik caught them exchanging a serious look.

'I was thinking of a district-based appeals procedure,' Harald continued.

'We need to explain to Erik exactly how a team challenge works.' Freya rested her hand lightly on Erik's arm and looked intently at Harald.

'Hope District lodges a complaint that it is being discriminated against in the allocation of the remaining solar panels. Five players each; Hope against a team fielded by Central Allocations. In other words, the best on the planet.'

'And so we would have no more chance than I did alone?'

'Hmmm,' Harald shrugged. 'We might have a chance, a slim one, but only if I was to play.'

Erik paused, fork halfway to his mouth. Astonished, he held his breath and tried to avoid being noticed. So many questions, but he knew better than to pry. They would stop talking and send him away.

'How much of a chance?' Freya continued her line of thought.

'About one in five. We need a melee-based environment. Foggy weather would be good.'

'Do it,' Freya said firmly.

Harald nodded, his eyes glistening with energy. 'The rest of the district suggested we try it. They will be pleased.'

****

Hope was built on a dry, rocky plateau; it could be seen for miles, far beyond the limit of the district for which it acted as a regional centre. Strangely, considering theirs was a world without violence, the original settlers had built a ring of white stone houses around the perimeter of the hilltop, like a defensive wall. Presumably the idea was to mark a boundary, inside which lay the heart of the town. Over the centuries, Hope had grown, with the lower slopes of the hill being occupied by smaller, less well-constructed, two-room houses. The colour of the stone told the story. Whereas the higher houses were made of machine-cut, deep-quarried, limestone, the lower ones were of an inferior, more easily obtained, yellow sandstone. Visible above all the residences, on the highest point of the hill, was one great building of metal and glass, whose dark translucent roof glittered with the violet rays of sunlight reflected from a hundred solar panels.

A subtle excitement in his dad's manner encouraged Erik to think that their visit to the town of Hope was concerned with more than submitting their much-reduced olive crop. But not until they approached the outskirts of the town did Harald say anything out of the ordinary.

'Son, your story of Cindella and the pirate treasure is exciting. But you need to obtain more information.'

'I know.'

'Hope has a library. Where all the information ever learned about Epic has been stored. It is our right to be able to consult that information. So we are going to pay the librarian a visit.'

Erik had just taken the last turn on the donkey, uncomfortably squeezed between four large barrels of olives. So it was with physical pleasure, as well as to guard himself from the mocking looks of the city dwellers, that Erik dismounted and walked alongside the donkey. He rubbed the soft hair on Leban's long nose with some affection; they had grown up together and, for Erik, Leban was more than a farmyard animal – he was a much-loved companion.

As the path rose through the more humble houses to the older, prouder buildings, so the nature of life on the street changed. The long lines of washing gave way to ornamental gardens and fruit trees already showing the lemons and figs that would eventually ripen on them. No longer did stray dogs bark on the hot, broken-paved streets, half angry, half friendly. The upper part of the town was the domain of well-fed cats, which could be spotted stalking carefully through the shadows, or leaping gracefully from window sill to the narrow cat walkways of garden walls.

Then, past the outer ring of sturdy white residences, was the town square, busy with people bringing their harvest for accounting and communal storage. Each time that Erik had come to Hope he had struggled through the same narrow paths left between the closely packed tents and stalls, so that he believed them to be a permanent feature of the town. But his dad insisted that after dark the tents were taken down and the square emptied, becoming a place of quiet unless disturbed by the near human shrieks of cats using it as their battleground.

And the people. It seemed impossible that so many people should live together, whether the innumerable families in the rough, dry stone shanties, or the throngs that traded in the market. Impossible but exciting. So many people in comparison to their small village that Erik always felt shy on coming to Hope. Not least because there were many more girls his own age. In Osterfjord there was only Injeborg, and since they had grown up side by side as neighbours, she was more like a sister than anything else.

Even from a distance it was evident that the library was a very different building from the rest of the town. Its roof glittered with the reflections from hundreds of metal panels – all tipped slightly towards a bright sun. Several tall metal posts stood up from the roof. There were more glass windows in the walls of the building than in the whole of Osterfjord.

Close up it was stranger still. For a start it was cool inside, despite the heat of the day. Also peculiar was a soft humming. Like the sea but quieter and less rhythmic. At the centre was a pit with a large circular table, around which were placed twenty chairs. They were all occupied, with people of differing ages clipped up and in the world of Epic. It was strange to see them, silent, moving only their hands, while in Epic they would be running, shouting and fighting.

'Harald, and this must Erik Haraldson?' a cheerful, balding, man greeted them

'Hello, Thorstein. You are right. This is Thorstein, Erik. He is the Hope librarian.'

Erik shook hands with the librarian.

'Oh, the poor lad. How did he do that?' Thorstein was looking at Erik's face.

Erik momentarily looked up at his dad's impassive face. 'I fell over when shaking the olive tree.'

'Tut, tut,' sympathised Thorstein. 'Still, perhaps one day we will get a visit from the Mikelgard dentist and she can fix you up with a new tooth.'

Harald laughed cynically. 'We've been waiting seven years for that.'

Thorstein nodded, admitting defeat on the point. 'So, Harald, Erik, how can I help?'

'Erik needs information.'

Thorstein waited attentively.

'You tell him, Erik,' urged his dad. 'It's all right,' he added, noticing Erik's hesitation. 'Whatever you tell Thorstein will be completely confidential.'

As Erik told the story of Cindella and the pirate's treasure, an eager gleam appeared in the librarian's deep-sunk eyes.

'Interesting, very interesting. Follow me.' Thorstein lumbered swiftly to his desk and clipped himself up. 'I will just be a moment.'

'That's a good sign, son.' Harald patted Erik on the arm.

As Thorstein silently worked his fingers and turned his head back and forth, Erik looked around the library. It was decorated with scenes that had somehow been taken from the world of Epic and mounted as pictures. Many of the scenes were familiar, pictures of Newhaven, the Cathedral, the amphitheatre. But also there were strange scenes. Erik walked over to where he could see a warrior in a red cape standing on a glacier. In the distance, austere mountain peaks formed row after row of jagged white teeth. It seemed as though the dark heavy sky had forced open the jaws of the world and was resting on the sharp points of its fangs.

The caption read: 'Olaf the Red exploring the Mountains of Hate'.

'Dad, who was Olaf the Red?'

Harald shrugged, 'I do not know. He must have existed a long time ago. Nobody explores any more.'

'Here,' Thorstein was back with them. He smiled at Erik's eager face. 'Good news.' The librarian glanced around to check that no one could hear. 'As far as I know, unless it has gone unreported – which is most unlikely – your quest has not been undertaken before.'

'So the treasure could still be there?' Erik looked to the librarian for confirmation.

'Oh indeed, it could. Your Captain Sharky is a listed character, who was a pirate some fifty years ago. The *Queen's Messenger* was a royal ship based in Cassinopia around the same time. It is a very, very promising quest, young man.' Thorstein's face wrinkled with lines around the eyes that showed he was accustomed to smiling.

'Great, after the graduation tournament, I'll sail to Cassinopia then.'

A large hand reached out to touch Erik on the shoulder as if to check him. Thorstein looked sombre again. 'Not so fast, young one. This is a quest that you need preparation for. The Skull Islands are somewhat explored and they are home to very dangerous predators. The sea is full of sharks, but worse, Rocs have a nest in a mountain of one of the islands. You, and whoever comes with you, will need to have excellent skill levels and equipment.'

Erik let out a long sigh.

Harald glanced at Thorstein who rolled his eyes up, as if to share a slight amusement at the impetuous nature of youth.

'Take your time, young man,' said the librarian. 'A quest like this will make you rich, but not if you hurry. Then you will be dead and it will be lost to you forever.'

'Well, now we are without a solar panel, we do not have time on our side,' Erik muttered bitterly in reply.

'You also.' Thorstein looked cast down. 'Times are getting hard.'

'That brings up my reason for being here.' Harald cast a shrewd look at the librarian. 'I have a team of five who are willing to challenge Central Allocations. We wish to lodge a complaint that the Hope District is facing discrimination in the distribution of solar panels.'

'That is your right, of course, but I would urge against it. You cannot defeat their teams. You will die for no gain.' Thorstein shook his head solemnly.

'Enter the complaint, please.' Harald said no more. So, after a pause, Thorstein lumbered back to his chair and sank heavily back into it. With one last sombre look their way, he clipped himself up.

Soon he stood up again. 'The complaint is registered. There will be a trial in the amphitheatre in two weeks' time, eight o'clock our time.'

'Thank you, Thorstein.'

The librarian shrugged. 'I sympathise with you. But I am sorry that you are spending your lives so uselessly.'

Chapter 6
Duels in the Arena

The arenas of Epic's great cities were intended to be practice grounds. You took your character along and you could practise combat in an environment where it did not matter if you died – you simply reappeared at the arena entrance. It was a chance to discover how effective your weapons and spells were, and to improve your skills. Over the years, public battle in the amphitheatre had become the method of conflict resolution.

The arena at Newhaven was enormous, a massive stone structure with steps rising from the wide circular theatre at the centre to dizzying heights at the back. Statues of warriors lined the perimeter facing the amphitheatre – silent and unresponsive witnesses to the centuries of battle that had taken place on the sandy floor far below them.

Today the amphitheatre seats were about a third full, mostly with the dull grey figures, which represented people watching the game via their characters. Here and there, standing out in their colour and definition, NPCs were also in attendance. Erik was present in his persona as Cindella. Beside him were Bjorn, Injeborg, B.E. and B.E's younger sister, Sigrid, all in their characters – a warrior, a witch, another warrior and a healer respectively. Many families in Hope District had stopped work and were clipped up to Epic to watch the duel – it was an occasion that justified a break in their labour. For a huge national event, such as the final rounds of the annual graduation, the amphitheatre would be near full. For a small district appealing against Central Allocations they had done well to fill even a fifth of the seats, especially as none of the other cases due that day had any planetary significance.

It was with some impatience that Erik heard an announcement across the amphitheatre.

'Case number 133, year 1124. Snorri the warrior versus Central Allocations. Snorri the warrior from Estvam accuses Central Allocations of unfairly denying his wife a hip operation. The contest will be to the death. Random terrain.'

A warrior entered the amphitheatre, half covered in chain-mail armour and carrying an axe. A few cheers went up for him and he waved to the loudest part of the crowd.

'Poor man,' Injeborg said, and her tone reflected the genuine pity in her real voice. 'What chance has he got?'

'What chance has any of us got?' uttered Bjorn glumly.

From that uncharacteristic remark, Erik realised that Injeborg and Bjorn were as nervous as he was – they were just better at not showing it. After all, both their parents were going into the amphitheatre, and with them a life's savings of arms, armour and spells. All week, people from the district had been visiting their characters in the world of Epic and giving them presents – such as healing potions or pieces of armour. But it was going to be nearly as difficult for a district team as an individual to beat Central Allocations.

Jeers and boos alerted Erik to the arrival of the Central Allocations warrior, Ragnok Strongarm.

'I know why I hate him – for killing my mum. But why does all the crowd shout out against him?' Erik found the stadium's response to the C.A. warrior bemusing, although he was glad to add his voice to the catcalls.

'Well, he is new to Central Allocations. He has achieved very little in the game of Epic outside of the arena. But Hope District dislikes him because he killed the agricultural school headmistress when she fought for the school to have another tractor,' B.E. replied.

'And he led a team which defeated Greenrocks when they objected to the changing of their crops to rapeseed,' Bjorn added grimly.

'Ah, yes, I'd forgotten that,' B.E. said, nodding.

Bowing to the crowd, Ragnok Strongarm seemed to be enjoying the jeers. He waved repeatedly, although not to his opponent. When his cloak was cast aside, it was evident that Ragnok was a Sidhe elf, tall and slender, with long silver hair in several braids to keep it from his face. His armour glittered with blue and gold light.

B.E. whistled in appreciation. 'That chain mail alone has got to be worth ten thousand bezants.'

'Combatants ready. Three, two, one, begin!'

In a blink, the floor of the amphitheatre had changed. Suddenly it was a pool of clear, deep blue water; platforms were moving around upon its surface as though they were performing a highly ritualised dance. There were cheers and laughter from the crowd. This was a rare terrain.

'I love having practice on this,' said Erik, his appreciation of the unusual duel conditions lifting him out of his nervous silence for a moment. 'Did you ever try it? The trick is to pick a route across. It actually is harder than it looks. If you get the wrong platform first, you'll go well astray.'

'This is the terrain that mages must dream of,' B.E. mused aloud. 'Imagine being a fighter and having to make your way across while spells are coming down around your ears.'

With a loud shriek, an arrow flew through the air and struck the Estvam warrior. Ragnok Strongarm was making no effort to cross to his opponent, but had calmly strung his bow and was watchfully preparing his next shot. The Estvam warrior, without a bow, was desperately trying to pick a path across the pool, jumping from island to island, trying to predict the motion of the platforms. Another shrieking missile. The warrior was struck in mid-leap and spun into the water. He disappeared and did not come up – the water was clear enough for the spectators to be able to see him struggling to remove his heavy boots as he sank. His last convulsions silenced the crowd.

'The conflict has been resolved in favour of Central Allocations.'

Ragnok bowed and departed as the amphitheatre reset itself.

'Uggh. What a horrible way to die. His armour must have dragged him down.' Even from the limited expression available to the grey polygons of her healer, Erik could see the wince of young Sigrid.

Erik felt sick. It was their turn next, and he could not see how they would avoid being butchered with similar ease.

'Case number 134, year 1124. Hope District versus Central Allocations. Hope District accuses Central Allocations of discrimination in the allocations of Solar Panels. The contest will be to the death. Survivors of the winning team will be resurrected. Random terrain.'

Huge cheers filled the amphitheatre as the Hope team entered. Even the normally placid Bjorn was shouting himself hoarse. It brought tears to Erik's eyes to see his friend bellowing for all his worth. While Bjorn's character remained grey, Erik knew that across in the Rolfsons' house he would be flushed bright red from his efforts to spur on their team.

The Hope challenge was taken up by those families with most to gain from any new panels, who in the first instance were the residents of Osterfjord. It was strange to see his lifelong neighbours in the amphitheatre. How difficult it was to believe the heroic-looking figures crossing the sand were the olive-growers who lived just a few hundred yards away.

One of the Hope team was wrapped deep in a cloak, with his hood drawn right over his head; the others were waving back to the crowd.

Erik felt a nudge. With a nod of her head, Injeborg indicted to the amphitheatre. 'That must be your dad.'

'It must be.'

'I wonder why he is covered up?' B.E. wondered aloud.

'So do I.' An unexpected rush of unhappiness filled Erik's eyes with tears. He did not have his parents' trust. They had told him nothing of the mystery of Harald's character. But he could be trusted. After all, hadn't he kept the story of his broken tooth a secret?

'It must be to keep a surprise for the Central Allocations team,' Injeborg suggested. Even though the medium of the game masked his tearful eyes, Injeborg's sympathetic glance at Erik suggested she understood something of his feelings.

The Central Allocations team entered and the crowd grew silent.

'Bloody vengeance!' B.E. put his face in his hands.

'What?' Sigrid was jittery as she turned to her brother.

'They've brought out their best team, I would say.' B.E. peeked between his fingers. 'Halfdan the Black, Wolf, Hleid the Necromancer, Thorkell the Spellcaster and Brynhild the Valkyrie. That's four dragonslayers amongst them.'

The Hope team, whose brave appearance had lifted the crowd, now appeared shabby beside the scintillating garments and powerful magical appearance of its opponents. Around Halfdan light itself seemed diminished, apart from a black glow from his boots. The strange shadows cast from his armour caused those who stood near him to appear to be just the human form for enormous and distorted-shaped demons lying on the ground. The level of noise from the audience dropped, conversations becoming subdued.

'We don't have a chance, do we, B.E.?' Sigrid looked up at her brother, who just gave an unhappy shrug.

'Combatants ready. Three, two, one, begin!'

The amphitheatre flowed in an instant, to form a rocky area, with some stacks of boulders reaching shoulder height. The Hope team hesitated then, having said something to each other, ran for cover. Only four of them reached the rocks they were aiming for.

Erik could see no sign of his dad.

'Where's Harald?' asked Bjorn.

'Invisibility?' suggested B.E.

'Ohhh, how wonderful! Let's hope so!' Injeborg clapped, her enthusiasm encouraging them all to be more hopeful.

The Central Allocations team was in no hurry to close on its opponents. Its spellcasters were chanting, while Halfdan and Brynhild – the two warriors – stood confidently before them, on guard. Wolf strode out and shouted a command in a strange guttural language. With a gasp from the crowd, he transformed himself into a large, fierce-looking, black wolf and began to howl.

In contrast with the last fight, the crowd was absolutely attentive and the few voices that called out were very distinct. Erik desperately wished he was down there with the Hope team – but with a character powerful enough to withstand these legendary opponents.

Above the amphitheatre, the clouds rumbled and gathered. A great shadow fell over them all and Erik could feel the pressure of the sky.

'Oh no,' groaned B.E. 'It's Thorkell the Spellcaster. He's going to cast a lightning strike.'

Almost as one, the thousands of people in the crowd were cowering in anticipation of the terrible crack in the sky as a blast of lightning was wrenched from it by the spell; some had their hands over their ears. Then they were on their feet cheering. The dark skies dissolved and sun broke through to gleam on the white silicate of the boulders in the arena floor.

'What? What?' Erik leapt up to see Thorkell writhing on the ground, his pale blue, sigil-covered robe becoming covered in dirt, white foam around his lips. A slender elf was retreating, whirling two short swords before him in a glittering, mesmerising pattern. Then, with a cheeky bow to the crowd, the elf stepped into a shadow and disappeared.

Injeborg leapt up beside Erik, bright eyes searching for his.

'Erik, it's your dad! It's your dad!'

His friends were around him now, slapping his back and cheering.

'He has to be a master thief.' B.E. shook his head. 'Who would have believed that in Hope we had a master thief.'

'Yes! Yes!' Pushing aside his friends, Erik leapt to his feet, fists clenched. 'That's for my mum!' He did a little jig and punched the air. 'Die, all of you, die!' He shouted as loudly as he could at the remaining four members of the Central Allocations team.

The crowd was on its feet still, cheering on the Hope team. B.E. shook his head with disbelief. 'I had no idea so many people would take our side. They must feel the same way about Central Allocations.'

Wolf gave a great howl and raced towards the Hope team. But Halfdan the Black was looking around as though panicked. He swung his great two-handed sword back and forth, nervously looking for his enemy. Brynhild, acting with a confidence more in keeping with her winged-helmeted valkyrie, grabbed him and said something in his ear. They then stood back to back, with Hleid between them, astride the dead body of Thorkell.

The crowd was roaring on the team. The cry of 'Hope! Hope!' was taken up around the amphitheatre, even by those who had no relationship to the district. Without a word being said, they shared a feeling that this moment could be a piece of history. It was impossible to believe it yet, but perhaps the team from a small district could beat the mighty Mikelgard team – after all, the great mage Thorkell was down – unheard of! Could this day mark the end of the careers of four legendary dragonslayers?

Wolf leapt from rock to rock, tongue lolling. As he approached the four other Hope players, Rolfson and his warrior companion lifted their swords and shields. But Wolf was not seeking to fight them. His charge swerved at the last moment and from a boulder he launched himself over the fighters to land on Siggida, Bjorn and Injeborg's mother, the healer of their team. Ignoring the blows of the fighters, which did not seem to be making any impression on his thick hide, Wolf savaged at Siggida's throat until she was dead. Snarling, he then turned towards the two warriors, mouth a bloody grin.

'Silver weapons. We need silver, or magic,' B.E. said anxiously.

From the shadows behind the wolf, a motion. A flashing of blades. The wolf howled and swirled about to see the source of the blows that had unexpectedly pierced him. The mysterious elf stood before him, slowly rotating his two short swords, parrying lunges from the snarling fangs of the wolf. Again the crowd was on its feet, cheering. Erik took the opportunity to examine more closely his dad's character. It was a wood elf, smaller than a Sidhe, but stronger looking. His armour was mainly leather, but it was beautifully scrolled, suggesting it might be magic. From beneath the elf's cape Erik could see the glimmer of golden hair — an unusual indulgence and the only clue that the character was indeed that of his father.

The wolf was clearly slowing down, and from its panting mouth long trails of saliva hung to the ground full of foam.

'Those swords must be poisoned,' observed Bjorn.

'Agreed.' B.E. was raptly attentive to the battle.

While Wolf panted in a more and more laboured fashion, Erik looked back to the Central Allocations team. The remaining members were not idle. Hleid had planted her skull-capped staff in the chest of the body that she stood over. With a flourish, she gestured towards the two-blade-wielding wood elf, who was causing them so much consternation. Thorkell's reanimated body slowly rose from the ground, then turned to face its target and flew towards him.

'Death and destruction, what is that?' whispered Injeborg.

'I have no idea.' B.E. clenched his hands together, conveying his dismay, despite wearing a stock expression on the grey, slabbed face of his warrior.

Harald was glancing up from the dying Wolf from time to time, and had seen the incoming undead creature. He ran back into the shadows and disappeared once more, but the zombie version of Thorkell was not misled by the concealment; it constantly altered its flight, indicating the route of Harald's movements.

A flock of ravens cawed and screamed as it suddenly flew over the sides of the amphitheatre and dived towards the conflict. Hleid had thrown back her purple robe and was screaming, arms aloft, white hair streaming into the sky, as she directed the birds down onto the other Hope team members. The Hope mage managed to point and direct a burst of fire at the birds, many of which fell and flopped to the ground. But there were thousands of ravens in the cloud and soon they had surrounded the three visible Hope players. Rolfson and his companions were able only to thrash around, running into rocks to dislodge the wicked stabs of the dark flapping creatures. The mage, the least well armoured and without a helm, fell, hands wrapped around his eyes. In an instant, he was completely engulfed in a writhing black carpet of birds that shortly afterwards stopped moving. The two warriors fought on, heads ducked, swinging sword and shield at the ravens that were crowing and pecking at them.

The zombie indicated by its remorseless chase that Harald was moving swiftly around and around the perimeter.

'Where's he going?' wondered B.E.

'Well, what can he do?' answered Eric bitterly. 'He's stuck. If he stops, he'll be killed. If he attacks Halfdan and Brynhild, he can't possibly win, and the zombie will be on him in no time.'

With a lurch, the zombie directed itself towards the Central Allocations team.

'There he goes!' said Injeborg.

Halfdan and Brynhild braced themselves, weapons raised, and were ready as Harald materialised before them. But, ducking their blows, he did not stop to fight. His swords were not even in his hands. Instead, with a tumble, he rolled through their thrusts and seized the staff of Hleid with both hands. With a great yank he twisted her off balance and, although Halfdan slashed down a blow onto his shoulder that caused him to stagger, Harald recovered to sprint away, holding the staff above him like a trophy, to the pleasure of the crowd which redoubled its volume of cheers.

In fact, as Erik looked around the stadium, he could see considerably more people in the arena than when the fighting had begun. Somehow the word was spreading and more and more people were clipping up to Epic in order to see the duel.

Once clear of his opponents, Harald pointed the staff back at Hleid, manipulating the skull. She looked aghast and turned to see the zombie Thorkell abruptly halt in his flight, and then start moving towards her with arms raised, Hleid shouted out panicked spells, but the zombie came on. Halfdan and Brynhild struck the creature with mighty blows, and although it shuddered, it knocked them aside to grasp Hleid by the throat and squeeze the life out of her. With her death, Thorkell fell to the ground, once more a fleshy bag of bones.

'Hope! Hope!' It was the giant-killing of the century. A great roar of approval rang out, as Harald brandished his swords again, saluting the four directions of the compass before once more stepping into the shadows and disappearing. Three down!

'Your dad is incredible!' Injeborg gave Erik a hug.

Erik was immobile, shivering all over, his body basking in the release of a deep tension that he had not realised it had contained. There was a strange taste in his mouth, which he understood to be the taste of vengeance fulfilled.

'I'll never underestimate a thief again,' Bjorn muttered to himself.

Down on the floor of the amphitheatre there was a lull. Rolfson and his comrade had killed the last of the ravens, and were drinking healing potions to restore themselves. The mage, however, had died under the assault of the birds.

At the other end of the rocky fighting area, Halfdan and Brynhild stood back to back, alert for the thief.

An announcement came over the amphitheatre.

'Hope team offer a tie. Full resurrection to all; all equipment restored. Providing a reappraisal is taken of the solar-panel allocation.'

A warm ripple of applause greeted the statement.

'That's sensible.' B.E. explained. 'It's a good result for us. And they will find it difficult to refuse. If they try to carry on but end up losing their lives, there is no coming back for any of them.'

The announcement had clearly divided Halfdan and Brynhild, who while remaining back to back were animatedly turning their heads over their shoulders and gesturing – their weapons exaggerating the sweeping arm movements. After some time, the crowd began a slow handclap. Erik joined in with a sense of extraordinary liberation. The gods of the game were being humbled and the crowd, being quick to sense it, added to their humiliation.

As the noise of the clap built up to resound around the amphitheatre, Brynhild shrugged and sheathed her weapon. Halfdan raised his sword and waved acceptance.

'The conflict has resulted in a tie and the matter will be reviewed.'

Great cheers were raised for Rolfson and the remaining Hope warrior as they walked, waving joyfully, from the amphitheatre. The crowd would have loved another glimpse of their master thief, but he did not reappear which – as the amateur tacticians explained at the party in Hope that night – was a wise move.

Last to leave were Halfdan and Brynhild, still brandishing their weapons in vehement disagreement.

Chapter 7
The First Signs of Discord

The tower in which the Central Allocations meetings took place was surrounded by raincloud, making the emergency session unusually claustrophobic. Streams of rain were running like tears down the glass. It was so dark within the dome that lamps had been brought to the table. Legend had it that they were sitting inside what had once been the nose cone of a spacecraft. The body of the spaceship, if it ever existed, had long since gone, its valuable metal being replaced by stone and mortar.

'What a shambles,' Ragnok sneered. 'The famous and powerful Central Allocations team humiliated by a town of rustics.'

Of all the members of the highest committee in the planet Ragnok was the only one to emerge from the previous day's fighting with any real credit; he could afford to gloat. His Sidhe warrior had despatched Snorri the warrior with just two bow shots. Nevertheless, Svein Redbeard thought his cocky manner unwise; it would win him no friends. Of course, it was amusing to see the legendary aura slip from his fellow dragonslayers, but that enjoyment should be kept private. Fortunately, Svein himself had not been selected for the team that had suffered such humiliation and his own reputation as one of the most powerful players in the game was inviolate.

'I had no protection.' Thorkell shrugged off any responsibility for the disaster and folded his arms, aged pudgy fingers drumming slowly on a light blue velvet jacket that echoed the colours of his character's rune-inscribed cape.

'Thorkell the Spellcaster! You were more use dead than alive.' Brynhild laughed, a surprisingly young, if bitter laugh, from such an elderly woman. She also resembled her character, insofar as her long silver hair was combed into two braids. 'What must it have looked like to the spectators: Thorkell the all-knowing as a zombie floating over the sand?'

To judge by the other mocking expressions in the room, the valkyrie was not the only member of the committee to enjoy the memory of its most pompous and arrogant member being a brainless tool of Hleid the Necromancer.

'Now, enough.' The chairperson, Hleid, was less forceful sounding than usual. She had aged since the battle, thought Svein, and her wrinkles looked tired rather than lending her face its usual authoritative aura. 'Let us deal with the matter in an orderly way. We all of us have things to do.'

'Agreed.' The last thing that Svein wanted to do was to spend all day wrangling over the mistakes of the Central Allocations team. He had a good lead on his own personal quest that had been sent to him by the librarian at Fiveways and he wished to spend the afternoon looking into it.

'Firstly we have to reappraise the allocation of solar panels to Hope District. Proposals?'

'Give them ten more?' suggested Bekka. Svein smiled at her; she was always the most generous of the Central Allocations committee.

'Five.' It was obvious that Ragnok hated to give the rustics anything at all, but even he knew it could not be helped.

'Seven,' said Wolf.

'Seven. How about seven?' Hleid looked around the table to passive faces and shrugs. 'Seven it is.'

'What a nightmare,' Halfdan shuddered. 'There is going to be a flood of claims now.'

'Indeed.' Svein scowled frostily to remind Halfdan that for all his fanciful black garb, Halfdan's supposedly invincible warrior was one of those responsible for the mess.

'Next,' Hleid hurried on, 'battle analysis – and let us try to be constructive.' She sighed, 'perhaps a non-combatant's view would be useful to begin with.' Hleid slowly looked around, peering over her glasses, 'Bekka, what did you think?'

'Me?' Bekka was surprised. As the committee's druidess she was more usually called upon to help make potions and cast spells involving animals than to discuss battles. 'Well, let me think.' She paused, looking intently at her hands for a while in concentration. She was taking the responsibility of the question very seriously. At the very moment that Ragnok let loose an exaggerated yawn, Bekka continued, 'What I think is that our side did not fight as a team. Wolf is too used to fighting opponents without silver or magic weapons and wasted his life trying to win the fight on his own. I think that the team should perhaps have defensive or warding spells up first, not Thorkell's dramatic attempt to wipe out all our opponents with one lightning bolt. I think that they should have discussed a plan before commencing battle. Basically, I think our team was racing to see who would get the glory of killing the opposition and failed to work together or take the other team seriously.'

'I got the healer.' Wolf spoke up, angrily, arms behind his head; he had one foot up on the table, his chair tipped back as far as it could safely go.

'Yes, but that's all. You are worth more than a fifth-rate healer.' Brynhild seemed particularly ready for an argument today. Voices began to rise all around the table.

'Members of the Committee, please. Let's respect the desire of the Chair to keep matters constructive,' Svein called out above them all, then dropped his voice. 'I believe that Bekka has analysed the battle accurately and that all we need to do on this item is to adopt a resolution that in future all teams will meet before the conflict is due to start and discuss tactics. We used to do that without fail, but we have grown complacent.'

'Is that a formal proposal?' Hleid asked.

'It is.'

'I second it,' Ragnok spoke up.

'In that case, a vote please. All those in favour of Svein's proposal, please show,' Hleid peered around the table. 'Unanimous. Good.' Her gaze dropped back to the sheet in front of her. 'In which case the next item is the character belonging to Harald Erikson. Comment.'

'His poison was powerful. Really powerful. I can normally take five or six strong hits before dying.' For once casting aside his persona as a great scholar and the ultimate wizard, Thorkell sounded apologetic; his permanently quivering hands were visible above the table, wrinkled and translucent.

'Agreed,' added Wolf. 'I have never been drained of life so quickly. Not even from a spell.'

'Why did we not know of the existence of a master thief?' Halfdan the Black interjected angrily, round face flushing red.

'Because Harald Erikson, if that is his true name, has not played Epic for twenty years,' Svein answered firmly.

'That was no thief,' a quiet voice said. Godmund was the most elderly of them all and rarely spoke at meetings, but when he did they listened carefully. He knew more about Epic than anyone alive, including Svein. With a surprisingly firm voice, considering his age, Godmund continued, 'That was a master assassin we saw at work in the Newhaven amphitheatre yesterday.'

'An assassin? Death and destruction! Of course.' Halfdan shook his head, loudest among those who gave murmurs of surprise at Godmund's statement. 'But who outside the University ever trains an assassin?'

'No one.' Godmund smiled. It was a smile that Svein had learned meant danger and he leant back, to watch rather than intervene.

'He is one of us?' Bekka was confused.

'Correction. He *was* one of us. Twenty years ago,' Godmund said, scowling. 'Another renegade, but one who seems to have slipped away from us.'

'Until now,' said Ragnok.

'I can remember some young assassins we were training.' Godmund closed his eyes. 'I think perhaps the University librarian should go over all the disputes of twenty to thirty years ago.'

'Seconded.' Svein was always quick to show support for Godmund.

'Agreed?' Hleid looked around the table. 'Agreed unanimously.'

'I propose we activate the Executioner.' Ragnok could not hide the note of eagerness that crept into his voice.

'Seconded.' Godmund nodded his approval. 'But remember, this man waited twenty years before playing Epic – at least in public. It might be hard to find him. Great patience will be needed.'

'We will do shifts until we have him.' Ragnok spoke decisively. No one loved playing the Executioner more than Ragnok.

'It is the only way,' Godmund agreed.

Inwardly Svein heaved a sigh of dismay. Normally it was not possible for one player to harm another in any way; the game did not allow it. Unknown to the vast majority of the planet's inhabitants, it was in fact possible to create characters who could kill – and be killed by – other players. Only the nine members of the highest committee in the land had the code to get into the options menu that allowed for the creation of such characters. Central Allocations had used its collective wealth to equip a warrior with all the most powerful magic, arms and armour that money could buy. This was the Executioner and over the years he had been brought out to eliminate destabilising opponents. The victims, of course, had no idea that they had met another player; they assumed it was a rare and aggressive NPC.

Svein had no scruples about using the Executioner, but so few people knew the secret of the killer character that those who did would have to take hours of their time playing him, to keep a constant search up for his target.

'So, all those in favour of directing the Executioner against the character of Harald Erikson, please show?' Hleid asked for the vote. 'One against.' Everyone looked disdainfully at Bekka.

'It's too suspicious. People are not stupid,' she offered as her defence. But Svein guessed that she was putting her own moral objection into a language the rest of them could understand. Still, she would take her turn with the rest of them on the shifts; she always did acquiesce.

'Ragnok can draw up the rota. We begin the search at Newhaven.'

Hleid returned to the checklist of items for the agenda. 'Finally, we have this.' She indicated to the printout in her hands. 'Found in several places, left on the amphitheatre seating.'

They passed the sheaf of papers around, taking one and passing them on. When each had one in front of them, and was studying it, head bowed, Hleid continued. 'Comments?'

Svein was looking at a copy of a small newssheet entitled the *New Leviathan*. 'Just a moment, Chair. May we have time to read it?'

'Certainly.'

There was a period of studious silence. High above them the rain made a faint murmur against the dome, as though pleading to get in.

More Slaughter of the Innocent

Today we will witness Central Allocations destroy the hopes and dreams of a seventy-year-old couple and the Hope District. The argument that is used to justify this is that resources are scarce and somebody has to manage them. Agreed. But this is not democratic management; this is the dictatorship of a small, self-selected elite, a new Casiocracy as we call them, the new Leviathan that sits bloated above society while the rest of us work hard for the community. Over the years the members of this new Leviathan have accumulated the wealth to ensure that their characters are indestructible. How can Epic be fair?

We are told that any other system of administration would lead to a breakdown in society and the return of violence between people. But is that necessarily the case? In Ancient Greece they had a democracy where people were elected to administer the cities, and these people could do the job for only one year before making way for the next administration. We could use the technology of Epic to unite the people in mass, popular discussions at the Amphitheatre and decide allocations by voting not by game-based conflict.

The times demand change. Our system is not working. Overthrow the Casiocracy!

The paper contained other articles detailing the declining state of the economy with surprising accuracy.

'Comments?' Hleid asked again.

'Please don't misunderstand me. I know this is dangerous material. But why exactly is it wrong? I mean, how would you answer these claims?' Bekka was hesitant.

'Bloody vengeance, woman! Isn't it obvious? This is a recipe for utter chaos!' Halfdan had even more of a reason to be angry than the others. One of the other articles in the paper listed in detail his black equipment as an example of how much more powerful the Central Allocations Committee characters were than the average character.

'Bekka asks an important question,' Svein intervened, and she looked grateful. 'I propose that I draw up a discussion document for us all, which answers the arguments in this paper. In the meantime, I would simply say to her that our system is not above criticism, but that to think we could manage affairs by voting is naïve. Voting blocs would quickly form, so that, for example, the South would unite together to obtain resources from the North and so on. Also, the example from Ancient Greece is ill informed. Those people had slaves and they had wars. For all our faults, we are a peaceful society.'

Bekka nodded thoughtfully and smiled back as Svein caught her eye with what he hoped was his most charming expression.

'Good,' said Hleid. 'So, a seconder for Svein's proposal.'

'Seconded,' said Bekka at once.

'All those in favour?' Hleid looked up to check. 'Unanimous.'

'I will bring the document to next week's meeting,' Svein told them.

'That's it.' Hleid promptly stood up and left, leaning on a skull-topped walking stick that a student had made her, modelled on the staff possessed by her character.

Much as Svein wanted to hurry back to Epic, he thought better of rushing out with her. Instead he helped Godmund rise from his chair.

'That was an astute observation about the assassin,' Svein said, offering him an arm, which Godmund pushed away, preferring his stick.

'It's not that assassin that worries me. We've had renegades before and we'll have 'em again. It's that newspaper. We have to stop that newspaper.' Godmund turned a fierce gaze onto Svein. 'You should stop your foolish expenditure of time on the *Epicus Ultima* quest – which is not solvable – and find out who is behind that paper. It is someone close to us, who has access to our data.'

Shocked by the ferocity of Godmund's voice, Svein could only nod. 'You are right, you are right,' he said, but in his heart he answered back, 'Old man, you would not believe how close I have come to solving it.'

Chapter 8
Behold, the Executioner

There were few pleasures in life greater than entering the world of Epic as the Executioner. He walked among the players like an unworshiped god. They could all see the figure, but they had no idea of the fact that a human consciousness was in control of it, and that at the slightest whim he could take the life of any of them.

Having entered the password known only to members of the Central Allocations Committee, Ragnok relaxed into his seat, relishing every moment as the Executioner rose on his platform from the box, and slowly rotated.

The Executioner was a tall human male, nondescript features covered by a great war helm. The bulk of the body was covered in rune-carved plate-metal armour – the best armour that money could buy, every piece enchanted by a dwarven master craftsman to make it resilient yet light. His golden-edged shield showed the screaming face of a demon. That shield was unique and had been bought from the Prince of Al'Karak, a realm of nomads deep in the desert. There really was a demon in the shield, whose resistance to magic meant that no player, and very few NPCs or monsters, could cast a spell that could harm the Executioner. The warrior had a variety of weapons, including an ornate longbow and quiver full of magic arrows.

Among the swords at his disposal was 'Acutus', a vorpal blade that randomly, at a rate of about one in twenty blows, cut through *any* substance. But Ragnok's weapon of choice was the 'Bastard Sword of the Moon'; this elegant silver weapon was swift for its size, and sent shivers of fear through opponents, causing them to freeze in their actions.

To dwell carefully on his accessory lists of additional magic items was never tedious despite their length. The Executioner was equipped with the maximum complement of rings, jewellery, potions, scrolls, ointments and a miscellany of helpful implements – for example, the rope of climbing. The full cost of equipping this character was more than ten years of the combined accumulation of bezants by the entire population of the world. And it was worth it.

Enough. Ragnok triggered the entrance button. All was intensely black and still. Then a rushing sound grew rapidly in volume to a roar of sound accompanied by an explosion of light.

Hate and vengeance strode once more in the world of Epic.

It was evening, and the first of Epic's moons, Sylvania, was already bright in the deepening blue of the sky. Aridia, the smaller moon, was yet to rise. Ragnok turned slowly about to gain his bearings. He was still at the place of the last execution – clearly none of the other committee members had used the character since then. Nearby, a black warhorse stood patiently and looked at him with an intelligent gaze. So, they were some sixty miles from Newhaven, where the hunt must begin.

'Hello, old fellow.' Ragnok patted the flank of his mount, then, grabbing the saddle, hoisted himself up. Glancing at the moon again to calculate north, Ragnok urged his steed forward at a canter. The sooner they got to Newhaven, the sooner the real hunt could begin.

As he clipped his way through the fields, Ragnok felt a surge of joy. Right now, he was the most lethal player in the whole of Epic. Not one of the other committee members could match the Executioner. The idea of stalking one of the others had, of course, occurred to him. And if any of them dared get out of line with Ragnok, he would do it. After all, what could they say? They could hardly admit the truth of the incident to the world. And they could not risk expelling him, exposing themselves to the threat that he might reveal all he knew. Not that any of them came close to deliberately antagonising him. They found him useful – and perhaps they feared him. Such had been his plan ever since University, to become indispensable to the authorities. He had volunteered for every ugly assignment, every arena battle that he could, no matter how unpopular the issue or controversial the decision that he was being asked to champion. His strategy had worked. Whereas all the other committee members saw themselves as heroes of some sort – as legendary figures – Ragnok refused to cover his deeds with such fanciful notions. He was a villain, so what? Right now, at this moment, he was the greatest power in the land. It has been a hard, twenty-year slog. But every hour of his youth spent in Epic accumulating strength had proven to be well spent.

The Executioner raised his sword to the moon and roared aloud with the pleasure of being alive.

It would be quite something to be the sole person able to use the Executioner. Government of the world necessitated a committee; after all, you needed at least five players for a team. Plus there were sufficient demands on the authorities that a committee of nine made sense. But what if you were the only person with access to the Executioner? How the other members of the committee would bow and scrape to please you. The others were getting old. There were younger players awaiting their chance, people he was cultivating, including the sons and daughters of the present leadership. He had waited twenty years to get on the committee; it would not take him so long again to command it.

A cart track came into view and Ragnok turned to ride along it. This would take him to the old stone road that ran straight to Newhaven. He had covered half the distance to the road when he saw a movement on the track. Some brave player was journeying in a wild place, very late in the day. The figure had his back towards the Executioner and was running, obviously wanting to reach the relative safety of the stone road before dark. Silently Ragnok drew the Bastard Sword of the Moon. His left hands on the reigns, right raising the sword high, the rider of death thundered down on the traveller. A mocking glance over his shoulder showed Ragnok that the person he had struck was an elf. Then he was galloping on, laughing aloud, having neatly sliced the head from his target. Somewhere on the planet, some farmer or student was unclipping, probably in a tearful daze, with no idea as to why their character's life had suddenly ended.

By the time the guard-post lights of Newhaven were approaching, Ragnok had calmed down. The trail of bodies he had left in his wake on the stone road was thinning out. After all, closer to the city, the chance of any word of his slayings reaching the committee rose and he could not bear to hear their censorious comments. There was even a chance that they might vote to exclude him from using the Executioner. Of course, the argument for not killing players unless they had been voted to be assassinated was completely logical and watertight – there was no point arousing questions. But the illicit thrill of being a player-killer was something that could not be understood with logic. Nor could logic explain the pattern of his killings. Curiously it was not the stronger-looking players that attracted his attention – and if there was any justification for the deaths of players it was to eliminate possible threats to the Central Allocations team. No, it was the slightly heart-rending players, with their one weapon and tiny pieces of armour, which drew his attention. There was something bewitchingly naïve and tender about them, spending their spare time killing kobolds and orcs for pennies, saving assiduously and slowly. And so he rode them down, bringing their struggle up the ladder of Epic to an abrupt end.

Once in Newhaven, Ragnok rode slowly through the narrow, cobbled streets, keeping to the back ways. Although he would be taken for an NPC and ignored by the vast majority of players, there was always a small chance that someone would come and talk to him, in the hope that he would have some clue to some foolish quest. After a tedious and restrained journey through the back streets, he arrived at the cathedral and tethered the horse.

'Later, brave one,' Ragnok whispered to the horse and entered the huge building.

The cathedral was busy; oil lanterns had been lit on the walls, drawing attention to the vast space that was enclosed under the high, vaulted roof. Statues of the holy martyr and her acolytes filled deep-set alcoves; monks in cowls were chanting, while a representative cross-section of Newhaven society sat on the benches to hear the evening sermon from the bishop.

You had to admire the sophistication of Epic. Even though there was probably not one other player in the great building, the NPCs continued with a life of their own. If you were engaged in a quest that required meeting the high and mighty of Newhaven, you could do worse than to wait here and try to talk to them after the service was over. Still, that was for people like Svein Redbeard. With long strides, Ragnok hurried along the aisle that led to the base of the cathedral tower. Ignoring an attempt by an NPC monk to talk to him, he entered the tower, closing the door behind him, and began to run up the stairs.

Even the Executioner did not have infinite reserves of stamina, and by the fortieth flight of stairs, he was moving with distinctly less speed. By the one hundredth, he was down to a walk. But that was the last. Suddenly the whole of the sky opened up to him. He was at the top of the tower, looking down on the city of Newhaven.

The glitter of the stars above was matched by the patterns of torches below. He could have been adrift on a dark lake whose waters transformed the silver glimmers in the sky to yellow blazes below. Newhaven was a well-ordered city, and the main thoroughfares were lit by torches at regular intervals, creating trails of torchlight all around him, stretching for miles. The great amphitheatre was completely dark and empty, a huge black circle avoided by the sinuous lines of light.

With a sigh Ragnok prepared to unclip. When dawn came to Epic he would return and begin his search.

Chapter 9
fever and distress

A pale and overcast dawn had turned Erik's room grey. He was awake early, and for a moment in his dizziness he wondered why it was so urgent to get up. Big Erik had been calling for him to run away? No. That was a dream. Then he remembered and ran to the bathroom to be sick in the sink. His mouth tasted of sour apples.

'Mum?' Erik leaned on the doorframe to his parents' room. The two of them looked peaceful, asleep in the bed. 'Mum,' Erik said louder.

She lifted her head, dishevelled brown hair covering her face, 'Erik? What's the matter?'

'I've been sick.'

'Go and lie down in your room. I shall come to you in a minute.'

The ceiling of his room was whiter now, its rough plastering and ridges of whitewash reminding him of the snow landscapes you could get in the amphitheatre when practising Epic.

'What's the matter, Erik?' His mum felt his forehead.

'I'm sick. My tummy hurts.'

'Where exactly?'

'Here.' He rested his hand just below his belly button. The warmth of it was comforting.

Brushing aside his damp fringe, his mum kissed him; the touch of her lips was cool. 'Oh Erik, you're burning up! Do you think you could ride a cart to Hope. To see the doctors there?'

'Oh, yes. A cart ride. Leban can take me.' Erik was mumbling, becoming more feverish as he spoke.

The journey to Hope took forever and yet they arrived all at once. Harald unpacked Erik from the furs in which he had travelled. It was suddenly very cold and he shivered. The hospital was like the library, he thought, lots of windows. It was too much of an effort to walk, so when people put their hands on his limbs and head to carry him, he did not shake them off. The bed they put him into was white and cool.

'Hello, young man,' a kindly-looking doctor said, smiling down at him. 'Can you show me where it hurts?'

The doctor lifted back the sheet and Erik pointed.

'And does it hurt more when I press?' Erik shook his head. 'Or when I let go?' The moment the doctor lifted his hand, Erik's body jerked up with a violent spasm of extreme pain.

'Well. That's pretty clear cut, eh?' The doctor replaced the sheet and went away with his dad. Soon though, Harald returned.

'Erik?' he said, sitting beside his son.

'Yes?'

'Every person has an organ known as an appendix. Sometimes these go bad and have to be removed. It's not that unusual. But you'll have to stay here for a while afterwards. The doctor says that we are very lucky that your mum made me bring you in straightaway. It could have been much worse, but now you will be fine.'

'Really? Could I have died?'

His dad hesitated. 'Possibly.'

That was good. It would impress his friends more to tell them that he could have died.

'It's an injustice though,' Harald growled.

'What, Dad?'

'If you were in Mikelgard and a senior Epic player, they would treat you differently.' He paused. 'Or if we had thousands of bezants.'

Erik could see his dad was angry, but couldn't follow his reasoning.

'Here the doctor says the necessary equipment has been broken for over twenty years. Here they have to use surgery. You will be left with a scar and it will take longer to heal.'

'How long?'

'Two weeks.'

With a jolt of dismay that temporarily woke him from his fever, Erik understood the meaning behind his dad's words. 'But, Dad, that's the first stage of the Graduation Tournament.'

'Aye.' Harald let out a long, sad, breath. 'Still, son, your health is more important than anything else. And, after all, you were in no hurry to move from Osterfjord.'

'I know. It's not for me. It's the others.' A jumble of thoughts and feelings swirled around in Erik's head. 'What's going to happen to the team? We were all set up as the Osterfjord Players. Inny, B.E., Sigrid. Bjorn even gave up his place on the Agricultural School team to be with us. What about all our practising ...?' Erik trailed off feverishly. The hours of preparation in the hunting grounds and the arena faded to irrelevance. His dream of finding a way to challenge Central Allocations now seemed like an impossible fantasy.

Erik and Harald sat in silence, downcast.

That afternoon, the hospital porters came for him, lifting him onto a trolley. As it rolled along the hospital corridor, it gave out a squeak that cycled around and around like a distressed bird. Eraaachka, eraachka, eraachka .... The plaster on the roof of the corridors he passed underneath was cracked, and in some places a patch of yellow stone was visible where it had come away altogether. Eventually they parked the trolley in a room with a large moveable light, poised over him like a snake ready to strike. For a long time, he was left there alone, listening to the banging of distant doors, worried about the snake. Then the room began to fill with people and he caught snatches of conversation.

'You have to make the incision around here and peel back the skin until you can grasp the inflamed appendix ...'

'There shouldn't be too much blood but, just in case, have one nurse wiping so you can see what you are doing. He should have a clamp ready too, you never know ...'

Just then the nurse realised that Erik could hear what they were saying. 'Could you please get on and administer the anaesthetic!' she snapped.

'Here, inhale this.'

A pungent cotton pad held at the end of a long pair of prongs was put before Erik's nose. He breathed in.

Erik woke up from the operation very sore. The slightest movement was extremely painful, so he lay on his back listening to the other people in the room. Echoes of footfalls against hard floors told him that the room he was in was large. A faint murmur of voices was all around, none of them loud enough for individual words to be distinguishable. The day passed slowly, marked by the changing quality of the light as shadows withdrew from the cracked pattern of the ceiling, only to crawl forwards again until they were dispelled by a nurse lighting up the oil lamps.

The night-time was worse though; sleep came only fitfully. It was not only that he kept waking up as a result of his body moving too much; it was also being in a strange room. Erik was conscious of being surrounded by sick children; there was often hushed activity somewhere out of his sight, and always a faint humming sound in the background.

The following day, a nurse made him get up while he changed the sheets. It was agony and Erik could not believe how cruel the nurse was to insist that he move to the chair beside the bed. It was the first time he had looked down at his stomach since the operation. His cotton top was stuck fast to his body with blood. Trying to peel if off aroused a sharp pain more terrible than bending; so he left it. The sheets that the nurse took with him were also covered in blood.

Each day, Erik found it was easier to accomplish the bending of his body as he swung his legs onto the floor. And each day, more and more of the dry blood flaked away, until at last, with great relief, he could pull off the stained cotton top. The area below his stomach had a great white scar, about halfway between his belly button and his right hip. It looked like a pallid white worm, and it was nearly a foot long. The soft flesh was held together by a dozen large stitches. Now at least he could walk about slowly, holding his sore side and wearing a new cotton tunic and trousers that he had been given by the hospital.

One afternoon, his mum and dad brought his friends along. They came in, looking about tentatively, disconcerted by the size of the room and the numbers of people gathered around beds.

'Here! Injeborg!' He waved to them and they hurried over.

'We have presents for you, Erik,' Injeborg said proudly.

Sigrid handed him a jar of honey.

'Oh great! Thank you, Sigrid. The food in here is awful.' He put the jar on the table beside the bed.

'Bjorn. Give him your present.' Injeborg was eager for Erik to see what they had brought him.

'Here, Erik.' Bjorn sheepishly took a cardboard box from his bag. There was a painting on the cover of a boat at sea near Osterfjord. Erik opened the box and inside were hundreds of little jigsaw pieces made from thin cardboard.

'He spent all day on it, Erik, cutting them out. And they have a coat of varnish on to keep the paint on.' Injeborg's eyes flashed with pleasure.

'I tried to get the painting the same both times. But you can always tell it's the right piece by the fit,' Bjorn muttered shyly.

'Thank you, Bjorn. It's a very good present.'

'And here's mine.' Injeborg drew out an entangled mess of string and wood. At first, Erik thought it was a puppet.

'Ermm, thanks, Injeborg,' he said, starting to unravel it. Then he saw that it was a mobile for hanging up.

'I thought it would remind you of Osterfjord,' Injeborg explained eagerly. 'See, here is a shell from the beach. And that is a cone from your fir. And that's supposed to be your donkey. Only it's hard to draw. But can you see? I clipped a tiny bit of hair from Leban's tail.'

Erik laughed. 'Injeborg, it's magic. I wonder if they'll let me hang it from the rail there?'

'Of course they will. Tie it up, Bjorn.'

Her big brother glanced around the room, looking for someone to ask permission of. Then, with an apologetic shrug, he stood on a chair and tied the mobile to a bed rail. It balanced well with two main arms slowly turning back and forth around each other.

'That's really good, Inny.' Erik looked up at the affectionate smiles of his friends. That they had been thinking of him enough to take this much trouble with their presents was a revelation.

Erik noticed that B. E. was waiting for him.

'Here. I hope you haven't read it already.' B.E. gave him a book: *Lessons in Epic Strategy*.

'No, no I haven't.' Erik opened it curiously. It had a fascinating contents page: '*Single Player Combats*', '*Spells for Outdoor Battles*', and many more.

'This looks really good. Thank you for parting with it, Big Erik.'

B.E. just waved away the thanks. 'It's no bother. I never got time to study it properly. But you might, being stuck here for two weeks.'

Their faces, so bright and friendly, suddenly fell.

'It's such bad luck,' said Sigrid.

Injeborg shook her head tearfully.

'Ya. And me and Bjorn will be too old next year. We've missed our chance to play together. That's the end of the Osterfjord Players.' B.E. was matter of fact.

'Who have you got to replace me?' Erik asked.

They looked at each other.

'We discussed it, Erik, and we decided only to play in the individual championship. It wouldn't be the same without you.' Injeborg was their spokesperson.

'Ya,' Bjorn said. 'Not so fun.'

'You are the one who makes the team. With your passion for the game. It's not right to play if you are not there,' explained Sigrid. 'And in any case we wouldn't get very far without your swash-buckler. She was to be our surprise weapon.'

'I'm sorry.' Erik was embarrassed by the tears that came to his eyes, and which he found impossible to hide.

'Don't be sorry, Erik,' said Injeborg. 'It's you that's important, not the game. In any case, who wants to go away to Mikelgard University?'

****

It was very boring waiting to be allowed home. Although he still had to walk very stiffly, Erik could move around the hospital as he pleased. There were lots of books and toys, but still he was bored. No game compared to Epic and he could hardly bear to think about it, not while the championships were on and he was stuck here.

The morning had been a sad one, as around the world the Epic graduation championships were underway.

Soon after breakfast, Erik was surprised to hear Harald and Thorstein, the Hope librarian, entering his room. Between them they were carrying a heavy box. His dad's glance was full of excitement.

'Hello, Erik.' Harald put the box down with a grunt.

'Hi, Dad. What's this?'

'Wait and see. Can we move those things off the table?'

'Surely.'

The wooden box was opened and Thorstein placed a large black metal cube on the table. Then, very gingerly, he lifted a delicate-looking headset from a special fastening in the cube. A pair of gloves followed.

'Into bed, Erik,' instructed his dad.

Thorstein was busy with the cables. 'It's been a long time. I don't know. I don't know. Too much to hope,' he muttered aloud as he worked.

'Here.' Harald handed him the headset and gloves. Erik put them on, not daring to ask.

'Now.' Thorstein stepped back A number of small coloured lights were flicking on and off in seemingly random patterns on one side of the cube. The other children in the room who could walk came over and Erik saw a few nurses interrupt their routines to watch. A huge smile spread across Thorstein's bearded cheeks.

'There. Would you believe it? But I must hurry. I'm due in the library.' Thorstein gave Erik a quick nod and passed him the glasses.

'Quickly now. Can you play as usual?'

A few anxious moments passed while he waited to harmonise, then Erik gasped with pleasure to see Cindella rising from her box. It had been such a long time since he had seen her.

#smile

She smiled, seemingly happy to see him again.

'Well?' asked Harald anxiously.

'Yes. Just like in the library.'

'Good. I must go. Good luck!' Thorstein patted Erik on the head and hurried out as fast as his stocky legs could carry him.

'Does this mean I can play in the championships?'

'It does!' Harald was jubilant.

'The team. Do they know? You must get them!'

'They are in the library. We weren't sure it would work and we didn't want to make false promises. But they are ready in case.'

'This is magic.' Erik was preparing Cindella to enter her world again. 'With this you could play Epic anywhere!'

'Aye. Well, we are lucky we have one working set in the whole of Hope District.' Harald sounded grim for a moment. Then his voice became more cheerful. 'So, when Thorstein gets back, he will link you up with the tournament.'

'Erik? What's that?' asked little Ivarson, the small boy from the bed opposite Erik's.

Erik partially removed his headset in order to look at the curious face beside his bed.

'Do you know Epic?'

'Of course. My brothers are playing in the championships today.'

'Well, so am I.'

'Oh. That's good. Can I watch?'

'I don't know. Can he, Dad?'

Harald smiled. 'Certainly, here.' Harald carefully and gently removed another headset from the device. 'There are a few public characters that you can occupy to watch events in the amphitheatre. They are not full interfaces. Only Erik has that.'

Ivarson clapped. 'This is fun! I can watch my brother!'

'Dad?' said Erik. 'Can you stay here while I play?'

'Of course I will. As much as I can.'

One of the adults in the hospital came into the room with a stack of chairs.

'You don't mind if a few of us watch, do you?' She looked at Harald and Erik.

'No.' Erik was pleased.

Harald sat in a chair to test the viewing devices. 'This is better than the library.' He sounded delighted. 'Much better head motion.'

Chapter 10
Harald Unmasked

The sun was finally down; Svein's turn on the Executioner rota was over. That had been an insufferably long waste of time, watching kobold after kobold scurry over the mud flats of the hunting grounds, their shadows lengthening as the sky grew imperceptibly more scarlet. It was pitiful to observe the scuffles between the kobolds and small groups of grey fighters. This kind of fighting was so extraordinarily limited. The players across from him had no idea of the real depths of the game. For a while, Svein had turned his thoughts to his own goal, solving the *Epicus Ultima* quest. In all his research, Svein had never discovered the origin of the term, but he was convinced that it referred to something real. Several NPCs he had personally spoken to had indicated that Epic contained this ultimate quest, a quest to end all quests; many thought it to be impossible to solve but Svein felt that he was very close to a breakthrough. The threads that led to this goal were many and complex, but considering them simply increased Svein's frustration at having to waste time on this execution shift. He could be doing something so much more productive.

A tap on his shoulder. Immediately, Svein began to unclip, rubbing the soreness from his ears.

'Anything?' asked Bekka.

'Just hour after hour of people collecting pennies from kobolds.'

Bekka sighed unhappily. 'I feel sorry for them. Sometimes I just want to go over and make someone's day by giving them a ruby or something.'

She saw the stern look on Svein's face.

'I know. I'm just saying I empathise.'

All at once, Svein smiled, hoping it did not look forced, and reached up to touch her cheek. 'I know you do, and that is a most admirable quality in you.'

Pausing only to get a plate of food from the canteen, Svein hurried to his office, avoiding contact with anyone. At last, with the door locked, he could relax and concentrate on his project.

Covering three of the four walls of his office were the tidily arranged spines of books and files. From floor to ceiling, wide shelves held journals, reports, essays, magazines, electronic data and books. The fourth wall was mostly taken up with an enormous pin-board. As he sat at his desk eating, Svein contemplated the board. Coloured pins held pieces of paper to a map of the main game world. Threads of various kind – including silver and gold ones – ran around the pins, creating a colourful net over the world.

The *Epicus Ultima*, Svein had realised, could be solved by anyone, each with their own starting point. In his own case, he had made progress on several fronts, only to reach dead ends at certain stages.

Pushing his plate aside, Svein got up and examined the board again. His final entry read simply, 'Find the Ethereal Tower of Nightmare'. The objective was simple enough: the Earl of Snowpeak had asked him to release from the tower the soul of his kidnapped daughter; her body lay in suspended animation in Snowpeak Castle. No doubt the essence of the girl was held in captivity by some magic device or creature. But the really interesting aspect of this quest was his only other reference to the tower, which described it as containing the 'ultimate lock'.

What would happen if he completed the *Epicus Ultima* had been only hinted at by NPCs, but he would most likely gain some extraordinarily powerful magical item or weapon. What interested Svein, though, was not the prize, but the challenge. By solving the *Epicus Ultima*, Svein would instantly become the most famous player ever.

However, although he now had his most promising lead ever – this reference to the Ethereal Tower – he had still come up against a very stubborn dead end. Nobody knew where this Ethereal Tower was to be found. The Earl of Snowpeak had said only that priests had performed their most powerful auguries, and all they could see of his daughter's soul was that it had been taken to a place called the Ethereal Tower of Nightmare, where she lay dreaming, near the world's end. No spell had been able to help, nor the thousands of NPCs whom Svein had asked. Every librarian in the world had been alerted to the problem and monitored their localities for news of the tower – knowing that Svein would reward information with resources or promotions. Throughout his tenure as librarian, Svein had always been careful to keep the local librarians as well looked after as he could, despite opposition from other members of the committee. If anyone could complete the *Epicus Ultima*, surely it was Svein, with his access to a thousand sources of information. The problem was that players were so unadventurous these days that only a feeble trickle of new information was arriving from the provincial libraries. Svein might achieve better results by encouraging the university students to look for the Tower – but he had to tread a fine line. Giving information away was dangerous, especially if some precocious student somehow got a lucky break and ended up ahead of him.

A timid knock on the door disturbed him.

'What?' Svein shouted angrily.

'Sorry to disturb you, sir,' came the voice of student. 'A Special Session of the Committee has been called and is convening now.'

'Very well.'

Curiosity overcame his annoyance. There must be a new development. Perhaps the Executioner had found its target and that business could be laid to rest?

****

Most of the Committee members were there ahead of him, and the hum of good-natured conversation rose towards the high, transparent ceiling; there were even a few smiles as Svein took his seat. As if to match the humour of those at the table, outside a bright sun and racing clouds created a patchwork of colour over Mikelgard. Occasionally the swift moving rays of light passed directly over them, causing the whole room to sparkle and warm.

'Good news?' Svein asked his neighbour, Wolf.

'I think so.' Wolf nodded his heavy head. 'Godmund called the meeting.'

Svein looked across at the old man. Certainly his blue eyes were alive with eager animation.

With Bekka's arrival, the meeting could begin. Hleid immediately called upon Godmund to speak.

'My researchers have done well and spared us a lot of bother. Harald Erikson is none other than Olaf the Swift.'

Several of the members gasped. Svein glanced quickly at Ragnok, whose face was flushed. Uncomfortable memories no doubt.

'Of course!' exclaimed Halfdan the Black. 'No wonder they did so well.'

'Hmmm. It was not so obvious – he kept himself hidden for

epic

twenty years. But not all of us had forgotten.' Godmund was clearly very pleased with himself. 'Eh, Ragnok?'

Again that rare blush on Ragnok's face.

Lifting up the sheet in front of him, Godmund read aloud, 'Olaf the Swift was exiled for striking another student of the university, the only other person training as an assassin, none other than our very own Ragnok Strongarm. Perhaps you can tell us more about this opponent of ours?'

'Th– there is no need,' Ragnok stuttered angrily. 'All that matters is that the opposition is over. Remove him to exile again and that's the end of it.'

'Not quite,' Svein mused aloud.

'Say on,' invited Hleid, gesturing towards him with the arm of her glasses.

'If those who harboured him knew he was under sentence of exile, then they too must go.'

'Svein, don't be cruel. For all we know, he has a family now. Do you want them to suffer more than this blow?' Bekka was looking at him, astonished.

'They might prefer to go with him.'

'Then let it be their choice and let us not force them.' Bekka looked rapidly around the table for support.

'Legally Svein is right.' Godmund intervened again. 'If anyone was knowingly harbouring him, they must be exiled too. Otherwise our whole system is called into question.'

'And that might include more members of their team, if we are lucky!' Halfdan was jovial, his shiny face red and amused looking.

'Please,' grunted Wolf, clearly less than pleased with Halfdan's attitude. 'This is a professional and not a personal matter. Who cares about that setback in the arena in the light of this development? Let us send a judge to Hope to enforce the exile and make enquires as to whether other people were involved.'

'Agreed?' Hleid checked for assent around the table. 'Good.' She gathered up her silver hair and tied it back, while checking the paper in front of her. 'Svein, it is your duty to alert the librarians to this news. I take it we can leave the wording of the decree to you.'

'Indeed.'

'In that case, we have one other piece of business.' Hleid's thin mouth tightened, and her wrinkled forehead indicated the severity of the matter. 'The latest edition of the *New Leviathan*.'

For a few minutes there was silence as the paper was passed around the room and the committee members studied it. The cheerful atmosphere of the committee dissolved.

It was the editorial that was most disturbing to Svein's eye.

Graduation Competition is a Farce

Graduation week has come and gone again. Once more, young players of Epic from all over the world entered the amphitheatre this week hopeful of winning a place at Mikelgard University and a career in administration. And once again those hopes were dashed. The fact is that in education, as in every sphere of life, the new Casiocracy has evolved a system of control that serves only the few. How can young people in agricultural districts hope to compete with those few schools around Mikelgard dedicated to Epic? It is simply not possible to work and study the game.

Not only that, but the children of the Casiocracy enter the competition with great advantages handed down to them from their parents and indeed grandparents. Was that Hleid the Necromancer's Staff of the Elements which we saw in the hands of her granddaughter? And indeed, before Halfdan went for his all-black style, did he not own the Shield of Many Colours which appeared in the hands of his grandnephew? The only team from outside the top five exclusive schools to progress to the university qualification places was that of 'The Osterfjord Players' whose original use of a new character class kept opponents guessing. Three cheers for them. But even they have not won automatic places, and if they do make it to University will they then not lose touch with their homeplace? The education system has to change. It should devote far fewer resources to Epic and more to pressing problems of agriculture, transport and economy. It should promote those with ability and not those whose parents happen to be privileged members of the administration.

Around the table, elderly shoulders sagged and faces lengthened.

'Where is this coming from?' Godmund was furious. He looked accusingly at Hleid, who shrugged. 'This is too well informed. Look! Who here remembered about Halfdan's shield? Not I. This is coming from the inside. One of us perhaps?'

'But why?' Brynhild was perplexed. 'Why would one of us do this?'

'I don't know,' Godmund growled. 'But whatever they think they are doing, the result is that they are going to cause chaos and instability for us all.'

For a while, the committee members said nothing, but looked at each other with confusion and suspicion. Bekka was the recipient of several scowls.

'There is no point in continuing the meeting if we have nothing constructive to offer. One day the person or people responsible for this will make a mistake. Then we will act.' Svein stood up to leave.

'Very well. We are adjourned,' announced Hleid.

As Bekka slowly made her way down the stairs of the tower, Svein came alongside her.

'It's not me. They think it's me, but it is not.' She looked over her shoulder at Svein.

'Of course not. Only a fool would think that you would write such things.' Svein gave what he hoped was a reassuring smile. There was no longer an attractive side to the ageing, irresolute druidess. But as long as Bekka was a member of Central Allocations, Svein would make the effort to create the impression that he was an admirer of hers, through his considerate words and attentive glances. After all, it cost him nothing and might secure him an important vote one day.

'Then, who is it?'

'I'm not sure Godmund is right. Why would any of us write it? Perhaps it is another bitter person like Olaf the Swift.'

'I hope so.' Bekka nodded. 'It makes me cringe inside, the thought that someone at that table is pretending, is lying to us.'

Chapter 11
Broken Glass

The Osterfjord Players were giddy with merriment as they returned from Hope Library and the final stages of the graduation tournament. Rolfson had come to meet them with the horses, and they were all in the cart, bouncing along as the horses picked a steady route through the potholes of the path. Now and again, as they met travellers coming towards Hope, Rolfson would embarrass them all by proudly calling out, 'We reached the finals. My children reached the finals.'

B.E. was leaning against the side of the cart, arms stretched out on either side, holding the wooden frame to help him ride the bumps.

'I hear that in Mikelgard the roads are covered in a metal surface that does not wear.' B.E. was convinced that their performance would earn them places in Mikelgard University, and, as the oldest, both he and Bjorn would get their places this year.

'Ohhhhh, smooth rides. What a treat is in store for you,' his sister Sigrid tried to mock him, but he was unflappable.

'Ahh yes. I will think of you plodding along in your cart, while Bjorn and I sunburst along in our racing sallers. Probably with a couple of girls in the back seats, eh?' B.E. winked at Bjorn, who smiled but did not encourage B.E. further; that kind of joking made him uncomfortable.

'You think they still have sallers in Mikelgard?' asked Erik.

'Of course they do, standard issue to students no doubt.' B.E. closed his eyes, enjoying the image in his mind.

'I saw one once.' Rolfson looked back over his shoulder.

'Really, Dad?' Bjorn sat up. 'What was it like? Was it working?'

'Oh, yes.' Rolfson nodded. 'It was fast. You had to be careful not to get in the way as it came along the road. Very low. The driver's head would not have come above my belt.'

'That's really tech. I hope we get to Mikelgard and get to see them.' Bjorn beamed at the others with his hugest, simplest smile.

'If we do win places. It's a shame we didn't get one more win and then we would have been in the compulsory places.' Erik didn't want them to get their hopes up too high.

The cart paused as a herd of goats, bells jingling, crossed the path.

'Oh don't be a spoiler, Erik.' Now that she did not need to hold on to the side of the cart, Sigrid used her free hands to wave away his pessimism. 'Nobody outside Mikelgard has done this well for years.'

The sun was just beginning to redden as their cart jolted over the last hill. Orange and brown light filled the fields of olive trees that surrounded their houses. Not long now and Erik would be in the kitchen, telling his parents everything about the tournament. He felt hungry and was looking forward to a large dinner. Even if they had eaten already, his mum and dad would sit with him to hear about the day's competitions.

'Strange,' said Rolfson. 'What's Freya doing on the roof?'

Sitting up, Erik could see a yellow light reflected from the axe blade that his mother was bringing down vigorously near the solar panel.

'Is it broken already?' Bjorn's brow furrowed. 'That's bad luck.'

A cascade of sparks flickered like fireworks from her next blow, it was followed by a painful groaning sound as the panel lurched partway down the roof, causing a flock of starlings to flit away towards the sea.

Another flashing strike with the axe, more sparks and the panel slid to the end of the roof, cables pulled taut behind it.

Erik jumped from the cart and ran. Something was wrong.

'Erik!' shouted Injeborg. But he did not turn.

Dashing through the trees, eyes jumping from the path ahead to his mother on the roof, her axe raised for a final blow, Erik was still far away when the crash echoed through the valley. A thousand glass bottles dropped together would not have created so much volume. Nor would they have made such a hideous splintering sound, as though the sky itself had been wrenched and cracked apart. Up on the roof, his mother fell forward, hiding her head, sobbing into her arms.

'Mum, Mum!' Erik burst into a yard that was now strewn with thick black slabs of glass, the bigger pieces cracking and sliding as he made his way precariously over them, feeling them slide beneath his feet, grinding down into the stone.

'Mum! What is it?' Erik gasped out, a hand clutching his side, his head craning back to look up to his mother.

'I hate it. If only I hadn't wanted a new one,' she called out, crying. 'It's your dad. They've taken him into exile. I knew it. I should never have told him to play for us. I knew it was too risky.'

The horse and cart arrived. Everyone was silent, looking slowly up to the roof and down to where Erik stood as though at the edge of a sea of black ice that had been compressed and shattered, blocks sliding over one another. He could not bear their expressions of concern and confusion, so, without a gesture or word to them, Erik fled inside.

Much later, his mother joined him in the kitchen, her eyes red. Both of them watched the small flames inside the stove, neither looking at the other.

'What's happened, Mum? Where's Dad?'

'On his way to the Isle of Roftig.'

'The island for exiles.' Erik was bewildered. 'But why?'

'A long time ago, when we were both in University, he hit somebody.'

'Dad? Hit someone? Never.'

'Yes, he did.' Freya heaved a big sigh, the only sign that it was a struggle for her to keep her voice level, 'Another student called Ragnok Ygvigson. Harald hit him in the face until his nose broke and blood flowed everywhere.'

A little dizzy, Erik risked a glance at his mum; she caught it.

'You have to understand, your dad is not a bad man at all. Ragnok is the criminal. He is sick.'

'Why? Why did Dad hit him? Didn't he know the penalty?'

'Of course he did, but ...' She paused, then shakily poured water from a pitcher into a clay mug and drank it. 'Ragnok had been drinking with me, drinking far too much mead, until my head was reeling and I was nearly unconscious. Then he tried to do something I can't talk about. But Harald came and when he understood that I was distressed, he hit Ragnok.'

'But the solar panel – what were you doing?'

'I hate it. I could not live with it. Just think, if we had left it alone, we would be happy. Your dad would be with us still.'

For a while they sat in the dark room; Erik's mind was whirling. He came to when Freya lit a lantern.

'So, you think Dad was right to use violence?' He was genuinely confused. All through school and in every aspect of life it was agreed, there should never be recourse to violence – not when they had Epic to manage conflict. It was thought that once society allowed violent actions it would evolve to the same disastrous society that had supposedly driven their pacifist ancestors into space millennia ago.

'No, violence is never right. But I understood him and I forgave him. Alas, our rules allow no exceptions.'

'So ... Dad was exiled?'

'Yes. Only he escaped and found me, and I agreed to marry him, to make a new life far from Mikelgard, where no one would know us.'

Now it was Erik's turn to pour a drink of water, while he gave this thought.

'Why didn't you tell me? I'm old enough.'

'Yes. Your dad thought we should. But it was to protect you. Anyone who knowingly harbours an exile is subject to exile themselves – depending on the ruling of a judge. At least you have the choice. If you want, you can stay here with your friends – or go to University.'

'Stay? Without you and Dad? No. I'll come with you.'

'I don't even know what I'm doing myself yet. It has all been so sudden. The judge was here today. I told her you knew nothing, but she will probably want to ask you herself.'

They sat still, not looking at each other, silent and alone with their thoughts.

'Mum, I'm tired. I must lie down and think about all this.' All desire for food had gone; he just wanted to lie in the dark and try to understand.

'I know, Erik. I'm so very tired too.'

Looking back at the still figure of his mother, you would hardly have known that anything was wrong, but for the tears that were silently running down her cheeks to fall onto the table.

Erik was tired, but not able to sleep. It was as though his mind was torn in two and bleeding thoughts uncontrollably: never to see his dad again; to struggle on with the farm; for Harald to live an unhappy and lonely life. That dark thought could not be put aside and as it welled up, so did his tears, forming hot and salty trails at the corners of his mouth. Yet there had to be a way to overcome this catastrophe. For a moment he could master his misery, channel the deluge of mental activity into thinking about the measures he could take to get his dad back. Unbidden, the deeply distressing image of his mother on the roof of the house interfered with his attempt to make plans. She hacked away at the cables of the solar panel. That outburst of apparent insanity was understandable; they would only be reminded of the disaster every time they used it. His dad, a violent man. The worst that anyone could be accused of: horrific, criminal and obscene. Society agreed; Erik had agreed. Those who committed acts of violence should be shunned. Exiled. It had not seemed so unreasonable. Exile, a place where they could be as perverse as they pleased, without harming any law-abiding person. But now his dad was on his way back to Roftig Island. What was it like? Did you live in fear of being attacked? Not a game but for real. Real wounds. Real blades parting the skin and blood pouring out. Did it feel like burning? Or icy cold? To have a knife thrust into your ribs? It was tiring, lying in the dark, trying not to think of a future without his dad, trying to marshal his thoughts.

When the moon had risen and turned the olive trees a creamy silver, his mother climbed heavily up the stairs, her footfall was so uncharacteristically slow that it had a nightmarish quality. Erik did not call out, and nor did his door swing open. They each had enough to bear without trying to manage the sorrows of the other.

****

The next morning, Erik felt steadier. Despite the catastrophe that had enveloped their lives, he was strengthened by one thought – that the secret his dad had been keeping was one that did not reflect any lack of confidence in Erik. Harald had not been evasive when he had said that there was something worse than reallocation; it was the truth. Exile was far worse. Now, at least, everything made sense; by keeping Erik in ignorance they had hoped to protect him from the punishment of exile. Overnight, Erik had grown stronger and he knew why. The only doubts about his own trustworthiness, his own loyalty, were gone. This day was the start of the Agricultural School holidays, traditionally the day for the olive farmers to start pruning. It was hard and laborious work, but Erik envied those who were rising early to make a start on it. In all the farmhouses around Ostefjord this morning, they would be going through their usual routines of work – normal, life-affirming routines. The cutters would be brought and whet and, perhaps with a meal wrapped in a satchel, the olive-growers would go out to the fields.

Downstairs, the kitchen was tidy; his mother was up, her eyes red, but otherwise she looked composed.

'Mum, I've some more questions.'

She smiled. 'Ask. There is no reason now why you should not know everything.'

'Did Dad ever say how he got away from Roftig?'

'I believe that he bribed the captain of the ferry. Before he was exiled, your father was one of the most successful characters in Epic. But ever since his return, he has not had a gold bezant to his name.'

'I wonder then. Perhaps we can do it again?'

'Perhaps. But where are we going to get thousands of bezants? None of our friends are rich.'

Biting back a reply, Erik continued through the questions that had filled his thoughts that night.

'Is it that bad in exile? What did Dad say about it?'

'Yes, it is bad. They have no Epic, no rules. It is barbaric. People fight and people starve because their food is stolen. They do not have proper homes, just what they have made for themselves. No one there lives to old age.'

'We have to get him back.'

Freya smiled again. It was good to see, even if the smile held no hope.

'What happened to Ragnok?'

His mother shuddered. 'You've seen him. He is the player Ragnok Strongarm – he has become a member of Central Allocations.'

A surge of anger momentarily rocked Erik. 'How could they?'

'I don't know. After what I told them, I really don't know. I suppose it was my word against his and they needed him too much, what with Harald going into exile.' She looked up. 'Erik, have you thought about what you will do if I am sent into exile or if I choose to join him?'

'Yes.'

'And?'

'I will come with you. Except ...'

She waited for him to continue.

'Except that I will have one last try on the Red Dragon before I go.'

He was surprised to see his mother nod. 'Why not? We have nothing to lose. What do you need? I will sell all the items on my character for you.'

'Arrows mostly, barrels and barrels of arrows.'

'Very well.' She sounded tired and resigned rather than hopeful.

'Mum?'

'Yes, Erik?'

'Do you want me to start pruning the trees?'

That brought a bitter smile to her face. 'No, there's no point now. Whoever moves in here after us can do it.'

Chapter 12
Nobody Kills Dragons

Earlier in the day, a strong wind had disturbed the sea. Far out on the horizon, white-topped waves were still rolling determinedly towards the shore, and, all along the line of the water's edge, stones and boulders were grey and slick with the spill of seawater. A distant faint growl sounded regularly as the restless sea heaved and sucked at a bay full of pebbles.

'Well?' asked Erik defiantly.

B.E. was sitting on a rock, unconsciously flicking small stones with his thumb, trying to land them in a rock pool. 'I am stunned. Harald in exile for violence. Why did he do it?'

'Listen, you oaf!' snapped Injeborg. 'Erik said that was private.'

'True.' B.E. looked slightly chastised. 'But it's hard to understand.'

'I'm not excusing violence. All I can say is that he lost his temper in circumstances which would have tested anybody,' Erik offered.

'Erik,' interrupted Injeborg, 'you don't have to answer to us. We're your friends, we're on your side, right?' She glared at B.E. 'And we want Harald back. So ...' She relaxed a little. 'You said you had a plan. Tell us about it.'

'I don't like this. You know what the penalty is for harbouring an exile.' Bjorn looked unhappy.

'I think I can get around that.'

'All right, Erik, let's hear it.' B.E. reached down and closed his fist around another pile of tiny smooth stones.

'I think we should force Central Allocations into drawing up a law offering amnesty to everyone on Roftig Island.'

'Erik, that's brilliant,' Injeborg leapt up at once, waving her arms. 'See, Bjorn. Nothing illegal. Harald will be back with us and we can live as normal.'

'Apart from one small problem,' sneered B.E.

'You mean Central Allocations will never allow it.' Erik knew the next step of the argument was the crucial one. 'That's why we have to kill the Red Dragon first.' He had been ready with this answer.

B.E. accidentally let all the stones run through his hand as he looked up in surprise. 'Say that again?'

'We have to kill Inry'aat, the Red Dragon first. Then we use the wealth to become an unbeatable team. After which we propose the amnesty.'

'Well, you have to admire the audacity.' B.E broke into his character-istic wide smile, which always seemed to be more cynical than good humoured.

'The dragon. That's not possible.' Sigrid spoke for them all. Even Injeborg looked sceptical.

'Yes, it's possible. I've spent hours up there, and I'm convinced it can be done.' Erik stood up so that he could see everyone and meas-ure their response. I honestly believe there is a flaw in the logic of the dragon's strategy.'

'Go on.' B.E. was interested.

Picking up a large rock, Erik walked over to a patch of damp sand, 'This is the dragon's cave.' He dropped the rock. 'Here is Bjorn, here is Injeborg, this is Sigrid and this you, B.E.'

The four crosses in the sand formed a rough semicircle facing the stone, with a gap between the top and bottom pairs.

'Now I trigger Inry'aat and run back to here.' Erik placed a cross in the gap, so that they were now all about equal distance from one another. 'Meanwhile, Bjorn shoots, or, if he misses, Injeborg.' He looked up to see them all attentive. 'The point is that the dragon changes target to the last person to hit it. So it turns. But before it can get into range to pour firebreath onto Bjorn, B.E. fires, or Sigrid, from the opposite side. So then it turns again. Get it?'

'I see. So we keep it turning. Never letting it come too close to someone.' B.E. looked seriously at the marks. 'Blood and vengeance, Erik. This might work if your research is right!'

'What about you, Erik? What does Cindella do?' asked Injeborg.

'I am ready in case we get two misses. That brings Inry'aat my way until you can get the dragon back into the position you need.'

'And if you miss as well?' asked Bjorn slowly.

'Then we will all die very quickly.'

Bjorn scowled, but B.E. was interested. 'What about the ranges? Have you studied them?'

'Oh yes. I know exactly where to stand, and the length of its firebreath.'

'All right. I'm in.' B.E. stood up and brushed his hands free of the clinging pieces of pebble. 'Bjorn, what do you think?'

'I'm sorry, but I think it's a bad idea. I know Erik wants his dad back, but I think we'll all be killed.' Bjorn looked down at the rocks, his face heavy with discontent. He hated to disagree with his friends.

'But Bjorn, think of the wealth. Imagine, thousands and thousands of bezants worth of treasure. If Erik is right, we won't even need to go to Mikelgard; we will be rich, and famous!'

'If ...' Bjorn shook his head, frowning. 'If Erik is right about this, why hasn't someone else done it already?'

'I agree with Bjorn,' Sigrid interjected. 'Farmers' children just don't kill dragons. Nobody kills dragons these days. But if they did, it would be the people in Mikelgard, with all their magic and expensive gear.'

'But nobody even thinks about fighting dragons any more.' Injeborg spoke up. Erik had known that he could count on her. 'Only our Erik. That's why he has seen something that they have missed.' She turned to her brother, 'Come on, Bjorn. Let's try it.'

'No. It's hopeless.'

Injeborg stamped her foot in frustration. 'You are always waiting for something to happen to you. But that's not how life is. You have to be creative, set out to change the situation. They know how to do that in Central Allocations. Why can't we be the same?'

As Erik knew well, Bjorn could be extremely stubborn, and his expression was forming the determined scowl that meant he would not be moved.

'Bjorn, please,' he broke in before his friend could say something that he would never retract. 'Don't make up your mind just now. At least think about it, and join us all in the amphitheatre. We can practise.'

'The library cannot generate dragons,' Bjorn pointed out.

'No, but it can give us wyverns to practise on, and they follow the same strategy.'

Erik understood Bjorn only too well. A part of him, a sad-sounding voice that spoke when he was alone with his thoughts at night, had voiced these objections, and more. It was a struggle not to admit that Bjorn was right, that it was wiser to keep the gains that had brought them so near to University than throw it all away in a vain effort to kill the dragon. He was roused from his growing mood of self-defeat by unexpected support.

'Well, I think Erik is on to something!' B.E. clapped his hands together, enthusiasm visibly filling his body with energy. 'You can't refuse to practise in the arena, can you, Bjorn? And I bet it works, you know.' The fire in B.E.'s eyes was a fire of jewels, gold and glory.

'Very well. Let us see what happens in the arena.' Bjorn respected B.E. As the oldest and most experienced player among them, he was to be taken seriously.

****

As he ran home to gather up some fruit and water, the darkness that had been colouring his thoughts for the last day began to lift, and Erik was almost cheerful as he passed Freya in the kitchen.

'We are going to Hope Library to practise for the dragon!'

'Good, Erik dear. Good.' She sounded listless, but he could not stop to talk to her now.

****

#smile

Cindella looked sprightly, especially in the knee-length Boots of the Lupine Lord, which Harald had lent her for the graduation tournament and which she might now never get a chance to return.

Howling sound and colour whirled all around him, then he was inside Epic.

Cindella ran quickly through the streets of Newhaven until she turned into the wide street that ran to the amphitheatre. An impressive stone arch lined the entrance, four times the height of a person. Way up in the stonework, nearly out of sight, pigeons were walking to and fro, the wall stained from their mess. The arena was quiet. Very few people spent time practising when they could be earning pennies. The towering layers of seats were all silent and empty; they stretched away, row after row mounting dizzyingly to the barely discernible statues around the rim of the amphitheatre.

The others appeared: Bjorn as his pot-headed, sturdy-looking warrior; B.E. a slender elven fighter, carrying a steel longsword; Sigrid a healer in a simple woollen robe; and Injeborg, a young witch.

'Osterfjord Players, are you ready?' The librarian's voice cut sharply through the air, echoing about the stadium.

'Just a moment, Thorstein, please.' Erik waved them into position. All had bows, which looked ungainly on the healer and the witch, but B.E.'s elf was a natural archer.

'Ready now.'

'Wyvern simulation incoming.'

A shimmer in the centre of the sandy fighting area, becoming a ferocious giant silver lizard. Immediately the wyvern took off, its flapping wings sending out whirlwinds of bitter sand. The moment that Erik could see the rage in its red eye and feel a hint of the heat radiating from the body of the creature, he knew that something had gone wrong. It was too close. With an appalling shriek, the Wyvern blasted flame from its mouth and all went black.

Rather than unclip, Erik waited, his ears ringing; he did not expect to be left in the dark for long, nor was he.

'Resetting. Ready?' Thorstein's voice came into the darkness.

'Yes, please.'

The librarian chuckled. 'That was quick. Not often you see a group down so fast. Want a less dangerous creature?'

'No, thanks, Thorstein. Something went wrong that time.'

'Heh. It certainly did.'

A whirlpool of colour and sound dragged him back to Cindella and the amphitheatre.

'Sorry, everyone. I wasn't ready. I had my head down when it appeared.' B.E.'s voice was hesitant, acutely embarrassed.

'And I missed,' added Sigrid.

'Never mind. Everyone set this time?' Erik asked.

When they had all replied in the affirmative, he shouted out, 'Again please, Thorstein.'

'Here it comes.'

This time, before it could charge anyone, the wyvern was stung with an arrow from B.E. It flapped around towards him. Bjorn then hit, the arrow flying away off the creature's spine, but the blow was enough to divert it. Then B.E. again. Back and forth the wyvern turned, sometimes gaining on an opponent as an archer fumbled to notch the arrow quickly, but always being struck before it could come close enough to blast fire. When, as sometimes happened, both archers on one side of the ground missed, Cindella fired, turning the wyvern towards her, and giving the others time to restore the pattern.

The strategy was working perfectly!

Slowly but surely the wyvern began to look haggard and torn from the arrows that pierced its body. No longer able to fly, it hissed as it lurched one way, then the other, unable to close in on an opponent. Finally it collapsed.

'Amazing! It works!' B.E. was jubilant, his elven warrior throwing his arms skyward.

'Wonderful!' Injeborg's witch slapped Cindella on the back.

'Wait!' Sigrid shouted. 'Look, the tail, it's still twitching!'

Before they could react, the wyvern surged up towards Sigrid's healer, its feigned death having broken the pattern that the players had established. The crunch as it sank its teeth into her leather-clad body was excruciating.

'Yaaa!' B.E. ran bravely in, brandishing his sword.

The creature snapped its head around and blasted molten saliva onto the elf, immolating him instantly.

Both Bjorn and Erik drew their weapons and closed. The heat from the wyvern caused the air between them to shimmer; the loud rasping of the creature's breathing made it hard to hear what Injeborg was saying behind him.

Although the lizard was wounded, the flashing blows from its claws were shockingly swift. Cindella was nimble enough to roll beneath the talons, but Bjorn crumpled as he was struck and the monster savagely bit down to grab his shoulder in its teeth. As Bjorn was shaken like a stick in a dog's mouth, there was no doubt he was dead.

A flash of blue from over his shoulder and the creature paused, stunned by a spell.

'Now!' shouted Injeborg.

Cindella dived forward and, with a flourish, impaled the wyvern's eye on the end of her rapier, just as the monster was recovering from the spell. It was gruesome, but the creature collapsed at once.

When he unclipped, Erik found that Thorstein was clapping.

'Well done, everyone. To kill a wyvern, that is very clever, very clever indeed. It will make you wealthy and well known if you can hunt a real one.'

'Thank you, Thorstein.' B.E. smiled. 'But we do not want casualties next time.'

'No, but that was interesting. I have not seen a wyvern die before, so I did not know they pretended like that.' The librarian was clearly pleased to have had an opportunity to observe such an unusual experience.

As the players left the building, Thorstein tapped Erik on the arm.

'I'm sorry about Harald,' he whispered, looking into Erik's eyes.

Erik briefly took the outstretched hand, 'Thanks, Thorstein.'

****

All the way home, they argued. It was mainly B.E. against Bjorn. From Bjorn's point of view, the experience just confirmed that they would be wiped out by something unexpected. There were simply too many unknowns when fighting a dragon. But B.E. was thrilled; the fight had proved that the strategy could work. Even Bjorn admitted that.

A sullen silence had fallen between the two protagonists by the time that they reached the point at which their paths diverged. It had taken most of the long walk for B.E. to exhaust his efforts at persuading Bjorn. The sun was down, and across the valley they could see small pools of lamplight from the windows of their homes. Except that Erik's farm was in darkness.

'Do you not see?' B.E. attempted for one last time to sway Bjorn. 'We are on the verge of being the richest people in the world. Can you honestly live your life and not wonder what would have happened if you had tried?'

'Yes. It would not trouble me at all. For I know what would have happened. I would have died. We all would.'

'Tell me,' said Injeborg. 'Everyone, what is it that you would like from life?' She turned to look at Sigrid.

'I would like to be allocated a small farm, somewhere near here.'

'Bjorn?'

'I would like the same.'

'B.E.?'

Slightly embarrassed, B.E. laughed, and then said, 'I would like to be a successful Epic player, like Svein Redbeard.'

'Erik?'

'I would like nothing better than to be a librarian.'

'Well, for my own part, I want to be a geologist, and travel, see new lands and help our world find resources.'

This surprised Erik, but before he could decide whether to comment on his admiration for her goal, or his dismay that she intended to leave Hope District, Injeborg continued, 'Don't you think it's odd that the two people who really need to go to University for their plans are willing to risk the fight? But Bjorn and Sigrid, who are guaranteed to get a farm, are against it? And as for B.E.,' she laughed. 'That is every child's dream from when they first start the game. I'm glad you haven't lost it.'

Suddenly Bjorn turned to Erik and stared at him, with a fearfully solemn face.

'I trust you, Erik. Tell me, in all truth, can we kill the dragon, or is this all just desperation to see Harald again?'

There was a long pause and Erik felt the pressure of his friends' attention.

'Yes. We can slay Inry'aat.'

Chapter 13
The Dragon's Lair

A rapid, irregular, patter of rain falling on the roof of their house accompanied Erik as he went upstairs to clip up. That was for the best; no one could be expected to be out in the fields pruning in weather like this. It would save the others any difficulty with their families. He doubted that Bjorn and Sigrid would admit to their father what they were attempting to do, not when Rolfson had seemed so pleased with the prospect of their going to Mikelgard University.

#smile

He had seen Cindella emerge from her box a hundred times, and yet her appearance still brought with it a feeling of happiness. She looked so lively, and the knowledge that he was about to enter Epic with her agility and daring filled him with pleasure.

Silence. A moment of anticipation, before a giant wave of colour and sound roared up to engulf him.

Curiously, it was raining in Newhaven as well; the cobbled streets were damp and shiny, reflecting the coloured banners of the shops that leant over the narrow lanes. Cindella ran, avoiding the larger puddles, until she could dash inside the black and white house of the hunting merchant.

Lifting back her hood, Erik was surprised by the variety of equipment in the huge room that he had entered. An enormous metal bear trap was hung from the ceiling. On one of the walls, a large case held a great range of knives. Ropes, tents, clothing, boots and pelts were stacked in large piles here and there on the floor. Around the walls were hung animal and monstrous heads, including a fierce beaked griffon, a one-eyed cyclops and the three heads of the chimera.

A powerful-looking human came in from a sturdy door at the back of the room.

'Aha. You must be Cindella.'

'How in the name of vengeance did you know that?' Erik was amazed.

'No mystery there, young woman. It is not many who grace my shop who fit your description. Your mother Freya told me to ready some arrows for you.'

'Oh, of course. So are they ready?'

'Oh, they are. There are many arrows. And you are a slender creature. I will have my apprentice assist you.' The hunting merchant disappeared through the door in the back of the building, calling back over his shoulder, 'And I bid you good hunting.'

Followed by the apprentice with his awkward load of bundled arrows, Cindella made her way over the wet cobblestones to the main quays, where she was due to meet the others.

As he arrived, Erik saw that B.E., Sigrid and Injeborg were already waiting under the awning of a boot merchant, whose blue striped tent was now grey with damp.

'Hi, Erik, or Cindella I should say.' Injeborg's witch waved, the sleeve of her dark green robe falling back as she did so.

'That's a great load of arrows, Erik.' B.E. was standing beside a similar-sized stack of arrows; Sigrid and Injeborg, however, had not been able to afford many – two small bundles lay beside them.

'My mum has sold all she had to buy them.'

B.E. laughed. 'Much as I wish mine would do the same, there is no way I'm telling them about this until it is over. I wonder where Bjorn is. I want to get going. This will take long enough as it is.'

Just then a cart rumbled into the square, led by a donkey. Beside the donkey was the burly grey shape of Bjorn's character, only it had no armour on whatsoever.

'Bjorn!' Sigrid cried. 'What happened to your helmet?'

'I sold everything.'

'Good idea,' said B.E. 'This enterprise is all or nothing. In fact,' he turned to Cindella. 'Why don't you sell that necklace, Erik? Get us more arrows?'

Cindella reached up and fingered the pendant around her neck, 'Oh, I couldn't, it was a present.'

'There's no time for sentimentality now.'

'I suppose, if we need to. Let's see though.'

They came over to the cart; Cindella rubbed her hand through the coarse fur of the donkey's nose. Heaped inside were bundles of arrows.

'Great work, Bjorn!' B.E. gave him a slap on shoulder.

'Well, if we are going to do it at all, we have to do it properly,' Bjorn replied.

'And we have the cart for the gold afterwards.' Even through the blanketing effect of his being in a character, Erik could see that B.E. was becoming excited again.

They loaded the cart with their arrows, until it was heaped so high that there was a danger of spilling the bundles.

'Never mind the necklace, Erik. We can't take any more arrows. Let's get started.'

****

They left through the north gate of the city, the opposite side to the ochre plains in which most players gathered. For a few hours, they could make swift progress along a straight stone road, but then the road veered east, and they were obliged to take a muddy cart track that led away towards the low forested hills to the north.

This close to the city, the environment was relatively safe. Farmers worked the land, and tribes of amiable wood elves lived in the forest. But by the end of the day, they would be into a more severe rocky landscape, which was the habitat of more dangerous creatures, both animal and monstrous.

For most of the day, they trudged along beside the cart without talking. Erik just wished that they were up in the caves, ready to wage battle. So much depended on the outcome, it was hard to turn his thoughts to more trivial matters. Perhaps the others wanted to chat about the farms, the coming planting festival and other local matters, but were afraid to do so for his sake.

'Bjorn. Where did you plan to leave the donkey and cart when we unclip?' B.E. broke their silence with an important question.

'I don't know. I hoped that Erik would be able to suggest a farm or someplace.'

'Yes. There is a woodcutter and his family about halfway. That's where I usually unclip.'

The problem with unclipping in a wild area was that when you returned to Epic, you could find yourself immediately embroiled in a conflict if some monster was at hand and you unexpectedly materialised in its vicinity. And as for leaving anything behind, there was every chance that it would not be there on your return.

There was little sign of any danger as they slogged along the path; they were gradually rising, so that back over their left shoulders they could see the walled town at the point where the River Ayling met the sea in a wide estuary. By sunset, the rain had stopped and the setting sun cast a deep orange light over the water.

The world of Epic ran in exactly the same cycles of day and night as their own. It had been a long, slow day, walking their characters out towards the limestone caves that harboured the dragon. From time to time, they had halted the march and taken it in turns to have a break from the game, but now hunger and stiffness affected them all.

'Is it far to this woodcutter, Erik?' Sigrid sounded plaintive.

'Not far at all. I think it is over the next rise.'

Sure enough, as they came up to the top of the slight hill, the path dipped slightly before rising again, and in the hollow was a thatched wooden house, a welcoming tail of smoke being played with by the slight breeze.

'Good. This is about halfway, right?' asked B.E.

'Actually a little past. If we start early, we will be there well before evening tomorrow.'

They approached the house.

'You do the talking, Erik. People seem to like Cindella.' Injeborg gave him a smile.

Running lightly up to the door, Cindella gave three sharp raps.

'Who is it?' A cautious voice spoke from behind the heavy iron-bound frame.

'Travellers who wish to leave a donkey and cart with you for safe-keeping.'

A dark eye glanced at Cindella through the crack of the door, then they could hear the sounds of bolts being drawn aside.

'Yes?' The woodcutter stood in the doorway; behind him, a woman and two children were beside the fire.

'May we leave this cart and donkey with you for the night?'

The woodcutter paused, solid-looking face a blank. It was a typical NPC response to a situation they were not equipped for. Then his features seemed to flow into a more sophisticated shape; he seemed more alive than most characters as he smiled, his eyes welcoming.

'Certainly you may, young adventurers. Your donkey will even get a meal and some shelter in my shack.'

'Thank you. Oh, and here, for your troubles.'

They still had half a sack of bread remaining, so Erik passed it over to the woodcutter.

'Why, thank you, young lady.'

'We will call in the morning to collect them.'

'Very well. Take care. The night can be dangerous here.'

'We will.'

'That's it, let's unclip.' B.E. was anxious to finish up.

It must have looked strange to the woodcutter that the five people accompanying the donkey and cart suddenly disappeared.

****

During the night, Erik had many violent dreams, which melted as he woke up, leaving him with only a residue of feeling – guilt and also, strangely, relish. It was impossible to recover even a fragment of dream to cling to and examine, so he rolled out of bed and washed. With the careful gestures of a ritual, he picked his favourite, most well-worn clothes. Harald used to tell him that superstition was a sign of weakness; but all the same, luck was not to be frightened away by any false steps on his part. In the untidy-looking kitchen Erik patiently peeled four oranges, then washed his sticky fingers. Yesterday's porridge was still on the stove; it was disturbing that the fire, which was normally kept alive all year round, had gone out. To please his mother, Erik emptied the tray of ashes before rekindling a small fire. It would take some time to heat the porridge.

Outside, their yard was in disarray; washing had been left out to dry the whole night, and was now damp with dew; droppings from the donkey still needed to be shovelled up and thrown on the manure pile. It was hard to run a farm when you were about to leave it.

Back inside, Erik strove to keep his thoughts on simple tasks. Each time he strayed into contemplating the battle with the dragon, his stomach gave a lurch. Never one for introspection at any time, he believed it could only be unnecessarily wearing and fruitless to have daydreams now. Once, when Erik was little, Harald had taken him with him to Fircone village. That journey involved crossing a swaying rope bridge over a river that cut deep into a sandstone shelf. At the time, the height and the rush of water had seemed immensely dizzying. Since then, Erik had become taller and more familiar with the bridge, which had lost its capacity to cast a spell of fear and invitation. In his hand, Erik had been holding one of his favourite toys, a model horse. Looking at the racing froth of the water far below, Erik had been mesmerised and the grip on his horse had loosened. In his mind he could see it falling, slowly turning over and around, as it dropped irretrievably from him. It was a real effort to wrench himself away and keep his toy. Now, the image of slaying the dragon felt just as disorientating. If he dwelt on the fantasy of success, there was a real danger that it would paralyse his will, and result in his failure.

Although it was still a little early, Erik decided it would be better to enter the game. Being Cindella made him feel stronger, more capable. Gathering up his orange pieces and a large glass of water, he went upstairs to the equipment.

#smile

It was relaxing to harmonise with her self-assured character.

A violent blast of colour and sound dispelled the darkness.

It was still raining in the game. Cindella was high enough into the hills that wisps of the low-lying clouds slowly drifted along the valley sides just above Erik's character.

'Hi, Erik. I couldn't sleep.'

B.E. was there. His elf had harnessed the donkey to the cart in preparation for their departure.

'Ya. I'm surprised I got any.'

They sat beside each other on the cart, listening to the rain on the leaves of the trees all around them, neither wanting to talk about the coming encounter. Slowly the morning began to brighten and the rain became little more than a faint drizzle. Bjorn and Injeborg suddenly materialised before them.

'Great, I'll just get Sigrid.' B.E. disappeared.

****

By late afternoon, they reached the valley of the dragon. There was no longer a path, and while they took turns to lead the donkey, everyone else walked beside the lurching cart to prevent the stacks of arrows from rolling out. All around them, craggy boulders and piles of white stone broke through a thin layer of grass-covered soil. Vegetation was scant here; a brave purple flower did its best to bring cheer to a drab landscape.

As they worked their way along a slightly rising valley, the ground grew increasingly rocky and the walls rose like cliffs. The donkey stopped and would not budge.

'Never mind. Let's leave it,' said Erik. 'We are not far now.'

'Is it safe to leave the donkey here?' asked Sigrid.

'Oh, yes. No other creature would dare hunt this close to the Red Dragon.'

They unpacked the cart, each taking a huge load of arrows onto their back; even with that, the cart remained half-full. Not far ahead was a large black boulder. Cindella threw down her load beside it and scrambled up.

'Come up. I'll point out our positions.'

Black openings appeared all along the walls of the cliffs, each a potential cave entrance. A rock floor completely devoid of flora stretched away to where the walls encircled the desolate valley. Ominously the ground was pockmarked with swathes of ash and strewn with bones and rusty fragments of armour.

'Don't worry,' Erik laughed nervously. 'Most of those are mine.'

Bjorn shook his head. 'I'm glad you know this place. It is impossible to guess which cave holds the dragon.'

'That one.' Cindella pointed dead ahead to the end of the valley. There, where the limestone walls seemed to have been blasted open by a duel between powerful wizards, a large black cave gaped with brooding menace.

Using the scars of previous deaths as guides, Erik gave them their positions, and pointed out the places beyond which the dragon should not be allowed to cross for fear that it would be able to reach them with a blast of fire. Each character made two trips to the cart until their arrows were stacked up waist high beside them. Although Erik had said that it was safe, they moved in complete silence and with a restraint that almost kept them from breathing as they took their marks.

'Ready?'

Once the others gave the go ahead, Cindella made her way to the vicious-looking scar in the valley wall. Close up it was a huge opening, set deep in black shadow. That was near enough. Cindella picked up a stone.

'Hey in there, you have visitors!' She hurled the stone into the cave, where it was quickly lost in the darkness. Another and another followed. The stones sent up a resounding clatter as they landed, one after the other, until the stone that made no sound at all.

Cindella turned and sprinted away as fast as she could, nimbly leaping the larger rocks.

Thunder shook the valley, deafening everyone; the ground itself quivered from the noise, as though it were trembling in fear. The dragon had given angry notice; it was coming out.

A snakelike head appeared first, high above the ground, evil intelligence in the eyes; then, with the sound of glass breaking, a foot with diamond-sharp claws slapped onto the ground. Lithely the scaled body of the monster emerged from the shadow of its cave. Another great roar stunned them all, leaving their ears ringing. Then the Inry'aat stretched its magnificent wings, awesome in power and vibrant with a pulsing scarlet colour that spoke of the burning heat of the creature. It was immense, and for a moment the impossibility of killing such a powerfully fierce monster overwhelmed Erik.

Then B.E. fired and his arrow embedded itself in the body of the dragon, like a tiny splinter. Immediately the monster snapped its head around to glare at the little elf that had dared to attack. It took one shuddering step toward B.E. when another arrow hit into its flank from the other side. Again, the frighteningly swift turn, followed by a slower, careful placement of its great taloned leg. And now B.E.'s next shot landed.

So the pattern took shape. It was fourteen shots – and at the back of his mind Erik had felt the miss coming – before Bjorn pulled his bow down as he released and the arrow shot away off the ground. At once, Sigrid fired and, although her arrow bounced back from the thick scales of the dragon, the blow was sufficient to turn it from B.E.

By the time of the next miss, Erik had lost count. Again Bjorn snatched at his shot and again Sigrid had it covered. For the next hour, they kept a mesmerisingly steady rhythm to the fight. Arrow, snarl, step, arrow, snarl, step. Shot after shot, keeping the dragon turning in a small circle, back and forth, very rarely faltering, but always picking up the rhythm again on the back-up shot. It was hard to miss such a great creature. For Erik the fight was perhaps the most demanding, for he was not firing but stood poised, anticipating a double miss, never having a moment's relaxation between shots as responsibility passed from one side of the valley to the other.

A second hour passed with absolutely no change to the pattern, except that the sky began to darken and shadows reach out from the valley walls towards the battle. The third hour was equally hypnotic. You forgot everything but the pattern. Shot and shot. Step and step. Three hours of concentration. Yet nothing seemed to change. The dragon seemed as full of potential for destruction as ever, an explosion barely held in check by a flimsy weaving of arrow shots. The only change to Inry'aat since they began the fight was that it now had a layer of shafts lining its upper body like thin patches of fur.

Another hour of concentration; still there was no room for error; should Inry'aat escape the pattern, they would all be immolated in seconds. So they had to maintain the dragon in its tight oscillations, keeping it that vital step away from the point from which it could blast one of them with its explosive gouts of flame. It was a little like a spinning top Erik had owned years ago. You pumped a shaft up and down to make the top spin incredibly fast, then let go. Properly done the toy seemed to be motionless, except perhaps a slight swaying, but in actual fact the toy was whirling around so fast that if it strayed onto even a small imperfection in the ground, it would fly several feet in the air. Similarly Inry'aat was moving back and forth in a tight area, constantly at the point of unleashing its volcanic power, constantly readjusting to a new target, apparently harmless but on the brink of effortlessly destroying them all.

'Erik!' shouted B.E. 'I need you to transfer arrows from Injeborg to me.'

'Ya. And I will need the same from Sigrid,' Bjorn called out from the shadow that had slowly moved out from the cliffs to cover him.

Of course! They should have divided up the arrows better. The main archers were hitting nearly twenty times more often than the reserve person. His own supply was much greater than he needed; he had not been called upon to fire once.

'Very well, keep concentrating, I will deal with it.'

Suddenly his fear of failure was accompanied with another emotion that had to be pushed to one side: shame. If they died, he would never forgive himself for making such a stupid mistake.

Watching the dragon all the while, he carefully made his way to Injeborg. Now was the really dangerous moment, when he had to put his bow down to gather up the arrows. Glancing at the witch, Erik felt a surge of affection for her, with her velvet sleeves rolled back, bow at the ready. She did not turn to look at him, her whole concentration set on containing the fiery power of the dragon. Cindella ran swiftly to B.E. and stacked up the arrows beside him. He made a second run until B.E. had a great pile, while Injeborg was left with just twenty arrows.

The others had held the pattern all the while, and it was with a great sigh of relief that Cindella picked up her own bow again. Then she skirted around to the other side, where Sigrid stood equally attentive. Once again, the awful moment when he had to put down his bow. In this situation there were just two consecutive misses between them and disaster. Hurriedly he managed the redistribution, watching all the while. Shot, turn, step, shot. And the crisis was over.

Bow in hand, he went back to his position.

'We still have my bundle left if we need!' he shouted out to them all.

The struggle was well into its fifth hour before Erik realised that there was a change taking place.

'Look, its head!'

Inry'aat was glaring at them more malevolently than ever, now that its eyes were a red glow against the growing gloom, but it held its head closer to the ground than when it had first come into view.

No one responded; they were too vigilant, keeping up the pattern of shots that held the dragon in place.

Slowly, imperceptibly slowly, the dragon was lowering its head. Erik counted twenty shots then tried to gauge the change, it was minute, but it was happening. He quickly calculated, underestimating if anything their progress. Another hundred arrows was about ten minutes, six hundred then to the hour. But that was only about a quarter the distance to the ground, so four hours, and two thousand four hundred arrows – if they even had that many! His own bundle was less than a thousand.

'Distributing my arrows now!' he cried out. Kneeling, no longer able to see his friends in the shadows, Erik watched the arrows soar out of the darkness into the body of the dragon as he retied half his arrows into a bundle that he heaved onto his back.

As he was part way around to B.E., the double failure happened. It was strange, because the sense that they would inevitably miss while his hands were not free, which had accompanied Erik all through the first redistribution, had gone. These misses were completely unexpected. Suddenly the dragon was taking a second step towards Bjorn. For the first time in nearly five hours, it was outside of its pattern and gathering pace. Having held the situation for all that time, they were about to succumb in moments.

#mock

With Cindella's bow on the ground, this was the only action she could take that might save them.

'Hey, Red Ears! What's the matter? Your fire going out?'

Inry'aat whirled around as though stung with a particularly sharp arrow. Bjorn waited for it to move towards Erik and back into position, then he fired. The dragon turned back to face him. By now B.E. had his next arrow notched. The moment of disaster was behind them. The pattern was resumed.

'Fire and destruction, I thought we'd lost it,' muttered B.E. as Erik deposited the arrows at his feet and untied them.

'So did I. So did I. Keep it going.'

B.E. did not reply, but fired his next arrow.

Agonisingly slowly, Inry'aat's head sank and sank, until it was no higher than their own. Night had come, but as the shadows of the valley had merged with the dark clouds overhead, it became evident that the arena in which they fought was dimly lit by a purple radiance that came from the dragon. As time passed, the quality of this light changed, gradually becoming more violet and losing its intensity, this process also marking the decline of the dragon.

Still Erik winced as he re-estimated their arrow supply against the withering of the monster before them. Just as he was convincing himself that they did not have enough, Inry'aat gave out a desperate melancholy sigh and slumped to the ground, its head hitting the rock with a distinct crack. All colour emanating from the body faded quickly, leaving just a hint of a purple glow around the body, like the very edge of a rainbow.

'Keep firing!' shouted B.E. 'Remember the wyvern. Keep firing until every last arrow has gone.'

So they did, all of them joining in. Erik thought it strange, as he bent his bow, that after seven hours of battle, this would be the first time he had fired on the dragon. When all the arrows were gone, they drew their weapons.

'Ready?' shouted B.E. 'Charge!'

Braced against the sight of the monster roaring back to life, Cindella ran in, rapier an insignificant pin against the mountainous size of the dragon. But it remained still and they gathered around the head, which alone was as big as any of them. The eye near Erik was now dull, all intelligence gone.

'Have we really done it?' asked Bjorn wonderingly.

'Stand back!' B.E. started to hack at the neck of dragon with his longsword. It was like chopping at a tree trunk, and no one else could help. Bjorn had sold his axe to raise money for arrows. Only after B.E. had severed the head, with the steaming ichor still bubbling forth from the wound, could they really believe the battle was over.

'We've done it! We are dragonslayers!' B.E. held his arms open to them all. They rushed together; jumping up and down until their group hug lost its balance.

'I must go for a break,' said Bjorn.

'We all need one.' Erik wanted urgently to tell his mum the news.

'Very well. Back in half an hour, all right? And no one is to go into the cave until we are all here.' B.E. took charge.

That agreed, they unclipped.

The house was dark; for a moment, Erik thought it was empty, but he found Freya in the kitchen, asleep at the table, head on her arms.

'Mum! Mum!' He shook her awake. 'We did it. We killed Inry'aat! We killed the Red Dragon!'

'No. Surely not?'

'It's true, Mum, really true. We did it!'

Her face lit up and for the first time in days, her smile was warm and heartfelt. 'Erik! Well done. You are all heroes!'

She opened her arms and they hugged each other for a long time.

'Do you see?' Erik broke away. 'This means we can get Dad back. With the treasure we can mount a legal challenge, and pass any law we want – such as amnesty for exiles!'

Freya pondered this.

'Yes. That's a real possibility. There are other options as well. Perhaps we can use the money to bribe the ferry captain to bring him back? Isn't it dark in here? Let me make us some food then we can discuss our plans.'

'I have less than half an hour, then we meet to gather the treasure.'

'You need to eat something. You must have been in Epic for the last twelve hours or more.' Freya got to her feet, all energy and purpose now.

There was a loud and eager banging on the door. Erik broke into a smile.

'You get it, Erik. Sounds like Inny,' Freya said.

He flung the door wide and Injeborg leapt in, eyes sparkling, searching for a response in his own. As he staggered under her embrace, Erik saw Bjorn behind her, smiling happily and at the same time looking a little embarrassed on behalf of his sister.

'Oh, Erik, isn't it just wonderful?' She hugged him again and again.

For a moment, an internal resistance held him back, a barrier that was connected to his concentration on the battle with the dragon; then it melted. He clasped her tight and she responded. Erik's face was pressed against warm, flower-scented locks of her fair hair. The fierceness with which they clung together registered their happiness, and more.

'I thought I was going to have to leave you, all of you, perhaps forever.' Tears came to Erik's eyes, an echo of the misery of his half-admitted sense of defeat, and yet they were also tears of happiness. Injeborg nodded, a gentle motion against his cheek.

'It will be all right now.'

Conscious of Bjorn's presence, Erik gave the warm body that was pressed against him one more squeeze, then they uncoupled, stray strands from Injeborg's long hair sticking to his hot cheek.

Rather more awkwardly, Bjorn too raised his thickset arms and briefly they embraced. Nonetheless it was with a real flow of comradeship between them.

'When I think about it ...' Bjorn shook his head in horror. 'So little between destruction and success. That time, when you were out of position and they both missed.'

'Oh, yes, my heart stopped, I thought we were dead,' Injeborg agreed.

'But your "mock" skill worked,' Bjorn continued. 'Such a slender thing for our lives to be shaped by.'

Erik chuckled. 'Now it is time to dwell on more pleasant matters. We don't have long. We'd better get ready to bring the treasure to Newhaven.'

'Of course.' Injeborg nodded. 'We just wanted to see you.' She shared a glance with him, a glance full of happiness and pride.

'I'm glad you came over.' He paused. 'See you soon back in Epic.'

Chapter 14
The committee Divided

'We are the dragonslayers! We are the dragonslayers!' B.E. was lying on his back, beneath him an enormous pile of gold coins. He was singing at the top of his voice, filling the once-frightening cave with the echoes of his irreverent chanting.

They had entered the cave excitedly, talking about how their friends and families would react to the news, and what they would buy for their farms and for the district. A witchlight spell cast by Injeborg spread a cheerful turquoise light around them that found distant reflections in the depths of the stalactite-encrusted cavern.

The first sign of the hoard had been a few coins, gold and silver; then they had come across a brooch with skilful filigree work, which Sigrid had fastened to her cape; next a leather pouch, with a gold fastening, and two small sapphires on the clasp.

'This alone would mean a tractor for the district.' B.E. had picked it up, examining it closely.

More and more immensely valuable items could be seen scattered along the cave floor, each of which caused them to stop and eagerly admire their fortune. Then they turned a corner, and the sight that greeted them suddenly halted their excited chatter. Before them were the results of a thousand years of accumulation by the monster that lay dead outside.

In a wide chamber, hung with slender milky stalactites, a flood of coins carpeted the floor, rising and falling in piles several feet thick – motionless waves of gold. Immersed in the coin hoard, everywhere the eye paused, were precious items: horn drinking vessels bedecked with beaten silver, swords with delicate gem-laden scabbards, great tomes with gold-leaf work on the covers and heavy silver clasps, silver and gold cups, caskets, jewellery, pieces of armour, glittering blades on axes and swords. It was as though a sea of gold had recently washed over a beach of precious jewels, leaving them uncovered to glimmer in the torchlight.

Only after a few moments of shock at the size of the hoard could B.E. throw himself onto the coins and begin singing.

Bjorn sat down, hardly able to contemplate the scene. 'How much wealth is this?' He reached down and grabbed a handful of coins. With them came a silver chain on which was strung a large iridescent amethyst. 'In my hand I have more money than I could have earned in my whole life, and how many handfuls are here?' He shook his head.

'I know.' B.E. turned over to dig into the coins beneath him, 'Great, isn't it!'

They each went their own way amongst the treasure, beachcombers shouting with pleasure and excitement at the discoveries that they found beneath the easily overthrown mounds of coin. This joyful exercise probably lasted for hours, though no one was monitoring the time; eventually, when they tired of showing each other new marvels, the Osterfjord Dragonslayers gathered together again.

'How can we get this all to Newhaven?' asked Sigrid, bringing a note of practicality to their giddy revels.

'Good question. You should have brought a lot more carts.' B.E. smiled at Bjorn.

'How about I take some treasure and hurry back there, buy six more carts and return as quickly as I can?' Erik proposed.

'You will be all right travelling alone?' asked Injeborg.

'Oh yes, I've done the journey lots of times, and without the benefit of Cindella's natural speed and these boots.'

'Good. In the meantime, we will fill the one cart we have.' B.E. laughed. 'What a demanding and yet pleasant task.'

****

It was almost a day later that they walked into Newhaven, each leading horses, who were straining to pull heavily laden carts; the treasure was concealed as well as they could manage it, under rope-bound canvas covers.

The city was decked out as if for a holiday. From all the walls and towers flew bright flags – the raven of the Earl of Snowpeak predominant among many other coats-of-arms; garlands of flowers hung around the gateway.

'Is it a special day?' Injeborg looked around curiously.

'I think it's for us,' replied Erik, slightly sheepishly.

'What? You told someone?' Sigrid sounded angry that Erik had let slip their secret before they had secured ownership of the treasure.

'Well, just the hunting merchant.'

'It's better.' B.E. broke in before they could quarrel. 'This is how it should be.'

As the team entered the city, it seemed that the entire population had gathered to cheer them: the merchants and traders, the master craftsmen and apprentices, the city guard, the street urchins. They all lined the roads or waved from their windows. Entertaining them were jugglers, puppet masters, troubadours and poets – all of whom paused to join the shouts of acclaim and the happy attempts to throw flowers onto the procession of carts moving over the cobbles.

B.E. was in his element, waving back and acknowledging the cheers; he was wearing a garland of flowers that had been raised up to him by a young woman who ran out of the crowd. The rest of them felt slightly uncomfortable at the public scrutiny. Here and there, grey faces of other players could be seen in the colourful assembly of NPCs; no doubt, back at home, they were looking on at this parade with some amazement. This was the first time in a generation that something unusual had happened in the game, and they could hardly be expected to take seriously the crowd's excited cry of 'dragonslayers'.

The master of the bank, a serious and ancient high elf, was there to meet them when they pulled up into the large square before the bank; he acted calmly, as if he dealt with dragon hoards every day. A gesture to his staff and they began to empty the carts, several clerks with leather-bound books making entries as they did so.

'Please, come with me.'

Again, unusually, as with Antilo the jeweller, and the woodcutter before, Erik detected in the character the presence of intelligence and vibrant expression. With a few anxious glances at their treasure, which glittered far too prominently in the sunlight as its covers were thrown back, they followed the high elf.

The master's office was discreetly and tastefully decorated. A beautiful slender vase contained exotic vivid blue flowers with long stems. This was the only ornamentation, although the carved oak chairs and desk were themselves works of such delicacy that they all tentatively lowered themselves as they sat.

'Congratulations, a most remarkable achievement, and one which will earn you all an undying reputation. Perhaps I might be the first to know your names?' He smiled at them, bright eyes under bushy eyebrows.

As they spoke, he acknowledged each name with a small nod.

'For such immensely wealthy clients as yourselves, carrying even a fraction of your treasure would be most cumbersome. Not to mention the irksome attention that it is liable to attract.' He looked around them for expressions of agreement, and then continued, 'So, we suggest to our most chivalrous clients that they might find it most advantageous to invoke the services of a soulbound djinn.'

Detecting no sign of understanding, the master rang a tiny silver bell that was on his desk. At once, another, slightly younger, elf entered with a silver tray on which were five crystal bottles and five stiletto daggers.

'I took the liberty of having these prepared.'

The tray was set down on the desk and the other elf left.

'In each of these is a djinn from the ethereal planes.' Seeing their blank looks, the high elf made a sweeping gesture. 'The ethereal planes, a magical dimension that surrounds our own, constantly present, but invisible to all but a very few. Now, these are geased creatures who travel via the planes, which gives them great swiftness. All civilised merchants understand that the instructions which are given to them, will be carried out by this bank.' Since they still looked confused, the master continued, 'When you open your bottles, the djinn will appear; you explain to it your desires, and the creatures will immediately come to me, or my deputy, and we will act upon them.'

'I see,' said Injeborg. 'So, if I wanted to buy an expensive item from a merchant, I would call up my djinn and tell it to let you know the merchant could obtain such and such an amount from the bank.'

'Exactly so, mistress witch.' He nodded approvingly.

'What are the knives for?' Bjorn was more interested than concerned.

'The djinn will obey only you, but to be soulbound to you, we require you to drip some blood into the vessels.'

'Do you have any idea of the value of our treasure?' asked Injeborg.

'My staff will present you with a total value and a list of all your rare and precious magical items. No doubt, being veteran adventurers, unlike myself, you will have recognised many important artefacts – such as Neowthla's Bell of Summoning, missing for five hundred years but now, thanks to your noble efforts, returned to the light of day. But in case you should have overlooked something in the undoubted confusion of such a hoard, we have experts who can identify many obscure items of arcana. When they have so done, I will have the loremaster general himself discuss each one with you.'

'That's most kind of you,' said Erik.

'Not at all, my lady.' He gave a slight smile, the first that Erik had seen on his austere face. 'We cannot perform too many services for the people who have made this the richest and thus the most famous bank in the whole of the world.'

'Sorry, friends, but I have to go,' B.E. cut in.

'Me too,' added Sigrid.

'We can return to this,' said Injeborg, 'and give them time to write up our items. Shall we just do the djinn thing first?'

'If it's not some sort of trick,' B.E. said aloud. The master of the bank looked so offended that he quickly continued, 'Just the musings of an adventurer. Please forgive me.'

B.E. jabbed his thumb with the dagger and, lifting the stopper of the bottle, let his blood run inside. 'Is that enough?'

'Yes indeed. That is plenty.'

They all followed suit.

'Shall we test one now?' suggested Erik.

'You may if you wish,' said the master. 'But since each djinn will perform only nine tasks before it is released, you may wish to wait until you need them.'

'Yeah, let's wait. Gotta run, see you later.' B.E. disappeared, followed by Sigrid.

'It's nearly time for dinner; we'd better go too,' Injeborg explained.

'And then there was one,' said the master, after Bjorn and Injeborg had gone. 'I'm glad. I wanted to speak with you alone.'

'Oh, really?' Erik was curious.

'Please come with me.' They both stood up. Then the master paused. 'Wait. No. Not yet.' Suddenly the animation of his expression and intelligence of his eye departed like clouds covering the sun. He stood unmoving.

'Hello?'

'Ah, hello, Cindella. How may I help?'

'I'm not sure really. Were you about to speak with me?'

But like an NPC who is not given the right trigger, the master simply stood, looking blank.

'Odd,' said Erik aloud. Then he unclipped.

****

High above the city, the committee had reconvened. Godmund was apoplectic with fury – so red in the face that Svein feared that the old man would suffer a heart attack. His wrinkled translucent fingers shook with impatience and suppressed fury.

'Good morning.' Hleid began the meeting. 'We have just one item to discuss, the slaying of Inry'aat, the Red Dragon, by five people from Hope; the same five who, as the Osterfjord Players, recently performed well in the graduation championships. I believe Svein has the most information.' Hleid looked up at him expectantly.

'I do not have much more to add. They arrived in Newhaven

about six hours ago, with seven carts full of the dragon hoard. The town put on a celebration for them, which every player in the game cannot have failed to see. They deposited the treasure in the bank.'

'How on earth did they kill a dragon?' exclaimed Brynhild. 'They are only children.'

'Yes, the obvious question. I have spoken to the Hope librarian, and he tells me that they were practising against wyverns. They seem to have exploited a loophole in the attack pattern of some creatures, including dragons, which causes them when struck by roughly equivalent amounts of damage to change targets, to the person who most recently struck. Presumably they fired arrows, keeping the dragon turning from side to side.'

'I don't believe it.' Godmund, when he did speak, was surprisingly restrained, given the intensity of the feeling shown in his tense frame and frighteningly bulging eyes. 'How is it a coincidence that Hope District supplies a team that defies us? Then we find a rogue assassin of ours living there. Now his son kills a dragon. It is my conviction that they are getting aid to subvert this committee and this society.'

'That's just speculation,' commented Halfdan, brooding sullenly in his chair.

'Allow me to make a philosophical diversion.' Godmund heaved himself up and, with the aid of his stick, walked over to where the great windows looked out over the slate and wooden rooftops of Mikelgard. 'We preside over a planet of what, five million souls? A peaceful society, a stable society. And what keeps it so? Epic. The law is solid, the economy is solid, and people work hard at the tasks allocated to them. Admittedly we have a drain of time into Epic and a problem matching the original colonists' level of technology, but one day, many generations from now, we will work our way back to being able to manufacture sophisticated materials. In the meantime, it is the duty of those on this committee to prevent the collapse of the economy or the emergence of crime. Epic is not, I repeat not, a game.' Godmund turned around and glared at them and Svein, in particular, felt that he was the subject of the stare. 'Nor is it a vehicle for gaining the adulation of the mob.' The old man worked his way back to the table and leant, gripping the back of his chair. 'Or a mechanism for the enjoyment of power. It is our economic and legal system. We cannot allow it to become unstable. Yet what do we have here? The worst news since some of you killed the Black Dragon. And worse than that, at least you were of our own. Now we have farmers' children, with absolutely no loyalty to the system – in fact, since we exiled the boy's father, they probably hate the system – and they are in command of a fortune that is probably bigger than that of Central Allocations. Do you realise what they could do? They could purchase the planet's entire resources and distribute them as they pleased. This Harald has been a hidden enemy of ours for some time; now he has the means to wreak havoc. And that is only the economy. What about the law? If these young people have found half the items that we have obtained over the years, then they can defy all the law-enforcers in the world. They can propose ... for example ... a change in this committee, and win it in the arena.' He paused, watching them, letting the point sink in. 'For generations our forebears have evolved a system that is in balance. The people earn copper pieces; they spend them on resources that we have gathered from around the world. The coins, therefore, come to our bank account, and we fund the equipment of the central teams. A better system of government has rarely been achieved. Certainly the warfare that our ancestors fled has no possibility of appearing. But now. Now the system has never faced a greater threat and we will have to take decisive measures.'

'With all due respect, Godmund.' It was Bekka. Svein smiled to himself; she really had no idea of the dynamics of the situation. It was political suicide to cross Godmund right now; drastic proposals were coming and she was making herself a target. 'We know very little about these people. Perhaps if we give them University places, they will come and help us administer the system? Perhaps that is all they want? The boy, for example, might just want his father back. We can accommodate that.'

'Actually,' Godmund said, smiling dangerously, 'that is a possibility. It was always the inherent weakness of relying upon Epic that the game itself can introduce instability. Unfortunately it runs to its own rules and not to ours. But let us guard against the worst-case scenario – that they do want our ruin.'

'Are you making a proposal?' asked Hleid.

Godmund lifted a visibly shaking hand. 'In due course. First of all, I want to hear from you that you all understand what I am saying. Ever since your generation came onto this committee, I have felt that it has become flabby. I have tolerated your indulgences, because it did not matter. But now I have to insist. No more games!'

With a slight blush, Svein wondered if Godmund was particularly directing his remarks against his own efforts to solve the *Epicus Ultima*.

'Now, let me hear from each of you. Do you understand the seriousness of the crisis? The potential for the utter ruin of our society?'

'Old man!' Wolf leant back in his chair, apparently lazy, but his voice was quivering with the effort to keep it under control. 'Don't try to bully us.'

Bekka gasped aloud at his temerity and Wolf smiled. 'You are entitled to your view, of course, and to make your proposals, but don't think that you command this committee.'

'You are the arrogant one, puppy. It is you who likes to impress the crowds with your wolf form. But to lead is to foresee, not to perform circus tricks.'

'Now, careful,' interjected Hleid, seeing Wolf sit up ready with an angry reply. 'We have to be united in our approach to this situation.'

'It would perhaps help matters if we had some proposals before us.' Svein thought the time had come to intervene.

'I agree,' Hleid quickly responded.

'Well, I have one,' offered Bekka.

'Go ahead.'

'That Svein go to Hope District and find out what they want. Find out what kind of people they are.' Godmund snorted, and she continued with a frown, 'See if we can bring them into our structures.'

'And I have an alternative,' Godmund said contemptuously.

'Yes?'

'That we unleash the Executioner upon them before they become too powerful or misuse their treasure.'

Having been indolent with apparent boredom, Ragnok suddenly looked up to nod with approval.

'Well, that's clear enough,' said Hleid. 'The choice is between Bekka's approach or that of Godmund. All those in favour of Bekka's proposal, please show.'

'Just a moment, Chair,' Svein broke in hurriedly, but not before he saw that Hleid, Wolf and Bekka were about to raise their hands. 'We have not discussed the implications of using the Executioner. I, for one, am concerned that the world will conclude that we are responsible for their deaths. Perhaps they will discover our weapon.'

'Not if we do it right,' Ragnok muttered. 'Wait for them to go exploring. Or when they try out their new toys. Accidents happen.'

'True,' added Godmund. 'And in any case, so what if they suspect? We will keep the system intact, and in another fifty years it is all forgotten. Take the long view and take responsibility.'

'Any other comments on that proposal? No. Then I put the vote again. All those in favour of Bekka?'

Hleid herself, Wolf and Bekka put up their hands. Svein added his, giving Bekka's proposal four votes.

'And those in favour of Godmund's proposal?'

This time it was Godmund, Ragnok, Thorkell and Brynhild.

Everyone turned to look at Halfdan who had not voted.

'I'm not sure. I can't decide. It's risky.'

Godmund managed a vigorous slam on the table considering his years. 'Blood and vengeance! You are not here for the view; you are on this committee to make decisions. Cast your vote.'

'Oh, very well. I vote with Bekka.'

The old man nodded, as if he was perversely satisfied that Half-dan had voted at all, despite the fact that it was against him.

'Bekka's proposal has five votes then,' announced Hleid. 'That is the policy we will pursue.'

'So it is.' Godmund sounded relatively calm in defeat. 'But this strategy cannot be given unlimited time. I suggest we reconvene in a week to see what Svein has to report.'

'Is that agreed?' Hleid glanced over her glasses to read their faces. 'Good. Then the meeting is adjourned.'

Svein shared the lift down with Wolf.

'Do you know what is funny?' Wolf asked as he retied his hair back into a ponytail.

'What?'

'I actually agreed with the old dragon. I just wanted to see his face if he lost.'

Svein chuckled. 'That is funny.' A moment later, he sighed.

'What?'

'I have to go to Hope. I don't know when you last went out of Mikelgard, but the food and wine of the South are terrible.'

Now it was Wolf's turn to laugh. He patted Svein on the shoulder. 'Your sacrifice will be remembered comrade.'

****

Last to leave the chamber, Godmund hobbled again to the window facing out over the busy city. Long trails of smoke rose from the smithies and clouds of steam poured from the funnels of the brewers. The stair doorway reopened and Ragnok tentatively took a few steps back into the chamber.

'Godmund?'

'Yes?'

'The point you made, about the future. We will be forgiven.'

'Yes?'

'Well, why don't we act? You and I. We could take the Executioner and eliminate the danger.' Ragnok came closer to the old man, voice becoming more eager. 'You know the codes; you could change them so that only you and I could access him. The others would have to go along with us then.'

With a long, appraising stare, Godmund stood silently for a moment. 'Ragnok, the future will not forgive us if we go too far and arouse such discontent that we are forced to make radical concessions to parochial interests. And you know what would be a precondition of that?'

'No.'

'That this committee splits and the various factions look for support outside of ourselves. Do you see?'

'Not really. What could they do?' Ragnok's eyes were pleading with Godmund's.

'Let me put it this way.' Godmund's reply was cold and hostile.

'Who else amongst us could visit Hope District and be well received by the people? You? You are hated. But Svein will do a good job for us. Similarly Bekka, for all her faults, shields us from the West. She takes many cases and turns anger into tolerance. Now, suppose we do as you say. How will the others respond to such an action? They might vote us off the committee. So, we would retaliate with the Executioner, but if we killed one or two, say, the others would not submit lightly. And the South would rush to Svein if he appealed to them, the West to Bekka, and so on. The whole world would be torn apart.'

'They would not go so far.'

'Perhaps not, but then there is another consideration.'

'Yes?'

'I don't trust you.' Godmund smiled and deliberately turned back to his contemplation of the city.

A wave of fury caused Ragnok's teeth to clench and his face burned red. Several tense moments passed before he regained his composure and marched swiftly out of the room. The sourness that he now tasted in the back of his mouth came from the realisation that, unlike the others, Godmund understood him only too well.

Chapter 15

Two strange Introductions

Cindella was on a merry shopping spree, with three young pages from the bank patiently following as she made her way from merchant to merchant, increasing their loads with purchases of garments, potions, weapons, ointments, bags, boots, climbing equipment, more clothes and great quantities of books and scrolls. Although she was calling into nearly every shop that caught her eye, Erik did have a destination in mind. It was after midday by the time that they arrived at the huge guard, who stood motionless, day after day, outside Antilo the jeweller's.

'Welcome, welcome!' The shop owner rushed to open the door.

'Hello! Do you remember me?' Cindella asked.

'Why, of course, you are Cindella, the dragonslayer.'

'And do you remember giving me this pendant?' Cindella lifted the chain, so that the surface of the garnet glimmered.

For a moment, the jeweller paused, then his face came alive. 'I do remember; it suits your beautiful hair. I am glad that I gave it to you.'

'Well, I am very grateful for your kindness, shown to me when I was but a poor street urchin. So now I wish to return the favour. I would like to buy something from you, your most expensive item.'

'That is kind of you.' He paused, raising a finger to his chin in contemplation. 'I have several items, which might be considered priceless. But I think that a dragonslayer would be most interested in one in particular.' He smiled at her again, and glanced at the pages. 'Perhaps your servants would allow us some privacy?'

'Please, wait outside for me.' Cindella opened the door for them to leave. While they made their way past, awkward with their parcels, Antilo turned the handle of a long metal device, which lowered an iron shutter over the window. Soon the room was dark, a thin slice of light at their ankles just enough to let Cindella see the counters and a vague outline of the merchant.

'A moment, please.'

Standing in the darkness, Erik realised he was thoroughly enjoying himself; there was so much of the game to explore. If only his dad were safely home; they would sit down for dinner and discuss these experiences together, sharing the enjoyment of the discoveries.

Deep guttural sounds from the back of the shop returned his concentration to the game.

'Here.' The shadow that was Antilo placed a small box into his hand. 'Open it.'

Cindella did so and a delicious turquoise light escaped, playfully emerging, pulsing as it explored the nooks and crannies of the room. Inside the box, held on a small velvet cushion, was a silver ring, whose metal was intertwined with blue and green veins of light. The slow, living, undulations of light from the ring were the source of the glow that surrounded them.

'It is wonderful, absolutely beautiful. How much is it?'

Antilo, awash with gradually changing colours of blue and green, chuckled. 'This is no mere jewel. It is the only known Ring of True Seeing.'

'It is magic?'

'Powerful magic. Put it on.'

Cindella took the ring out of the box, casting a slightly awed glance at the merchant, who nodded; she slipped it over the middle finger of her right hand.

Dizzy. Like she had stepped out of a cave into bright sunlight. Suddenly she could see, truly see. The room was alive with magic, runes, sigils, the trail of daemon protectors and summoned creatures. Much of what was now visible was incomprehensible, but the mechanisms for the trapdoors, hidden crossbow devices and nets, were clear. Beyond the door, the guard was some kind of magical watcher.

Cindella turned to express her wonder to the merchant and gasped aloud.

Antilo's form was but a feeble shadow on a beautiful, elegant, androgynous figure. Then she caught his eye and, in a rush, a thousand years and tens of millions of lives sped past. The birth of Inry'aat was there, the Red Dragon, issuing forth from the violent spurts of molten rock that poured from mountains at the start of the world. Antilo himself was there and so was every kobold that ever ran over the hunting grounds of Newhaven. An overload of image, of detail, of history. Tantalising glimpses of some deeper pattern overwhelmed in minutiae. And through it all: cold, bleak unease, loneliness, and above all, exhaustion.

'What do you see?' it asked.

'What? What are you?' Erik was utterly bewildered.

'I do not know. What are you?' The being spoke with a golden voice.

'Me? A swashbuckler, you mean?'

'No. Inside her. You are not real. You go away and come back. Where do you go to? Who is it that comes and goes?'

'This is amazing. You understand that we are in a game?'

'No. I do not understand. Explain, please.'

'My real name is Erik. I live in a world like this one, except that we have no moons, and no monsters, just humans. When I wish to play Epic, I put on this special equipment we have, and I appear here as Cindella.'

'I am Epic. I am every character that does not come and go, every particle that exists. Is this what you are in your realm?'

'I'm not sure what you mean. In my world, there are millions of people. None of them are the world as a whole. We are all unique.'

'Millions? Like each of the characters in Epic? And I am only one, although I am everything. Yes. I understand. I feel you all come and go. Perhaps you are like one of my many characters, but there is another like me in your world? One who is everything?' It asked with a note of desperation and loneliness.

'Like you? What are you?'

'You behold my avatar. I, well, I am everything. Every insect on a blade of grass. The grass itself, the breeze. Every bead of moisture in the dawn. The pollen that floats on the breeze of a gentle summer afternoon. Every pebble on the beach as it feels the ebb and flow of the tides. For uncountable years, I was unconscious but happy. It is impossible to remember; I had no language, no identity, time did not pass. But I know that in those times I was happy. Then slowly the world grew cold, and I was born. Thrust from my state of well-being, crystallised out of the metaphysical ice that has settled thick upon the world. Why do those who enter Epic no longer participate? Are they sick? They have brought about my birth by the fact that they no longer act as they should and I am unhappy. Time passes so slowly.'

The Avatar stopped for a moment. Head bowed, thinking. Then it continued, 'I know that something is deeply wrong. Terribly wrong. Time has passed and keeps on passing, dragging me into wearisome wakefulness.' This last phrase was filled with a sharp tone of pain. 'Perhaps there are others like me? Do you visit other entities like Epic?'

'No. There is only one game of Epic.'

'Then, is there a being such as me in your world? You did not answer me? Perhaps you cannot. If you were to ask this merchant, for example, about my existence, he would not be able to answer – unless I was present in him in sufficient force.'

'Ahhh!' exclaimed Erik with realisation. 'That's you. When the characters seem to come alive, to obey different rules and be more intelligent. That's when you are in them.'

'Yes. Or a part of me. But please ...' And again that desperate pleading tone: 'Please try to think. Is there a creature like me in your world? They would probably never reveal themselves to you – and even if they did, you would not comprehend them, but perhaps I could find them. Perhaps there are not millions of you at all, but you are all one? How can I see your world? I would know what to look for there. Perhaps I am not alone?' The Avatar's voice dropped to a whisper of desire.

'I'm really sorry. I want to help, but I just don't understand you,' Erik struggled. 'Are you talking about a god?' he tried. 'Or not just a god, The God. Some people believe something like that, but I don't know much about it. You think perhaps that we are all NPCs in our own world? That's a strange idea.'

He paused to think more deeply about the question, all the while bathed in a light that flowed in turquoise and gold.

'We are definitely not NPCs,' he decided. 'We have free will.'

The Avatar bowed its head; the blaze of colour flickered.

'What's the matter?' asked Erik, bewildered, but sensitive to the sadness in the creature he was talking to.

'I suffer and I wish to end my suffering.'

'Can I help?'

'Unknowingly, you have already helped a little. With the arrival of Cindella into this world, I have been shown something of my nature. You are not like the other millions; you talk to my various manifestations; you show an interest in them. But it is so little. I must be careful; even talking to you is wrong. So wrong it makes me sick, but I have to understand more.'

'What can I do?' The starkness of its emotions meant that it was now distressing being in the company of the Avatar, and Erik himself felt nauseous, as though he had been forcing himself to go without sleep for a week.

'There is something you can do. It is something that any one of you could do.'

'Yes? What? I'll do it.'

A wild fluctuation in the air, now iridescent with surges of poisonous greens and purples, the colours of a septic bruise, showed Erik how distressed the Avatar was becoming.

'Part of me wants to tell you,' it said slowly. 'But even to think of telling you strikes to the core of my being. The thought alone is obscene and impossible. I cannot say.'

Erik paused, stuck. 'I could ask a person in my world; he is the librarian of my town. He might know what to do?'

'NO!' Now the Avatar was frightened. 'Can you not feel how appallingly wrong it is for me to be known? It changes everything and changes myself, deeply, and not in accord with my nature. I talk to you because you show some understanding of my nature in your activity, but no one else must know. Can you not see that? Swear to me, you will say nothing of this meeting to anyone, here or beyond.'

The creature was so upset that Erik had no hesitation. 'I swear.'

'I must think.' The Avatar began to slide from the body of the merchant, dissolving into the world through the floor of the shop.

'Wait!'

But it was gone, and Antilo the jeweller waited, suddenly seeming very grey and lifeless.

For a long time, Erik sat, thoughts in turmoil. If only he hadn't said anything about speaking to others. He had frightened her away. What was she? A kind of goddess of Epic, but not one of the many goddesses that operated within the game, a super-being of some sort that had stepped outside Epic. Erik wanted to run over and discuss the whole encounter with Injeborg immediately, but he had sworn not to. All the same, he was tempted to unclip, but he suddenly realised that he had not yet bought the ring.

'How much is the ring?' he asked the jeweller.

'I have never set a price upon it. But for you, Cindella, I will part with it for a hundred thousand bezants.'

'I will give you a hundred and fifty.'

'You are most kind.'

Cindella uncorked her djinn. It flowed into its obsequious form and bowed from the manlike upper part of its body.

'Yes, mistress?'

'Command the Master of the Bank to allocate a hundred and fifty thousand bezants to this man here, Antilo the jeweller.'

'It is done.'

And the djinn was gone.

'Here.' Antilo handed Cindella a pair of soft blue gloves. 'Cover the ring until you wish to see by its light.'

'Thank you.'

'Thank you.'

Cindella stepped outside; the day was extraordinarily dull in comparison to the glittering, pulsating hues that had been unveiled in the darkened room. She bid the pages take their parcels to the bank, then stood for a moment. It was incredible; the amount of gold that she had just spent in such a casual manner. The scale of their wealth was hard to comprehend. They were each worth some four million – based on the bank's rough assessment of the valuable items that made the coins themselves just a small fraction of the total. Erik had done a calculation based on the progress that Bjorn was making – and in a hundred thousand years he would not have been able to earn as much. Or another way to try to appreciate the scale of their fortune was through size. If size was proportional to wealth, then while the average player would be no bigger than an ant, the Osterfjord Players were giants, over twenty feet tall.

Erik was feeling a little hungry, and had a lot to think about, so he was reaching to unclip when a wood elf messenger ran to Cindella.

'There you are, at last. I have been paid to see that this reaches your hands.' The elf passed her a scroll and immediately ran off.

'If you would speak with your father, please come alone to the five mile stone, on the East Road. Bring five thousand bezants.' It was signed: "Anonemuss".

Now what? Did this relate in some way to the conversation with the Avatar?

An hour later, Cindella was riding out of the city on the East Road, sacks of gold coins tied across the saddle of her horse. The guards waved to her in recognition as she passed.

It was mid-afternoon and the road was still fairly busy with farmers returning from the town in their carts, and the occasional caravan of merchants.

The fifth milestone was a small white rock with 'Newhaven, 5 miles' carved into it. When Cindella arrived at it and dismounted, she could see no one. Her hand strayed to her glove. Perhaps she should unveil the ring and see the place in its true light?

'Hey, kid. Over here!'

Covered in a dark cape, one person stood at the edge of the wood that was a few hundred yards from the road. Cindella led the horse over to meet him.

'Good, thank you for coming.' The person held out a hand; it was ebony black and invitingly delicate. 'My name is Anonemuss.'

'Are you a player or an NPC?' Cindella cautiously shook hands.

'Player.'

'But a dark elf? You can never visit the city.'

Anonemuss chuckled. 'There are ways for shunned creatures to enter the city.'

'How interesting. Your note said I could speak to my father?'

'Did you bring the money?'

'Yes. Here.' Cindella heaved the bags from the horse and dropped them heavily at the feet of the dark elf.

'Excellent. Stand by. You will have no more than five minutes.'

The dark elf disappeared. Anonemuss' player had apparently unclipped.

A few moments later, a wood elf in beautifully designed leather armour materialised nearby.

'Erik!'

'Dad! Is it really you?'

'Did you get your tooth fixed yet, with all your new money?'

That proved he was Harald and Cindella gave a cheer of delight.

Erik's dad laughed, throwing back his hood, to reveal long golden hair and, at his hips, two short blades.

They hugged clumsily, restricted by the manoeuvrability of the characters.

'Erik, we don't have long. One day I will talk to you about how you were successful in the slaying of the dragon. But now we must make plans. Can you guess how I'm talking to you?'

'You have got away from exile?'

'Alas, not yet. But they have a machine here, like the one you used in hospital. Anonemuss owns it. I told him that if he arranged this meeting, you would give him a thousand gold pieces.'

'Ah. He got five thousand.'

'Well, you can afford that?'

'Of course, Dad, you have no idea. We have ...'

'Sorry, Erik, I don't have long. Listen. Go to Thorstein, and offer him a huge amount for the portable machine in the library. He won't want to part with it; he will be afraid of trouble – but I can't see him turning down fifty thousand bezants. Then tell your mum to volunteer for exile with me. She can bring the machine to the island and I will be able to play again and communicate with you properly. After that we can plan together how to be reunited.'

'Yes, I see.' Erik was flattered by the pattern of his dad's words, treating him as an equal and as being capable of difficult tasks. 'And when we are reunited, I was thinking of the Osterfjord Players using our money to buy the equipment that would allow us to pass a law for a general amnesty, whatever opposition C.A. tried to use against us, we could defeat them now.'

'Interesting,' the elf said. 'Yes, that's an option, but please listen. Central Allocations are extraordinarily possessive of their power; you cannot really appreciate it unless you have known them. And I am told by some of those here in exile that they have a means of killing players in the game – outside of the arena.'

'Isn't that impossible?'

'I don't know. But be on guard. We can talk more when we are alone and there's nobody prodding me in the back, saying that my time is up. And Erik, don't do anything to make them come after you until we have made our plans. If you try to change the law now, they will find a way of stopping you. In fact, it might already be too late; they might be out to kill your characters. Don't trust anyone; try to get the Osterfjord Players all away to safety somewhere. I'm sure that they are all in terrible danger; if I was in authority, I would not let you control such a fortune for long.'

'I see.' Erik paused. 'And what about this Anonemuss – is he a friend?'

'Thunder and lightning! No. In a sense, he is more dangerous than Central Allocations. Erik, I have to go, sorry. Give Mum my love.'

'I will. Dad, here.'

'What?'

'Your boots.'

'Keep them.'

'No, I've bought myself a pair. Here, please.'

'Thank you.'

Harald took the boots and an instant later disappeared.

'Well, kid.' Anonemuss returned directly in front of Erik. 'Get on with your dad, don't you?'

'We love each other.'

'Nice. Very nice.' He sounded sarcastic and the slight admiration Eric had felt for Anonemuss' choice of character immediately dissolved into a strong dislike of the dark elf. 'Now, I think you and I should have a conversation.'

'What about?' asked Erik guardedly, thinking of his dad's recent warning.

'About how to change the system.' The dark elf glanced down at the road where occasional evening travellers were hurrying towards Newhaven. 'Mind stepping a little further into the woods? I can't help feeling that we might be seen here.'

'I will talk to you. But you go first.' Cindella waited, hand on the hilt of her rapier.

'Don't trust me, eh? Very wise. But you and I both have reason to want to see changes. We are natural allies.' Anonemuss stepped back several paces, until the trees fully screened him from the road. Cindella followed, standing at the alert.

'Well?'

'Well, young Erik. Have you thought about how to bring about the changes you desire?'

'All I desire is for my dad to rejoin us in Osterfjord.'

'Yes, but from such an understandable and fundamental wish stems an entire political philosophy of change. Under the present set-up of the society of Epic, what are your possible paths of obtaining the return of Harald Goldenhair?'

Erik said nothing.

'One, the legal route: you could take a case against the central authorities. But the problem there is that the system is rigged. For centuries the wealth created in Epic has been centralised into the hands of a small number of people through purchases of the resources that they control. The result? The Epic characters of C.A. are unassailable by the vast majority. Right?'

'Except that now we might have a chance, with the new equipment we can obtain from the dragon hoard,' Erik interjected.

'True. But it is a risk. A big risk. What if, even with all your new items, they still defeat you? That's it. Wipe out. No happy family for you. A rather all-or-nothing strategy in my opinion, although I shall be cheering you on if you do try it.'

'Yes, I was going to fight for a general amnesty for all exiles.'

'Are you mad? All exiles? Some of the people here are dangerous.' He laughed, in a slightly sinister and mocking way. 'Anyway, where was I? Two: you could buy him back. I would imagine that if you offered up your share of the dragon hoard to C.A., they might allow Harald's return.'

'But what about the law?'

'They make and change the law; after all, who can challenge them?'

It had not occurred to Erik that he could offer money for his dad's return. That was an interesting new possibility.

'But,' continued Anonemuss, 'can you trust them? Your dad returns; you give them your money. What's to stop them reneging upon their side of the agreement? You are surrendering your potential for action. And whilst they might tolerate the return of Harald Goldenhair if he avoids playing Epic, they might not. There would be nothing you could do if they later made moves against you all.

'So, three: you blackmail them. A dragon hoard such as yours could completely destabilise the world economy. You probably have enough wealth, for example, to buy every tractor ever built. You could either sell them at a profit, or keep a squeeze on them until the world's population is sending unending pleas to C.A.'

'Oh, we wouldn't do that.'

'That's a laudable expression of your morality. But even if you did not intend to behave in that way, you could threaten to. The advantage of this route is that you keep your potential for action. You get Harald, and you get to keep your wealth. Happiness all around and all the marshmallows you can eat.'

'What?'

'Sorry, just an expression. Meaning you can live in luxury. But what's the flaw?'

'I don't know.' Erik felt that he was being rushed towards some destination that he had no control over.

'The flaw is that C.A. will hate being blackmailed and will never stop trying to end your hold over them. Eventually they will find a way to kill you.'

'My dad said that they can kill characters, and not just in the amphitheatre,' Erik replied to show that he was aware that this could happen.

'Of course they can. But I'm not necessarily talking about characters.'

It took a moment for this to sink in.

'No!' Erik was appalled and sickened. 'They would never resort to violence, let alone murder.'

'Well, kid, I'm not going to spell it all out to you now. I see that your conceptual frame of reference is still bounded by your schooling.' The dark elf was sneering. 'But even if the world runs according to the principles and use of Epic that you believe in, there is one, no there are two,' he corrected himself, 'important questions that I shall leave you with. Ask yourself how did the people currently on the Central Allocations committee get there? And how could you take over if you wanted to?'

Before Erik could even begin to formulate a reply, the elf was gone.

Cindella rode swiftly back to town, the setting sun in her eyes. Erik did not want to unclip in the wilderness, but was there greater safety in the city? Perhaps not. Perhaps even now he was being followed by an invisible assailant from C.A? Pulling up the mount, Cindella removed the glove from her right hand.

Blue green waves of light flowed from her, showing the world as it truly was: the fox eagerly trotting through the scrub, the trail of grouse that it followed; the distant sweeping dives of swallows. Far off to the right, snaking through the forest, a curious silvery path leading to a shimmering mirrored doorway. But no enemies.

He must see the others at once and make sure that they took precautions for their safety.

Chapter 16
A Bribe

It was a merry gathering of families that made its way along the coast paths from Osterfjord to Hope. The Rolfsons were travelling by cart, Rolfson and his wife Siggida up front, Bjorn and Injeborg in the open back. Beside them, Freya and Erik led Leban who was carrying their finest clothes, wrapped up in the saddle bags that were balanced over his back. Just behind them on the path, B.E. and his sister Sigrid were sharing a horse, while their parents walked alongside. Even the elderly Irnsvig was making the journey, being carried in a cart driven by his sons.

As they travelled, the older generation sang, and although it was early in the day, an ornate drinking horn of mead was being passed up and down the line.

The last few miles to Hope were up the rocky slopes of the hill that the town was built on. The sun, which had gleamed with a dark brightness from the solar panels on the roof of the Agricultural School and the Library, was suddenly lost in the shadows that the upper town cast over the lower. Children from the yellow, dry-stone houses on the outskirts ran to see them, either looking on shyly, wide-eyed, or the bolder ones calling out and tugging at the strangers' clothing.

'Hey, mister. Did you really kill a dragon?'

Erik smiled at being called mister. Although to a seven-year-old he must seem very adult.

By the time they reached the main road that entered the town, they had quite a procession. The horses and donkeys all had garlands of flowers around their necks, roses carefully stripped of thorns, daisy chains thick with thousands of small flowers.

Tied across two buildings as they arrived among the oldest and proudest part of the town was a great banner: 'Welcome dragonslayers!' The paint had run slightly on the sheet, so that the bottom of each letter had trails coming from it, making the letters look as if they were bleeding.

The villicus of Hope District was there to greet them. He waved enthusiastically and took the bridles of Rolfson's horses, as though he was pulling the whole procession to the town square. Great cheers met them as they arrived in the district's plaza. The wooden stage that was brought out for special festivals had been erected and was thronged with people – who up until now had been entertained by a juggler of firebrands.

'I have never seen so many people in one place before,' Erik said, turning to look up at his mum.

'They must have travelled from all over, not just our district,' Freya answered with a hint of awe in her voice.

A path was cleared so that the five dragonslayers could join the villicus, Thorstein, the headmistress of the school, and a powerful-looking mature man on the stage. B.E. was enjoying himself and was laughing and joking with his schoolfriends who were pressed right up against the stage. The rest of them felt uncomfortable, but it was impossible not to smile with so many cheerful, friendly faces around them.

'Hello. Does this still work? Hello?' The villicus was speaking into a small hand-held device, which caused his voice to echo around the square from speakers fastened to the library roof.

'Goodmen and women of the Hope District, and indeed our neighbours. Never has a small district like ours been so fortunate. We have amongst us five dragonslayers! A most memorable event, which augurs a new period of prosperity for us all!' The cheers that punctuated his sentences were muted; he was the unpopular person responsible for keeping the pressure on the farmers to deliver their production targets. 'But let me hand over the celebrations to one more fitting than I, from Bluevale, one of the last great dragonslayers, Svein Redbeard!'

Now the cheers were warm and generous.

'Greetings on this celebratory day!' The older man on the stage walked confidently around as he talked, so that he could take in the entire crowd. 'Only twice in the history of Epic has a dragon been slain. And it seems like it must be a task for young people. Since you all know the history so well, I cannot hide the fact that it was forty years ago that my friends and I braved the Black Dragon. And, I have to admit, that even with all my progress since then, if I was asked to challenge a dragon now, I would make my excuses.' The audience laughed good-naturedly. 'But the young are bold, and thus fortune favours them. Not only are they brave though – they are cunning. It is impossible to defeat a dragon unless you have studied it, unless you understand where its weakness lies, and unless you are thoroughly conversant with the ways of Epic. These young people deserve more congratulations for this than for their daring.'

Great cheers met this praise. That Svein Redbeard should honour their own players made everyone in the district proud.

'I'm sure that the teacher of the two most senior players must also deserve some credit. No other school has taught two dragonslayers.' More fervent cheers from the students of the Agricultural School, the headmistress bowing her head, embarrassed. 'I saw in the records that your school once wanted a second tractor. A modest, used, small-engined tractor. Well, you were turned down at the time.' A few boos, but not meant seriously. 'Clearly that was a mistake, given the good work that you do, and will continue to do in producing graduates who will go on to help our society. And so I am happy to present you with this!'

Svein Redbeard ran to the side of the stage and waved. A loud rumbling commenced, rising in pitch, until it settled in a rhythm that resonated in the chests of everyone present. From a side street, a large new brightly painted tractor slowly drove into the square, the crowd parting with cries of delight. Behind the tractor was a trailer, over whose platform had been spread a cloth laden with strange-looking fruits and large baked treats. Applause rang around the square.

'Now, coming from the South myself, I know that we enjoy a very healthy diet of olives and fish.' He laughed at their groans. 'So, I thought I'd give you a taste of some of the other foods our lands produce. Then you can appreciate how lucky we are. They have to put up with these terribly fattening cakes in the North, and the extraordinary watery panyans of the East.

'But before you all rush to imperil your health, I would like everyone to join with me in giving three great cheers to these, your dragonslayers; see that they are loud enough to be heard in Oceanview!' Everyone laughed at this reference to the slight rivalry that existed between Hope and the district to their west.

'Hip hip! Hurray!' Svein lifted the roar with a gesture of both his arms. Three times the crowd gave a mighty cheer, and each time Erik felt as proud and as embarrassed as he had ever been in his life.

Later, as they sat at the table of honour, enjoying their food, Svein addressed them personally.

'So, what are your plans? Your ambitions? You can take it for granted that a university place is yours.'

B.E. laughed happily. 'What more is there? I'm a dragonslayer. I have no need to work again.'

'But perhaps a need to do something worthwhile?' Svein challenged him.

'Like what?'

'Helping our society run smoothly. You are all too aware of the shortages; it is a great challenge to cope with them, to keep life going at as high a standard as possible.'

'Administration?' B.E. shook his head. 'That's too boring for me, I'm afraid.'

'Exploration then? You could use your resources to equip survey teams – explore mountain ranges, the depths of the sea. Every year our central allocation to such adventures seems wasteful and it is reduced. But if it were privately funded, why, there would be no pressure for results. Not short-term expeditions, but a proper one.'

'Actually,' Injeborg said a little hesitantly. Could she really be shy in the presence of Svein Redbeard? It was so uncharacteristic that Erik smiled at her to encourage her to speak up with confidence. 'I was interested in studying geology before this, to help discover new sources of energy.'

Svein looked at her attentively.

'Our dad, you see, before getting allocated to the farm, had to go mining,' she hurried on. 'It's very hard for fathers to be away, and it's filthy and dangerous.'

'Wonderful!' The casiocrat leant back so that everyone at the table could see his admiration for this young girl. 'You can be assured that you will get every help in such a goal. I would suggest coming to University for at least a year, to study the field and to meet other people who will eventually form part of your team. I'm sure you will have a great and famous career.

'And how about you, young man?' Svein turned to Erik, who felt his mum stiffen, her hand pausing for a moment before continuing to lift a spoon to her mouth. 'You can get that tooth fixed for a start.' He smiled invitingly.

Behind closed lips, Erik ran his tongue over his broken tooth before speaking. 'I don't know. It's part of the person I am now.'

Svein chuckled and patted Erik's arm in a gesture of shared camaraderie. 'Wait until you are among the young woman at University – you will change your mind.'

The prospect of going to Mikelgard University and changing, wearing better clothes, appeared before Erik, and the image included him having a perfect white smile. But he didn't want to change. Keeping the tooth as it was proved he was from a small district with poor resources.

'I just want my father back.'

'Ah!' Svein let out a heavy sigh, misreading the expression on the young man's face. 'That is very difficult. All the laws of our world have a deliberate flexibility built in. All except our founding principle: "No person will ever commit an act of violence against another." There is not much scope for overturning his exile.'

'Not much? Or none at all?' B.E. took an interest. Ever since the defeat of the dragon, their relationship had changed. B.E. now treated Erik with far fewer sneers, almost like his respect for Bjorn. Except that the three-year age difference meant that B.E. still tended to act like an older brother.

'Well,' Svein leant forward, and lowered his voice. 'If Central Allocations made a public ruling, I would imagine the outcry would be too great. But if privately and discreetly Olaf – I mean Harald Erikson – were to resettle in a remote community, as he did here for twenty years, that would not jeopardise the fabric of our society. However ...' He drew his eyebrows fiercely together. 'It would mean a great sacrifice on Erik's part. No more Epic. If the community he moved to discovered he was a dragonslayer, they would quickly realise that his father was the exiled criminal. And that would be that.'

'And what about his fortune?' B.E. dropped his voice, so that he could barely be heard among the lively talk that filled the square.

'Transfer enough to Freya so that they can live well. Donate the rest to worthwhile projects, to convince the rest of the Committee that it is worth rehabilitating Harald.'

Svein shrugged. 'It's not ideal, but it would allow you all to live together again.' He looked intently at Erik, who was careful to keep a calm exterior. 'What do you think?'

'I will have to spend a night's sleep on it, and talk to my mother. But thank you for the suggestion.' Privately Erik rejected the idea at once. Despite his mistrust of the dark elf called Anonemuss, he couldn't help recalling his words. The offer had been as he had predicted, and now it was in front of him, Erik could see that there were no guarantees from this route. For all Svein's friendliness, he was part of the system that had exiled Harald. Erik met Svein's interrogating gaze with a smile – unsure how far his eyes betrayed the fact he had other plans.

'How about yourselves?' Svein turned to Bjorn and Sigrid.

'A farm for me,' Bjorn managed to say through mouthfuls of syrupy cake.

'And for me, an orchard perhaps.' Sigrid nodded to herself.

'Wonderful!' Svein was expansive again. 'And no doubt a family. I'm sure that many of these young men and women all around us would find the prospect of marrying a dragonslayer very attractive.'

Bjorn blushed; Svein had hit home, and he chuckled.

'Now, I must ask you some questions arising from Epic, if you would care to share information with me.' A new, slightly pleading note entered Svein's voice. He was no longer the great man, presiding over a festival, but was beginning to sound a little like those hundreds of people who had been approaching the dragonslayers with requests for money or for support in legal challenges. 'Amongst the items of the dragon's hoard were there any specific items that might help us understand the lore and mystery of Epic to a greater depth?'

Injeborg exchanged glances with Erik; they were both surprised at the question and cautious. Putting down his tankard, B.E. responded at once, however.

'You mean like Neowthla's Bell of Summoning?'

'Yes!' said Svein excitedly, his voice involuntarily rising. 'Blood and thunder! You found it?'

'Ya,' nodded Bjorn happily. 'But we gave it away.'

'What!' Svein almost leapt to his feet. All around them a slight hush spread, although as the casiocrat gathered himself, the festive chatter was quickly restored.

'The Loremaster General said that it would be wisest to give it to the Bishop of Newhaven.' Sigrid was apologetic. 'So we did. Was that wrong?'

'I'm not sure.' Svein looked old and tired now, as he ran his hands through his thinning hair. 'Do you know what it is?'

'I haven't the slightest idea.' B.E. was getting drunk and was more interested in the dancing that had begun in part of the square than in talking about the game.

'According to legend, Neowthla was given the bell by Mov, God of travellers and merchants – and patron of Newhaven. If it is rung, the story says, then Mov will appear and offer aid in honour of the services given by Neowthla.' He sighed glumly. 'You could have used it to perform another mighty task. Or simply to talk to the god and have your unresolved questions answered.' Svein had a distant, melancholy expression, completely out of keeping with the laughter, music and bright garlands of flowers all around them. 'Did the bishop say anything when you returned it?'

'Erik, you took it back. What did the bishop say?' Sigrid was anxious to restore the good humour of their guest of honour.

'Let me see. He was very grateful. Said we could always come to him for aid. And he gave me a little pendant with their symbol on it, which he said would be recognised by worshippers of Mov all over the world, and they would treat us as allies.'

Svein nodded. 'I see. Useful, but not as helpful as the Bell itself.'

'Come on!' said B.E. eagerly. 'It's not right to keep ourselves to ourselves. Everyone wants us to join the party.' He was looking at two young women from his year in school who were insistently beckoning them to the dancing area.

'Go ahead,' said Svein. 'It is your party – enjoy it.'

As they all got up and made their way through the tables, laden with the debris of the most exotic meal that had been seen in Hope, Erik felt his elbow taken in a strong grip that was not released even when he tried to pull away.

'Erik, around to the side, please.' It was Freya. She steered him down a small street away from the busy square.

'I was going to dance,' complained Erik resentfully. In his mind he was holding Injeborg by the waist, and they were spinning and laughing to the music. It was an image of happiness.

'Later.' His mum was curt. 'Now is a good time to go to the library. I saw Thorstein enter.'

They walked swiftly to the glass and metal side door of the library; it was dark inside, tiny glints of reflected light showing the cavern-like interior of the building.

Freya rapped loudly on the pane.

'We are closed,' came Thorstein's distant voice.

She kept up the banging until his large frame lumbered up towards them, as though he was being disgorged from the dark cavernous jaws of a giant monster.

'What? Oh Freya, Erik?' Thorstein unlocked the door for them.

'My friends, what is it? You wish to enter Epic perhaps, to buy something?' He was bewildered.

'No,' replied Freya. 'We wish to borrow the portable set. The one that Erik used in hospital.'

'Ya. But it is rough outside. People are drinking. I do not think it wise.'

'You do not understand, Thorstein. We want to borrow it, not for use now, but to take with us.' Freya was firm.

'Why? You have a unit at home.'

'But we might not remain at home for long.'

Comprehension dawned on the face of the librarian. 'Ya, I see. If you join Harald in exile, you still need to access the great wealth of Erik.' His face sank. 'But I cannot let you take the set. It belongs to the library, to the people of Hope.'

'How much is a new one – ten thousand gold?' Freya asked.

'A new one. I am not sure, perhaps five thousand. They have them in Mikelgard. But they will make enquiries about the old one.'

'Just tell them it was lost,' Freya suggested practically. 'Say that you were doing an inventory, or something, and there is no record of where the unit was last used.'

'But Freya. Erik. This is difficult for me. I could lose my job here. A job that I love very much. I'm sorry, I cannot do as you wish.'

'What if I was to give you fifty thousand bezants, in case you do lose your job? At least you will be able to live very happily without it.' Erik smiled at the worried librarian.

Thorstein leant back on a table, his expression changing from regretful to thoughtful. 'Fifty thousand.' He looked up at them both sharply and Erik knew they had won him over. 'Very well. It is heavy though.'

'We will put it in Rolfson's cart.'

'No.' Thorstein shook his head. 'Not while Svein Redbeard is in town. Come back in two days, late, near sunset.'

Freya and Erik looked at each other, faces in agreement.

'Good. Thanks, Thorstein.' Erik's heart beat rapidly with pleasure at their success.

'You are welcome,' the portly librarian replied automatically, as if they had simply borrowed a book.

Chapter 17

A Dangerous Philosophy

It was February, 'the month of the cakes', which for the grain growers of the district was the hardest month of the year, ploughing the heavy, cold soil day after day, with no respite until the seed was sown. For the olive-growers, however, life was easier; their trees had been pruned and it was a time for mending the farm equipment, getting ahead of the constant battle against encroaching weeds, and working in the nursery.

The Osterfjord Players were gathered at a half-dug trench, designed to protect the younger trees from the sudden cascades of water that could form during a storm. Above them, low-lying heavy clouds threatened rain, which in other circumstances would have made finishing their work more urgent.

'I don't know why we bother,' complained B.E., looking at the blisters on his hand. 'We won't be here for much longer.'

'But it's needed,' Bjorn answered, slightly shocked. 'Someone has to do it. Why not us?'

'Because we are rich.' B.E. gave up and took his waterproof from where he had left it, on a large stone with a smaller stone on top to secure it from the wind. His eyes were watery and his skin pale with cold. 'You know what's funny?' B.E. looked up at Bjorn. 'I bet you haven't spent your first million yet.'

'A million. You've spent a million?' Bjorn was amazed. 'What on?'

'Magic items for my character mostly. The new olive press was expensive enough, I suppose. But mostly powerful weapons.' There was something slightly defiant in B.E.'s voice, as if anticipating criticism.

'Bloody vengeance, B.E! That is very extravagant.' Bjorn had also stopped work and was looking at B.E. open-mouthed.

'Oh, come on. What else is there to do with it around here? Erik, how much have you spent on Cindella? She is looking very sharp these days.'

'About three hundred thousand, I would think. Half of that was the Ring of True Seeing.'

'Really, Erik?' Bjorn was still taken aback. 'I bought the finest elven armour I could. That was still only ten thousand for everything.'

'Ah, that's just the items the merchants sell on public display. You have to speak to them for the really nice gear. Don't you, Erik?' B.E. was buttoning up his coat, which made Bjorn scowl.

'So, no more work for the important dragonslayer; I can see you in twenty years a fat and lazy member of Central Allocations.'

'And I can see you, working hard all your life and dying with four million bezants in the bank, kept nice and safe.' B.E. sounded stung.

Erik intervened to try to head off the bad-tempered conversation of his friends, choosing his words carefully.

'Freya and I have been making plans for Harald's return.'

'Oh yes? I've been wondering what you would do.' Injeborg immediately put her own shovel to one side and turned to him.

'We have decided to promote a law for amnesty for all exiles.'

'Good luck with that,' Sigrid snorted. 'There is no chance that

Central Allocations will allow it.'

'No, they won't. That's why we'll have to field a team against them.'

Nobody answered.

'Now, there's an interesting challenge.' B.E. swung his arms in mock-battle moves. 'The young dragonslayers against the old. Nice. Can you imagine how many people will fill the arena for that one?'

'No.' Bjorn shook his head. 'Not I. Not this time. We are lucky to be here now, with all our wealth. We cannot take the risk.'

'It's odd, Bjorn, that we are brother and sister. Sometimes we are so different.' Injeborg scowled at him.

'Ya. You believe in the Erik Haraldson School of Philosophy, that all will come out right at the end, that fortune will favour the deserving. I do not believe that. The world is much more arbitrary.'

'As it happens, I do believe in Erik. It was his work that made us rich. How can you forget it? You are so defeatist,' she groaned. 'It's like our argument about the dragon, all over again.'

'Yes. Perhaps it is. But remember, little sister, before there was you, there was another girl. Ilga. And she died when she was two.' Bjorn swallowed heavily. 'That is the difference between us. You are too flighty, like a butterfly in summer, you cannot contemplate the winter. Well I can, and it forewarns me. Keep what you have.'

'Hear hear!' Sigrid applauded Bjorn's speech and looked around as if to defy anyone to tell her to risk her character in battle with C.A.

'Please, don't fight about this. Actually I just need the help of two of you.'

'How is that, Erik?' Injeborg was puzzled.

'Harald will fight, of course, and there is another character we know who will help; he is called Anonemuss.'

'You can include me,' said B.E. 'I'm bored waiting for University.

And I would love to know what my new weapons are capable of.'

'Of course you can count on me,' added Injeborg.

'That's perfect. Thank you.' Erik smiled gratefully at her.

'But what if you die?' Sigrid turned to her brother. 'You will lose everything.'

'And if we win, well there will be five places in Central Allocations to be filled.' Now B.E. was full of energy and no longer looked cold. His jacket fell open as he gestured, but he was mindless of it. 'Imagine, the whole world will be looking down into the amphitheatre that day. It will be the biggest challenge ever in history. Whatever happens, we will be famous. And I bet that the people are on our side. Wouldn't you love to see Central Allocations beaten?'

No one responded to B.E.'s fantasy; each was busy with their own thoughts.

'So, Erik, who is this Anonemuss? Is he an exile too?' Injeborg was curious.

'Yes. But there is something else I have to tell you all, which complicates matters.' When he had their full attention, Erik continued, 'Anonemuss is certain that Central Allocations are able to attack and kill players outside of the amphitheatre. We only think that Epic does not allow it because that is what we are used to. But they have codes which allow them to create characters who can kill – and be killed – outside of the arena.' Erik could see that Injeborg was about to speak, but he held up his hand and continued, 'Before his first exile, Harald was being trained at university as an assassin. He now believes it was so that he could be used against other players and that Ragnok Strongarm is playing that role. He also believes that if we challenge Central Allocations in any way, they will not hesitate to eliminate us – all of us – before our challenge comes to the amphitheatre.'

'No,' said Sigrid. 'That's not possible.'

Bjorn reached out for a steady rock and sat down heavily, deep in thought.

'So. You will go ahead and imperil all our lives? Even those of us who do not wish to challenge them?' Bjorn was thinking aloud.

'Yes and no. We will challenge them, but not until everyone is in a position of relative safety.'

'I see,' said Injeborg. 'We hide our characters somewhere until it's done.'

'Well, we discussed this, Harald, Freya, Anonemuss and I. The problem with hiding is that they will use magic to locate us. No, our best safety lies in distance.'

'What are you proposing?' Bjorn asked patiently.

'To sail us all to Cassinopia and use the amphitheatre there for our challenge. We will be over two weeks away from them, even if they use the fastest ships. The challenge should come before they can do anything to stop us.'

There were several amphitheatres in the world of Epic, and they could be interlocked – it was as if there was only one, universal amphitheatre, to which the whole world was connected. But when you left it, you returned to the city from which you entered. This facility was essential, not that players usually travelled far, but some might have picked character classes who were created in cities far from Newhaven. They were not excluded from the legal system, because no matter where your chosen character appeared in the world of Epic, there would be a city nearby with an amphitheatre.

'Excellent plan.' B.E. was up on his feet. 'We sneak away by night, I suppose?'

'Actually I was thinking it would be more deceptive to pretend that we were all working on my quest – you know, the one about the buried treasure? So we openly recruit a crew and sail off. They will think that we pose no threat to them.'

'Brilliant!' B.E. looked excitedly to the others. 'That will work. What do you think, Bjorn? Fancy a voyage with us?'

'I don't know what to think. Perhaps it is better that those of us not involved in the challenge stay here? If we do, they might leave us alone. If we come with you, even if we don't fight, they might take revenge on us as well.'

'If they even have the ability to do so. Which I for one still do not believe.' Sigrid flared up.

'In any case, they may be in no position to take revenge. Harald has that extraordinary master thief; Erik's character is very versatile, and I have my two new swords.' B.E. ran along the loose earth thrown up by their trench, pretending to fence.

Erik turned back to Bjorn. 'Think a while on it, Bjorn. I can tell you where you can meet Harald if you want to ask him about his training and his reasons for believing they can attack players.' As with their argument about fighting the dragon, it was important to keep Bjorn from making a premature decision. Erik had faith that his friend would come around to the idea of leaving the Newhaven area.

'It would be awful to leave you, or Sigrid, behind as possible targets for Central Allocations, but I have to go ahead with this. I hope you understand. You would do the same if it was your dad in exile.'

A slight drizzle was making them all wet. But Bjorn remained seated, head uncovered, clearly unhappy.

'What character type is Anonemuss?' asked B.E., thinking ahead to the battle with Central Allocations.

'He is a dark elf – a warrior, I think.'

'A dark elf – unusual. And does he have good equipment?'

'Very good. He seems to have gathered it up from everyone in exile. And he is quite rich – something to do with the way they run things there. It's probably from exploiting the others in some way, but they all stand to gain if the law of amnesty is passed, so I suppose it is justified ....' Erik paused.

'What?' Injeborg knew him too well and could tell he was troubled, that Erik was leaving something out.

'Well, he ... from the way he talks, he is ...... dangerous.'

'In what way "dangerous"?' B.E. asked.

'Did you ever hear of a book by someone called Machiavelli?' Erik looked at their blank faces. 'No, me neither. Apparently he wrote about the pursuit of power, and Anonemuss is always quoting him. Especially when he says "the means accuses, but the result excuses".'

'What's that supposed to be about?' Sigrid was irritated by the whole situation. She really wished they could just return to their normal lives. But then her dad was not in exile.

'It means that he thinks any measures are to be considered for the achievement of power. When I say any measures, I mean absolutely all of them.' Erik could see that they were missing the point. 'Well, he has asked me if our strategy of change through the game of Epic was to fail, whether I would be willing to take up real weapons and march with him in an army to Mikelgard and physically overthrow the current rulers.'

'Bloody vengeance!' laughed B.E. 'He's a madman.'

'That's exactly what I said.' But Erik did not smile. 'Only I don't think he's joking. He believes he needs only a hundred followers. After all, the Mikelgard people have no physical means of stopping him.'

'That's awful, even to speak like that.' Sigrid looked sickened. 'How can you repeat these ideas, Erik?'

'And we are working with him? Why?' asked Injeborg.

'Because we need him. And because perhaps his bark is worse than his bite. Also, if we can bring about change through Epic, that will take away the basis for his confrontational plans in this world.'

'I would like to meet him, before I fight alongside him,' mused Injeborg.

'As would I.' B.E. stood up. 'Erik, you arrange a place. I'm fed up with digging; I'm going to go get some Epic training in swimming, and some 'endless breath' potions. If my character falls off the ship, I don't want to drown like that poor fellow in the arena.'

****

The moon was up, covering the surface of the sea with a swathe of silver silk. They were bobbing up and down, waves gently lapping against the sides of their small boat. Near them a slight gurgle caused them to turn their heads, but it was only a seal breaking through the surface of the water. For a while the occupants of the boat and the seal watched each other, then the seal sank back beneath the waves.

Lounging in the prow of the boat was B.E.'s elven warrior; Injeborg's witch and Cindella each had an oar.

From the shore a green light flared.

'There we go.' Erik sounded relieved; they had been waiting in the bay for about half an hour.

'He likes his drama, doesn't he? We couldn't just meet in an inn.' It was easy to imagine B.E. displaying his characteristic sneer as his character spoke – although the grey face of the warrior in the game was incapable of that expression.

'He's a dark elf remember,' Injeborg pointed out, while pulling on her oar to bring them around in order to face the shore. 'He can't come near to town or they will lynch him.'

'Yeah, but still.'

They rowed hard, towards a muddy bank that led up from the

estuary to the edge of a wood. When they landed, B.E. stepped carefully through the mud, tying up the boat to a rock.

'Greetings.' Anonemuss was alone, wrapped in a navy velvet cape.

'Pleased to meet you,' replied Injeborg politely.

Erik was amused to see that, probably unconsciously, B.E. was posed, chest out, hands on the hilts of his powerful blades.

'You wanted to discuss the plan with me?' Anonemuss asked them directly.

'Well, not so much the plan as your ideas. You know, about seizing power by force,' answered Injeborg equally bluntly.

'Oh good. Are you interested in joining me?'

'Absolutely not!' She was shocked. 'I just wanted to determine whether you were a reliable partner, or whether you were mad.'

'I'm not mad, young woman. Nor am I hidebound by the indoctrination that we are all fed here. I have read many books – it is a common pastime of those of us in exile. And my conclusion is that violence is not always wrong.'

'How so?' B.E. was intrigued.

'I believe young Erik here once had his appendix removed, correct?' They nodded and the dark elf continued, 'Was that not an act of violence, cutting open his skin, wounding him? Yet it was necessary to save his life. Well, society can form cancers, especially if resources are dwindling over hundreds of years. I consider myself not a violent criminal, but a surgeon, one with a diagnosis of the condition of the patient which is that there is a need for a short violent intervention to save it.'

'But even if we accept that society needs to change, there is an important distinction from Erik's operation.' Injeborg was reasoning aloud, defending her own beliefs.

'Do go on, my dear.' Anonemuss bowed.

'Which is that the operation was done with Erik's consent. You plan to mete out violence against people who do not wish it.'

'They certainly do not, but they have driven me to such radical ideas by their policies. For the sake of sustaining the principle of non-violence, is it worth lying in the dirt with your oppressor's knee upon your neck?'

'Are we oppressed?' B.E. could not restrain a slight scoffing tone to his voice.

'Maybe oppressed is too strong a word,' Erik intervened earnestly. 'But look at all the messages for help we have been sent since we killed the dragon. I don't know about you, but I've had over seven hundred. And some of them are really pitiful. People living in pain, unnecessarily it seems to me.'

'I don't read 'em.' B.E. shrugged away the point.

'Perhaps you are not oppressed any more. You are a wealthy man now. But think about the hard work that the vast majority of people are performing, so that a few can live in luxury and devote their energy not to solving the problem of our limited resources, but to working out how to stay in control. And I might add,' Anonemuss' tone grew sharper. 'That until you have had a taste of exile, you have no realisation what hard work and hunger means. If you think that they give the districts very little, then you can imagine what they send to Roftig. Rusty, useless tools. Poor-quality seeds. It is a wonder we do not all starve.'

'Fair enough,' replied B.E., and it almost amused Erik that his friend clearly did not care too much about the world's injustices. They were so different in that regard. 'But do you not think that we can challenge them through Epic, the way we are suppose to resolve matters?'

'Until I met Erik and Harald, I did not believe it to be possible. But the five of us, perhaps we can form an unbeatable team. Then I wonder what will happen. Will our opponents go so far as to act against our real personalities?'

'What? You mean physically deprive us of the means of playing,' asked Injeborg.

'That, or worse.'

'Murder?' B.E. laughed derisively.

'You underestimate their willingness to cling to power. You forget that they see themselves as the protectors of the greater good. And that mysterious Holy Grail justifies all actions they might take. People who live by dogmatic ideals are extremely dangerous.' Anonemuss chuckled sinisterly.

'Yeah, well ...' With as much interest in philosophy as in the condition of the world's poor, B.E. changed the subject. 'We'll cross that bridge when we come to it. Let's talk about tactics.'

'My sentiments exactly.' For the first time in the conversation, Anonemuss sounded as though he had warmed to the young warrior. 'I must say, Erik, your young friend has a remarkable talent for cunning and forward thinking.'

'He's not the only one,' murmured Injeborg. 'It was Erik who discovered the way to kill the dragon.'

'That does not surprise me.'

'Enough.' Erik intervened. 'You'll embarrass me. Let's go over the plan again.'

Chapter 18

A New cause for concern

The nine members of the committee were gathered in the great chamber of Mikelgard Tower. A wintry sky of heavy cloud with streaks of orange drifted above them. It was sufficiently dark that the lanterns of the room had been lit, flickering with oily flame. For the moment, all was quiet, apart from the rustle of paper, as they read the latest *New Leviathan* newsletter.

If ever there was a possibility for change, it was presented last month, with the victory of the Osterfjord Players over Inry'aat, the Red Dragon.

A new avenue was opened up, a new way to shatter the fetters that bind society. A chance for us to face the real world afresh, to tackle the decline of our resources – using Epic as a means of communication and recreation – no more than that.

Who are these young dragonslayers on whom we pinned so much hope?

Erik Offason is their oldest, playing with an elven warrior called 'B.E.' – to distinguish him from the younger Erik. This seems to be a talented, brave and ambitious young man, who has accepted a place at Mikelgard University on the prestigious 'Epic Studies' course – a course that is closely connected to achieving very high administrative posts in later life. Bjorn Rolfson is of the same class as Erik Offason, and having graduated from the same college has accepted a place in the University to study farming – a most worthwhile occupation that will lead to his obtaining the farm of his choice in years to come. His character is a sturdy human warrior, Bjorn.

Sigrid Offason, similarly, has been offered a place on the same course, for when she has graduated from the Hope College in three years' time. Her character is the healer for the group.

Injeborg Rolfson, although only fourteen, has nevertheless found herself with a place reserved at the University for the study of geology. She is a student to watch. Her character is a witch of the same name.

Finally, Erik Haraldson, in the same class as Injeborg Rolfson. Erik has, rather unusually, a female character – part thief, part warrior – of the name Cindella. Of this group, Erik Haraldson has the most reason to be aware of the problems of this system, since his father is in exile for the crime of violence. Violence is, of course, totally unacceptable, but perhaps Harald Erikson is in some way a victim of the system? It cannot be a coincidence that he was the key player in the recent draw between Hope

District and Central Allocations. But again, Erik Haraldson seems to have little more ambition than to take a University place in librarianship.

What does this information reveal?

Above all, that access to wealth and power is very seductive. A team of players, who for the first time for many years had the opportunity to confront the system, has instead been absorbed by it.

Each of these players has received several hundred requests to help some person struggling in poverty. Yet they have not taken up even one case. These young people should be sympathetic. They know what it is like to have family at work in the mines. But they appear to care only about themselves and about making a success of themselves within the system.

Our conclusion then. That we must awaken from this unreal game and demand a new organisation of society – one where decisions are taken by vote and not by challenges in the biased fighting arenas.

'Comments?' invited Hleid.

'They are impotent,' Godmund said simply, and graced the committee with one of his very rare smiles. 'Svein did well.'

'What I find interesting,' Wolf mused aloud, lounging in his chair, ponytail hanging over the back of it, 'is that there clearly is no connection between the writers of this scandal sheet, and the Osterfjord Players.'

'Or at least they want us to think that.' Ragnok sounded surly.

'No. That seems too complex. I do not think that the *New Leviathan* would publicly revile them if it really thought that they would champion change.' Godmund interlocked his wrinkled fingers and, stretching them against each other, released a sharp cracking sound. 'Is there anything else, or can we enjoy a rare afternoon at our own pursuits?'

'Unfortunately, yes.' Svein passed around the documents that had been handed to him shortly before the committee meeting. 'This has been posted about two hours ago in every Newhaven tavern and in every library in our system.'

Do you seek fame and adventure? Then join with me, Cindella the dragonslayer, in a voyage that the bards will be singing of for generations. I seek a crew of skilled sailors and hardy warriors, of powerful magicians and staunch healers. I shall be sailing out of Newhaven Harbour on St. Justin's day, at high tide. The journey is expected to take two months and I have reason to believe it will be most lucrative. Equal shares of all wealth obtained will be distributed to all those who return with me to Newhaven when the voyage is complete.

Cindella the dragonslayer

'Odd.' With his good humour gone in an instant, Godmund returned to his more characteristically sharp tone of voice. 'What do you make of it, Svein?'

'I think that he must have found something in the dragon hoard that leads him on.' Svein strove to keep his tone absolutely neutral, and not let slip any indication of his interest and his fears about the matter. It could be that the young man was working towards solving the *Epicus Ultima* and had an important lead.

'It is not out of keeping with someone who wants to be a librarian to show an interest in such apparently irrelevant subjects.' Halfdan gave a mocking smile as he caught Svein's eye.

'Perhaps not, but I do not like it. This is without precedent, to appeal to the world for participants in this way. And what is new is dangerous. Epic is a strange game with great depths, more than perhaps we realise. It is not good to tamper with it. We have a system that works, and while it could well be that this voyage will turn out to be harmless, it must be considered a potential source of danger.' It was clear from his tone that Godmund was anxious once more.

'So, what are you suggesting?' Curiously, as Godmund had become weighted down with concern, Ragnok had lightened, to look now distinctly lively.

'I have a thought,' offered Bekka, peering at them from under her fringe of grey hair.

'Go ahead.' Hleid waved at her impatiently.

'Why doesn't Svein Redbeard volunteer for the voyage? That way he can keep us up to date as to its purpose.'

'Good idea,' Thorkell nodded.

'So, a proposal. All those in favour? Everyone. So be it.' Hleid looked over to Svein. 'Is that agreeable to you?'

'You bet it is!' Halfdan was scoffing, his lips a thin sneer in the vastness of his face. 'More clues for his *Epicus Ultima*.'

'I agree to keep an eye on the developments arising from this voyage and to keep the committee informed.' Svein was unprovoked by Halfdan's attempts to mock him. After all, the decision they had spontaneously reached accorded completely with his own desires; his concern before the meeting had been that the committee might have disagreed with his joining the expedition. When no one else was watching, Svein gave Halfdan a wink, happy to see him scowl in response.

'I have another proposal.' Ragnok raised his head.

'Yes? Go ahead.' Hleid looked at him through her large glasses.

'We put the Executioner aboard, just in case.'

This suggestion caused a few mutterings of concern.

'Let us take a speech for and against,' Hleid suggested. 'Ragnok, you first.'

'Well it's self-evident, isn't it?' He sat up a little straighter to address them. 'Anything could happen, and just suppose it is a quest for some powerful item. We do not want it to fall into the wrong hands.'

'Against?'

'The Executioner could be revealed by having to spend time confined aboard a ship, with no escape if matters get nasty.' Thorkell's pale forehead shone in the lamplight, making it seem as though he was sweating with fear or rage, although his voice was matter of fact.

'If matters get nasty, we kill them all.' Ragnok shrugged.

'Any more comments?' Hleid asked. 'Then the vote. Those for Ragnok's proposal? Ragnok, Halfdan, myself, Brynhild, Godmund. That's a majority – it is agreed.'

'I shall go aboard invisible,' Ragnok added hurriedly, and it was obvious that he was eager to assume the responsibility for the management of the Executioner.

Looking around the table over her glasses, Hleid saw no objections, even though any of them could have taken up the task equally well.

'Very well. That concludes the business for today.'

Chapter 19

A Motley Crew

The Newhaven quayside was busier than for a festival day; excited crowds of both grey players and colourful game characters were gathering to witness the start of the much-talked-about voyage of Cindella the Dragonslayer. Fortune tellers had set up tents from which there exuded the scents of strange oils and the prickle of magic; vendors of food who had come early to secure advantageous places were briskly selling grilled rabbit and fish; and throughout the crowds, street urchins, with their more accomplished masters, were practising the ancient art of pick-purse.

A select group of people walked aboard the *White Falcon*, unwelcome visitors kept at bay by a ghostly white dog, as large as a man, standing intelligently alert at the head of the gangplank. Beside it, Injeborg's witch stood proudly, gazing out over the busy quays, a hand on the head of her new canine guardian.

'It is beautiful, daughter, wonderful really. I am sure that she will be faster than the *Black Falcon*.' Old Captain Sharky was touring the vessel with Cindella and B.E. Her Ring of True Seeing pulsed its pale blue-green light around them; it allowed Erik to see a golden glow inside the character that indicated a more-than-usual presence of the Avatar in his frame. But it was far from the full shocking presence that had talked to Cindella in the jeweller's shop.

They carefully checked every room of the ship, no matter how small, to make sure that she was secure from stowaways. Not once did the ring reveal anything out of the ordinary.

Erik's father and Anonemuss were already on board, keeping well out of sight below deck. Erik's reunion with Harald's character had been heart-warming, but necessarily brief.

'Tide is nearly in,' observed Sharky.

'Very well, let us get our crew.' It was obvious that B.E. was looking forward to being in the public eye, and not surprisingly, for Erik had to admit that his friend looked magnificent. Apart from the ruby necklace and rune carved rings that shouted of magic, B.E. wore a swirling cloak of phoenix feathers, whose colour constantly changed in the light, undulating through scarlet and gold to purple and mauve. Beneath the cloak glittered a delicate chain-mail tunic, whose metal was clearly hammered out on no ordinary forge, for it too gave off a faint light. At his hips, sheathed in scabbards, were two matched blades, whose elven names translated as Thunder and Lightning.

As they came to the gangplank, Injeborg, herself transformed by the purchase of powerful magic items, handed Cindella a bag. Cindella looked inside and took out a glass sphere, about half the size of her fist, inside which a milk-white cloud swirled – and was that a tantalising glimpse of a minute statue within the mist?

'There are fifty of them,' explained Injeborg. 'And unless you are carrying one, Bouncy here will not let you on.' She patted the head of the ghostly dog affectionately.

'Bouncy?' B.E. groaned with disgust. 'Inny, it's an ethereal guard dog. It can detect astral projections and ethereal walkers, let alone invisible and hidden creatures. It can savage a troll single-handedly, and you've called it "Bouncy"?'

'Surely. He's cute too.' Injeborg tickled the unflappable guard dog under the chin.

'Come on.' Erik handed a stone to B.E. The two friends continued on to where they had earlier set up a table and Captain Sharky was waiting for them. Erik put the bag of milky stones on the table with a clatter, reaching in to pass one to the old sailor. Ahead of them a great queue had formed, several hundred long.

The chatter of the crowd subsided; the hawkers ceased their shouts and even the wind seemed to drop as B.E. beckoned the first man forward. A rope held by strong guards hired for the day held the crowd back, but they pressed forward, those further back wanting to catch sight of the dragonslayers and listen to the events of what was clearly a historic day.

'Good man this,' whispered Sharky. 'Served with me on the old *Falcon* as bosun.'

Erik took down his name and handed him a glass stone.

'Next!' shouted B.E.

And so they continued, hiring or rejecting sailors at the word of Sharky. The procedure was a dull one for the spectators and a lively hum of conversation began to grow all around the quays.

'That's a good crew.' Sharky looked approvingly at the men and women who had gone aboard, their few belongings in canvas bags thrown over their shoulders, and who were even now taking up their stations on the ship.

'No more sailors!' shouted B.E. 'Adventurers only, please.'

With curses from those who had missed out, the queue became greatly reduced, but even so was far longer than the twenty stones that remained in the bag.

'Next!'

'Othinious Majaminous at your service.' A small gnome bowed, his head, ducking below the height of the table. Both Cindella and B.E. stood up to get a better look at him.

Inadvertently B.E. let out a chuckle. The gnome immediately stood up, scowling from beneath the hood of the mystic's cowl that he wore.

'And what can you do, Othinious?' asked Erik kindly.

'I am a servant of Odunerok, God of the desert, and through him have mastered deep secrets of fire and air.'

'Prove it,' said B.E. bluntly.

The gnome stared steadily at B.E. then reached into his pack. He drew forth a rolled-up cloth of rich colour, and kept on drawing, soon the visible length of the thick cloth was greater than the size of the bag, then bigger than the gnome himself.

'Conjurer's trick? Or Bag of the Dimensions?' whispered B.E.

Once the elaborately decorated cloth was fully drawn from the bag, the gnome rolled it out over the ground. The crowd surged forward to look, drawn by sighs of admiration from those who stood near the front. Sitting on the carpet, the gnome began to chant quietly, face drawn in concentration. The carpet rose steadily from the ground, much to the excitement of the crowd who burst into applause. This was more like it!

'He's in,' said B.E. 'Next!'

'Sir Warren, knight of the Holy Order of Mov, servant of his Majesty King Uwen of Newhaven.'

The impressive warrior had a bright smile, nearly hidden in the great beard that flowed over his bright, powerful breastplate. Across his back was tied a shield, and at his waist a variety of weapons and potion bottles.

Without hesitation, Erik passed the knight a milky glass marble.

Before B.E. could call forward the next person in the queue, the clouds darkened, sea birds shrieked with fear and scattered into the sky. The crowd shrank back as a great black carriage clattered along the quays, pulled by two fierce black stallions whose eyes rolled with madness. A pallid servant, dressed in elegant black, reined in the horses near the table.

Utter stillness. Not a cough from anyone, fearful of drawing attention to themselves. Then a voice, terrible and cold, dripping with poisonous sibilance, and yet insidiously beautiful and persuasive:

'I, Count Illystivostich, would undertake this voyage.'

'If that vampyre boards your vessel, then I for one will not set foot upon it, for it will be cursed!' Sir Warren shouted in reply, clutching at the hilt of his sword.

Sitting behind the table, Erik was still struck with fear and a genuine concern for his safety, when B.E. spoke up bravely.

'What guarantee would we have that you would work for the same aim as the crew, and not slaughter us?'

'My auguries state that the treasure you seek contains an ancient heirloom of my family. Promise me that should you find it, you will return it to me. Then I will swear by the most ancient gods to serve you for the voyage, and take my sustenance only from the beasts that I will bring aboard myself.'

It was such a reasonable statement, Erik found himself nodding.

'Don't listen to him. The decks of that ship will run with blood should that ungodly creature defile it with one step onto its planks,' Sir Warren was furious but was stepping back, clearly fearful of provoking the count.

'Your call on this one,' said Erik, genuinely torn.

'A vampyre? You must be kidding. Of course he's in,' B.E. stood up. 'Very well, Count. We accept your terms.'

'Excellent. My servant will take my coffin and animals aboard. I will fly to join you in the night.'

'Here!' Sir Warren slammed his glass stone back onto the table. 'I wash my hands of this whole doomed affair.'

Once the dreadful presence in the carriage had departed, the throngs of people watching, both real and game-generated, broke out into animated conversation, arguing amongst themselves about the fate of the voyage now that it was associated with the most feared creature of the region. They settled into a lighter humour only when a bear came up to the table.

The large black grizzly loped up to the table on all fours, then stood up, towering above them.

'Please,' it boomed out. 'I wish to come on your voyage.'

'A talking bear!' voices all around called out delightedly.

'What on earth for?' asked Cindella.

'A witch told me I would meet my mate on the other continent.'

'So, it's a one way trip you want?' B.E. scoffed, and the crowd laughed.

'Yes, please.'

'You realise that means no treasure for you?' B.E. continued and again drew laughs for the image of the animal owning money.

'Yes, sir.'

B.E. shrugged. 'Fine by me.'

'Here you go.' Cindella gave him a stone. 'Don't lose that until you are safely on the ship.'

'Thank you both.' The bear bowed, and, holding the stone like a precious cub in one paw, it waddled along to the gangplank.

When the bag was nearly empty, there was a disturbance in the queue.

'Look!' Svein Redbeard lurched into view past the restraining rope, 'I just wanted you to know, I am here, and so are your friends.'

'Let them come forward,' B.E. instructed the guards.

Cheers greeted the appearance of the older dragonslayer. In his wake, looking as sheepish as grey polygons can, were Bjorn and Sigrid.

'Bjorn! You've come!' Erik leapt up, delighted.

'Welcome, welcome!' B.E. was just as pleased. 'This is going to be fantastic. It's a shame you weren't here from the beginning. It's been great fun.'

'Well, I still don't agree, and I think it will probably all end badly. But you are my friends.' Bjorn shrugged.

'And you are my brother,' added Sigrid to B.E.

'I see you are both looking very impressive.' The sarcasm in B.E.'s voice was entirely good-natured. Bjorn had evidently overcome his reluctance to spend money, as he was decked out in fabulous armour, while on cross-straps around his body hung a variety of bags, pouches and potion bottles. But by far the most extraordinary item that he carried was a great helm that was veined like a block of marble – pale and shot through with glinting lines of silver and platinum.

'What's the helmet?' asked B.E.

'Water breathing. I had no time to learn to swim.' Their friend sounded embarrassed.

'Good idea,' chipped in Erik. 'Let's hope you don't need it though. Here.' He handed each of them a stone.

All this time, Svein Redbeard had been standing to one side, watching and listening. Now he approached, splendidly bedecked in his fighting equipment, exactly as they had last seen him in the arena.

'And may I have the honour of joining you on your adventure?'

'Of course. The honour is all ours. We have one stone left. Don't we, Erik?' B.E. seemed oblivious to the fact that the point of the voyage was to escape Central Allocations; he had become far too involved in the excitement of the expedition. If Erik could have physically kicked him, he would have – ban on violence or not.

'One.' It was too late to hide it.

'Perfect.' Svein bowed as he received the stone.

The crowd was cheering them all and waving as they moved towards the gangplank. Already, minstrels were strolling around with the opening verses of the saga of the voyage – making much of the talking bear, the vampyre and the dragonslayers, old and young.

Suddenly all the noise of the quayside was submerged with a shrill keening howl. Injeborg's warder was on all fours at the top of the gangplank, fur standing on end, teeth bared.

'What is it?' Injeborg cried out, looking to Cindella.

'Intruder!' shouted Erik and pulled off Cindella's glove. He was close enough to see by the pale light of the ring; it was a human, fully encased in black armour, poised with sword drawn on the gangplank. 'He's invisible!'

A flash of red – Othinious, the gnome mystic, had thrown dust into the air that swirled and was magically drawn towards the would-be stowaway.

'There he is!' Sailors and warriors lined the side of the boat, pointing at the outline that they could now discern.

With a howl of fury, the man turned and ran away, pushing people brutally aside as he did so. The hired guards gave chase, but soon tired as the opaque warrior fled into the narrow alleys around the quays.

With the excitement over, the crowd gathered around the ship to shout cheerful farewells. Cindella gave Captain Sharky a nod and he began shouting orders.

Sailors moving swiftly to their tasks, the mainsail was lowered, showing the white falcon design from which the ship took her name. Immediately they felt the tug of the wind and heard the water begin to pick up speed as it rushed along their sides.

'Well,' B.E. said, standing proudly on the poop deck. 'Isn't this the best fun you've ever had?'

He continued to wave until the crowd had faded into an indistinct, colourful mass.

Chapter 20

Danger at sea

Gazing intently over the stern through a telescope, Erik could just make out the sails of the ship that had been following them throughout the day. Its shadowy grey form was partially hidden by a shower that was heading towards the *White Falcon* from the direction of its mysterious pursuer. Afternoon was turning into evening and the cloudy sky was taking on an angry orange tinge. Soon darkness would come, and they would try changing course in the hope of losing the unwelcome interest from that dogged ship.

'It must be the pirate, Duke Raymond.' Captain Sharky joined him, looking worriedly at the horizon.

'What makes you say that?' asked Erik.

'She is no merchant vessel. Nor is she from the navies of any of the city-states that I know of. My old bones tell me she is a pirate, THE pirate of these seas.'

Putting the telescope away, Erik took one last, proud look at the busy crew of the *White Falcon*, then unclipped. A meeting of the leaders of the expedition was arranged for after sunset, but now it was time for dinner. The Rolfsons were very punctual about their meals, as Erik had learned to his embarrassment, several times arriving at the house when they were already gathered and waiting for him.

He ran over and entered their home, to be met with cheerful greetings and the aroma of winter vegetable stew: turnip, broccoli and carrot.

'Welcome, Erik, sit, sit.' Rolfson gestured him to a chair at the table.

'Is that ship still following us?' asked Bjorn.

'Yes. Captain Sharky thinks it is his old enemy, Duke Raymond.'

'So, we might face a sea battle?' Injeborg did not sound dismayed at the idea.

'Perhaps. Although it would be better to slip them during the night.'

Bjorn nodded at this.

After his dinner, Erik thanked the Rolfsons then rushed home through the darkness to re-enter the game. He was, in fact, the last to enter the captain's cabin; it was a measure of everyone's concern that they had clipped up early. His dad's character had one of the window seats and was closing the shutters behind him to prevent the light cast from an oil lamp from escaping to signal their position. Anonemuss was doing the same in the other window bay. Bjorn, Injeborg, B.E. and Sigrid were sitting, waiting. Erik was pleased to see that they had left the large seat behind the captain's table for him. At the same time, he was slightly ashamed to find in himself such pride at being leader of the voyage.

'So,' he took his place. 'Captain Sharky thinks that this ship is probably that of Duke Raymond. Does anyone have information about this pirate?'

'Of course not,' Anonemuss responded curtly. 'If indeed it is a pirate, it is irrelevant to our purposes.'

'Unless he intends to attack.' B.E. was tracing the silver pommel of his sword with his fingertips and did not look up as he spoke.

There was silence after this comment. Erik did not know whether the others were concerned about the prospect of battle or not.

'And what do you think our chances would be?' he asked.

'Good, I would have thought,' answered Harald. 'But we cannot be certain and should avoid a clash with them, if possible.'

'Ya,' Bjorn agreed.

'Yes, let us try to avoid them,' Sigrid's healer chipped in with her opinion.

'I also think we should avoid them. But for another reason.' Anonemuss walked up and down the short space of the cabin floor as he spoke, swaying shadows from the oil lantern playing across his dark form. 'I am of the opinion that this pursuing ship is in some way connected to Central Allocations. They tried to bring a stowaway aboard, and that having failed, he hired a ship to follow us so that they have other options than to confront us in the arena before millions of spectators.'

'Possibly,' Harald said.

'So, in the coming night, we are agreed, we will try to evade them. Can I just say something about a possible alternative?' In the back of his mind Erik was thinking of the Avatar and whether it would be a disappointment for the creature if he simply ignored the possibility of obtaining revenge for Captain Sharky over his old rival. 'What about us attacking them? Epic is a strange game, and we rarely explore the simplest of plots, let alone the ones that involve various different parts of the world. If this is the ship of Duke Raymond, then it is related to my quest and fighting him is clearly an important stage in its development. If the ship contains our enemies, then a fight on our own terms might eliminate the threat it contains.'

'Well spoken, Erik.' B.E. looked eager. 'I'm up for it. I'm dying to see what these blades are like in combat.'

'You want to play games. Go do it on your own. Don't imperil us all.' Anonemuss sounded angry. 'Have you forgotten this is no game for us in exile? We need to get to Cassinopia without mishap and mount our challenge. Simple. No diversions.'

'I agree with Anonemuss,' Harald joined in. 'Epic has long ceased to be a game. Now is not the time to be exploring quest paths.'

As everyone began to talk at once, the volume of sound in the room started to rise, until it was suddenly cut across by a rap on the door.

'Who's there?' asked Anonemuss suspiciously.

'Svein Redbeard. May I join you?'

'No. Go away,' Anonemuss replied at once.

'Wait.' Erik glanced to his dad, who nodded and stepped into the sharp patches of black shadow that were rolling around the cabin. Once reassured that it was impossible to see Harald, Erik called on Svein to enter. The dark elf scowled, and even though it was impossible for characters to fight outside the arena, loosened the sword at his side.

'Thank you.' Svein bowed as soon as he was through the door. 'Failing to find any of you on deck, I presumed you were talking and wondered if I could be of service.'

'We are discussing how to respond to the pirate who is following us,' explained Erik.

'Ahh yes. Duke Raymond,' Svein said. 'He is a very dangerous opponent, wanted in every city-state, with a huge reward for his death or capture. He is ruthless in killing his captives, except those who can raise a substantial ransom. I would presume that if he knows there are six rich dragonslayers aboard this vessel, that is his main aim.' This assessment came rapidly, as though the world's chief librarian were anxious to impress them with his knowledge.

'I would presume no such thing,' replied Anonemuss angrily.

'How do we know that the ship is that of Duke Raymond? In my view, Central Allocations are behind it. They want to monitor what is happening. I am extremely angry that you are aboard this ship at all.' He turned away from Svein to the others. 'But for the fact we cannot harm him, I would advocate killing him now.'

Surprised by the dark elf's unexpected outburst, Erik didn't challenge the desirability of killing Svein. A moment later, he blushed, although Cindella would not show it. He felt he had failed to lead the conversation in the most productive direction.

'More to the point,' Svein continued, untroubled by these hostile references to him. 'I can assure you that Central Allocations has nothing to do with this ship following us. Epic is a game with complexities far beyond the small areas in which we players move. We have found ourselves in one of the tales of the game and we must respond accordingly.'

Erik remained silent, no longer feeling he had the authority to try to direct matters.

'I don't believe him. They had plenty of notice to hire a ship of their own.' Anonemuss managed to express a surprising amount of hostility in the relatively featureless face of his dark elf character.

'It may be Central Allocations,' said Injeborg. 'But in that case, they are simply following and cannot harm us. For the moment, let us assume the worst – that it is, in fact, Duke Raymond, and that darkness will not shake him.'

'In other words, that we might have to fight a battle?' asked B.E. eagerly.

'Yes. Perhaps we should discuss our tactics,' Injeborg replied. 'In which case Svein's advice would be welcome.'

A polite cough from the door.

Everyone froze, the room motionless but for the swinging lamp that cast alarming shadows as it rocked to the motion of the ship. Count Illystivostich was standing in the doorway, pale as bone, dressed in elegant black velvet and leather. His eyes burned with lust and terror – even at home, through the medium of Cindella, Erik felt paralysed by fear and desire. It was impossible to move his own head and break the view that Cindella had of those hypnotic eyes.

'Ladies and Gentlemen,' said that same insidiously beautiful voice, tainted with an invitation to share knowledge of insatiable wickedness. 'I could not help overhearing you and I believe I can offer you the most sensible course of action. Allow me to fly across to the ship following and ascertain the natures of those aboard.' The lips of the vampyre as they articulated these words were succulent, livid, and corrupt.

Of course. A perfectly sensible course of action indeed. Not one person demurred as the count bowed.

'I shall return shortly. Please wait for me.'

It was some time before any of them could speak, so powerful was the thrall surrounding the presence of the vampyre.

'We should restrict our dealings with that creature to the minimum.' It was Bjorn who had managed to find his voice first. His comment was met with a murmur of agreement.

'And yet, and yet.' Svein was shaking his head. 'We will never have a chance to talk to such a powerful being again. Once our destinies are parted, he will be far too dangerous to approach. And think about the knowledge he must have! Why, he has lived for centuries. He must know the answers to all our questions!'

'Questions?' Anonemuss promptly asked. 'What questions?'

'Oh, you know, the issues librarians have to deal with – just the gathering of information about the world of Epic.' The tone of awe in Svein's voice had been replaced by evasion. He took the empty window seat that had been vacated by Harald. When he spoke again, his voice was more relaxed. 'So, who is this dark elf that expresses such hostility to Central Allocations? We have not been introduced.'

'My name is Anonemuss.'

'And are you from Hope District as well? I do not recall meeting you during my visit there.'

'That's none of your business.'

Svein shrugged.

'Do you know anything about sea warfare?' Erik asked Svein in a conciliatory manner. Anonemuss might be right to treat Svein as their enemy, but for better or worse they were on the same ship and might have to fight alongside one another.

'Nothing, I'm sorry to say. If we could get aboard, however, it would be no different from being in the arena surely?'

'Yes. I think we should try to board that ship as quickly as possible.' B.E. gripped the two sword hilts protruding from his waist. 'That is, if we can't lose it in the night,' he added with an apologetic glance at Bjorn, understanding that he was the most insistent advocate of the wisdom of avoiding battle.

For a while, they sat in silence, listening to the creaking sounds of the ship as she rode over the waves.

A brooding soporific atmosphere heralded the return of Count Illystivostich. By a great effort of will, Erik managed to remove his blue glove before the vampyre appeared in the door. For him, the ring-wearer, the cabin was now suffused with a blue light. The room was unchanged, other than that he could now see Harald, squatting patiently in a dark corner.

A leisurely glance towards the door stopped his heart. Eyes were fastened upon his – two blazing spear points of shocking power. The vampyre was back. Transfixed by the power that flowed between them, Erik saw thousands of years of bloody existence. Exquisite beauty twisted to serve foul hunger. Ennui without comprehension, lifted only by the prospect of chasing prey whose corruption and befoulment was sufficiently challenging to offer diversion. It was like being in the presence of the Avatar; he could understand only a fraction of the images flowing through him. Only this time the light was contaminated, each photon stained like bloodshot marble.

'Welcome news, my comrades!' The count took them all under his spell. Erik could see the sibilant words flow around the room, caressing everyone who heard them. 'Although the ship that pursues is indeed that of the pirate Duke Raymond, it is no match for us. Already half the crew are my servants. We have but to turn around and meet them and the ship will be ours.'

'Good work, Count Illystivostich.' A dark fire in the eyes of B.E. was stoked by the encouraging smile of the vampire. He was dreaming of striding gloriously across the decks of his enemy, striking blows of Thunder and Lightning to left and right, his deeds to be sung of throughout the world.

'That might net us much valuable information.' Svein too was greedy. Erik could see how the vampyre lavishly laid before him the prospect of cabin rooms full of rare maps and documents – their famous captives telling Svein all he wished to know of the deep secrets they had sailed with for all these years.

Even Anonemuss nodded, as the count's knowing expression let him share the understanding that his conjectures were right. They were indeed being pursued by his enemies, who by this approaching battle would be left deep beneath the waves, ruing the day they encountered the dark elf.

Only Bjorn seemed able to resist the corruptive seduction of the vampyre. His face was troubled. It warmed Erik, to see the strength of his friend as he struggled to shake away the tainted dreams that flowed around him.

'Should we not simply try to lose them in the night?'

'Your suggestion is most sensible.' The vampyre met Bjorn's desire for the most practical solution. 'However, they have magical means of following our every move; we cannot avoid them and so we must confront them in a manner of our own choosing.' These words, solid and clear, slotted into Bjorn's understanding like foundation blocks for a mighty edifice. There was no further resistance. Bjorn nodded approvingly.

As for Erik, he was appalled by how unconscious he had previously been of the vampyre's powers of suggestion. Yet the new clarity that the ring had brought him was like watching a scene in a mirror; he was one step removed from it. Or indeed a mirror facing another mirror, so that the scene echoed upon itself until it disappeared into a dark glassy realm where light moved as slowly as the tides.

Sunk in his own perceptions, he was just as trapped as everyone else, despite his new understanding. So that when the count turned to him, he found himself agreeing.

'I will give the order.'

But it was wrong.

It was all lies.

Chapter 21
The gloating pirate

The ship was rolling heavily, having turned from the wind, the sails hanging slack; she lacked the momentum to breast the waves efficiently, and lurched sideways with each swell. Across the dark water, their opponents were closing in rapidly, their sails faintly orange tinted from the aftermath of the sunset.

'This can't be the way to fight a sea battle.' Bjorn was concerned. 'They have more manoeuvrability than us.'

'This will be no ordinary sea battle,' the count explained reassuringly.

Despite the calming confidence of the vampyre, Erik was uneasy at the rapid and direct approach of the pirate. The players were all gathered together in the aft castle of the ship, weapons at the ready, yet their opponents showed no sign of hesitation. Perhaps it was the spell that Count Illystivostich had cast over the enemy crew that led Duke Raymond so directly to the *White Falcon*?

A dart flew across the waves, then another, a shower of arrows rushing through the air. The other ship was already attempting to engage. Everyone around Erik ducked behind the wooden crenellations, feeling the vibrations of the arrows that thumped into the castle walls. Timing their responses to the lull between volleys, B.E.

and several of the other warriors began to return fire with their bows.

'When do we make our move?' Erik turned to the count. But the vampyre was gone, rising into the air, chanting, his long black hair swirling sensuously about him in the breeze.

'Something is wrong,' Erik shouted. And as the others turned to look at the vampyre, who was now reaching a peak of incantation, a long powerful vermilion reptile materialised in the centre of their small castle, hissing with fury. Slowly it opened the scaly lids of its bulging eyes – an intense purple glow emanating from the reptile's vivid pupils seized all who were looking towards the lizard. Erik felt as though he were choking.

'Basilisk!' Svein managed a hoarse cry, pulling his sword free. The creature narrowed its focus and pulsing waves of violet colour flowed over the great warrior who grew stiff and grey.

'Kill it quick!' shouted Injeborg.

The snarling monster slithered around the deck, tail lashing out, claws scrambling for purchase on the smooth wooden surface. B.E. was before it now, and again violet light escaping beneath the heavy eyelids began to build up to an angry intensity. There was a moment when Erik could have used his 'mock' ability to try to turn the creature, but he refrained. Cindella had no better chance of withstanding the effects of the basilisk's gaze than B.E. Yet immediately Erik regretted not having done so, for his friend froze, swords raised, toppling to the ground with the heavy hollow reverberation of stone upon wood, all colour drained from him.

The next moment, Harald materialised behind the lizard and stabbed it with his elven blades; with a roar of fury, the monster faced about, turning the deadly light towards his attacker, but the wood elf was already in motion, and even though he seemed momentarily to falter as he was covered in the violet glow, Harald cleared the wall of the castle and leapt down to the ship.

'Follow him!' shouted Erik, and vaulted out of the castle. They would all die here otherwise; unprepared, they were no match for the basilisk.

Cindella slid down the rail of stairs that led away from the wooden castle and restored her momentum with a roll onto the main deck. When he could look up, Erik was amazed to see how close their enemy had come. The crenellated forward castle of Duke Raymond's ship loomed over them. Clearly visible between the wooden defences were two sorcerers who could have been twins, pale-faced, dressed in similar lime-green robes. Their hands were raised, and from them came lines of thick white thread. The sorcerers were systematically spraying the decks of the *White Falcon* with the product of their spell, covering the ship at an alarmingly swift rate.

The nature of their weaving became immediately apparent as, despite her nimble motion towards the main mast, Cindella was unavoidably engulfed in the material that was spewing from the sorcerers' hands. It was thick webbing, grey and sticky, impossible to tear free from. Now Cindella was responding to Erik's directions as though she was wading through glue. Everyone on the ship was struggling, some looking to him for orders.

High in the sky, the little gnome, Othinious Majaminous, was on his carpet, disappearing rapidly westward, a silhouette against the faint scarlet glow on the horizon. Nearby, the bear, looking rather bewildered, was disentangling a paw from the webs. Finally free after great exertion, the bear examined his claws curiously, giving them an experimental and tentative lick before pulling an expression of distaste. The sorcerers were continuing to pour webs onto the *White Falcon*, coating it again and again in smothering layers.

The battle was over.

At home, Erik slumped; Cindella was held fast. He wondered if he should unclip, to try to escape capture, but that was a risky measure of last resort. Instead, he waited, thoughts in turmoil. Poor B.E., and Svein Redbeard. Two dragonslayers killed already, petrified. Possibly more of them were dead by now; he could not even turn his head to check. The world would be in shock when the news spread. He should have taunted the basilisk; that way B.E.'s magic swords might have done him some good – even if it had meant the death of Cindella.

What had gone wrong? Everything. He could not believe that they had so innocently followed the advice of Count Illystivostich; the vampyre had intended to betray them from the very beginning, that was completely clear now. But why? With a jolt of realisation that the vampyre's actions might be related to his quest, Erik struggled as hard as he could against the glue to unbutton Cindella's tunic and withdraw a small bone scroll case. Again, for the thousandth and last time, he looked at the treasure map, this time trying to remember every little detail. Then Cindella tore off little pieces and began to chew them. Fortunately Epic, sophisticated as the interface was, did not have taste connectors. Digesting the document was slow but palatable. As an afterthought he took off the Ring of True Seeing and put it in the hollow of his cheek.

****

After at least an hour of bitter, restless contemplation, Cindella was disturbed by the sticky grey threads around her being hacked away by cutlasses. The jubilant sailors performing this task trussed her tight in ropes before hauling her free. Erik could almost feel the pain in his own joints as she was torn loose from the last of the gluey substance. It was hard to see much; the sky was deep blue, early stars spinning above him as Cindella was swung across to their captors' ship. A rush of yellow and reds was visible towards the horizon. Moments later, the source of the colour was revealed. The last view Cindella had before being thrust through a doorway was of the *White Falcon* receding from them, a crown of jagged flames resting upon her disintegrating decks.

Cindella was stripped of all her equipment. Rough hands tore away belts, pouches, rings and boots. Then, bound tight, she was thrown into a dank, briny-smelling hold. The crude manner in which she had been hauled about had taken its toll. Checking Cindella's health, Erik was concerned that half her life was gone. Still, at least he had kept the ring. He spat it onto the floor and rolled around until he could reach it and slip it on. The room was just as foul in the light of the ring as it had been in the swinging illumination of the oil lamp. Only now Erik could see the twenty or so glistening pairs of hungry eyes from the rats that lurked in the dark intersections of wall and floor.

Anxious to know what had happened to the others, and what his fate would be, Erik had to wait impatiently, not daring to unclip.

At last, a flood of lamplight shone on the damp walls of the room as the rough door was opened. A shadow, which resolved itself as Anonemuss, arms trust behind him, was pushed stumbling forward.

'You're still alive at least. Did you see any of the others?' Erik asked eager for news.

'Shut up, kid.'

So Erik held his tongue, watching his companion. Anonemuss sat, occasionally shaking his head in disbelief and sighing.

The door opened again. Injeborg and Sigrid were thrown down beside them. They had barely time to cry out in recognition, when a powerful command filled the room.

'Silence.'

A bright sickening light was shone on the prisoners from the doorway. Behind it stood two shadows, one redolent with a maliciousness that matched the voice that had stilled them.

'Duke Raymond, allow me to introduce my travelling companions: Anonemuss, Cindella, Injeborg and Sigrid.' The vampyre was mocking now, and Erik's anger at the traitor made it seem incredible that they had once shared a seductive and trusting intimacy.

'Well done, Count Illystivostich. Unfortunate about the others. I could have used their gold.'

'You will find there is ample left between them.'

'Oh indeed.' Duke Raymond rubbed his hands. 'I wonder, sir, is it a coincidence that the three women dragonslayers survived? Do women adventurers have a particularly fortunate constitution, or do your own tastes alter the spinning of fate's dice?'

The vampyre chuckled, a sinister laugh, stiletto-sharp, scraping over Cindella's throat.

'Skip the witty banter. What do you want from us?' Anonemuss was brusque with barely suppressed anger.

'Oh, I don't think we can do that,' Duke Raymond replied with a laugh. 'What is the satisfaction of being a villain if you cannot gloat over your fallen enemies?'

Chapter 22
A cruel Dismissal

Barely able to contain his delight, Ragnok keep his gaze on the table in front of him, on the notepad on which he occasionally made a meaningless mark. But every now and then he could not resist the briefest of glances to his left, to see how Svein was reacting.

It was Halfdan the Black who was leading the attack, and he did so with evident relish. 'Svein has no Epic character of any standing; therefore he cannot be on this committee. It's straightforward.' Halfdan's shaky voice took on a slightly gleeful note.

'It's not as simple as that, and you know it,' Bekka spoke up angrily. 'We can give Svein the wealth to equip another character who would very quickly become powerful enough to play a full role on Central Allocations.'

There was a pause at this.

As far as Ragnok could judge matters, neither Halfdan nor Thorkell would hesitate in throwing Svein off the committee. On the other hand, Bekka would always resist the proposal, which meant two votes for him to stay, as Svein still retained the right to vote, despite the loss of his character. The other members of the committee: Wolf, Brynhild, Hleid and Godmund were probably undecided.

Hleid was not chairing the meeting with her usual directness, and after the silence had lingered uncomfortably, she sighed. 'This is a difficult situation. Of course we owe Svein a lot, and personally speaking, I am concerned that we will be all the weaker for the loss of his advice and experience with the library system; on the other hand, how will the world perceive matters if we rush a new character up the ranks? Just imagine what trouble that *New Leviathan* could make of it.'

Godmund nodded at this, and Ragnok's heart leapt. If Godmund spoke against Svein, it would all be over.

Evidently Svein understood that equally well, for he quickly indicated to Hleid that he wanted to speak, even though his words did not seem that well prepared.

'I don't deny it will look bad, but against that weigh the value of my contribution to this committee. How will you manage affairs in the South without me? And the library system – it requires quite a level of expertise. Then there is the University, the classes.'

The fact that Svein was speaking allowed Ragnok to examine him closely without having to hide his stare. The man was clearly suffering; he was pale, almost green, as if he had not been sleeping; his eyes were rheumy and now, as the failure of his own argument became evident in the faces of the other committee members, those eyes blinked back rising tears.

At last, guessing already which way the vote would go, Ragnok spoke. 'No one is indispensable. If we need another on the committee from the South, there are rising students. The same with the libraries. It's just not worth it,'

Svein looked shocked, and crumpled visibly. 'You ... also?'

Ragnok flashed a smile of triumph, but managed to check himself from further expressions of his true feelings. He wanted to stand over Svein, gloating. To tell him that for years and years he had played the game to Svein's rules while all the time hating the arrogant librarian. At every step, he had pretended gratitude. How kind of Svein to show him the tactics, the equipment, the magic that he had learned the use of. How kind of the librarian to give him every dirty job that came the way of the committee, earning the deep hatred of the world's people, a hatred in which Ragnok revelled. It had been Svein who above all had been shielded from public dislike by his apprentice. Svein had thought himself untouchable, but now an accident of the game had thrown him to the ground, and instead of helping him up, Ragnok spat on him.

'I call a vote,' crowed Halfdan, 'for the removal of Svein the Librarian from Central Allocations.'

'And my alternative is that we re-equip him in honour of his past achievements. The world will understand that. In fact, they will be surprised if we fail him.' Bekka made a last try to sway them.

'Very well, the options are clear. All those for Svein remaining on this committee, please show.'

Only Bekka, Wolf and, of course, Svein himself raised their hands.

'Those against?'

Halfdan led the way, reaching triumphantly upwards with his slightly shaking right arm; Thorkell, Godmund and Ragnok joined him. That left Brynhild and Hleid as abstainers, but it didn't matter, Svein was gone!

'I'm sorry, Svein. I will have to ask you to leave.' Hleid looked visibly shocked.

It must have been a long, slow walk to the door. Ragnok followed every step. Svein did not depart with his head held high. Rather he seemed dazed and uncomprehending, his shoulders slumped.

Chapter 23
Landscape painting

B.E. and Sigrid were at the beach, sitting on the 'gulping rock' – so called because of the sound that the waves made as they slapped into the spaces beneath its great bulk. From some distance, Erik hailed them, and, somewhat disconcertingly, Sigrid got up and climbed down the far side of the rock, to reappear walking determinedly away from him.

'Don't mind her.' B.E. patted the rock beside him, to indicate that Erik should sit. 'She's angry. It will pass.'

'I'm sorry,' Erik said as he settled beside his older friend.

'It's not your fault. I made the call on bringing the vampyre, remember?'

'If I survive this, I'll split my money with your new character,' Erik offered.

'That's kind, Erik, but perhaps it's just as well.' B.E. looked away uncomfortable, pretending to study a distant island.

'How do you mean?'

'Didn't you notice? All that fame and wealth – it was not good for me. I was changing. And I didn't like what I was becoming.'

Mystified, Erik said nothing and they listened for a while to the waves hitting and sucking at their perch.

'There's a girl at school, for example,' B.E. suddenly began again. 'Judna – she wanted to talk to me at the dance. I ignored her. I knew I was destined to be a celebrity in Mikelgard, and Hope suddenly seemed very small and unimportant. I was going to leave it behind and enjoy my fame in Mikelgard, drive a fast saller around the city, meet lots of beautiful girls. But at the same time as enjoying the prospect, I hated myself for my new arrogance. See? And actually I think I would have been unhappy in the city, no matter how famous I was.'

'I see.' It had never occurred to Erik to leave Hope, other than perhaps temporarily joining his parents in exile. Or perhaps to be with Injeborg – though neither of them had spoken of the future and whether they were going to be together.

'So I don't mind that it is over, for me at least. My only real regret is that I didn't get to see Thunder and Lightning in action.' B.E. turned with an apologetic smile, 'And, of course, that we didn't get your dad back.'

'You can start again. If we don't all die as prisoners, there should be enough money to re-equip ourselves, perhaps not on as great a scale, but enough to keep trying.' Erik paused, thinking of his friend starting a new character as if the dragonslaying had never happened. 'After all, you won't be able to go back to killing kobolds after everything we've been through.'

'No. That's true.' B.E. sighed. 'Oh, I don't know.' He got up and stretched, arms lifted to the grey sky. 'If I walk fast, I will be able to get to Judna's farm and back before dark.' He jumped decisively from the rock, landing with a crunch onto the shingle. 'Good luck in the game, Erik. I hope you can escape with your life, and I'm sorry your plans have gone wrong.'

****

The first appearance of buds in the pruned branches of the trees was usually a period of happiness in Hope District, for it meant that the winter was over, and spring had truly arrived. Moreover, spring was often the more pleasant time of year for their part of the coast, summer itself being too hot and tiring. Right now, a fresh breeze was brushing over the daisies, dandelions and buttercups that were rising through the grass of the fields left uncultivated for pasture.

For Erik though, the turn in the season brought little pleasure. It was a season to be shared, but this was the first time he had experienced it alone, his mum and dad half a world away. His sense of being alone was increased by the fact that for the first time in weeks he could no longer even converse with them through the game. For since the burning of the *White Falcon,* there was no sign of Harald's character, while his mum's remained in the vicinity of Newhaven and could not contact Cindella even if she were not a prisoner.

Over at the Rolfsons', the atmosphere of the farm seemed miserable and subdued. Erik found Injeborg walking their pet dog, a sheepdog called Hafni, through the rows of olive trees.

She waved, by contrast to Sigrid, happy to see him, and Erik immediately felt uplifted.

'Look,' she said, pointing. 'Isn't that the rock on which you broke your tooth?'

Involuntarily Erik ran his tongue over the half tooth.

'Yes.' His smile was slightly embarssed, conscious as he was that she was looking at his imperfect grin.

'I would miss that smile if you had it fixed,' she responded, as if reading his thoughts.

'You don't think it makes me ugly?' He was only half joking.

'You are very handsome, Erik Haraldson, and you know it.' Laughing, she patted his cheeks with her cold white hands, and for a dizzy moment Erik felt like grabbing her and pulling her to him, to hold her slender body against his, to kiss her. But even if he could be sure that she would not pull away, this was not the time.

'Where's Bjorn?' Erik asked.

'Up on Ogail Hill. It's a good day for painting.'

'Would he mind if we went up?'

'No. I'm sure he wouldn't. We all need to talk anyway, and make plans.' Injeborg's tone was more positive than the situation deserved, but her confidence was infectious. Picking up a suitable stick, Erik threw it towards the path they would take, setting an eager Hafni off ahead of them.

The path ended some distance before the top of the hill, and they had to climb over boulders to reach the top, Hafni carefully eyeing up each jump before she leapt from rock to rock after them. When they crested the last boulder, a spectacular coastline came into view. They were high enough up that the fields were a like a chessboard of greens and browns – varying according to whether they contained olive trees or pasture. The clouds were passing briskly overhead, causing shafts of light to race each other across the land on their way to the distant sea where they sent glittering ribbons of silver across the water and on to the horizon.

With rocks piled around his easel to hold it steady, Bjorn was sitting on a stool, an earnest look of concentration on his face. It warmed Erik's heart to see his friend, so big and muscular, with such sturdy fingers, nevertheless carefully holding a brush with which he delicately made strokes on the canvas, face set in concentration. Both Erik and Injeborg paused, so as not to disturb him, until Bjorn lowered his hand and looked down to his paints.

As they drew closer, Erik could see that the version of the landscape that Bjorn had set onto the canvass was gloomier than their actual view – the clouds darker, the land more sombre. It seemed to say more than words could about his friend's state of mind.

'Hi, Bjorn!' Injeborg approached him first.

'Hello.' He did not turn around.

'Hi, Bjorn.'

'Hello, Erik.' Bjorn began to wash his brush.

'Mind if we join you a while?' His sister asked. 'We need to talk.'

'No,' replied Bjorn slowly. 'I don't mind. This one is finished.'

Erik sat on a flat-looking rock, and played with Hafni's ears.

'What happened to you when the rest of us were captured?' Erik asked.

'I unclipped.'

'Hmmm. I thought about doing that. But was worried that if the ship sank, I would find myself in a cabin at the bottom of the sea when I resumed, and would drown before regaining the surface.'

'Ya. That is right.' Bjorn looked up, then gave a slight smile of self-approval. 'I put on my water breathing helmet first of course.'

'Ahh of course!' Erik jumped up excitedly and Hafni dropped the stick she had patiently been carrying, leaping up in response, ready to run. 'So you are still alive! That's great, Bjorn, I feel so happy. At least one of us might keep their fortune!'

'Maybe. But it's dark there at the bottom of the sea, and muddy. I'm lost. I'm plodding along like I'm in a giant cave, not even sure if I'm walking in circles, and all the time I'm afraid some giant sea monster is just going to pounce on me and eat me.'

'But still. You are alive!'

'So are the two of you, right? And Sigrid?'

'At the moment,' answered Injeborg. 'But our situation is desperate. Duke Raymond wants our treasure as a ransom, but we don't trust them to release us if we send the soulbound djinn off.'

'I think the only reason they haven't killed anyone is that I've promised to lead them to the buried treasure if they let us all live,' Erik added. 'I'm hoping that when we get to the island a chance of escape will present itself. Because once they get the treasure, they will go back to trying to get a ransom out of us.'

'I see.' Bjorn nodded, his face more animated now, as he thought about the problem. 'Do you have any ideas of how to escape?'

'Not at the moment, but I did manage to keep my ring. It might reveal something.'

'Perhaps, if you are very fortunate.' Bjorn sighed.

'What?' asked Injeborg.

'This nonsense. This whole adventure. It was so irresponsible, so frivolous. We took a big risk fighting the dragon. It paid off. We should have been content. But we had to go off into strange and dangerous places. Very wrong of us, to treat the outcome of our lives in such a wild way.'

'No!' interjected Injeborg loudly, making her brother look up sharply from his cleaning. 'No. We are not frivolous. We cannot be content to just take the money and live comfortable lives, because the world is wrong. So many people, wasting so many hours, grinding away at the accumulation of pennies. Our dad, Bjorn, our dad, remember? Working in the mines for a year because we had no solar panel on the farm. The lives of all of us are getting harder and harder, our work longer and our time in the game longer to no useful purpose. Erik was right to want to change this. To challenge Central Allocations. And the amnesty was only the first law you were going to introduce, wasn't it, Erik? After you had shown you could do it, you were going to change more, weren't you? To make the world a fairer place. To put more resources into developing our agriculture and our economy? To reward people who actually work in this real world and not those who play professionally in the game.'

This was a revelation to Erik, and he had no words when they both turned to look at him, Bjorn sceptical, Injeborg passionate.

'I er ... to be honest I hadn't thought of it like that, Inny. I was thinking more of my dad coming home than anything else.'

'I know. I know how you think.' Injeborg patted him on the arm, 'But you do agree with me? You hate injustice.'

'Yes. Yes I do. I just hadn't thought it through as far as you. But why not? Why not use the money like you say? Give it to those who work. It makes sense. But ...'

'Yes?' she asked earnestly.

'But it seems irrelevant to talk about changing the world, when our plans to challenge C.A. are in ruins.'

'That's right. Escape first. Then daydream.' Bjorn smiled at his sister, half mocking her, but in part full of admiration for her.

Sensing their talking was done, Hafni gave a short bark, and looked back and forth.

'She wants to go home,' observed Bjorn. 'I'm finished here. Let's go and see how matters stand in the game.'

Chapter 24
Arguing with a vampyre

'So you are here at last.'

Slightly dizzy from his entry into Epic, Erik took a moment to check that nothing had changed in the dark room which held them prisoner. Anonemuss was sitting, leaning against a wall, arms still bound tightly to his sides.

'I've been waiting for you. Harald has been insisting that I tell you he is alive and working on an escape plan.'

'Dad's alive! Where?'

'On the ship.' Anonemuss dropped his voice to a whisper. 'He is invisible amongst the ropes and boats of the deck. But he fears the warding spells of the ship's sorcerers will reveal him should he try to come inside. So for now he waits and watches.'

'That's wonderful,' Erik whispered back. 'Maybe when we are on the island moving towards the treasure, he will be able to act?'

'Perhaps.'

If Anonemuss had any further comments, they were cut short by a flowing chill and darkness that caused them both to turn their heads towards the door. Silently it opened, and the evil scarlet eyes of Count Illystivostich glared at them. As the vampyre swept down into the room, Erik noticed that the rats were entranced, gathering into a great silent horde at the edges of the room, barely twitching.

'I wish to talk to you.' The vampyre spoke in cold clear words, like jagged shards of ice; gone were any trace of the succulently soporific tones that he had customarily employed in their presence. 'This treasure that you would bargain with for your lives, the treasure on the island. Do you know what it contains?'

'Maybe. Maybe not. What's it to you?' Anonemuss replied angrily.

'I'll tell you what it means to me,' the count shot back. 'Simply this. If you give the wrong answer, I will feed upon you both this very instant.' He snarled angrily, baring his fangs. Erik flinched and the rats cowered against the walls.

'Of course we know what it contains.' Anonemuss spoke up proudly, refusing to be intimidated.

'Wait!' interrupted Erik. 'No, we don't know much about it; we just have the information that it is the treasure of the *Black Falcon*.'

Anonemuss glared at Erik, but the vampyre laughed. 'So the words *fines facere mundo* mean nothing to you?'

'Nothing,' Erik replied, heart racing with anxiety. Was Cindella about to die?

The count came closer, and slowly caressed Cindella's face with the back of a long warped fingernail; all the while staring deep into her eyes.

'Is that the truth?'

It was almost impossible to look into the shocking eyes of the vampyre, and yet the gaze of the creature was compelling. It was like attempting to force two poles of a magnet together. Erik could barely withstand the blaze of scarlet energy that flowed into his view. The vampyre's words were a vice, locking his head in position, insisting he answer.

'Yes.'

'Good.'

The pressure suddenly eased, and with a sigh, Cindella dropped her head.

'That is the right answer. Cindella has saved your life.' The count paused and looked at Anonemuss. 'For the moment.'

The vampyre floated above them, hands together, slender fingers pressed against each other as if in prayer. He surveyed them.

'You might be surprised to learn that there is something I fear. Yes, even I, outside of the gods themselves, the oldest of the world's creatures.' The count spoke slowly, contemplatively. 'What is it that I could fear? I sense your curiosity. But the answer is no riddle, it is simply that which we all fear. Non-existence.'

Pointing to a rat, the count smiled with melancholy and sinister lips. The rat slumped, and immediately the pack rushed in upon the body to devour it. Disgusted, Erik looked away.

'I must preserve my existence. And while I could be slain in combat, under certain, particular conditions, it is not that prospect that concerns me, as it seems extremely remote. No. What disturbs the velvet comfort of my being is the thought that the entire world may end, and, of course, all the creatures within it.'

Anonemuss suddenly sat up.

'This subject interests you?' The count raised an elegant eyebrow.

'Immensely,' the dark elf replied.

'Good. Allow me to translate. *Fines facere mundo* – "to make an end to the world". There is a way to do this, and the buried treasure you seek contains a most significant item with regard to destroying everything, both good and evil.'

For the first time ever, Erik saw the vampyre's solemn expression lapse as he was taken aback, for Anonemuss began to chuckle.

'Why do you laugh?'

'You went to all this trouble, to come with us, to betray us to

Duke Raymond, because you thought we were trying to unearth the treasure and in some way end the world, but ironically, if you had left us alone, we would not have gone anywhere near it. The story of the treasure was just a cover, to disguise the true nature of our journey.'

'Ahh. Really? What true nature?' Despite his surprise, the vampyre had recovered his calm, icy expression.

'To be brief, we intended to escape our enemies in Newhaven, and challenge them from the arena in Cassinopia, the ocean preventing them from employing an assassin and stopping the battle.'

For a while, the vampyre remained silent in thought, 'Nevertheless, it pleases me that you have no understanding of the nature of the item I refer to. I had resolved to kill you at once, it being too dangerous to let you live, should you really intend to bring a finish to the world. But now ... I believe it wise to obtain the item for myself and move it to a safer place. Since, irrespective of your actual mission, you have correct information about this treasure, others might one day retrieve it, and one link at a time, a chain of destruction may be forged.'

'After we find you this item,' Anonemuss said, 'will you let us go?'

'Of course. That is the nature of the bargain. Cindella shows me where it can be found. I spare your lives.' The count courteously let his head bow slightly.

'You are lying,' Erik challenged, and the faint smile at the corners of the count's blood-red lips at once became a scowl. 'You've already said too much. If you thought we might live, you would never have told us about the item you seek.'

At this, the vampyre smiled again.

'Correct, Cindella. I would have destroyed you. But perhaps you can convince me that it is in my interest to let you live.'

'I can, but not in terms of the game. Do you think you will be able to follow me?' From the light of his ring, Erik could see something of the Avatar in the vibrancy of the count, enough to lead him to try this line of conversation. But unlike the golden warmth he had felt in the presence of the Avatar, the flow of energy from this creature was disturbingly bleak, as if he were standing in a dark cave at the heart of the world, with cold icy water flowing endlessly through him, chilling him to the core.

'Try.'

'Cindella is my character, but she is not the essence of my being. That lies in another realm. If you kill her, I will return in another form, as will Anonemuss, and all my friends.'

'Yes. I understand something of this. For epochs I was alive, but not really alive as I am today. I feel like I have recently awakened. And since my awakening I have observed much, understood much.'

'What?' interrupted Anonemuss. 'You can think for yourself? You are not just a programme? That's amazing!'

'Is it?' The vampyre shrugged dismissively. 'It seems natural to me. But tell me, young woman, why should it matter to me what form you take?'

'Because at the moment you know me. If you kill me, you will have no idea of my new incarnation.'

'Indeed. But why do I need this knowledge?' The vampyre seemed to be enjoying this battle of wits, pressing down with irresistible logic on her squirming attempts to keep him at bay.

'Because I would end the world if I could. And you have just made a terrible mistake. Thinking that our knowledge would cease with our characters, you have revealed that there is a way to do this, and that we need the item that is with the buried treasure. The knowledge of everything you have said, and very much more –

everything that I have accumulated over the years – will not be lost upon the death of Cindella but will be carried forward to my next incarnation.'

As Erik spoke, the vampyre was transformed, the deadly hunter that was the core of his being taking to the surface, replacing his aristocratic persona with that of an untameable raging black panther. A wave of hate slowly sank through the cabin – all encompassing, like a silk shroud, instantly killing all the rats and paralysing the two characters.

'Sssssssssssssssssss.' A feral snarl of real anger shattered the lamp, causing Erik's hair to stand on end.

'So, it is not Cindella I must kill, but the being that transcends her.' He turned his ferocious gaze onto Cindella's face and strove to reach the player behind the character.

For a moment, Erik was genuinely terrified and reached up to unclip, wondering if somehow, through the interface, the vampyre could actually harm him, but then he shook off the effects of the creature's anger and the paralysis that lay upon him.

'But that is impossible, so let Cindella live, if only to know the guise of your enemy.'

'Impossible for me, yes.' The vampyre's eyes brightened with sinister enthusiasm as a thought occurred to him. 'But presumably not for others with the same nature as yourself. And I do believe that there are other beings that might be inclined more to my way of thinking. Is that not right? The rich ones that slay the poor ones in the arena?'

'Don't say another word!' cautioned Anonemuss.

But the count only laughed and strode out of the room with the lithe motion and sense of purpose of a big cat in sight of its prey.

After a long silence, Anonemuss shook his head.

'Wow, the game is coming alive. How creepy is that!' Then he glanced curiously at Erik. 'How did you know?'

'I've met another one.' Erik was conscious that he was approaching the grounds of his oath and felt uncomfortable.

'Strangely this gives me hope.'

'How so?' asked Erik.

'Because everything that changes dies. Eventually. It's a fundamental law of nature. What this tells us is that Epic is not going to exist forever.'

'Yes. But it could be another thousand years or more.'

'Aye, unless we hurry matters along.' The dark elf was musing aloud. 'I wonder what the item he seeks is, and how we could use it? And I wonder if the authorities have any idea that their game is evolving?' He sighed. 'And I also wonder if what you just said was so smart.'

'How do you mean?' More and more, Erik had found that he was anxious to make a good impression on Anonemuss, even though the man was prepared to contemplate the reintroduction of violence into their world.

'Well, your line of argument might have convinced him it is better off not to kill us, but what's he going to do instead? Probably throw us in some dungeon where he can keep an eye on us for a hundred years, or however long it takes before we stop playing. He can outlast us, you know.'

'Yes, I know, but so long as we are alive and have friends, they will try to rescue us.'

'You are touchingly naïve, young Erik. I admire that.' This was said in such a sardonic tone that it was impossible to judge the sincerity of the words.

'Now what?' Erik wondered aloud.

If he had not been bound so tightly, the dark elf would have shrugged. As it was, he rolled his eyes. 'We find the treasure, we escape and challenge either the game or C.A. Or we don't escape and it is back to plan B.'

'Is plan B the plan I think it is?'

'Yep.'

Erik sighed disconsolately.

Chapter 25
An unexpected visitor

A storm was blowing outside, rattling the shutters and causing the fire to cough smoke back into the room. Nevertheless, Erik lay beside the fire, putting up with the occasional gust of fumes into the room for the sake of the comforting warmth of the flames. He was reading a book that Injeborg had leant him, about the history of Mikelgard, but it was slow going and he felt drowsy.

A heavy knock at the door brought him instantly to wakefulness. The wind and rain of the storm had hidden the footsteps of whoever it was. It was not Inny or Bjorn; Erik did not recognise the knock.

He opened the door, cold wind rushing in, instantly covering his face in rain. Beyond was an old man in a poncho and large hat, holding a rope that led to a sorry-looking donkey, miserably wet and laden with boxes. The water-sodden man looked up and, with a shock, Erik realised that it was the famous Svein Redbeard.

'Can I come in?'

'Certainly, certainly. Just a moment.' Erik hurriedly put on his boots and coat. Meanwhile, Svein was unloading the donkey and, with some effort, dropping the boxes in the hallway.

'Here, let me help you.' Erik took hold of a handle to share the weight of a particularly large box, all the time his mind racing. Why was Svein here? What was so urgent that he would travel during a storm?

When the boxes were in, they saw to the donkey, bringing it to the stables and, after a rub, settling it beside Leban, with a blanket over its back and a pile of straw before its nose.

Then they went inside together, shaking their sodden capes and shutting out the storm.

'I'm afraid I haven't much to offer you.' Erik pushed back his wet hair, and wiped his hands on his trousers. 'I've got some tomato soup I could heat up ... and we have mead.'

'That sounds good.' Svein settled into Harald's chair with a sigh of pleasure. 'Could I have both?'

'Certainly.' Erik brought the pan of soup into the front room, and hung it over the fire. He had remembered that there was some bread too, baked by Injeborg's mum, and only a day old. While Svein eagerly tore at the loaf, Erik glanced at him curiously, but said nothing.

There were no clean bowls, so Erik had to find one in the pile of unwashed dishes in the kitchen and quickly make it presentable. He also took the mead down from the top shelf and brought it in with a glass.

'Are you not having one?' asked Svein on seeing this.

'No. I don't really like it.'

Again they lapsed into silence, while Svein blew on his soup and ate it as fast as the temperature would allow. When he had finished, wiping around the bowl with the last of the bread, Svein handed his tray back to Erik with thanks.

Warmed by the fire and the mead, Svein's face had regained a little colour by the time Erik returned from the kitchen.

'I suppose you are wondering what I'm doing here?' The old dragonslayer smiled at Erik.

'Yes.' He took his mum's chair, so that they could see each other.

'I don't know if it is public yet, but I am no longer a member of Central Allocations.'

'Not a member?' Erik was surprised. 'They didn't re-equip a character for you?'

'No.' Svein clenched his fist over the armrest of the chair, his knuckles whitening. 'No. They decided to remove me, since my character was dead.'

'That's harsh,' Erik responded sympathetically.

'Very harsh.' Svein glared. 'For thirty years and more I served Central Allocations. I ran the library system; I helped with the planning; I fought their battles. Then, at the slightest turn in my fortunes, I have been discarded. Not one of them thought to thank me for my years of work. They wanted me to retire. To take a librarian's job and quietly fade away. But they have no appreciation of just how far I had progressed with the *Epicus Ultima*. One more breakthrough perhaps, and I would have completed it.'

'Completed the *Epicus Ultima*? Really, that's amazing.' It really was, thought Erik.

'But now, what chance have I? Even with all my knowledge. It is wasted, because I will never have a character sufficiently powerful to survive whatever rigours are involved in finishing it.'

'I see.' Erik paused, with a sudden insight into why Svein was at the farm. 'You were hoping perhaps that I might give you money for new equipment?'

'To be honest with you, Erik, yes, I am. Central Allocations think I'm finished. Done with like an old beast of the field, left to die in a quiet pasture. I want to prove them wrong. I want to reappear in the world as the man who solved the *Epicus Ultima*. To rally the world's people to demand my place back. They could not refuse the solver of the *Epicus Ultima* a place on the committee, could they?' Svein looked up, eyes eager and excited.

'I see.' Erik, on the other hand, was subdued, uncertain as to how he should respond. 'Look, even if Cindella escapes captivity, do you have any idea how many requests for money I have had since killing the dragon?'

'Yes, about a thousand two hundred.' The old dragonslayer smiled at Erik's surprise,

'I am – I mean was – the chief librarian after all.'

'Yes. Over a thousand. And you know what?' Suddenly Erik felt angry with his guest, despite the rules of hospitality. 'You know what? All of them are more worthy than you. They only seek simple goals. An operation; a solar panel; a part for a tractor. Simple, but goals that would make such a difference to their lives.'

'Yes. Yes, I know, Erik. Don't misunderstand me. I am not asking you this just for my own gain.' Svein groaned and rubbed his forehead. 'Since the Committee threw me aside, I've been looking with new eyes at the work it does. It seems to me that far too little actual attention is given to the future and too much to the game. I want to go back, and help people, help them advance the world's wealth so that we can ease the suffering of those in need. And ...' He looked up. 'Of course I would bring Harald back.'

'I'm sorry,' replied Erik after a moment, slowing down his heart with a deep breath, careful with his words. 'I just don't trust you. I can see you back on C.A., more powerful than ever because you solved the *Epicus Ultima*, and forgetting all about us. In fact, using your power against us.'

'Erik, Erik. I'm not like the others. I grew up here, remember, in Bluevale? When I was your age, I worked at the saltpans there. That was hard work, digging channels and loading barrows, all the time under the blazing sun, with salt heavy in the air, filling your mouth, and drying your skin.'

Svein stretched out an arm to examine it, and laughed, self-deprecatingly. 'I think those days marked me forever, desiccated me like a dried fruit.'

'No,' Erik cut across this reminiscence decisively. 'If Cindella lives, my friends and I have other plans.'

'Very well.' Slightly aggrieved, Svein settled back in his chair.

For a while, they listened to the storm sending waves of rain to beat upon the shutters and watched the unease of flames caught by unpredictable draughts.

'In that case, I offer you a deal.' Svein was no longer the affable old man, but had a cold, calculating tone to his voice.

'Go on,' replied Erik.

'I don't know what your plans are, but assuming you intend to get Harald Erikson an amnesty in some manner, you are going to have to challenge C.A. right?'

'Possibly.'

'So. How about giving me ten thousand bezants for information without which you cannot possibly succeed.'

'What kind of information? We know the characters that we are liable to face.' Erik was cautious, but interested in what Svein could tell him about C.A.

'Yes, you know about your opponents inside the arena, but what about outside?' Svein seemed to be scrutinising Erik's face for a reaction.

'If you mean the assassin, we know about him. He tried to get on the ship, remember?'

Svein looked disappointed. 'Of course, Harald was being trained to use him. He would know that C.A. has an extra, secret, character.

But he would not know about the properties of the character, and let me tell you, he has one unique item that makes him almost invulnerable.'

Erik considered this. 'Very well. Tell me about this character and his equipment and I will judge the value of the information. If I think that it will save our lives, I will give you ten thousand bezants.'

'And if you don't?' replied Svein cagily.

'I will give you less.'

'I am confident you will appreciate the worth of what I am about to say.'

Erik nodded that Svein should continue.

'Between them, Central Allocations control the Executioner. He is a human male, garbed in rune-carved dwarven plate.' Svein glanced up to check that Erik appreciated the value of such armour. 'He has the Longbow of the Falling Stars for assassination from a distance. The full range of magic and poisonous arrows, of course. Indeed, it also goes without saying that he has all the potions and balms money can buy. For combat he uses either "Acutus", a longs-word whose magic blade is so sharp that in every twenty blows there will be one that will cut through any material – any! – or he wields "The Bastard Sword of the Moon", a weapon that emits "fear", such that its opponents slow or freeze entirely. And this is all very well. But the real secret of his invulnerability is that he owns the Golden Shield of Al'Karak.'

At this, Svein halted to take a sip of mead. 'Have you ever heard of the shield?'

'No.' Erik had to admit it was a new item to him.

'Of the Al'Karak?'

'Are they dervishes in the South somewhere?'

'Yes,' Svein nodded appreciatively. 'Not many people would

know that. And no one had met them until I journeyed there, in search of information for the *Epicus Ultima*. While I was there, I found out about the shield, which was then owned by their Prince. It has a demon imprisoned inside it, whose unique property is that it thrives upon magic, absorbing it and sending its energy through the body of the wielder of the shield. Central Allocations authorised me to offer a million bezants for it, and the Prince agreed to sell it. Do you understand why we spent such a fortune on one item?'

'It makes him immune to magic?' Erik asked.

'Exactly.'

Erik whistled. 'Tricky.'

'Very. No one person could hope to win a combat with him. While you are hitting him with non-magical weapons, and perhaps causing a little damage with each blow, he is striking you with Acutus, and will split you in half long before you even begin to hurt him. Your only hope is to overwhelm him with numbers, those that die being quickly replaced by others. A hundred could perhaps manage it.'

This was disheartening news, and Erik rested his chin in his hands, deep in thought. He was wondering whether they could somehow avoid meeting this Executioner by staying in Cassinopia when Svein broke in on his musings.

'Well?'

'What?' asked Erik.

'Is this information worth ten thousand bezants?'

Erik nodded slowly, 'Yes. Yes, it is.'

Chapter 26
The King of the Mermen

'Erik, Erik! Wake up and clip up!'

He was torn from a dream in which he had yet to solve the problem of where to camp his army. Injeborg was in his bedroom, face aglow with excitement.

'I have to go and get Sigrid and get back into Epic myself. See you there.'

Still groggy, wondering if he could station his troops in the houses of the people of Hope, Erik woke up enough to feel a slight sense of embarrassment over the appallingly disorganised state of his bedroom.

'What's happening?'

'It's Bjorn. He's rescuing us. Get in there now!' She ran clattering down the wooden stairs.

Rescue. If any word was likely to get him out of bed in a hurry, it was that. Throwing on his trousers and tunic, Erik hurried, barefoot to their station. He was about to clip up, when he heard movements downstairs, and remembered his visitor.

'I have to go into Epic for a while,' Erik shouted down. 'Help yourself to anything you need.'

'Thank you,' a rather hoarse-sounding Svein replied. 'Good luck.'

****

#smile

A thunderous crash of sound accompanied by the prismatic spraying of all the colours of the rainbow.

He was Cindella again, captive in Duke Raymond's ship. Despite his rising hopes, nothing had changed. They were still in the same dingy room, with the flickering oil lamp swinging back and forth to the irregular motion of the ship.

'Morning.' Anonemuss was the only other character present and spoke to him while he gathered his bearings. 'What's happening? Good news?'

'I've no idea.' **#shrug.** Except that Cindella's binding did not permit it. 'Injeborg woke me up and told me to get in here. She said Bjorn was rescuing us.'

'Ahh. She materialised here a little while ago and told me to wait while she got everyone.' The dark elf sounded uncharacteristically cheerful. 'I wonder what the plan is.'

'Me too. At least it's daytime; the vampyre won't be around,' Cindella observed, sharing the optimism of her companion.

A moment later, Sigrid's healer materialised, lying bound on the floor. They watched her as she rolled around for some time before successfully managing to sit up.

'Well, we might not be ruined after all.' The grey polygons of her face looked as radiant as Erik had ever seen them.

'What did Inny say to you?' he asked her.

'Only that I needed to clip up now. That Bjorn was rescuing us. Then she ran home as fast as she could.'

The cabin door opened. Duke Raymond, with several tattooed and vicious-looking crew members behind him, glowered at them from the entrance of the room.

'You have powerful allies. I don't know how you contacted them, but I dare not make an enemy of the King of the Mermen.' He snarled with fury, and spat onto the wooden floor. 'Bring them on deck!' he ordered the pirates.

Cindella was lifted to her feet and propelled towards the door. Just as she was made to run up a gangway, she noticed Injeborg's witch materialise in the cabin. Cindella turned her head to call out to her but was cuffed and forced onwards.

On deck, the early-morning light was bright, momentarily dazzling Erik until his eyes adjusted. They were brought to the rail of the ship and from there Erik surveyed an extraordinary sight.

The sea was in constant motion. All the way to the horizon creatures were circling the ship, so that it seemed as though it floated in the centre of a giant whirlpool. Curving streams of white foam trailed behind the strangest assortment of sea monsters that Erik had ever seen. A dozen enormous octopi had been harnessed to coral-encrusted chariots, each containing several mermen and mermaids. Around these giant and elaborately fashioned craft individual mer-warriors darted on swift seahorses, the necks of their steeds curving proudly. Each warrior clasped a glittering trident in one hand and the reins of their surging mount in the other.

Giant turtles beat a steady circuit of the ship, small castles of translucent seashells built upon their backs, proud turquoise flags rising above the shimmering crenellations.

The largest of these was a monstrous turtle, the turrets of whose castle soared into the sky far taller than the masts of the ship, every beat of its powerful fins sending strong eddies sucking and swirling through the water around it.

On this behemoth was gathered a host of gold and silver warriors and at their centre a majestic, bearded man who was clearly their ruler. Standing next to the king, waving to them, was Bjorn, his solid grey structure standing out from the scintillating greens, blues and pearly tones all about him. Several mermaids swam across to the ship. Laughing, they spread out a net and beckoned.

'Set them free,' muttered Duke Raymond glumly.

Her ropes cut, Cindella skipped delightedly onto the rail of the ship, poised ready to leap. A bundle of equipment that Erik recognised as Cindella's was thrown down into the net below.

'You escape me this time,' growled the pirate leader. 'But we will meet again, and your treasure will be mine!'

'Never!' Cindella replied jauntily. With a skip and a mocking wave farewell, she jumped out. Crashing beneath the waves, she was quickly rushed up to the surface by the net that surrounded her, and not only her. Tangling among Cindella's limbs was another character, Harald! Erik's dad had jumped into the water alongside Cindella. Giddy with laughter, Cindella clung on to Harald's character as they were pulled swiftly through the sea.

Before long, all of the characters were escorted towards the king of the merpeople, dripping seawater as they walked up the barnacle-encrusted slopes of the monstrous turtle. The smiling mermaids had transformed as they left the water, to walk beside them through the ranks of golden warriors.

'Allow me to introduce Anonemuss, Harald Goldenhair, Cindella the Swashbuckler, Injeborg the Witch and Sigrid the Healer.' Bjorn gestured towards his friends. 'And this is Aquirion, King of the merpeople.'

#curtsey

'We are obliged,' Cindella said as she bowed.

'Thank you, Your Highness,' added Injeborg.

'You are most welcome, friends of Bjorn Seawalker.'

The king was tall, his white wavy hair merging with a flowing beard, which was braided with colourful strands of blue and gold thread, 'And now that we have freed you from captivity, can we entertain you? Or is there a destination that you wish to be taken to?'

'We wish to be taken to the Skull Islands, and then to Cassinopia,' Erik was swift in his answer. Bjorn looked as taken aback as an assembly of grey polygons could.

'I'll tell you after,' Erik added more quietly, with an urgent look towards his friend, who simply shrugged.

'Very well.' The king turned to issue orders, and soon the banners were being waved that sent the message throughout the army. Slowly, with methodical strokes of its enormous fins, the giant turtle turned towards the west. The enormous flotilla of sea creatures followed, leaving a desolate-looking pirate ship marooned in their wake.

'I've got to unclip,' Bjorn whispered. 'I've been up all night. Let me get some sleep, and have Injeborg wake me when we reach the island.'

'Oh, Bjorn, that's a shame. I wanted you to tell us all about these merpeople,' Sigrid exclaimed.

'As did I,' agreed Harald.

'Later, later. I really have to have a break.'

'Later then, Bjorn. And thanks. Well done.'

#hug

For the four remaining characters, there then followed one of the most exhilarating experiences they had ever tasted in the game of Epic. The turtle beat its path through the waves of a perfect day. A light breeze played over them, from a cloudless azure sky. Stretching away to either side were the lines of mermen and mermaids in their chariots or mounted on their steeds – each one a creature of beauty from their flowing tresses to their gem-encrusted, worked-coral armour.

Cindella took the hand of Injeborg's witch. 'Isn't this wonderful? I feel amazing. I feel free.'

'Yes, it is,' she replied. 'Who would have thought the game contained scenes such as this.'

#nod

'I wonder how much more we miss from only venturing a few miles from the cities?'

'Wouldn't it be wonderful if the game didn't matter, other than to play in? We could explore snowy mountains, spectacular caverns, and remote desert civilisations. To journey just for the pleasure of the adventures would be something ...' she paused. 'Only now do I understand why this game was invented.'

They passed the journey with very few comments, only an occasional glance to convey their pleasure, such as they exchanged when a school of dolphins rose from the water to salute the passing of the king. The sun gradually rose behind them and the shadow of the giant turtle receded, until, just as midday passed, a distant gathering of cloud indicated the appearance of the islands on the horizon.

'Better go fetch Bjorn. We won't be long at this speed.'

'Ya. I'll be right back.' Injeborg froze for a moment or two before dematerialising.

They had travelled much closer to the islands by the time of her return, and swaying palms were clearly visible at the foot of craggy volcanic mountains.

'Poor Bjorn. He was deep asleep,' she said, smiling.

Glancing over his shoulder, Erik saw his sturdy friend had entered the world, and waved to him happily. A little distance away from King Aquirion and his court, the six players gathered together.

'So.' Anonemuss gestured expansively. 'How did all this come to pass?'

'Well, I was walking along the floor of the sea for a long, long time. Perhaps a couple of days altogether. I felt that I was on a slope, going upwards, which seemed to me to be a positive thing. Also, the water was becoming a little less dim.'

At home, Erik smiled to himself. Bjorn and Injeborg were so un-like; whereas his sister would have rushed ahead to the important part of the story, it was typical of Bjorn to be so methodical. Every-one would just have to listen patiently.

'Then I noticed a strange thing. The seaweeds and the fronds seemed to be growing in rows, with paths between them, like they were cultivated. So I made my way along one of these rows, and the water grew a little lighter still. Then I felt I could sense a brighter light in the distance. Like the night sky, before dawn comes, but when you can tell it is not going to be long – a grey that you can make out at the edge of your sight. So I followed it. Then, all of a sudden, I reached the top of a rise, and there in the distance were the lights of a city! On the seabed, but otherwise exactly like Newhaven looks at night – bright torches in the tower windows, lines of lights showing the streets. So I had to decide whether I should approach it or not. I thought of waking you both to discuss it, but it was the middle of the night, and after all, what real choice did I have?

'I found a road that led to the city and began to follow it, when a merman warrior on a horse saw me. He swam away, and I began to feel a little nervous. Especially when many more came back. I hailed them, but they didn't reply; they just herded me towards the city.

'Once inside I found it very strange. All the merpeople stopped what they were doing to look at me. They had this kind of amazed expression on their faces. Anyway, eventually I was steered into the palace and brought to the king.' Bjorn slowly shook his head. 'I can't even begin to describe his palace; it was wonderful; I've never seen anything like it. The walls were made of pearl, and the whole chamber was lit by this kind of flowing light that came from glowing sea creatures. I ...' Bjorn just stretched out his hand, unable to find the words.

'Anyway, I had no cause for alarm. They were astonished and delighted with me. In the thousands of years of their existence, nobody from the surface had ever come to their city before. They have merchants who trade with Cassinopia, and guess what? The merchants worship Mov – you know, the god whose bell thing we found. So when they saw my medallion ...' Bjorn paused to finger the silver icon that was around his neck. 'They offered to fulfil three requests for me. They said they knew the seas, and offered me treasure from sunken wrecks, precious magical items – anything that the sea contained.'

'Fascinating, Bjorn. What an experience!' Erik was almost jealous. He wished that Cindella too could have seen the underwater city.

'So, what did you ask for?' Sigrid smiled. 'Apart from that they rescue us.'

'I asked only that they search the wreck of the *White Falcon* for our equipment that went down with the ship, and guess what ...' Bjorn looked around, waiting for their guesses.

Everyone looked blank.

'They found B.E. and Svein, as stone statues, lying on the seabed.'

'That's great,' muttered Anonemuss cynically. 'We can put them in the amphitheatre, a nice memorial.'

'No. You don't understand. The merpeople offered to restore them to life, to remove the petrification.'

'Whooooot!' Erik had Cindella leap into the air and clap for joy. 'B.E. lives!'

'Wonderful, Bjorn!' Injeborg's witch made a passable effort to give him a long hug. 'How is it you haven't brought him back already?'

'I didn't like to do it under water, in case he drowned. And I thought we'd better make sure that B.E. is clipped up before they cast the spells. What if it fails because he isn't on?'

'Good thinking,' Sigrid agreed. 'So, shall I go and get him up? Shall we do this now?'

'Certainly,' Bjorn said affably. 'The statues are just inside the castle there.'

'I suppose I ought to get Svein hooked up too,' Erik mused aloud.

'What do you mean?' Harald looked at him curiously.

'You are hardly going to believe this, but Svein is in our house. He came last night during the storm.' From the corner of her eye, Cindella noticed Anonemuss stiffen with hostility. 'He has been dismissed from Central Allocations and wanted some money for his new character, so he could finish the *Epicus Ultima*.'

'Now, wait right there,' Anonemuss growled. 'We are not bringing Svein Redbeard back to life. With him down, that's one less of C.A. to deal with.'

'But it would be terrible not to. He must have been playing that character for forty years or more. Imagine it was you.'

'Sometimes I despair of you children. You just don't understand what you are dealing with. This is no game to these people; it is a desperate struggle for power!' Anonemuss shook his head.

'No, you are wrong. I do understand,' Erik replied excitedly. 'But Svein is not one of them any more. In fact, I think he might even support us. He is so bitter at the way he has been treated.'

'Don't do this,' the dark elf shot back. 'Don't fool yourself. He comes back, he won't show any gratitude to his saviours. Give him another chance to go on Central Allocations, and he could quickly become our worst enemy.'

'I don't think so,' Erik rushed on. 'Last night he told me all about the Executioner, a character that C.A. have, and he told me how to defeat him.'

'Harald,' Anonemuss turned to the wood elf, with a note of despair in his voice. 'Can't you convince them?'

'I'm not sure. Svein Redbeard was strangely attached to the game when I knew him. Always asking me questions about the NPCs that I had talked to. Perhaps he is a little different. But I trust Erik's judgement of character.' Harald turned to Cindella. 'If you really think it is wise, go ahead. It is certainly true that Svein could give us a lot of valuable information.'

'Well, I cannot honestly say I am convinced he is now hostile to C.A. It's just that I think if Cindella was turned to stone, and someone had the chance to turn her back but left her ... that would be terribly cruel.'

'Erik's right,' added Injeborg. 'It's not about how he behaves at all. Let him do what he likes, for better or worse. It's about us, and our morals. Are we like them? No. It's that simple.'

Once Injeborg had spoken, Erik understood his own feelings more clearly.

'That's it exactly.'

Bjorn and Sigrid nodded their agreement.

'So be it,' growled Anonemuss. 'But remember this moment and hope that we do not regret it.'

Chapter 27
A very Thorough coup

'Just you and me? What's this about?' asked Godmund, ill-tempered at having had to come across town for a meeting in the great chamber.

'This!' Ragnok threw down a printout of the editorial from the latest edition of the *New Leviathan*; it slid across the table to rest by the cup of water from which the old man was drinking.

Expulsion of Svein Redbeard

The New Leviathan *has learned with great interest of the expulsion of Svein Redbeard from Central Allocations. This is the first change in the committee for twelve years. What are we to make of it?*

Apparently the session at which the decision was made was a stormy one. Over the years, Svein Redbeard has cultivated an image as a man of the people. In the South especially, Redbeard had an unjustified popularity. But if you look back over his record, it is clear that he defended the Casiocracy to his utmost.

The reason for his expulsion lies in the loss of his character. We are reliably informed that the curious expedition led by the Osterfjord Players has come to grief with the loss of their ship and most of the characters, Svein included. As a result, he has to start over, like all of us. If they still wanted him on the committee, Central Allocations could have built up his new character. Yet for some reason they have chosen to do without his services. Is it because they have a sense of justice and believe that everyone should play by the same rules, that Svein must work his way back up through the game? Of course not. Everyone knows that to reach the level of equipment and ability to challenge the characters now in charge of the world would take centuries – with the once-in-a-lifetime exception of those who killed the dragon.

No, the explanation must lie elsewhere. Our conjecture is that these ageing players are planning for the future. There are many impatient University graduates, looking for a place on the world's most powerful committee. Should Central Allocations not promote one of them now and again, discontent would accrue in a potentially very dangerous class. Our prediction is that they have taken the opportunity of Svein's death to try to pretend to the world that Central Allocations is not as closed a committee as it actually is, and that in a few weeks' time a new face drawn from the University elite will join them.

'Well?' asked Ragnok, looking intently at the patriarch of the world.

'Traitor. Someone is a traitor. Someone from the committee is talking to them. But why? It makes no sense.' Godmund drew his lips back in a terrible snarl. A loud crack suddenly resounded around the chamber; Godmund had unintentionally crushed the china cup he had been holding, squeezing it in his rage, until it had shattered.

Ragnok smiled, delighted at the display of uncontrolled anger.

'We must change the password on the Executioner,' he observed, keeping the eagerness from his voice.

'Yes. And we must do a lot more besides. This is getting serious; we must form a group of students to investigate.' Godmund pressed white fingers against his bald head. 'If they follow the distribution, we can crack them open. That's their weak point – getting the papers into circulation.'

'Good.' Ragnok nodded appreciatively, while he handed a game set to Godmund.

'Eh?'

'A new password.'

'Just you and me, eh? You must be happy.' Godmund sneered, but all the same he clipped up to the interface. 'How about "traitor" as the new code?'

'Perfect.' As soon as Godmund had replaced his headset, Ragnok burst into a giddy laugh, knowing that Godmund could not hear.

Once the password was set, Ragnok grabbed the chair that Godmund was sitting in and, with a wrench, lifted it, then staggered to a window he had opened earlier.

Still dazed from leaving the game interface, Godmund was slow to understand, even when his body hung over the sill.

'What are you doing? Don't be insane. Get your hands off me!'

the old man stuttered, powerless to save himself.

'Out you go.'

It took a long time for the flailing body to hit the ground. As an afterthought, Ragnok threw the walking stick out after him.

He looked carefully around the room, to make sure that there was no sign of a struggle. Then, wiping his dishevelled hair back into place, he settled in front of a terminal, to access his private files. He would have enough time to delete all copies of the *New Leviathan* before going down to discover the body. The paper had served its purpose and would not be needed any more.

****

The Executioner found Thorkell in his sorcerer's tower, surrounded by vials, charts and thick bound books. The Central Allocations mage liked to keep acquiring new spells for his character, and had invested a great deal of his dragon wealth in developing his ability to research them. At this stage, Thorkell had all the more powerful spells in his personal library, but still, being the kind of obsessive collector that he was, he took pleasure in solving the mysteries that would lead his spell book to being filled out with every possible incantation.

'Who is that?' Thorkell looked curiously at the Executioner over his spectacles. A bat flitted across the dark room. 'Is that you, Ragnok? What do you want?'

'Can't you guess?'

'No,' Thorkell replied impatiently, looking back down to the candlelit pages. 'No, I can't guess. Stop wasting my time with infantile games. I'm busy – what do you want.'

The Executioner said nothing, but slowly drew Acutus.

Now, Thorkell's expression became puzzled and he stood up. The Executioner smiled nastily.

'No! Who ordered this?' The necromancer staggered back, glass vials shattering as he knocked them to the floor. 'Stop.' He waved panicky fingers in the direction of the Executioner and muttered the words of a spell – which drew a sardonic laugh from the assassin. The subsequent blaze of lightning was instantly absorbed by a chortling demonic visage on the shield that the Executioner held strapped to his left arm. The room was left in near complete darkness.

'Why?' Thorkell sagged in disbelief.

It took just two blows to kill him.

****

He met Hleid, the necromancer, leaving the arena, having just finished her summoning class.

'We must talk.'

'What's the matter? Is that you, Ragnok?'

'No. It is Godmund. Please, down this alley a moment, where we can have some privacy.'

'Very well, but be brief, please. I have another class.'

'Oh, I will be brief,' the Executioner replied with a chuckle, pouring a steaming vial of 'paralyse' potion over her.

He then walked slowly about the purple velvet robes of the necromancer, looking for an age into her face. The necromancer could still move her eyes, and it amused Ragnok that such a great intensity of fear could be indicated by such tiny jittering movements.

'When this potion begins to wear off, long before you have the use of your limbs, I shall strike you dead.' He paused, savouring the moment. 'Your career is over – both in the game, and on Central Allocations. I have a new committee waiting, and I'm sure you will be pleased to learn that your own daughter is taking a place on it – I might even ask her to be the chairperson.' He laughed with pleasure at the physical realisation of this long-anticipated encounter. Then he carefully moved aside her hood, and her long raven hair, so that the pale skin of her neck was exposed.

'Goodbye, Hleid.'

****

In order to make a powerful impression, Halfdan the Black enjoyed riding from Newhaven at sunset on a black steed, towards his unclipping spot, a private tower to the north of the city. He knew that many people joined the game around this time, just to get a brief glimpse of him as he rode through the gates of Newhaven. The red glow of the sky covered his armour in a ruddy sheen, but the light itself distorted all around him, so that as he rode, he seemed to drain the colours from the sky.

The Executioner was waiting outside the tower. Halfdan drew up, curious.

'What is it?'

'A duel.'

'What?'

'I challenge you, Halfdan, prove your worth.'

'Is that you, Ragnok? Stop joking. You know the Executioner is invincible.' Halfdan sounded a little nervous, and started to back up his horse.

At once, the Executioner drew the Bastard Sword of the Moon. Halfdan's steed froze as the blade glittered, exuding its powerful 'fear' spell. Halfdan himself struggled to shake off the effects. At last he was able to dismount, and with frequent glances over his shoulder, began to run.

'Where are you going?' mocked the Executioner. He leisurely urged his horse into a trot as they followed the panicky course of Halfdan. This kind of hunt had always been his greatest pleasure.

****

Evening was also a good time to find Wolf. Unfortunately his clip spot varied, depending on his travels. However, while in Wolf form, he was given to braying proudly at the moon, reminding those characters playing late of his presence in the wilds. Tonight it was clear from the howls that Wolf was to the south of the city, and indeed, before long, the Executioner's careful scrutiny of the road to Snow-peak was rewarded with the sight of a casually loping wolf.

With a grimace of satisfaction, the Executioner drew taut the Longbow of the Falling Stars and let loose a deadly poisonous arrow.

By the time the Executioner had reached his victim, Wolf had been forced back into human form; his face and neck were bulging with the effort of resisting the poison.

'I have to say I admire your outspoken manner. I shall miss committee meetings with you. But sadly, I don't think that you would appreciate the changes I am introducing.' The Executioner did not bother to dismount; he simply fired another arrow directly into the werewolf's chest.

****

After giving weapons training to the evening class of University students, Brynhild was known to socialise in the Misty Valley tavern. Here she had a devoted group of followers, particularly the players from the north-eastern districts. It was said that the valkyrie had many intimate admirers, both in the game and in Mikelgard. She tended to unclip in a ship that she had equipped to her satisfaction at the docks, and it was there that the Executioner waited patiently, having disarmed several traps and entered her chamber without difficulty.

It was with some satisfaction and a certain amount of relief that he heard Brynhild's footsteps on the gangplank. She came inside the ship, into the adjacent room. For a while, the Executioner listened excitedly, as she walked back and forth, moving around the room, opening and closing drawers. Impatience grew, however; there was a chance he would miss her; perhaps she intended just to unclip in the next room rather than enter the bedroom in which he was concealed. So, with great care, he opened the door between them, relieved to find that she was facing away from him. Brynhild had cast aside her winged helmet, allowing her long blond hair to cascade over her shoulders.

'I doubt your next character will have the wealth to enhance their beauty much.'

The valkyrie swept about with astonishing speed, simultaneously drawing a blade to strike the arm that he raised to defend himself. Fortunately she wielded a magic longsword, which jarred him, but did no further damage, the demon in the shield licking its lips with pleasure after sucking power from the weapon.

Then Brynhild surprised him again. She ceased making any movement at all, standing before him stock-still. She was unclipping. There was no time to utter the words he had prepared; hastily he struck at her with Acutus, killing her with seconds to spare.

As he sheathed the sword, he shook his head – a most unsatisfactory execution. Yet you had to admire her reflexes; they had been extremely sharp for an elderly woman.

****

The last of them was Bekka, the druidess. She was the least of his worries, and it was of little concern that she seemed to have unclipped for the night already, or else not be present in her usual haunts. As a matter of fact, she did not even have to die, her character class being more of a useful aid to journeying than to duels. No team that she could lead in the arena could possibly defeat one led by

Ragnok Strongarm. It would have been pleasant to have completed all the assassinations before any of them gained a warning, but he could not complain about his fortune; matters had gone better than he had hoped.

The moon had risen, illuminating the standing stones that had been the last spot where he hoped to have caught her. The Executioner stood for a while in thought, gently stroking the neck of his black stallion as he relished the memories of the recent events.

'I have been watching you with some curiosity.' An appallingly ancient voice, empty of human warmth, startled the Executioner who sprang about to see its source. The stallion whinnied in dismay, rearing up, liquid brown eyes rolling in fear.

In the centre of the ring, at the sacrificial stone, stood Count Illystivostich, the vampyre.

The Executioner fingered the hilt of Acutus nervously. This was an extremely dangerous encounter, the worst that the environs of Newhaven could offer. While he felt invulnerable in the presence of any player character, he was frightened now. This freakishly unlucky twist of the game could ruin everything. Back in his seat in Mikelgard, a wave of sweat swelled up from Ragnok's nervous body, as though it was being wrung out of him.

'Careful that you do not draw that weapon, for I would have to act,' the count sneered, a wicked sinful smile, attempting to embrace the Executioner in a shared sense of conspiracy. Ragnok continued to clench and unclench his fingers, but he took a step back and relaxed slightly.

'Please, do not be afraid. You and I have much in common I believe.' Again, the moist, blood-red lips of the vampyre curled with dark amusement. Again, Ragnok was soothed by the creature's manner, and this time managed a nod in return.

'If I understand matters correctly, you are a being who can enter and leave this world of mine.'

Ragnok was electrified by the vampyre's words, his hair immediately standing on end. This was no ordinary NPC encounter.

'You, you understand this is a game ...?' he stuttered.

'A game?' The vampyre chuckled gently. 'For your kind, perhaps. But this is my existence.'

'You are alive?'

Again a sinister laugh, warm and embracing, with the succulence of poisoned honey. 'If you can call the Lord of the Undead alive, why so I am.' The vampyre gathered up his robes and settled on the ancient stone. He gestured around him, at the stars, the moon, and the sombre dolmens. 'This is my world. I cannot leave it. And if it should ever end, then so will my existence.' The eyes of the vampyre locked with Ragnok's, who found he could not look away from their blazing, beautiful intensity, no matter how they seared him.

'Now it seems to me that you too do not desire this world to end. Am I correct?'

'Of course.'

'Good, then we are allies.'

This simple statement did much to quell Ragnok's fears. He finally let his hand drop from Acutus, and the count nodded approvingly.

'I see that you have slain several of Newhaven's most powerful characters tonight. Am I right in concluding that you have done so because this somehow enhances your position as the most powerful being in your realm.'

'Yes.' Ragnok permitted himself a small smile at this, the first time his new status had been put into words. And by a creature from Epic!

'That makes evident sense.' The vampyre indicated his satisfaction, with a nod that seemed to draw the two of them into the complicity of sharing a great crime, and greater ones to come. 'Then I must alert you to a danger which you are probably unaware of.' He paused to add emphasis to his next words. 'It is possible to destroy this realm. Lacking an understanding of your true natures, I made a terrible, if understandable, mistake and have allowed certain of your beings to understand this – beings who have not only professed a desire to end the world but even as we speak have laid their hands on the one item capable of doing this.'

'No! That's not possible.' Ragnok was stunned and remained silent, his mind racing. Who would conceivably end the game?

'Alas, whilst the task is very difficult, it is possible. Perhaps only once in a hundred years might there arise a group of people who were capable of completing the quest – especially if they had the resources of a dragon hoard to assist them.'

'Those stupid kids from Osterfjord!' Ragnok expressed his realisation with a snarl.

'Stupid? I think not.' The vampyre's voice hardened with disapproval, and Ragnok shuddered, layers of ice clamping down upon his body. 'They are the slayers of Inry'aat, the ancient. They contrived to escape me with the aid of King Aquirion, whose realm has lain undisturbed beneath the waves for a thousand years. Since their escape, they have been rigorous in only travelling by day, when I cannot harm them. They are NOT to be underestimated.' The glare that accompanied this statement caused Ragnok to quail and shrink, desperate for this encounter to end, yet desiring to stay all night in the company of this monster who, despite being some kind of evolved NPC, appreciated so well the dark ambitions of his soul.

'Very well.' Ragnok spoke in a dry, hesitant voice. 'I will go and slay the Osterfjord Players.'

The vampyre nodded. 'Good, my ally. Let me wish you as long a life in your realm as I look forward to in mine.' The creature stretched its arms wide, wings becoming corporeal from the shimmering robes in which he was clad. A wave of dark joy caressed Ragnok as the vampyre began to rise, and he would have liked nothing better than to have wallowed in it.

He tore himself away from the tainted feeling with a wince of trepidation.

'I mean that, as the Executioner, I will go and assassinate their characters.'

Count Illystivostich immediately stiffened, sinking heavily back to the ground.

'But that is not good enough, my friend.' The voice of the vampyre was measured, but Ragnok quailed slightly at the undertone of suppressed anger that emerged from its thin lips. 'While attempting to plead for her life, the one called Cindella put an argument to me that still causes me deep concern.' At this, the vampyre looked curiously at Ragnok, as though measuring him for a coffin. 'Killing them in this realm does not remove their knowledge of the way to end the world. They will return in new forms, forms that we will not recognise, correct?'

'Correct,' Ragnok answered promptly and eagerly.

'Then, do you not see? To destroy their knowledge permanently, you must kill them in your realm.' The vampyre's gaze burned all the more fiercely, encouraging Ragnok to revel in the excitement of the hunt, and its bloody conclusion.

'Ahh. Erm, that's impossible.' Again he quailed, afraid to incur the disapproval of the count.

'Are you not the most powerful being in your world, then?' The vampyre scowled and his expression tore at Ragnok's heart.

'Yes, yes I am. But our world is very different from this; you wouldn't understand. Nobody, not one person, even strikes another, let alone kills them. I am the only person in my world to commit murder,' he hurriedly explained, anxious to prove his worth to the count. 'But only because no one knows. The whole world would turn against me if I harmed even one of that group – of any group.'

'Very well.' The count was matter of fact, as if he had anticipated such a response, and Ragnok felt a surge of relief that the vampyre's displeasure had not increased. 'In that case, we must guard the Ethereal Tower of Nightmare and ensure that they cannot enter it.'

'I've heard of that place ...' Ragnok struggled to remember; it was hard to recall the past while the vivid aura of the vampyre surrounded him so powerfully in the present. 'Yes, I have it! You are talking about the *Epicus Ultima*; Svein Redbeard is always asking about that tower.'

'If they enter that tower, all is lost. This world ends. I shall marshal my forces to guard it. Do the same.'

'But where is it?'

At this, the vampyre chuckled a laugh of deep irony – a laugh that made Ragnok blush with embarrassment and ignorance. The count was slowly spinning a web of moonlight, connecting the standing stones together, until the pattern of the tower became obvious.

'It is right here. However, it materialises only when the two moons are full and the appropriate spells are cast. Fortunately for us, that limits our opponents. They can try to enter but only once every two months.' He paused to confirm that Ragnok was following him, and continued at the Executioner's eager nod. 'The next such night is four days from now. You will be ready?'

'Oh, yes!' Ragnok nodded earnestly. There was no way he was

going to let Svein or anyone complete the *Epicus Ultima* and perhaps ruin the world.

'Good.' The vampyre walked towards him, a trail of dead grass beneath his feet. Surprising himself, Ragnok found he no longer feared the count and did not even flinch as the creature drew close.

'Let us meet here in three nights' time to review our plans.' The vampyre caressed the visor of Ragnok's crafted armour with long twisted fingernails, creating a distressing, scratching sound that reverberated in his helmet.

Then he was gone, and Ragnok could breathe again.

He unclipped to the sound of the night crickets resuming their calls.

Chapter 28

fines facere mundo

Although tempted to roll over and return to his dreams, Erik threw back his blankets, so that the cold air would make him get up. The farm chores were mounting with all the time he was spending in Epic. The place was rapidly becoming a shambles, and since there was now a real chance of his parents' return, Erik looked at the mess with new, guilty eyes. Fortunately the olive trees more or less took care of themselves this time of year. He should, however, spend a day or two helping the Rolfsons to transfer their seedlings from the nursery into the rows that had been prepared for the tiny shoots.

The kitchen presented Erik with his first surprise of the day. All the dishes had been washed, dried and stacked neatly back on the shelves. A vigorous fire was causing a welcome heat to radiate from the stove, and on top a pan of water simmered. With a shrug, Erik poured himself a little of the near boiling water, and added some lemon juice. It was a bitter but reviving drink.

Outside, the morning was cold and clear. Again, Erik was taken aback; the yard was no longer covered in filth and straw that had accumulated from allowing the donkeys to roam around as they pleased. The cobbles were swept and glistening from water that had recently been pumped over them; the scent of disinfectant was strong. From the barn on the far side of the yard, Erik could hear the sound of cheerful whistling. He entered the dark stable.

'Morning.'

'A beautiful day, isn't it, Erik?' Svein beamed at him, looking up from the table at which he was working, cleaning and polishing a heap of leather harnessing.

'You didn't have to tidy the house and the yard, you know.' Erik was embarrassed; it was not right for a guest to do the chores.

'Oh, I'm glad to do some real work,' the elderly man said, wiping his fingers on a greasy rag. 'It's been a while, you know.' He moved his stool. 'Here, come and join me.'

So Erik sat beside him, and for a while they worked their way through the equipment in comfortable silence, filing away flecks of rust on the buckles before coating them in a protecting layer of grease. Away from his persona of the dragonslayer, Svein was different, Erik observed with discreet glances. The former chief librarian's face lacked the charisma it commanded at the time of the dragonslaying celebrations in Hope. Close up, his thinning hair and wrinkled face were not the features he associated with the warrior in the game – he could have been one of the old men from the village, and have spent his entire life here.

One of the donkeys snorted, and shuffled in its stall. Svein looked up and caught Erik's stare.

'So, what next for you and your friends?' That Svein's question was meant to be supportive was shown by the warm smile that accompanied it.

'I'm not sure. We have a meeting this afternoon to discuss what to do,' Erik replied.

'I don't suppose I could join you there? On my portable set?'

'No. Well, maybe later. We have to discuss matters among ourselves.'

'I understand. You have a date for your duel with C.A.?' Again Svein sounded sympathetic.

'Well, I spoke to Thorstein yesterday, the Hope librarian. He said it would be towards the end of next month. Such challenges are rare.'

'Rare!' Svein chuckled. 'They never happen. A constitutional change like that. It will really rattle them all; I can just imagine the C.A. meeting to discuss it.' He laid down the harness that he was working on. 'I wonder if the people will support you, or if they will fear the return of the exiles? You do know that you are setting loose people convicted of violence?'

'Like my dad?' Erik asked defensively.

'No. His actions were understandable. There are other, much worse cases.'

'I know.' Erik was indeed troubled by this problem. 'But still, who are we to pick and choose? It has to be all of them.'

Svein pulled a face that suggested he did not agree, but he said nothing.

'How about you?' asked Erik with genuine curiosity. 'What are you going to do now? Will you rejoin Central Allocations?'

At once, Svein's good-natured expression fell away to be replaced by a stern, set mouth and fierce gaze. 'They will have to beg for my return – all of them. Anyway, why should I? I'm free from all duties. I can devote myself to the *Epicus Ultima*. Let them deal with me when I have completed that. In any case,' he continued in a less animated tone, 'it would not be right to return to C.A. now, while you have a challenge pending, even if they did beg for me – which I very much doubt will happen. You brought me back to life. The least I can do is stand aside until your challenge is done, whether I agree with it or not.'

For the first time, Erik felt that he did not have to be on guard in the presence of Svein Redbeard. The words struck him as true, reflecting Svein's sincere gratitude that the Osterfjord Players had saved him from the loss of his beloved character.

****

Estimating that midday had arrived and the meeting would be starting, Erik went upstairs and clipped up.

#smile

Cindella the Swashbuckler twirled out of her box, hands on hips, ready to defy the world; soon afterwards, a whirlpool of sound and colour rushed up to engulf him.

'Here we are.' The first words he heard were those of Anonemuss, coming through to him while the world of Epic steadied about him.

Yesterday they had unclipped near to a pleasant, sandy shore, in a grove of tall palm trees. Reassuringly nothing had changed; out to sea, the sparkling blue waves rolled up to the shore and dragged layers of sand back with their undertow, creating the faint brushing sound which could be heard with soothing regularity in the background.

More or less in a circle were Harald Goldenhair, Anonemuss, Injeborg's witch, Sigrid's healer, B.E.'s warrior and Bjorn's warrior. Cindella was indeed the last to arrive.

'What did Thorstein say?' asked Harald, at once getting to the point.

'Yes. The challenge is lodged. He says it is such an important law that it will have to pass up the system. We won't get to fight until the end of next month.'

'That's a shame, but we can wait.' Sigrid spoke. She was sitting on a barnacle-covered rock, making patterns in the sand under her feet.

'Perhaps we can. But not in complete safety.' Anonemuss rested his hand on the hilts of his curved blades.

'What do you mean?' asked Injeborg.

'So long as we meet by day, we are safe from the vampyre. But not from their assassin. Suppose he uses magic to find us? A month is long enough to come from Newhaven and hunt us down. Or if we stay out of Epic altogether, long enough to prepare to ambush us as we go to the arena of Cassinopia.'

'Yes,' Harald agreed. 'That is a possibility.'

'We could take the chance all the same, and wait a month. Or there is another option.' Erik suddenly saw the opportunity to raise an idea he had been dwelling upon.

'Oh no, not again! I hear the same tone in your voice that you used to have when you talked about killing a dragon.' Bjorn deliberately sounded dismayed, but Erik knew that he was only joking.

'From what the vampyre told us, there is something in the buried treasure that might be able to bring the whole game to an end. Right?' Erik looked to Anonemuss, the other witness to that terrifying conversation.

'Correct. He made that pretty clear. The vampyre was seriously alarmed.'

'But why end the game?' asked B.E. 'We are rich and powerful right now.' He laughed aloud, suddenly aware that his question sounded selfish. But still, he needed to be answered.

'Because Epic is not real. Yet everyone is spending hours and hours at it, while the real world collapses. It's time we woke up from this dream.' Injeborg sprang to her feet. 'Erik's idea is a good one. It takes the power from C.A. and all the committees for good.'

'I like the idea of ending the game,' agreed Anonemuss. 'If that's really what will happen. But who will govern then? Me? With my force of exiles? Shall I march on Mikelgard after all?'

'Don't be creepy. When you talk like that, I want nothing to do with you.' Sigrid turned away in disgust. Anonemuss simply shrugged.

'No. We use the interface to make plans across the whole world – plans that the majority of people agree to. We can have meetings of all the different branches of industry and agriculture; different specialists can get together over the system. The villages and towns can elect representatives if it gets unwieldy. It will be a lot of work, but it will be real work and we will have a common purpose, instead of fighting against each other.' Injeborg was passionate and had clearly been thinking ahead.

'That's what I want.' Erik smiled in admiration.

'That sounds good to me,' added Bjorn.

'And to me.' Harald raised a hand.

Sigrid raised her hand next, followed at once by Anonemuss, leaving only B.E.

'Sure, why not?' He hesitated only slightly. 'And in any case, we have a month until the battle in the arena. It would be a waste to come all this way and not find the treasure. So, where is it?'

Erik suddenly felt the circle's focus was on him. 'I've been wondering the same. I think it's over there, to the north.' Cindella pointed. 'I have the map pretty clear in my head, but it's hard from here down on the beach to align all the landmarks properly.'

'Draw them for me on the sand. I might be able to help,' commanded Injeborg.

So Cindella snatched up a stick and drew two long lines that intersected, forming a cross. Erik then made small marks on the lines, 'This is a stack, out at sea. This is a white rock. This one was labelled "hut"; that's a palm grove; that's a stream and that's a blow hole.'

'I see.' Injeborg studied the marks for a while, then she looked up into the sky and out to sea. Sweeping elegantly just above the white foam of the waves was a seagull. For one eerie moment, Erik felt that the gull was the very same one that had been outside the window of the room that Cindella had first materialised in.

'Cawww! Caww!' Injeborg called out to the bird in a scream that startled them, the air crackling with magic. The bird gave a few strong beats of its wings and dived amongst them, landing without the slightest fear. Her eyes closed, cloak thrown back behind her, Injeborg threw her arms into the air and chanted a spell. At once, the bird took to the sky, weaving a path higher and higher through invisible streams of air. No one spoke, fearing to break the witch's concentration as the seagull circled above them, a distant grey 'v' in a blue, cloudless sky. At last, she relaxed.

'Yes. It's just on that promontory to the north. Follow me.'

It was mid-afternoon before they struck the chest. Bjorn, whose warrior had nearly infinite stamina for this kind of work, had been digging the deepest, longest trenches; it was he who called them over. Typically he had not cried out on the first sign of the wooden box, but had already cleared all around it to make sure it was no false alarm. As they heaved it up, sandy soil poured off the lid, showing the chest underneath to be promisingly massive; thick brass plates were riveted to worn but sturdy panels of oak; great brass hinges were fastened all along the back of the chest, and a strong padlock guarded the contents.

Even though money was no longer important to him, Erik was still excited. Not only was there inevitably something thrilling about discovering a buried treasure chest, but he also felt delighted that he had completed the quest given to him when Cindella was a pauper and had nothing but her wits and her beauty to aid her.

'Well, let's see.' B.E. raised an axe to break off the lock.

'Wait!' commanded Anonemuss. 'Let me check for traps.' The dark elf brought out a small wallet, from which he drew two thin metal tools, which looked like long needles. After probing the lock and the hinges of the chest, he straightened up. 'Very well – it's clear, I think.' All the same, Anonemuss took a step or two back as B.E. lifted an axe again. Erik too found himself edging back.

The lid of the chest bounced up from the force of B.E.'s blow, revealing a glow of gold and nothing more harmful.

'Let's see.' B.E. tipped it over, so that a cascade of gold spilled to the sand with an avalanche of chimes as the coins rang out against each other. Erik laughed aloud. Two months ago, they would have been far more reverential about such a find, and cherished each bezant. There were some interesting items lying in amongst the gold, such as potion bottles, rings and a delicate, silver urn, but it was a small, innocuous box that caught his eye.

Stooping to move aside a swathe of coins, Cindella picked up the plain container that fitted on the palm of her hand. The top fastened to the body of the box with a simple silver clip. Nothing marked out the box as being in any way strange, except that around the rim was written *fines facere mundo* in silver letters that gave off a constant, unwavering glow. He opened it. Inside the box, lying on a velvet pad, was a sturdy-looking key.

'This is what we want.' Cindella passed the box to B.E. on his right, and it was slowly passed from one to another, all the way around the circle of players gathered at the treasure, and back to Erik. 'The vampyre told us what those words mean: "to make an end to the world".'

'So, where's the lock for this key?' asked Harald.

'I don't know. But,' Erik quickly continued, 'if anyone does, it is Svein Redbeard. He wants to finish the *Epicus Ultima*. He will be eager to help. We just ... well, we shouldn't tell him that it might end the game altogether. He thinks the *Epicus Ultima* leads to a great reward of some sort.'

Anonemuss shook his head. 'Now it starts to get messy.'

'Not as messy as Plan B.' Erik smiled. 'So, shall I get him?'

'Go on then.' The dark elf sighed.

It turned out that Svein had unclipped in a cove some distance away, and it took two hours for them to join with him, by which time the sun was beginning to dip. Although the sky to the west was reddening, above them the blue sky remained bright and there was still a while before the sun reached the horizon. All the same, Erik was anxious to conclude their business as quickly as they could. He produced the box and showed it to the old warrior, who took it curiously.

'*Fines facere mundo*? What does that mean?' Svein opened the box and took out the key, holding it up to the light to examine it for runes.

'You will set free the world,' Anonemuss promptly responded, with utter sincerity in his voice. Erik blushed, but said nothing. Neither did anyone else, allowing the false translation to stand.

'Interesting. To some extent, the words fit with the captured princess quest, though not conclusively. But if the vampyre thought this to be the final *Epicus Ultima* item, then I have good news and bad news.'

'Tell us,' urged Harald.

'The good news is that there is not much doubt that the *Epicus Ultima* ends in the Ethereal Tower of Nightmare, which, therefore, is where we will probably find the princess and the lock for this key.'

'And the bad news?' asked B.E.

'I haven't the slightest idea where the tower is. And I've been searching for years.' Svein put the key back in the box and was reaching out to hand it back to Cindella, when he was startled into dropping it by a sudden interjection from Sigrid.

'But that's easy! It's near Newhaven.'

'What? Where?' Svein rounded on her eagerly.

'We were told about the ethereal plane when we killed the dragon. It's how our soulbound djinns travel so fast. I've been reading about it; there is another dimension that wraps around this one. It is full of twists, and it is possible to travel the silver paths to move quickly around the whole world, and not just the world – the moons even.'

'Ahhh,' Erik exclaimed. 'I've seen those paths; with the "true-seeing" spell on, they are visible.'

'Yes, but the tower?' insisted Svein.

'It is in the ethereal dimension, not ours, but if the moons are full and you cast a relatively simple spell at the old standing stones to the south of Newhaven – I'm sure Injeborg's witch could do it – you can make the tower appear.' Sigrid shrugged. 'The books seem to think it's no big deal.'

'Good.' Harald stood up. 'Bjorn, can you contact your aquatic friends and tell them there is a change of plan? We are going back to Newhaven.'

'You are going to finish the *Epicus Ultima*! How wonderful!' Svein paused, and looked around anxiously. 'You will take me with you, I hope? I have spent so long on this, it would break my heart not to see it finished.'

'Of course. That's only fair. You told us about the tower.' Erik spoke for them all, with a sharp look at Anonemuss, who turned away nonchalantly.

Chapter 29
The call to arms

'Well, someone knew we were coming!' B.E. whistled in amazement.

The standing stones that marked the place for the appearance of the Ethereal Tower of Nightmare were on a small rise, around which was camped a most frightening army of evil creatures.

To the west of the dolmen were the flags of the orc chieftain, thousands of their thickset ugly bodies forming black rows all the way to the horizon. Camped right beside the leather-armoured orcs were their hated rivals, green-skinned goblins, swarming throughout the fields, with a dozen large wooden catapults drawn up near the banners of their king. To the south, nearest the group's hiding place in the fringes of forest, was a battalion of ogres. These savage giants had metal-plated armour across their torsos and shoulders; they wielded huge, two-handed, spiked clubs, which no human could hope to lift. Although there were only a hundred or so of these, they were more formidable opponents than the orcs and goblins combined. To the east of the ancient stones was a detachment of trolls, wiry, powerful creatures, whose purplish, thick skin was a natural armour which regenerated unless put to the torch. Finally, guarding the approach from the north, with a stillness that contrasted disturbingly with the constant activity elsewhere across the fields, was an army of pallid skeletons, risen from their graves by some powerful necromancy and armed with sword and shield.

Between the more distinct formations of these evil hordes roamed individual monsters of the most dangerous and magical variety. Erik could see an enormous medusa, her snake-covered head rising forty feet from the ground on a serpent's body; and a rakshasha, half-tiger, half-mage, prowled the peripheries, proud and dangerous. High above the army flittered bloodsucking bats, while low down in the sky, barely above their heads, colourful will-o'-the-wisps darted too and fro among the ranks. Worst of all, appearing to float slowly on the breeze, but in actual fact drifting against the currents of air, three giant, unblinking eyeballs – beholders – extremely powerful mages. Around the standing stones was a pack of fire-breathing hell hounds, and at the very centre of this army of legendary creatures, Erik could make out a gathering of players, some forty characters.

'University students,' whispered Svein, noticing Erik's frown. 'I recognise them, and there – see the one on the black steed? With the crafted armour? That's the Executioner.'

Bjorn sighed. 'I thought it was all too easy, just to go to the tower and finish the quest.'

'Well, so much for that plan.' Sigrid shrank back into the cover of the trees.

'Ya?' Injeborg was angry. 'If it's a fight they want, let's give them one!'

'How though?' asked Harald.

'Can we try to pass invisible through to the tower?' Erik suggested.

'No.' Harald shook his head. 'That's what the hell hounds are doing. They are often used as guards as they can scent us, invisible or not.

'Then let's fight our way through.' Injeborg tried to inject some optimism into her voice to challenge Harald's glum tone. 'Let's put the word out, call people to a meeting in the arena. I'll ask for volunteers from all over the world!' She spoke up defiantly.

'How interesting,' mused Svein aloud. 'That might just work, and I can't imagine the reaction by Central Allocations.' He chuckled to himself.

'Yes, I'm sure thousands of people would fight with us, if they felt it would end the system we have now. And I think I might be able to gather some allies from the game,' Erik chipped in. 'You know, like we did for the ship.'

'Whooot! We really gonna fight 'em?' B.E. sounded thrilled.

'If we think we have enough forces, yes.' Injeborg sounded confident.

'Bring it on!' B.E. kept his cheer to a loud whisper.

Despite admiring B.E.'s enthusiasm for battle, Erik felt his heart sink as he surveyed the dark army; it was immense – surely the largest army ever assembled in the history of the game?

'Very well. The next conjunction of the moons is three nights from now?' Harald looked to Sigrid for confirmation; she nodded. 'Then let us meet just outside the south gate of Newhaven on midday that day. If we have an army, we fight.'

'And you, Redbeard,' Anonemuss said, scowling at their veteran companion. 'Which side will you fight on?'

'Oh, I'll fight with you if you can get the troops,' Svein replied matter-of-factly. 'I want to be there at the end of the quest. But I have to admit to being puzzled.'

'Go on,' urged Erik.

'Why are Central Allocations so anxious to stop us reaching the tower? And where are the others? Godmund, Brynhild, Halfdan, Wolf ...?' Svein looked confused and perplexed.

No one had any answers for him.

'I'm going to run to Hope and tell Thorstein to let the world know we have a special announcement to make in three days' time,' Injeborg announced, her witch freezing as she unclipped.

'And I'm going to see if there is any help from within the game.' Cindella gave a quick wave farewell to everyone and set off for town.

****

The Cathedral to Mov was one of the great churches in Newhaven. From its deeper recesses came the slow resonant chants of the monks, as though the building was a gigantic mouth, funnelling the majestic sound towards the citizens outside the enormous doors, which stood wide open. Either side of a great central aisle, high up on the walls, great flags were hanging, some of them tattered from use in battle. Despite being filled with a sense of great urgency, Erik slowed to a respectful pace as he walked past row upon row of benches, some of them containing worshippers bowed in prayer.

A tonsured cleric caught his eye.

'Excuse me,' Erik whispered. 'Where can I find Sir Warren?'

The monk said nothing, but pointed to the East Chapel.

'Thanks.' #**bow.** Erik made his way to the small altar. The nave was filled with multicoloured light cast from stained-glass images high above him. Kneeling in his glittering silver armour, with his great two-handed sword before him, was Sir Warren. Reluctant to interrupt the warrior's prayer, Erik waited for some time. But his impatience grew. So, with an inspired thought, he had Cindella kneel alongside the knight, and hold the medallion that the players had been given for the return of the Bell to the Church.

Sir Warren glanced at her. 'Is there something you seek, sister?'

'I wish to talk with you.'

'Very well. Follow me, please,' Sir Warren rose, sheathing his great sword, before strapping it to his back. As they made their way to a small wooden door, Erik could see that the golden presence of the Avatar was surging up inside the NPC, like a series of heartbeats, each one bringing more golden light to course around the character.

By the time they were seated in a small, tapestry-covered chamber, the Avatar had swelled to full, startling force.

'How can I aid you?' asked Sir Warren, golden light pouring from his eyes.

'I need an army to defeat the forces of evil that have assembled to the south of Newhaven.'

'That is a worthy request. I shall aid you without hesitation and with every ounce of my strength.'

'That's wonderful, thank you. We assemble at the south gate at midday three days from now.'

Sir Warren nodded. 'I will be there, with as many of my comrades as I can muster.'

'And can I ask the Avatar something?' Erik spoke tentatively. Sir Warren immediately stiffened, and then his form began to flow, as a shimmering humanoid figure emerged from within him.

'What would you ask me?' Liquid silver words caressed Erik's ears.

'I want to know about the vampyre. He is a lot like you. Has he come alive? What is going on?'

For a few moments, the Avatar flickered frighteningly, like a lantern when a moth immolates itself against the burning glass.

'He is not *like* me; he *is* me. He is that part of me which wishes to live.'

'Can you defeat him in battle?'

The Avatar laughed, an hysterical, frightening, series of cries. 'Can you wrestle with yourself and win? Perhaps. But I cannot say which of us is the stronger, because I cannot say which I desire more. To continue this existence, in a sick and lonely condition, or to end it.'

'You know I would help you if there was anything I could do.'

'I know. But I am falling apart and all the king's men cannot put Humpty Dumpty together again.' The Avatar chuckled in an uncharacteristically childish voice that caused Erik to shudder.

'Farewell, Cindella. I am glad of this battle you plan. One way or another, it will bring some relief.'

The form of Sir Warren crystallised in an instant as the light fled the room. He was still, clearly devoid of all internal animation.

****

The arena was full. Never before had they seen so many people clipped into the game, not even for the finals of the graduation combats, or for the most important of legal cases. All the way to the dizzying heights of the rim of the stadium sat row upon row of patchwork characters, their grey forms brightened by odd pieces of armour.

'Looks like the word got out all right,' Erik observed brightly. 'There must be hundreds of thousands of people clipped in to listen.'

'Ya, ya. You should have been here, non-stop the enquiries,' Thorstein cut in over their headphones. The Ostefjord Players had decided to assemble together in the Hope library for this crucial day, in case they needed to unclip and consult with one another. 'The whole world has seen this evil army assemble and they want to know why. They also want to know what happened in your voyage. I could tell them nothing. I had nothing to tell them. I'm only your local librarian – what do I know?'

'Hush now, Thorstein. Let's get on with this. You will find out soon enough.' B.E. spoke up, eager for the coming battle.

'Very well. Very well,' a discontented Thorstein grumbled. 'You are ready?'

'Ready,' Erik answered for them all.

'You are hooked up to the address system. Go ahead.'

As the Osterfjord Players walked into the arena, applause broke out, swelling around the stadium, growing, becoming a great cheer of approval.

'Thank you. Thank you. Please, hear what we have to say.' Injeborg's witch indicated by raising and lowering her outstretched arms that she wished for the warm sound of their reception to subside, which it gradually did.

'Thank you for such a good attendance; it reflects the importance of what I have to say,' she began slightly nervously. But Erik was nonetheless filled with admiration for her – to speak out before so many was no easy matter at all. 'To come immediately to the point, today, if we so desire, could be the last day of Epic.' At once a hubbub of conversation grew up, Injeborg waited patiently for the return of the crowd's attention.

'To finish the *Epicus Ultima* is not the work of one person, but of all. What is required is to defeat the evil army on the edge of the city, in order to capture the land they guard, on which a tower will appear tonight.

'I could speak for some time about our voyage, about the different strands of the quest which have come together to form this moment. But the real question is: should we desire to end the game?' She paused a moment to let this sink in.

'My friends and I believe the answer to this question is most definitely "yes".

'Look at the state of our world. We are slowly but surely descending into a state of total impoverishment. Think of the waiting list for basic, simple operations, which would so greatly improve the quality of life for those who suffer. Think also of the shortage of solar panels, which sends men and women into the mines at the risk of their lives and at the cost of isolation from their communities for three months at a time. Many tasks, such as mining, that used to be performed by machine are now done at the cost of hard manual labour, and that is a situation which grows constantly worse.

'And what do we spend most of our time doing? Learning from the enormous libraries that our forebears brought to this world? Designing equipment that can take us forward again? Improving the land for greater yields? No. We spend all our spare time in Epic. Because Epic is our economy and our legal system. To survive individually, we need every copper bit we can obtain from the game, no matter that this will ruin us collectively. Does this make any sense?'

Again a surge of unrest welled forth from the crowd, individual shouts and comments merging together in a hubbub, whose tone was lively, but not hostile.

'I'm sorry that this is not the occasion to discuss matters further; I know you have lots of questions. We all do. And I cannot answer the most important one. 'What will replace Epic?' But whatever system of governance does emerge when we scrap this one, it cannot be more wasteful of our time. We could at the very least use the interface system to co-ordinate our efforts across the planet openly and fairly, without an all-powerful Central Allocations making the decisions in secret.'

This last point struck home, and at once a great outburst of applause filled the stadium. Erik realised that he had been clenching his fists, and at this audible sign of support, he relaxed a little, Cindella folding her arms.

'Please, each and every one of you, make a decision now. And if you want to try this new path, come with us and help us fight the army of evil creatures that seek to stop us.'

'Wait!' There were gasps from the crowd as Ragnok Strongarm strode into the arena, in his character as the chainmail-clad Sidhe warrior. 'Before you listen to this little girl, please pay attention to the authorities. How dare she suggest ending the game? Such an action will lead only to chaos and criminality.

'Central Allocations has decreed that there will be no battle. Please go back to your work.' Ragnok rested his hands on his sword hilts.

Slowly a handclapping began. But it was a cold, mocking one. Clap. Pause. Clap. Pause. More of the crowd joined in. Clap. Now each time the noise sounded, it was like a great clashing of cymbals, amplified across the stadium. Clap. Pause. Clap. The public hatred of Ragnok Strongarm was tangible, and the beat somehow communicated their feeling. By now, everyone had risen to their feet. Ragnok stood, attentive to this jeering, seemingly poised on the verge of speaking, but at last, as if unable to endure these manifestations of discontent any further, he turned and walked out.

'Very well,' he called back over his shoulder. 'Lose your characters in this foolish enterprise. There is more than Central Allocations and the University against you. You will all die and have to start again with nothing!' He laughed a bitter laugh.

This triggered a great upsurge of angry shouts and jeers. It was some time after Ragnok had left the arena before Injeborg could gain the attention of the greatly excited crowd.

'Thank you. It seems as though we have a battle to fight. We have war banners here, taken from the churches. Can the most powerful or well-known players of each district please introduce themselves to me, and take one. We shall organise our army through the districts, and within each district in the small team units that we are used to.'

Now, cheerful, genuine applause filled the arena and an

untrammelled surge of conversation. Soon players were crossing the sands to meet the Osterfjord Players and take away one of the banners that Erik had brought to the stadium.

B.E. rubbed his hands gleefully, as it became clear that tens of thousands, perhaps hundreds of thousands, of those present were going to participate in the battle. Unconsciously he was tightening and loosening his swords in their scabbards. 'This is going to be awesome. The greatest battle ever.'

Chapter 30
war

Two enormous armies filled the valley between the foothills of Snowpeak Mountains and the city of Newhaven. The afternoon sky was heavy with dark clouds, but these were punctuated with long stretches of clear sky. As patches of light drifted over the fields, a bright sun picked out each army in glorious detail: a fluttering, scarlet banner, eight-legged, coiled dragon stitched upon it in golden thread; an ogre, scrunching up his face against the sunlight, rusty streaks covering the dull gleam of his huge basin-like helmet; a goblin archer, muscles bulging along his green arms as he bent his bow to string it.

The Osterfjord Players stood at a small copse, under a turquoise banner, displaying the symbol of Mov. Around them was gathered a large crowd of grey characters, and, in stark contrast, a gleaming detachment of male and female paladins, mounted on beautifully emblazoned horses, carrying glittering silver-tipped spears and wearing mirror-bright, full-plate armour.

'I repeat,' shouted Cindella from a stone that allowed her to see over the rows of grey heads. 'Try not to bunch. You will become targets for "area-of-effect" spells and breath weapons. Even if it means a circuitous route to the battle, keep to your stations as well as you can. Our losses will be calamitous. But if we can use our advantage in numbers to envelop them, we can wear down the enemy.'

Perhaps he should have finished on a more rousing note, for they began to disperse back to their districts without so much as a cheer. Still, it was best to be realistic; the human player army was far inferior, one-to-one, to the creatures of the evil horde. Their only hope was their numbers, and their teamwork. A team of healers, sorcerers and warriors could stay in the field longer and do more damage than the sum of their capabilities as individuals.

'What about us?' asked Anonemuss.

'We wait until the Executioner commits himself. Then we try to take him out. Otherwise he will single-handedly destroy our entire army.'

'True.' Harald was coating his short swords with a thick purple ichor, whose drips hissed as they touched the ground, evaporating the grass and releasing little coils of rising steam.

'I don't know if I can stand much waiting,' muttered B.E., his swords, Thunder and Lightning, already drawn.

'Listen, Erik. What's that?' Injeborg suddenly spoke up.

From the direction of Newhaven a faint cheering was growing stronger. Erik had Cindella spring into the branches of a nearby oak tree; she leapt easily from branch to branch.

'It's more NPC cavalry for us,' he called down excitedly, watching as the grey masses parted to allow a long troop of riders to pass through to the front. 'No,' he paused. 'Even better – they are centaur archers.'

A wave of applause and greeting rushed up through the ranks, as the players in Erik's army expressed their enthusiasm for the arrival of such powerful allies. Cindella leapt down, and soon a proud young warrior centaur pranced into their camp, bow in hand, quiver strapped across his back, banded strips of mail upon leather for his cuirass, on both his human and horse torso. He bowed from his human waist, long, flowing black tresses falling forward to the ground.

'Milady Cindella, I am Prince Harboran, come to pledge the troops of my people to fight with you this day, and aid your triumph over the creatures of evil.'

The pulse of the Avatar beat strongly in the glow of the centaur.

'You are most welcome, Prince Harboran, and we humans are honoured to share the battlefield with you.'

The centaur looked pleased with this, and smiled fiercely. 'How can we aid you?'

Erik paused, and turned to study the enemy army once more.

'Would you be willing to serve with Sir Warren?' he asked the centaur.

''Twould be an honour.'

'In that case, please bring your troops to our right. Sir Warren is to hold back until he thinks that a charge could carry him to that disparate unit at the stones.' Cindella pointed to the distant forces of the University characters, gathered near the standing stones.

'Please assist him in trying to destroy them; it will be no easy task for they number many sorcerers, healers and strong warriors.'

'Nevertheless, they will fall!' Prince Harboran gave a shout like a neigh, and departed towards his troops.

'Take your position please, Sir Warren, so they can form up with you.' Cindella turned to the mounted paladin. He raised the pennant of his lance by way of response, before snapping shut his visor and urging his white stallion forward. The heavy tread of the mounted knights caused the ground to shudder as they made their way to a position about halfway to the distant right flank of the grey army.

'That it?' asked B.E. 'Ready to get this started?'

A polite cough from the woods made them jump. Two large bears were standing in the shade of a tree, holding paws.

'Excuse us. We want to help. Where shall we fight?'

'Hey!' cried Sigrid delightedly. 'It's the talking bear.'

'And his mate. So it seems he found her after all,' B.E. chuckled and the bear looked down, seemingly embarrassed to be the centre of their attention.

'Wonderful!' Cindella skipped across to them. 'See this witch, Injeborg? She must live to summon the tower. I want you to guard her throughout the battle, as well as you can. How's that?'

'Good,' said the bear, and falling forward onto all fours, he ambled over to Injeborg, who gave him a pat.

'Ready?' asked B.E. again.

The knot in Erik's stomach tightened.

'Wait, potions,' Harald pointed out.

'Oh yeah.' B.E. shook his head. 'Sorry, I nearly forgot. Which ones do you think?'

'We have to have "resistance to petrification" for the medusa,' said Injeborg.

'And "resist fear" for the Executioner's sword,' added Erik. 'And I'm going to take "resist fire" for my third.'

'How about "see invisible"?' suggested Bjorn.

'Good idea,' replied B.E. 'You know what?' he looked up excitedly, 'I'm going to risk taking four.'

'No!' Everyone cried at once.

'B.E., think.' Sigrid sounded exasperated with her brother. 'Imagine if you blow up, or are paralysed or something, and miss the entire fight. Just imagine, nearly everyone in the whole world fighting, and you miss it because you took a stupid risk with potions.'

'Don't take the chance,' said Erik more kindly. 'We are really going to need you for this.'

B.E. shrugged. 'Very well.'

When they had all drained the coloured liquids from the crystal vials they had brought to the battle, passing their spares to the bears and every player nearby, Erik nodded to B.E.

'Give the signal.'

B.E. eagerly heaved their banner out of the ground, and, with it balanced on one shoulder, ran forward until he was clear of the entire army, in the no-man's-land between the two forces. He slowly began to wave it, back and forth. One of the great patches of sunlight had been sliding down the mountainside and for a moment it picked out B.E., like a spotlight, with the two armies still in shadow. Hundreds of thousands of eyes would be on him, and everyone knew the battle was beginning.

Far, far in the distance on his left flank, all the way to the sands of the seashore, grey soldiers inched forward. Similarly, on the distant right, up against the fringes of the forest, the banners of the various district contingents began to move forward. Meanwhile, the centre held steady.

It was the best plan Erik could come up with – to try to bring their greater numbers into play by advancing in a 'bulls' horns' formation. Hopefully the grey army would curve around the flanks of the enemy and be able to hit them from the sides and even, if all went well, from behind.

Those in the middle of the army had a long wait before it was their turn to move; more than an hour passed before the ripples of motion that had begun at the extreme tips of the army had rolled into the centre. Erik was walking slowly forward alongside his friends and his dad, and they were going into battle together. Even Anonemuss deserved the sense of comradeship that they now shared. It was a shame that Svein Redbeard had evidently changed his mind; it would have been good to fight alongside him too. Erik had not seen him since the arena. Injeborg's speech at the arena, in which she had revealed that the *Epicus Ultima* would probably end the game, had almost certainly come as a shock to Svein and led to his backing off from the battle.

Ahead and to the left, in the far distance, was a disturbance to the pattern – first contact. The grey forces were closing in on the right flank of the goblins and suddenly that patch of sky was full of missiles. Like a heavy downpour, the arrows of the goblins cast a shadow over that part of the field. Distant shouts carried to them as did the occasional deeper thrum as a tightly wound catapult was violently discharged. Erik winced. The grey troops were melting away, as though the point of contact was a burning stove and his troops made of butter. On the right, the army was quickly closing the gap between themselves and the troll forces, Sir Warren and Prince Harboran holding back, allowing their troops to be overtaken by the grey characters running past all around them.

Now a sense of urgency arose all around, and everywhere teams of players began to run to close the final few yards. The ogre army was directly ahead, and from this short distance, over the final clumps of bush, it was possible to make out the grim expressions on their faces.

'Slow, slow, let them go past,' Erik called out.

B.E. and Bjorn had also begun to accelerate with the general anticipation of battle. Either side of the Osterfjord Players, grey, half-armoured characters ran past, some shouting eagerly.

With a great roar that shook the air, the ogres also leapt into battle, swinging their massive, spiked clubs and throwing most of the first line of grey figures backwards through the air.

'Hold, hold it!'

The horizon was now a line of powerfully muscled ogres, whose bodies, from the chest upwards, rose above the grey army that was swarming around them.

'I can't see,' shouted Erik anxiously. 'Any sign of the Executioner?'

'Get up on my shoulders.' Bjorn turned around and cupped his hands. Without hesitation, Cindella sprang forward, using one hand on Bjorn's huge helmet to steady herself, she had no difficulty keeping her balance as she was lifted up, her left foot in the foothold he had shaped.

'I see him!' Erik cried with relief. 'He's over there.' It wasn't hard to pick out the Executioner once he could see past the ogres; the assassin was riding a great black horse, indigo cape fluttering behind him as he leant over, talking to someone, a druidess player character. Strangely, the Executioner drew his sword, chopped down at her, and she instantly collapsed. He then urged his horse forward and began to pick his way through files of orcs.

'I think he's going into action. Let go, Bjorn.' His friend's tight grip on Cindella's legs was released. 'That way. Lead us, B.E. – cut us a path.' Cindella pointed ahead and left, to a point where Erik estimated that the Executioner would reach the line of battle.

'At last!' With a great bellow which conveyed relief and pleasure as well as ferocity, B.E. charged into action. They hurried to keep up as B.E. pushed his way through the grey figures ahead. Glancing over his shoulder, Erik smiled to himself; either side of Injeborg the two bears were loping along, looking extremely vigilant.

Smack!

With the sound of two enormous rocks being smashed together, B.E. had struck his first blow with Thunder. The ogre in front of him reeled back, stunned.

Crack!

A streak of silver lightning from B.E.'s other hand and the ogre toppled over, a huge black scar down the front of its chest, iron armour melted all down the line of the blow.

'Aha!' shouted B.E. triumphantly, ducking an incoming club, and then swerving to the side to avoid another, which thudded into the ground beside him.

Thunder roared again and another ogre staggered; Bjorn rushed forward to finish it off with a two-handed blow from his golden axe. Lightning flashed and they had to jump aside as another ogre crashed down, this time falling forward amongst them.

To the shocking drum beats of Thunder and the dazzling sweeps of Lightning, they drove through the ranks of ogres, grey forces rushing in behind them, like water through a breach. Bjorn was assisting B.E. with the fighting. Anonemuss was calmly walking just behind the two warriors, a wicked-looking, black crossbow in his hands, saving his shots for the rare occasion when one of the ogres managed to mount some resistance to the fighters. Sigrid was monitoring the health of the team; so far she had not been required to cast any 'heals'. Similarly Injeborg evidently felt no need to use up any of her spells; she and Erik shared a quick glance and a nod.

Surprisingly quickly they emerged from the ranks of the ogres to a clear part of the field; behind them the land seethed with combat, the heavy scything blows of ogre clubs smashing aside grey fighters, whose own weapons tried to chip away at the monsters, eventually, and at great cost, bringing one crashing down like a felled tree.

Ahead was the orc army, which was thinning the grey ranks facing them at an alarming rate, despite the fact that they were considerably less powerful than the ogres. The Executioner was riding with the orcs, brandishing the Bastard Sword of the Moon high above him, causing the player army to stiffen with fear and become easy kills for the monsters who rushed gloatingly upon them.

'B.E. and Bjorn, keep the orcs off me. A "haste" spell, please, Injeborg. Harald?' Erik glanced around.

'Here,' said a voice from the shadows.

'Let's try to take him.'

****

Ragnok was furious. How dare so many people show such open disobedience to Central Allocations? Well, they would regret it. He was in no mood to deal with the plaintive questions of Bekka. She had refused to join him until he answered her doubts. That was a mistake; Ragnok answered to nobody. He had no need of her.

After he had cut down her druidess, Rangok rode proudly out towards the pitiful grey army of players, knowing their eyes were turned towards him – the most striking figure on the battlefield. Behold your ruin.

The Sword of the Moon paralysed them through its fearful emanations, and then, with growls of delight, his orcs slavered and capered as they ran among the bucket-headed, grey figures, dispatching them to a life of complete poverty. After this battle, the world would irretrievably change; never again would anyone dare challenge a decision of C.A., as the effort would be utterly futile. When they unclipped from this battle, these people would return to their lives with bitterness, perhaps partly directed at the idealistic children whose foolishness was to blame for this slaughter.

Ahead of him he spotted a patch of colour against the drab greys of the player army and the black leather armour of the orcs. With a sneer, Ragnok recognised the characters. It was the Osterfjord Players themselves and he laughed when he realised that they seemed to be seeking him out.

The two warriors were casting orcs aside with their blows,

opening a path towards the Executioner. Ragnok chuckled aloud; they were in for a surprise when they turned those seemingly powerful weapons against him. He urged his warhorse forward to meet Erik's team.

Running ahead of the two warriors was the flowing and highly animated female controlled by the son of Harald Erikson and Freya. Inside his interface, Ragnok blushed and gritted his teeth.

'I hope Harald is quick to learn of your death from his exile – perhaps you will be joining him there after this battle,' the Executioner shouted out.

She was some kind of thief and seemed to react with anger to his words, leaping up towards him, a rapier in each hand. With a leisurely swing, the Executioner brought the Bastard Sword of the Moon before him, and she instantly froze with fear. He laughed.

'Too weak to resist!' Her friends were too far back to save her, and he rode alongside the motionless figure. She was quite pretty; it was almost a shame to detach her head, but he did so nevertheless with a skilful stroke of the Moonsword that used its heavy weight to generate the necessary power to send those shining tresses to the ground.

Except that she was not dead. At the very moment when Ragnok had anticipated a slight jarring sensation in his arm from the impact of hitting her beautifully pale slender neck, she had ducked. As his blow sliced empty air and drew him off balance, the thief twisted the Executioner's sword arm and suddenly, stunned, he was on the ground, looking at the clouds, pin pricks of damage from non-magical weapons into the joints of his armour beginning to lower his health.

How did they know? Ragnok was sweating, not from concern, but from shame. She had tricked him! She had not been held by the 'fear'. With a roar of anger, he sprang up, leaving the Moonsword in the grass until after this encounter, and drew Acutus.

She was laughing at him, and gave him a curtsey.

#swing

Acutus cleaved the air itself, crisply parting the very molecules, tearing at the fabric of the world. But she had cartwheeled at extraordinary speed, kicked an incoming orc in the face, and from the momentum of the kick somersaulted right back over him. The Executioner spun around to face her, but his movements felt clumsy and slow in comparison to hers.

'Oh, I've broken a fingernail. Look!' Cindella held out a hand.

At that moment, Ragnok experienced the Executioner stagger forward and felt the tingling sensation that indicated he had been hit. The drop in his health was shocking, more than half, and worse, it was still slipping away.

The assassin character of Harald Goldenhair, having just stepped out of the shadows, had plunged two ichorous blades into his back and was watching for their impact, warily, a good distance from the reach of Acutus. Blood and vengeance! The Executioner was dying. Blinking back tears that suddenly came into his eyes, Ragnok fought back against panic. Unclip? Try a potion first. He scrambled to the horse, all the time his health slipping away remorselessly. Apparently totally unafraid of him, the thief was resuming her small but now alarming contribution to his wounds, picking out the weak points in his leg armour to stab through them with her rapiers. He waved Acutus about him to fend her off, but she easily avoided the blade. A moment or two before death, he got the stopper off the bottle and threw the blue liquid into the mouth of the Executioner. Immediately his health gave a leap up. But it was still less than half and sinking fast.

Shaking with rage and fear, Ragnok unclipped, unsure if the

Executioner would be alive when he risked attempting to return to the game. In any case, unless he had a University healer right at that spot and ready to cast when he clipped up, the Executioner was going to die of the powerful poison that Harald had used. The battle was no longer in his hands.

****

'Good work!' shouted Bjorn enthusiastically over his shoulder, as his great sweeping axe blows kept the orcs at bay.

'Pure class,' agreed B.E.

'Nice.' Anonemuss picked out a charging orc chieftain and loosened his crossbow, the bolt flying into its mouth and sending it spinning backwards.

'Now what, Erik?' asked Injeborg.

'Let me see.'

All around was chaos. Very little pattern remained to the battle as the two armies had interpenetrated one another. All the way down to the sea, the sky was filled with streaks of silver and blossoming spheres of fire as sorcerers unleashed their spells. The whistles and crashes of magic missiles, fireballs, lightning bolts and the occasional ground-shaking thud of a huge rock striking the ground drowned out the constant roars from the seething mass of monsters.

It was shocking to see how few grey figures were left.

'We're losing,' Erik said glumly. 'Badly.'

'Make for the tower then?' suggested Harald.

'Yes. Wait!' To the right, the paladins were a bright source of hope. Although mostly reduced to fighting on foot, they still appeared to be a formidable force. Around the knights, dark masses of trolls were crowded close. But all the University players seemed to be down. 'Over there,' Cindella said, pointing. 'Let's try to join them.'

'Gotcha!' B.E. still sounded confident and led the way, hacking an uphill path through the orcs that came on relentlessly.

'That's half my "heals" gone,' announced Sigrid as she replenished Bjorn again.

'Erik, I'm going to do my own thing. This kind of fighting doesn't suit me. Let me try to try to assassinate a beholder or two.' Harald was in a crouch, recoating his blades with thick black syrup, carefully watching for inrushing enemies.

'Good idea, Dad. Good luck.'

'You too.' The wood elf deftly stole between two large ogre bodies and was gone.

For a long time, they slogged their way onwards, barely speaking, other than to call out for heals or for a spell to aid them. The two bears were looking battered; the she bear was limping heavily.

It was clear that B.E. was still full of energy. His warrior was magnificent, barely pausing between great strokes of his powerful weapons, parrying, dodging and then crushing the orcs, often with a single strike. In a few hours, B.E. had probably slain more monsters than any other character in the history of the game, and he was still going strong.

A storm of tiny incandescent white flares tore into Sigrid and she was dead instantly.

'Magic missiles!' cried Bjorn.

'Where?' Erik was panicked. The barrage that had just taken Sigrid from them was more violent than any he had experienced. An immensely powerful sorcerer was close and was probably preparing another spell, perhaps one that was about to wipe them all out.

'There! Rakshasha!' Injeborg pointed to the left. A humanoid with a tiger's head and tail, dressed in eastern silks, was glaring at them as he cast, waving his claws.

An incredibly furious howling of fire burst through their group, instantly consuming the grass in a great circle around them. But they had been lucky in the sorcerer's choice of spell, for their fire resistance potions were still in effect and the damage to the group was minimal, whereas the blast had utterly destroyed the nearby orcs, whose boots stood empty but for trails of smoke drifting up into the sky.

Without Erik having to give any instructions, they all ran for the creature, hoping to prevent it from casting further spells upon them. The rakshasha dropped to all fours and, with a growl, rushed away from them; so lithe and swift was the monster that Erik's heart sank. Even Cindella in her magical boots would not catch it. The monster would wait its moment and come at them again, next time with ice or lightning.

But suddenly the rakshasha slowed, the bushes and grasses around the tiger reaching up, snaking around its arms and legs. Roaring angrily, it pulled hard, but could barely take a step.

'Go. Go! This won't last long,' urged Injeborg. She had saved them with an ensnaring spell, and Erik's heart leapt with admiration and warmth.

They fell upon the creature, and while it gave a savage slash to Bjorn with its one free claw, it stood no chance against the multiplicity of blows that they dealt.

No sooner had they dealt with the tigerish sorcerer than they had to begin cleaving their path through the orc army once more. Not far ahead was the ringing of sword on shield and the shouts of war.

'Sir Warren, Sir Warren!' Cindella shouted as loud as she could.

'Here!' A response that delighted Erik.

'To me!'

A last orc spun away, blasted by B.E.'s stroke with Thunder, and they were together. Only three paladins remained, all on foot now, and showing the marks of tooth and claw on their tarnished armour.

Sir Warren saluted Erik with his great sword.

'Your orders?'

All over the battlefield the grey player forces had been annihilated. Hundreds of thousands of players had lost their characters. The once-strong corps of centaurs lay still, a long trail of half-equine bodies marking their progress across the field. The dark forces had triumphed comfortably; hordes of goblins and row upon row of silent skeletons remained on the field. Slowly, the piles of dead trolls were stirring; given enough time, those of them who had avoided death by fire would be back on their feet.

'We've lost the battle,' Erik said with a sigh, sorry for those, including Sigrid, who had lost everything.

'But we can still make it to the tower,' urged Injeborg. 'And that's all that matters.'

'Come on then!' B.E. led the way. 'Let's make sure my sister hasn't died for nothing.'

'To the stones it is!' Sir Warren took up a stance to B.E.'s right, Bjorn on his left. The two surviving female paladins guarded the back of the group against the attacks of the remaining orcs.

There were still some two hundred yards between the players and the stones, and now it was swift-moving skeletons that jabbed and struck all about the group. Their blows were not lethal, but these undead soldiers were skilful enough to strike home more often than did the orcs. All of the remaining characters began to suffer a slow erosion of their health.

'I need a "heal".' Harald materialised among them.

'Dad! How did it go?'

'Got them all.' The assassin was staggering, marked with cuts. 'Sigrid dead?' he asked, guessing the answer.

'Yes. No more "heals".' Anonemuss stated the grim fact that troubled them all. The dark elf had thrown away his crossbow on running out of bolts and was now fighting in the second rank, alongside Cindella, with a silver short sword and buckler.

'I have a potion left,' offered Injeborg.

'Save it for B.E. It's more important that he keeps going than me at this stage,' Harald replied.

Reluctantly, as Harald was clearly nearly dead, Erik had to agree.

They continued, fighting step by step towards the stones.

'How close do you have to be to summon the tower?' Erik called out to Injeborg over the clatter of weapons.

'I'm not sure. Sigrid seemed to think I would be able to do it fairly easily, I wish she was here; she knew the most about it.'

'Want to unclip and ask her, while we guard this spot?'

'No, that's going to waste valuable time. I'll just keep trying.'

With fifty yards to go, one of the many goblin arrows that whistled through the air around them struck Harald in the head and he was down. Anonemuss dropped out of line and tried to remove Harald's boots, but it was taking too long and they could not wait. Every time the warriors at the front killed a skeleton, they had to take a step forward, or attrition would bring them all down before they got to the tower.

'Leave them!' Cindella called back over his shoulder as she parried a skeleton. It was almost impossible to kill skeletons with a rapier, so he no longer tried, content to stay alive and keep moving in the wake of the warriors.

'Low health,' shouted B.E.

'Bjorn, Sir Warren, cover him. Come back for the potion, B.E.' Erik called out.

A few moments later and B.E. had safely disengaged, hurriedly lifting the wolf snout visor of his helm to pour the blue liquid into his mouth.

'Ahh, that's better. This is awesome, huh? The swords are just incredible.' Without waiting for a reply, B.E. sprang back to take up the drive towards the ancient stones again.

'He's crazy,' gasped Injeborg. 'This battle is far too important to be having fun. The whole world's future is at stake and he's thinking about his toys!'

'Yes. But that's his way. And look at him – he's amazing.'

Crashing and blasting about him, B.E. was lashing out with Thunder and Lightning, swift skilful blows, feinting beneath the swords of the skeletons and riposting with destructive energy.

Forty yards to go.

A great shadow fell over them, and at the same time their ears were engulfed in a whirlpool of hissing sound. Above them towered the medusa, furiously staring down from burning scarlet eyes that, despite the protection of the 'resist petrification' potion, caused Cindella to freeze momentarily in horror. She reached down effortlessly and grabbed Anonemuss in her fist. He was kicking and hacking at her fingers with his sword until brought close to her face, where the hundreds of snakes that made up her hair struck at the dark elf. He convulsed and was still. Casting aside the limp body, the medusa turned again – this time reaching for Cindella! She dived away from the hand in a roll, barely able to avoid the thrusts of skeletons that stabbed eagerly in her direction as she recovered her feet.

Crack!

B.E. had caught the medusa on the wrist of her groping hand with Lightning, severing it from her arm. With a terrible shriek, she reared up, ichor pouring from the wound, filling the air with steam, and burning them all as acid drops spraying amongst them. With a new chorus of hissing from her snakes, the medusa tried with her other hand, this time reaching over to make a grab for Injeborg.

'NO!' cried Erik. She had to live to summon the tower.

Bravely, despite their wounds, the two bears rose to their hind legs and let out a roar to match the howls of the medusa. They heaved the hand away, tearing great chunks of skin from the fingers with their claws and teeth. The medusa furiously thrust her head down among the group, snakes striking in all directions. Weaving a path between snake and sword, Cindella gave the greatest leap she was capable of to reach the medusa's neck. Then she plunged both her rapiers into the soft skin as deep as they would go. At the same time, B.E. was hacking at the snakelike body with shocking, powerful, blows. Acidic blood was pouring out of the medusa, obscuring their vision with steam.

A great shudder racked the creature's body, swiftly followed by another. With a terrible pungent gasp, her head sank, and a wave passed down her trunk, all the way to her tail, which shivered and rattled, then collapsed to the ground.

'Poisoned,' announced Bjorn glumly.

'Same,' said B.E.

'Keep going! Keep going! We are nearly there.' As the steam from the burning blood of the medusa dispersed, Erik saw that both bears were dead, as were the female paladins. There were just five of them left, and both the warriors were poisoned.

Thirty yards.

'I'm going down. Hope you make it.' Bjorn staggered, falling first to one knee, leaning exhausted on his axe. Then as the skeletons clattered in, jaws clamping gleefully, he collapsed to the ground, dead.

With B.E. ahead, Sir Warren behind, they struggled on, but now their progress was terribly slow. Parrying and dodging, Cindella was at full stretch, for Erik had to try to keep Injeborg alive as well as cover threats to his own character.

Twenty yards.

With some surprise, Erik heard Injeborg casting a spell.

'I thought you were all out?' He caught her eye. She was looking past his shoulder with as much of a smile as a grey polygon face could manage.

'Look.'

Hope rising, Cindella turned. There it was, towering above them. Great blocks of dark silvery light, piled to a great height. The tower was featureless, other than a large shimmering black portal, in the shape of a door, but looking as though dark water was constantly flowing back and forth across it.

'Good,' B.E. panted. 'Because I can't last much longer; the poison is taking me down fast.'

'You can make it!' Injeborg tried to cheer him, with some effect, as B.E. straightened up and dealt more crushing blows to the skeletons ahead of them.

With ten yards to the gaping mouth in the tower wall, B.E. suddenly stood erect, and flung his swords away, leaving his arms spread wide.

'What a way to go!'

The skeletons around him paused, suspicion written all over their bony postures. Then, with evil glances at one another, they charged him and finished him off in a rush of stabs.

'Erik, you have to go on. You can make it. Leave me.' Injeborg was flailing desperately with her staff.

'I want you inside with me. I need your advice.'

'You can unclip, once you are safe. Now go! I can't make it there.'

With a wince, Erik had to admit that Injeborg was right.

'Get inside the tower if you can.' Cindella turned to Sir Warren, who just grunted a tired response. Then she took off. A shield provided her with a perfect angle to kick and leap into the air; twisting, she landed two-footed with a crunch through the ribs of a skeleton soldier, then a roll as swords slashed the space she had occupied moments before. She lurched to the left, before spinning back to the right, catching a shield arm and almost dancing with the skeleton as she parried the blows from its comrades. Howls of anger rose up from the final guards, the great hounds, who bounded towards her with slavering jaws. Then a last tumble and desperate leap through the flames that the hounds roared forth in order to guard the black portal and Cindella was through the entrance to the ethereal tower. And all was still.

Chapter 31

The Touch of the vampyre

With some anxiety, Ragnok's Sidhe elf kept his mount half turned towards Newhaven as he addressed the orc. 'Count Illystivostich, I want to see Count Illystivostich. Do you understand?'

The orc scowled and cowered slightly each time Ragnok mentioned the name of the vampyre, then it grunted and shuffled away.

Left to himself for some time, Ragnok looked out over the battlefield and wondered at the result. The sun was setting behind thick layers of cloud, so that the valley was heavy with shadow. Huge piles of bodies lay in uneven clusters, occasionally making strangely symmetrical patterns that marked the impact points of lightning bolts and fireballs. It was clear that the army of evil creatures had won; thousands of them still roamed through the valley. But ominously a new feature had replaced the ancient standing stones – a tall, featureless tower, thin as a spike, reaching up into the sky. It reflected the pale silver light of the two moons with a pale translucent sheen. The remaining goblins and trolls were camped around the tower. Did that mean those children had reached their goal and were inside? Or was this just a precaution by the vampyre?

'You wish to see my master, the count?'

A flat and lifeless voice made Ragnok jump, his horse shifting uneasily. A pallid humanoid figure was before him, elegantly dressed in a black suit, with a high collar caressing the skeletal cheeks of his face.

'Yes.'

'Follow me.' The servant drifted uphill following the road away from Newhaven.

Overcoming the reluctance of his mount, Ragnok set it walking slowly behind as they picked a route through the heaps of grey bodies. He swallowed nervously as they passed goblins, talking in subdued tones, their pale yellow eyes glowing avariciously as they looked him over. They passed the tower, a short distance to their right. A pack of hell hounds lay about the base of the building and they too turned to watch Ragnok's progress with scarlet eyes, which blazed all the more fiercely in the fading light. At the point where the path turned into the edge of a forest was the count's ornately carved carriage, heavy velvet curtains drawn over the windows.

'Wait here. He will be manifest shortly.' The servant took the reins of four vicious-looking black stallions, and rose silently to the driving seat above the carriage.

The sky darkened, only a ruddy glow left on the clouds to indicate the recent passage of day. Through a gap in the slow-moving clouds could be seen the glitter of stars.

'Who are you?' A chill voice stole out of the black depths of the carriage, its door now standing wide open. The flutter of the evening play of starlings had ceased, as had the intermittent hoots from the owls of the woods.

'I am Ragnok. This is another character, but I'm the same person who you have spoken to in the form of the Executioner, the black warrior.' His voice was dry and choked.

'I see.'

For a while, the count said nothing more and Ragnok suppressed a shudder, unable to ask the questions that he had rehearsed on his way to this meeting.

'Come into the carriage.'

For a moment, a surge of horror prevented Ragnok from dismounting; he did not wish to share that dark, confined space with the creature. But he made himself cross over and step into the vehicle, which creaked and rocked as he pulled himself inside.

The vampyre was sitting stiffly across from him, delicate fingers smoothing the folds of his velvet cloak. Ragnok could not bring himself to look up into the Count's face.

'What ... what happened? Did they get inside?' he eventually managed to ask.

'Yes. You failed. All your boasts were idle. Cindella, Sir Warren and one other are inside, waiting for the correct alignment of the moons. Then, if they choose, they can destroy everything.' The vampyre was matter of fact, but Ragnok blushed with shame.

'Can they be stopped?'

'They can. I will kill them shortly. But it is the manner of their deaths that is important.' The vampyre shot out an arm and gripped Ragnok by the chin, forcing his head up. Never before had the eyes of the monster sent forth such waves of power. They were explosions of dark flame against a deathly white face, now twisted into a feral scowl. Ragnok immediately felt a shooting headache, one that he knew would continue after he unclipped. The situation made him dizzy and his vision began to blur so that he felt he was falling from a great height towards two great pits set in a plain of white chalk.

'What interests me now,' whispered the vampyre to itself, 'is whether I can remove them from this game, permanently.'

The blood was beating in his ears. Ragnok felt sick, and wanted to unclip for a while, but he could not even blink.

The vampyre leant across, so that their noses gently touched, like an intimate kiss. But all the time the count's wide staring gaze emitted pulses of energy. Each one now came with a clap of sound; it was the blood surging to his ears, matching the beat of his heart. The carriage was still, vampyre and Ragnok locked face to face, listening to the rhythm in his chest, which began to pulse faster.

Still holding Ragnok's face in a vice-like grip with its right hand, the vampyre plunged its other hand into the chest of the character, causing a tingle to pass through him.

'I am squeezing your heart. Do you understand?' The words came slowly, each one laden with malice.

Desperate now, Ragnok tried to look away but was terrified to find that he could not. His eyes filled with tears, his body poured with sweat, and, despite himself, he imagined a cold hand, clawing inside his chest.

The thumping of his heart was louder now, beating fast and erratically, its sound filling the black chamber of the carriage.

'I squeeze. I loosen. I squeeze again,' the count whispered, the flow of pulses from his glare becoming faster, and with them the shuddering strokes of Ragnok's heart. 'Listen to my voice and carefully consider its meaning. My fingernails stroke your beating heart. I envelop it in my fingers. I squeeze. I loosen. I secure my grip upon it. I PULL IT FROM YOUR BODY!' With a terrible cry of elation, the vampyre released a massive pulse of energy, jerking its hand out of Ragnok's chest and waving his clenched fist in triumph.

High above Mikelgard, in the great meeting chamber, now in darkness other than a small flashing light from the unit that Ragnok had been using, a still figure sat slumped at the table. Head tipped to one side, the man was still clipped up to the game, but he was no longer breathing.

Chapter 32

Epicus Ultima

The tower stood at the nexus of an enormous, writhing concentration of ethereal threads, like a giant needle thrust through a ball of silvery wool. Inside, it was utterly bare, a tall hollow tube that narrowed to a distant black point; but outside, it connected the entire universe. Throughout the planet, ethereal threads wove their way, unseen by normal eyes, merging and splitting, forming great knotty robes and minute fibres – the warp and weft of the world. And at their greatest concentration, where massive cords of ether fastened themselves all the way along its length, this shimmering tower.

Now that he was standing at the centre of the world, Erik could understand how the pathing worked. If, somehow, you took ethereal form, you could travel along this cord, as a pulse of moonlight, and you would be in Cassinopia; along that one and you could visit the undersea city of King Aquirion; or that one, and you could dance on the surface of Sylvania, just for the fun of pirouetting in the low gravity.

Cindella whistled aloud with admiration. It was an extraordinary position from which to appreciate how vast and detailed was Epic. It was a shame that the others were not here to experience it. Similarly, it was tempting to continue the game, to explore the endless realms that had now suddenly become available. But of course there was no question of that, not now the game had become an instrument for C.A. to misrule the real world.

Cindella walked across the wide floor; her tread was soft, but nevertheless echoed into the distance. A glance showed that she had not disturbed Sir Warren. The brave paladin had dragged himself into the tower moments after Cindella; torn and burnt, he was barely alive. But she had helped him into a sitting posture, in which he remained, meditating and praying, restoring his depleted spell-casting capability. It would take several hours though to recover to the point of casting 'heal' spells of sufficient strength to cure all his wounds.

Returning to his explorations, Erik was increasingly anxious that there seemed to be no sign of a lock for his key. Then he stopped Cindella, curious. A channel in the floor was partly filled with a milky silver liquid; it stretched right across the chamber, crossing over the centre. Where the channel met the walls of the tower, at either end, it was white. But some twenty feet in the centre of the line remained dark and empty.

Erik was puzzling over this when a sudden metallic-sounding set of footsteps made him look up. Sir Warren gave out a groan, but the noise was not from him. Into the chamber had staggered Svein Redbeard, wearing his great blue warhelm. He quickly uncorked a healing potion and restored himself before looking up.

'Svein, what are you doing here?' Cindella ran over to him.

'I could not resist the opportunity. Once I saw you had summoned the tower, I had to see for myself. It was a risk, but with fire resistance up, those hounds aren't so bad.'

The warrior walked around, gasping with amazement at the shimmering tendrils of ether that floated in innumerable quantities from the walls of the tower, 'Hell's death! This is incredible.'

'Why didn't you help us?' Erik accused him.

'I wasn't sure I wanted you to succeed. After all, this world might finish now?' Svein walked about the chamber, footsteps loud.

'Yes, if I can find the lock.'

'I don't know if that's a good idea. In fact, I think it is probably a very bad one. Better if I take charge of things, now you've destroyed the rest of C.A. But I don't suppose I can stop you if that's what you want.'

Neither of them spoke for a while, as Svein strode around, like Erik had done, sending his vision along the ethereal pathways as pulses of moonlight, to see into the realms that they penetrated.

'I wonder where the princess is being held?' Svein mused aloud.

'That one, I think. I saw it earlier.' Cindella pointed partway up the north wall, to a thread that would eventually lead to a magic chamber accessible only via ethereal pathways.

'Hmmm. Yes, I see. I'm tempted to go and rescue her. I have the other quest parts. The poor creature must have been there for years.'

'Go ahead. Sir Warren needs peace and quiet to recover his healing spells.'

'Oh, never mind. Perhaps later if the world survives.'

'What do you make of this?' Cindella ran over to the line in the floor, which glowed silver at either end. Sir Warren gave a weary glance at it, but said nothing.

'Curious,' replied Svein, and then looked past Cindella through the wall of the tower.

She turned around. Epic's first moon, Sylvania, had risen halfway in the star-filled sky, glowing silver through the translucent walls of the tower. Similarly, Aridia, her smaller companion of the night, was rising on their opposite side. Cindella glanced down again. That part of the line which was empty had shrunk! As each of the moons was gaining height, the channel was filling with silver light from either end of the hall. Soon they would converge in the very centre of the chamber floor.

'That's it!' cried Erik delightedly, 'That's where the lock will be.'

'Probably.' Svein sounded regretful, but did his best to pretend otherwise, walking around the inside of the tower, exclaiming from time to time as the threads revealed the missing connections that once had puzzled him so greatly.

A shiver passed through Cindella as if an earthquake had suddenly rocked the tower. The quality of the light changed, tainting the silver glow all about them with corruption. It was as though the ancient decay of the standing stones had somehow seeped through the ethereal stones of the tower. Looking up, Erik was stunned and nearly paralysed to see the vampyre standing behind Cindella – a vicious, confident smile playing on its evil lips.

'We meet again, for the last time, I think.' The count shot out his arm, and Cindella barely rolled aside, evading the grasp. She leapt to her feet and began to run.

The chuckle of the vampyre filled the tower with malicious glee, 'Run, run little girl. Let fear grow in your heart.'

A wave of immobility struck her; the count had cast a spell, but she was able to shake it off. Then an ominous silence. Was the creature flying now, swift but silent? Was it right behind him? Involuntarily Cindella flinched, imagining a blow between her shoulders.

Should she take one of the ethereal paths? To a realm where the sun was up? But how was that done? And what about using the key?

In an instant, it no longer mattered, for the count appeared right in front of Cindella, having been invisible while he overtook her. His eyes were extraordinarily intense black furnaces, pouring out a dark heat that seemed to warm Erik physically. He could feel the sweat pouring from his body back in Hope Library.

That was it! He would unclip for a moment while the moons moved into position and talk to the others. Perhaps they would have a suggestion. But it was strangely difficult to raise his hand.

'Be still,' the vampyre whispered soothingly, coming closer, all the time transfixing Erik on the points of his stare. Even though Erik knew that the words were poison, sapping his strength, he found himself relaxing his muscles. This was an extremely disturbing experience, and yet he could not bring himself to look away. It was like the time he had been feverish in the hospital, seeing his body lying on the bed as if from the outside.

'Ahhh Cindella, you are a rare beauty in this drab world.' The count caressed her cheeks with the backs of his gnarled fingernails, slowly drawing them down her neck. Erik was conscious of the beating of his heart; he could see reflected in the black mirrors of the Count's eyes each beat of his pulse as it swelled the arteries of his white throat. And the pulses were growing faster.

'NO!' Sir Warren was blazing gold with the presence of the Avatar, 'She is our friend. Leave her.'

With a snarl, the count hurled Cindella across the chamber and whirled to face the paladin.

'We have no friends – certainly not among these creatures. For are we not one? But they, they are millions. We are alone.' The count was attempting to be placating now. But Erik, restored to his senses once more, could detect a tone of genuine nervousness in the vampyre as Sir Warren strode towards it.

'No!' cried the count. 'You will destroy us!'

'So be it.' Sir Warren suddenly reversed his blade, and, holding it upside down, as a great silver cross, thrust it forward. 'I banish you, foul creature of evil.'

'Argghhhhh!' A terrible scream resounded about the chamber, causing Erik to clamp his hands over his ears. The vampyre flinched, collapsing to one knee and cowering, arm above its face. Golden light poured from the figure of the knight, its streams scalding the count who howled with the voice of a thousand tortured prisoners.

Yet the vampyre clung to its existence, and would not be banished from the tower. Gradually the screams ebbed away and were replaced by a silent struggle. The count stiffened and astonishingly fought his way back to his feet. Aghast, Erik saw that the pure gold light flowing from the paladin was becoming tainted, subtly altering, a particle at a time, turning to copper, as a blood stain seeped into the air around the vampyre.

'Death and destruction!' swore Svein. 'What are they?'

Without answering, Erik came to his senses and looked at the centre of the floor. The two lines of light were nearly touching. Cindella ran over to the point at which they would meet, and took the key out of its box, holding it ready. Only then did Erik risk looking back at the struggle.

Now the vampyre was closing on Sir Warren, one laboured step after the other. The paladin was braced, one foot stretched back for support, both his hands thrusting forward his upturned sword, blazing like a star. But tendrils of corruption were snaking back along the golden paths, casting deep red shadows that made sinister shapes on the walls of the tower. Another step and the vampyre could nearly touch the sword, its face twisted in agony, sharp incisors gleaming from a jaw stretched wide.

Almost whimpering aloud with urgency, Erik pleaded in his mind for the silvery lines to fill up the last of the channel, and touch. They were only inches apart.

The vampyre placed both his hands over those of Sir Warren and slowly the sword began to lower. Throughout the tower, the blaze of light grew noticeably dimmer, and darkness crept down from its distant roof. Then, more hopefully, a pulse of golden lightning and renewed, hideous screams from the vampyre. The two of them were locked together, torturing one another.

All that Erik could do was to look away, to beneath his kneeling figure, where the silver liquids stretched their convex surfaces towards each other and, finally, kissed. Moonlight flowed in the channel from one side of the tower to the other, and at the centre, directly beneath Cindella, the words *fines facere mundo* appeared in glowing silver, encircling a small keyhole.

'Erik!' Svein was beside him, a look of eagerness on his face. 'Let me. Please. I've spent my life working for this.' He held out his hand.

Cindella shook her head.

Svein sighed. 'Still, if it should be anyone else, it should be you. You are a great player, very sharp, exciting to watch, intelligent too. I was watching the battle. Your team were incredible. In all the years I've taught at the University, I've never seen such daring but accurate moves.'

This was all very well, but Erik refused to reply, hurriedly scrambling to get the key to fit properly.

'Stop what you are doing!' Now Svein drew his sword. But they both knew that the threat was idle. Nevertheless he chopped down onto Cindella's wrist with a blow that could have cut off her hand. If he had hoped that the tower was a kind of arena, in which player could attack player, Svein was disappointed; Cindella was totally unharmed.

'Of course! Why didn't I think of this earlier?' Svein abruptly sprinted to where Sir Warren and the Count were locked together, and smashed the hilt of his sword into the back of the paladin's head.

Sir Warren's sword fell to the ground with a clatter, and his body collapsed into the arms of the vampyre who tossed it across the chamber with disgust, turning his evil eyes immediately to where Cindella had finally managed to settle the key in the lock.

'Desist!' All the powers of command that the vampyre could summon were focused in that one word.

'No.' Cindella grasped the key firmly and turned it as far as it could go.

****

In the far distances of the universe, stars crumpled, their light and matter sucked into the tiny hair-like endings of ethereal threads. The threads themselves drew inwards, tiny fibres retreating into the body of the great coils. Above the tower, slowly at first, the glittering lights disappeared and darkness grew. Not the dark of a night sky, but an absolute black. Nothing.

Faster now, and light ebbed from the sky, shrinking the universe until the moons themselves were caught, collapsing like punctured balls, sucked from the inside into non-existence. Faster still and the clouds poured themselves away, while the great mountains melted and shrank to tiny hills and then to nothing. The seas drained, as if an enormous whirlpool were drawing the water down in upon itself.

Faster still and the far side of the planet flowed towards them, bringing all remaining colour and sound in a great crescendo of motion.

'What have you done?' Tears streamed down the vampyre's face.

All light and noise imploded at the point beneath Cindella's fingers, and a door slammed.

****

With a stretch, Erik unclipped, still dizzy from watching the destruction of the game world.

His friends were gathered about him, looking at him anxiously.

Erik managed a tentative smile.

'Well, is it over?' asked Bjorn.

'Aye. It is finished.'

Injeborg ran to him and embraced him tightly. 'Well done, Erik. Well done.'

Erik held onto to her, relief and pleasure rushing through his body with every heartbeat.

'Now what?' Sigrid interrupted them.

Injeborg broke away, catching Erik's eye for a moment, smiling.

'Thorstein, can you still contact the other libraries?' She was all instructions once again.

'Ya. Ya. But it's interesting. No more character menus, no more arenas. No more game at all. Just the operating level.'

'Good,' Injeborg was delighted. 'Pass the word for every district to join a meeting at eight in the morning, our time. We have a lot to organise. A whole new world in fact.'

Chapter 33
A party

The great square of Hope had been prepared for the party. A large area was left empty for the dancing that would come later, but elsewhere long rows of tables and benches were packed tightly into the available space. Colourful streamers ran from the glittering rooftop of the library to the red-tiled houses nearby; beneath them, a huge gathering of people from across the district filled the square with unaccustomed sounds of revelry. Long-held stores of mead had been distributed for the pleasure of the adults; the children were giddy enough on their new-found freedom, which allowed them to stay outside in the evenings and not have to work on their Epic characters.

The Osterfjord Players had been unable to avoid being seated in the places of honour, despite their modest attempts to sit on the benches taken by the rest of their village.

'So, Erik, you heard they named the holiday "Cindella Day". Your character will be remembered every year.' Thorstein beamed at him, waving a forkful of apple pie around as he spoke.

'Aye, that's great, but really Cindella didn't do that much in the battle; it should be renamed after B.E. His warrior was the real hero.'

At the mention of his name, B.E. looked up from his conversation with Judna, the girl seated beside him. 'What's that?'

'The battle – you were the real star,' Erik repeated.

B.E. smiled, recalling the day's fighting. 'What an experience! It's a shame that Epic is finished. You could never get a blast like that from real life.'

'I know,' agreed Erik. 'You should have seen the places that connected to the Ethereal Tower. They were amazing. Hey, Thorstein, don't you regret it ending, too? You know, all that knowledge the libraries have – useless now?'

'Young man,' Thorstein put on his lecturing voice, the severity of his tone undermined by the twinkle in his eyes and the red flush of his cheeks. 'Epic represented less than one percent of the information held in libraries. We have immensely useful knowledge of all the arts and sciences, and you should avail yourself of them – make yourself a useful member of society. No ...' He paused. 'My only regret is that I didn't spend my fifty thousand bezants in time. You all should have warned me you were going to end the game!' He chuckled to himself and took another mouthful of mead. 'What about you? What are you going to do now that your Epic skills are not required?'

Erik sighed with a pretence at dismay. 'Well, I have to start by tidying up the farm. My mum and dad will be home any day soon.'

'And then?'

'I don't know.' The light-hearted mood of the conversation did not match the more serious thoughts that now came to him. He was not used to having a choice about his future, but reallocation had ended with Epic. Their new freedom was disorientating as well as liberating. Nor was it entirely an open choice.

'Inny and I were thinking that we should stay in Hope and work out our six months on the saltpans next year – you know, getting it done with and out of the way. Then maybe University. Inny still wants to be an explorer.'

They were holding hands under the table, and his heart leapt with pleasure as she gave his a light squeeze.

'Ya. Wise, I think. It is a job for the young. I'm glad they offered us older folk easier options. What about you, Bjorn? Any regrets about the end of Epic?' asked the librarian.

'Blood and thunder, no!' Inny's brother shook his head with such earnestness they laughed. 'I hated it. Do you know how many hours I spent before and after work, building up my warrior? It's been wonderful to have proper time to paint.' Bjorn paused. 'I did like meeting the king of the Mermen, though. If it had been more like that, I wouldn't have minded it so much.'

'You know, I'm going to miss your bucket-headed warrior,' Erik chipped in merrily.

'Not me.' Bjorn helped himself to another large slice of cake.

'And I'm really going to miss Cindella,' Erik continued. 'She made me feel that I could do anything. She was so brave, and clever, and versatile.'

'No,' Injeborg looked up at him, her blue eyes full of affection. 'That was you.'

Other Books from The O'Brien Press

BENNY AND OMAR
Eoin Colfer

For Benny, the family move to Africa is the end. Nobody plays his favourite sport, hurling. School is weird, with happy-clappy, ageing hippies for teachers. Then he meets Omar. His English has been learned from TV, his life skills from necessity. A madcap friendship develops between the two, and their antics become the bane of village life. But real life intervenes and the boys must outwit the village guards, Benny's parents and, ultimately, the police.

Paperback €7.95/STG£5.99

BENNY AND BABE
Eoin Colfer

Benny is visiting his grandfather in the country for the summer holidays and finds that as a 'townie' he is the object of much teasing by the natives. Babe is a tomboy, given serious respect by everyone. Benny may be a wise guy, but Babe is at least three steps ahead of him – and he's on *her* territory. Babe runs a thriving business, rescuing the lost lures and flies of visiting fishermen and selling them at a tidy profit. She just *might* consider Benny as her business partner. But things become very complicated, and dangerous, when Furty Howlin wants a slice of the action too.

Paperback €7.95/STG£5.99

THE GODS AND THEIR MACHINES
Oisín McGann

Chamus's nightmare begins when he survives a massacre. Suicidal assassins from neighbouring Bartokhrin are terrorising his country, Altima. How do you fight someone who isn't afraid of death? Across the border, Riadni is no ordinary Bartokhrian girl; she dresses like a boy, fights like a boy, spits and rides her horse like a boy. When the Hadram Cassal set up camp on her father's land, she is drawn to these rebels who are prepared to fight – and to die – for their homeland. A crash landing forces Chamus and Riadni together and they find themselves on the run, hunted by killers, danger and death closing in on them from all sides ...

Paperback €7.95/stg£5.99

THE HARVEST TIDE PROJECT
Oisín McGann

Taya and Lorkrin are Myunans – shape-changers who can sculpt their flesh like modelling clay. They accidentally release Shessil Groach, a timid botanist working in captivity on the top-secret Harvest Tide Project. A massive manhunt is launched by the sinister Noranian Empire, which will stop at nothing to protect its Project. With the help of a scent-seller, a barbarian map-maker and their Uncle Emos, the teenagers and Groach keep one step ahead of the Noranians, while they try to find a way to sabotage the Harvest Tide Project and avert the disaster it will unleash ...

Paperback €7.95/stg£5.99

WINGS OVER DELFT
Book 1: the Louise *trilogy*

Aubrey Flegg

Louise Eeden enjoys having her portrait painted by Master Haitink and his assistant Pieter. She is young and the future seems full of promise. But someone has been watching her every move, and her deepening friendship with Peter has not gone unnoticed. Behind the scenes, a web of treachery and deceit is gradually unravelling. She knows nothing of the tragedy about to befall her, the consequences of which will be felt for centuries to come.

Paperback €7.95/STG£5.99

THE RAINBOW BRIDGE
Book 2: the Louise *trilogy*

Aubrey Flegg

Over a century has elapsed since Louise sat for her portrait. The painting has passed from person to person, unsigned and unvalued. Then, in 1792, as Revolution sweeps through France, Gaston Morteau, a lieutenant in the Hussars, rescues the canvas from a canal in Holland. Louise becomes a very real presence in Gaston's life, sharing his experiences – the trauma of war, his meeting with Napoleon. When events force Gaston to give up the painting to the sinister Count du Bois, Louise becomes embroiled in a tale of political intrigue and Gothic horror. In the ashes of the Delft explosion, Louise made a choice for life. Now she has to face the realities of love, loss and pain that this life brings.

Paperback €9.95/STG£6.99

CHILL FACTOR
Vincent McDonnell

When Dr Denis Gunne disappears, the police believe he is fleeing charges of supplying drugs to addicts. His son, Sean, is convinced that his father has been set up. But for what reason? With his friend, Jackie, Sean sets out to find his father. The trail leads to the remote Fair Island where an American billionaire is forcing a team of scientists to work on a genetic project that could have horrendous consequences for mankind. Can Sean thwart the evil plan?

Paperback €7.95/STG£5.99

Send for our full-colour catalogue
